Falling Off The Planet

(Book 2 of Over the Moon Series)

By

DIANE DANIELS

This book is dedicated to my big brother, Blaine McClellan, who shared with me his love for literature and I am eternally grateful.

"Small as is our whole system compared with the infinitude of creation, brief as is our life compared with the cycles of time, we are so tethered by the beautiful dependencies of law, that not only the sparrows fall is felt to the uttermost bound but the vibrations set in motion by the words we utter reach through all space and the tremor is felt through all time."

—MARIA MITCHELL (1818-1889), FIRST WOMAN ELECTED TO THE AMERICAN ACADEMY OF ARTS AND SCIENCES.

"Forgiveness is the sweetest revenge."

—ISAAC FRIEDMANN.

CHAPTER 1

BASKETBALL

All the people in the Hurricane High gymnasium were standing on their feet with their eyes glued to number 10, my boyfriend, Andrew Martin. I had this gut-wrenching feeling that something was going to go terribly wrong. There was less than a minute left in this Regional Championship basketball game and I had just finished chewing all my fingernails off my left hand. My right hand had already suffered the same highly undignified plight. He had taken a hard foul from a huge, hulking, Desert Hills player who had shoved and tripped him in a futile attempt to thwart his not-so-easy lay up. The ball went in anyway, tying this extremely exciting and nerve-racking game at 70 all.

Andrew bounced up from the floor to take his shot from the free throw line. A normal athlete might have suffered a concussion from the force of his head connecting with those hard, wooden floorboards that smelled like floor wax mingled with healthy- teenage-boy-sweat. The sound of it echoed like an explosion through the building, causing all of us to gasp and then hold our collective breath as we waited. Was our superstar was alright? Of course, he was okay because he isn't normal. He is much better than normal. He's from another planet and yes, I mean that literally.

He glanced up to where I was standing on the edge of the bleachers, bounced the ball three times, mouthed "I love you" and arced it through the hoop. Swish! It hit nothing but net. Comforting warmth flooded my circulatory system. He always performs that ritual at the free throw line. I know it's sort of cheesy, but it always makes me feel like the luckiest girl on Earth or any other planet in our galaxy.

A raucous roar filled the air as we took the lead by one point. The Desert Hills Thunder-boys (I'm not kidding, that is what they call themselves) inbounded the ball and raced down with squeaky shoes to score once more. Their star center buried it, while their fans cheered them on with loud fervor. They were on top again. Desert Hills was highly favored to win this game with ease. They were ranked number one in our division. We were the underdogs in this contest. The Thunder had expected to dominate the scoreboard, so the closeness of the game had been a shockingly unpleasant surprise for them.

Our Hurricane Tigers ran the court, passing the ball to Andrew as they approached the three point line. The scoreboard clock ticked down to show three seconds remaining. Time stopped for a few intense moments as we all stiffened and ceased breathing altogether. He casually and confidently took the shot. The buzzer sounded as the ball once more found its home in the hoop. Game over! We were the 3A region champions!

We jumped, clapped, and screamed wildly. The Desert Hills fans moaned and cursed and then fell silent. Our "Tigers" had eaten their "Thunder." We, the team from a tiny high school in a dinky, desert town near the Utah-Arizona border, were going to the state finals. We had just beaten the best team in our division, the team who was supposed to take home the trophy. This was huge! Nearly everyone in our little city was here celebrating this remarkable victory. What else is there to do on a Friday night in February in a town the size of Hurricane, Utah?

Andrew was now the officially designated hero of Hurricane. He had been my own personal hero almost since the day I moved here from Chicago. He had saved my life three times so far. Once from being blown to bits in an exploding car after an accident, then again, when I'd been bitten by a rattlesnake. Finally, he had rescued me from extraterrestrial, cannibalistic terrorists, Hellites, who caught me and planned to kill and devour my body after Andrew's evil x-girlfriend had pushed me into their cruel clutches. My life is a lot more exciting than it used to be, since I fell in love with this amazing alien from another world. Yeah, I know some of that stuff is seriously disturbing, but I prefer to forget the bitter and focus on the sweet.

I twisted the delicate pinkie ring that adorned the little finger on my left hand. It was intricately engraved with a lacy pattern on silver and encrusted with tiny diamonds. The Valentine's gift from Andrew was a symbol of the unbreakable bond of love that we share. I know that sounds kind of mushy and way too serious for anyone under the age of twenty, but I swear this isn't your regular, everyday teenage crush. We are both in it for the happily-ever-after even if the happy part is interrupted from time to time. He had explained that this ring was a circle without end, so it was an eternal emblem of his endless love. It had been handcrafted by Helamite artisans on his home planet. It was also extra significant because it had belonged to his late mother.

I smiled as I remembered how eager he had been to give it to me a week ago. I gave him a heart shaped chocolate cake with whipped cream frosting and a framed picture of the two of us kissing in front of "Weeping Rock" in Zion National Park. (It's this giant sandstone wall that looks as if it's crying because the springs behind the many cracks and crevasses riddling the massive rock cliffs seep through and leak down to the creek at the bottom.) I fully realize that my gift was way outclassed by his, but he loved it anyway and insisted that my heart was all he really wanted from me, and I'd already given him that. I still sometimes find it hard to believe that Andrew loves me.

I was shaken out of my revelry by my brother, Mark, and his best friend and roommate, Jeremy, who were here on the bleachers with me watching this momentous game. I mean that literally, as well as figuratively. They were actually shaking me and hugging me. Their enthusiasm for the win was evident as they whooped and screamed and pumped their fists in the air. Both play basketball at UNLV and they take this sport very seriously. They were also extremely eager to watch Andrew win as Mark had encouraged him to try out for our high school team.

We made our way down through the crowd and onto the floor to congratulate our favorite star player. My heart skipped several beats and then began racing when his bright, turquoise eyes found mine. He flashed me his dazzling smile. I ran to him and threw my arms around his neck. Even hot and sweaty, he smells like cinnamon and cloves mixed with sunshine. Sunshine has a warm, musky, citrus smell to me. I'm not sure if he smells like that to other people, but to me his scent is irresistible. I'd recognize it anywhere. Oh yeah, I should also tell you, he has the most amazingly magnetic grin on the planet. He's six foot four, blond, blue eyed, beautiful inside and out, and he's mine. I have to pinch myself every once in a while to make sure I'm not dreaming.

"You were fantastic tonight!" I whispered in his ear as he drew me into his embrace.

"It was a tough game," he said hugging me tight against his broad chest and making me tingle from the inside out as that now familiar welcome warmth enveloped me. He gazed at me with a knowing look, telling me that he knew exactly how he made me feel.

"Maybe it was a little too close for comfort," he admitted.

"You're not kidding!" Mark exclaimed, slapping him on the back. "Next time try not to let it get that close! I was ready to tear out my hair! I was sure Tiana was going into cardiac arrest, and Jeremy nearly stroked out. He kept punching me every time they scored on you! I'm going to be black and blue tomorrow."

Jeremy rolled his eyes, "Man up, Mark. I barely touched you. I only did it because you kept shoving me off the bleachers. It was you who was thrashing around like you were having a seizure or something! Seriously, Andrew, that was way too intense. It was painfully hard for us to watch."

"I feel your pain. Thanks for the expert advice. I'll try to work on keeping the opposing team's points to a minimum. I admit defense isn't really my forte. I'm better on offense." Andrew said, grinning at my big brother and his best friend.

The crowd quieted as Coach Gordon handed a pair of scissors to Andrew. Someone had positioned a step ladder under the basket.

"We want you to cut it," Ryan, the captain of the team, said as he put a hand on Andrew's shoulder. "We couldn't have done it without you."

"I think you should do it, Walker," Andrew said as he tried to pass the scissors to the senior. Ryan held up his hands and shook his head, refusing to take them. Andrew sighed and climbed the ladder with resignation, cutting the net as was the tradition of the Regional Champs at the end of the championship game. I know this might be hard to believe, but Andrew doesn't seek the spotlight; it just seems to follow him around. He handed the net to Ryan, who presented it to the coach. We all cheered and clapped with all our most eager and energetic enthusiasm. This was an event of epic proportions for our puny, desert community.

The Desert Hills team quickly left for the showers. Their fans were rapidly escaping from the bleachers and pouring out of the building mumbling things like: "We should have won it! Who was that guy? He played like a professional. They say he's only a junior."

That's when I saw them, my two least favorite aliens. Psycho Sonya and her big-bad-brother, James, were coming directly toward us.

"Oh crap!" I said as Andrew returned to our little group and turned to see his gorgeous x-girlfriend and her incredibly handsome older brother threading their way through the fans still loitering on the floor. As I watched them strolling toward us, I had that "fight-or-flight" reaction, but my feet felt heavy and seemed to be frozen to the floor, so I couldn't run. Andrew had assumed his usual protective position, joining me and wrapping both arms around my waist tightly in an attempt to insulate me from the wave of negativity that I could feel rolling toward us. Our combined dread at the prospect of having to endure the influence of this terrible twosome hung in the suddenly icy air. He frowned and looked down at me with raised eyebrows.

"What are they doing here?" He tried to suppress the aggravation I couldn't help hearing in his voice. His fists were clenched and ready. I knew he'd like to punch James right in the middle of his annoying, smiling, movie-star-handsome face. James looks a lot like Antonio Banderas, only much younger. I cannot deny the fact that he is definitely eye candy. He's also suave, sophisticated and accustomed to having most girls bow down and worship him with dedicated adoration. He always makes me nervous, not because of his good looks, but because he strikes me as being some kind of cunning predator out for blood. Tonight he reminded me of a werewolf.

For some reason, he almost always seems to have his predatory sights set on me. I still don't understand why. I'm really not that appealing. I'm just an average-looking, teenage female with red hair, green eyes and very pale skin that won't tan. Well, Andrew thinks I'm beautiful. He's the only one in my world whose opinion counts.

Mark and Jeremy stared at Sonya like she was an exotic princess who expected and commanded their complete attention. She is almost six feet tall with strawberry blond hair that cascades in golden waves down her shapely back. She has a pretty face and an hour glass figure to die for, the kind of body that causes teenage boys to drop to their knees, lose control and start drooling all over the floor. She was dressed to impress in a low-neck, fuchsia cashmere sweater that clung to her curves and too-tight jeans that were tucked into pointy-toed, stiletto-healed, black boots. These are the kind of boots that can double as weapons if the need should arise. She expects everyone's undivided attention and sulks or comes unhinged when she doesn't get it. The unhinged part can be terrifying. I'm sure she knows how to use those lethal boots to take down her unsuspecting foes.

Andrew and I know she is pure evil through and through. She spit in my face the day I met her and told me that I was all wrong for Andrew. She has always operated under the erroneous impression that he should be with her, like she owns him or something, just because they grew up together on the same planet. To eliminate me as competition, she hypnotized me with her superpowers and pushed me into the hands of evil, extraterrestrial cannibals, hoping they would kill me and save her the trouble of having to do it herself. They had tortured me emotionally. I would have been the main entrée on their dinner menu if Andrew hadn't rescued me in time.

She had also used the same super-scary influence to convince me that Andrew was better off without me and that I should break it off with my soul-mate to save him from the guilt he'd feel when he broke my heart because he was "fated" to return to her. I was still waiting for the insincere apology that James had promised was coming my way. I guess that ship had sailed and sank before it ever reached me. I'm not sure the girl knows how to apologize. Why should she? In her mind, she is totally justified in unleashing the fury of her inner witch on my obviously inferior mind, seeing as I'm from Earth and she's not. That supposedly makes her far superior to those of us who actually belong on this planet.

All of my past experience with the girl makes her my least favorite person in the whole Milky Way Galaxy. All my worst, recent memories revolve around her. She fully believes she is the center of the universe. I think she's more like an uninhabitable planet orbited by sorry-satellite-boys who find it impossible to escape her gravitational pull before she drags them down to explode and burn up in the noxious atmosphere around her or break apart as they collide with her rock hard surface. Of course, many of them aren't struggling because they don't yet know that they are doomed.

I have to confess that I just wish I'd never met the girl. I've been trying to pretend she doesn't exist, but she keeps coming back to torment me. If I could, I would beam her and her big-bad-brother back to where they came from, and that would be the planet, Helam. It orbits the star, Vega, which is twenty five light years from here. I'm not sure that's far enough away to send them. A black hole somewhere out in the far reaches of deep space seems more to my liking or locked into an orbit around a distant star in a galaxy so far away, it can't be seen through the most powerful telescope on Earth. I would like nothing more than never to see their condescendingly smug faces again. Yeah, I guess you could say I don't like them much.

James had tried to convince Andrew that he should dump me, so he wouldn't put me in danger through my association with him, seeing as it's Andrew's sworn duty to protect Earth from subversive invaders from other planets. He planned to get rid of Andrew and clear the way so I would date him. I just don't get it. I think he stepped off the edge of sanity into that gray area where crazy people, who do things I can't understand, live. It didn't work. As if? He is a master manipulator. I want nothing to do with him.

If there's one thing I can't stand, it's people who try to make me do stuff by tricking or forcing me to conform to their own selfish desires. I don't like mind games. If someone can't ask me nicely, then my answer is a rebelliously resounding "no!" I'm pretty proficient at recognizing reverse psychology or any other miscellaneous manipulative methods designed to control me. Yeah, my parents tried using them all in vain. Finally, they gave up and just started asking nicely. I've been relatively cooperative ever since. I'm not usually unreasonable. I just like to be asked, rather than told what to do. Who doesn't?

James professes to be Andrew's friend. They've known each other since they were children. They are both aliens with superpowers, but aside from their extraordinary good looks, superpowers and ancestry, they are nothing alike.

"Good game, Andrew!" James grinned, showing us his incredibly perfect, large, white teeth, and put his hand on Andrew's back.

7

I'd suspect him of being addicted to tooth whiteners if I didn't know better. I wanted to say: *What big teeth you have Mr. Wolf* and I half expected him to reply: *All the better to eat you with, my dear.* Andrew turned away from his touch and frowned.

"Uh, thanks, I guess," he said. He completely ignored Sonya (Miss Manners would have been appalled, but I wasn't) and turned to me.

"Wait for me, Tiana. I'll hurry," he whispered in my ear, kissed my cheek and hugged me again, giving me a tight, apologetic smile. Then he ran off to the showers, leaving me to face the deplorable pair of Parkers. I would have rather braved the boy's locker room than stay here with these volatile siblings. I hoped they were going to act relatively civilized tonight, and I especially hoped they had left their mind control abilities at home. Perhaps the presence of Mark and Jeremy would keep them at bay. Not likely!

"Who are these delicious men, Tiana?" Sonya asked me with her sugar-coated, sexy voice. She acted like we were best friends. Huh? I thought her choice of words was appropriate. She looked as if she wanted to eat Mark right here, right now, in front of me. She's obviously still living in Looney Land with James.

"Sonya, James, this is my brother, Mark and his friend, Jeremy. Mark, Jeremy, this is Sonya and James Parker. They're old friends of Andrew's family." I introduced them as politely as I could manage. I amazed myself by keeping my voice fairly neutral.

I am getting exceptionally skilled at acting calm when I genuinely want to run away screaming, launch myself out the exit and never look back. I so wanted to lead Mark and Jeremy out of harm's way and explain that James and Sonya are insanely evil aliens who can't be trusted. Instead, I pretended to be perfectly at ease, a model of civility, while my stress level was climbing to dizzying heights.

I was glad they weren't especially adroit at reading my thoughts. James sometimes got bits and pieces, but not enough to panic over. They probably already knew what I thought of them anyway so why should I care?

I smiled pleasantly at them and tried to make polite conversation while I waited anxiously for Andrew to return. If he didn't hurry, I was going to march right into that locker room and pull him out, no matter how embarrassing that would be. I'd rather see a bunch of naked jocks than stand here too long, trying to act at ease with these crazy, poisonous, pretty people.

"Why didn't you tell me that you had such a luscious big brother?" Sonya just kept on using those food analogies. I wondered when I should have told her. Maybe, after she had attacked me at Zion National Park, I could have said, "You can't have Andrew, but I have a big brother you might like to torture, destroy and then devour" or maybe after she used her evil superpower of exploiting and controlling my mind to convince me that I was unworthy of Andrew, I could have offered Mark up as a token of my appreciation for her considerable kindness in explaining my inferiority to her supreme, highly evolved, alien race. She's a supreme, highly evolved, alien bigot. She and James both believe that we, Earthlings, are here solely to serve and amuse them. I don't find their prejudiced opinions at all amusing.

"You never asked," I answered while gritting my teeth and biting my tongue so hard it hurt as I was still trying to make nice.

"You are even more beautiful than the last time I saw you, Tiana. How is that possible?" James flashed me his best, brilliant, wolfish grin and put his arm around me which made me shutter involuntarily as I shrunk out from under its unwelcome weight.

He shrugged, turned to Mark and complained, "Did you know your little sister broke my heart? She won't go out with me, but I'm not giving up."

Jeremy pulled me away from James and said, "Take a number and get in line!" What was that supposed to mean? I felt like the rope in a tug-a-war between two opposing teams. Mark stepped in front of me and got into James' face.

"Sorry man. No offense, but you kind of remind me of the big, bad wolf. You need to back away from my little, redheaded sister!" Mark narrowed his eyes. Although his voice sounded friendly, I wasn't fooled. He was suspicious of James' intentions. This was one time I didn't mind that he was playing the part of the obnoxiously-overprotective, older brother.

I was taken aback that he apparently got that same weird-wolf-vibe that I was sensing. I could tell he didn't trust him, but he was thoroughly smitten by the alluringly lovely Sonya, our favorite, formidable sociopath. What was up with that? I knew she had some kind of power over men, but I'd never seen it work before. She had tried to captivate and possess Andrew, but lucky for me, he has some natural, super immunity that protects him from her mysteriously lethal charm.

"I can't believe you think I'd do her harm," James said and held up his hands while trying to look innocent. That was one look he could never quite get right no matter how hard he tried.

"I guess you approve of Andrew, our hero, golden boy, and knight in shining armor?" His voice seemed to drip with scorn and envy. That was it! His deviant behavior suddenly made sense to me. He didn't really like me. He just wanted to get revenge by hurting Andrew. I'm fully aware that revenge seems to be one of the top motivating factors for many of the permanent inhabitants of Crazy Town.

"So, do you both live here?" Sonya changed the subject, fluttering her much-too- long eyelashes at Mark and Jeremy. The two unsuspecting male victims immediately fell under her sordid spell. I waited, half expecting her to sink her teeth into their necks, paralyzing them with her poisonous venom. I could envision her as she lured them off to her hidden lair for a future feeding frenzy. I know, I know, I have an overactive imagination, but if vampires were real, the first two people I'd suspect of being blood-sucking parasites would be the Parkers. Of course, they could just as easily be werewolves who howl at the moon and viciously tear their victims' limb from limb, gulping down the gruesome remains. Sorry! I keep getting carried away with unpleasant imagery.

"No, we're just here for the weekend. We live in Vegas on the UNLV campus. We're living the entire college experience," Mark answered, grinning from ear to ear, like he'd never seen a pretty face before.

"They both play on the basketball team there," I bragged for them, so they wouldn't have to. I should have kept my mouth shut. What was I thinking?

"Oh, I just love athletes," the villainous vixen said as she felt their biceps appreciatively. "You have such ginormous muscles." She continued to flirt and bat her unnatural lashes at them both. I thought I might be ill if she didn't ease up on the sugary sweetness. She was so obvious; I couldn't believe they were buying into her bogus innocence. Why are guys so unbelievably clueless when it comes to beautiful women? How can they be so blind and stupid? If I knew the answer to that, I would be able to unravel one of the greatest mysteries of the universe.

After what seemed like a century and several decades, Andrew finally joined us. He pulled me into his arms making me feel safe and warm again.

I relaxed, letting my stress dissipate and disappear into the air like sun-kissed fog. I sighed audibly with relief.

"What are you two doing here?" He scowled at them. They are at the top of his "top ten list" of people to avoid like the black plague, terminal cancer or any antibiotic-resistant, skin-eating bacteria.

"Our parents are looking at real estate. They want to move to St. George," James explained. "I called your house and Evelyn told me about the 'important' game tonight."

"We just had to come and watch Andrew play!" Sonya added. "There's no way we'd miss seeing the big game." She made quotation marks around the word, "big." with her perfectly manicured fingers in the air.

"Isn't it great that we're moving here? We can all hang out together," she gave everyone her version of the toothpaste-commercial-smile so common in Helamites.

I was gagging on the inside, instantly wanting to throw up. I'd rather hang with rattlesnakes, tarantulas and Gila monsters than spend five more minutes with these fiendish frenemies from Roswell.

"Why don't we all go out for ice cream to celebrate? My treat." James said when Andrew and I didn't say anything in response to the woeful idea of hanging out with the pompous Parkers. My father's words spoke in my head *if you can't say anything nice, just shut the heck up!* I positively could think of any number of not nice things to say. I bit my tongue again to keep the bad words from escaping from my lips, marveling at my astounding self-control under these adverse circumstances.

"Tiana and I have other plans," Andrew said with a tight lipped grimace.

"We'll go," Mark answered the dynamic duo.

"Yeah, we never pass on free ice cream," Jeremy quickly agreed, nodding his head enthusiastically. It was painful to watch them trip over each other in an effort to please the hypnotic Miss Madness.

"See you at home, Carrot Top," Mark mussed my hair. I was too stunned to say anything. He and Jeremy followed the sinister siblings out into the dark and dreary night. I watched them go with my mouth hanging open, wondering if they would make it back alive and relatively unharmed. I wished I'd had a chance to warn them, but they probably wouldn't have listened to me. That beguiling witchy woman had already hexed them for sure. Curses!

"That can't be good," I remarked as Andrew led me out to his red Mustang convertible. "Mark doesn't stand a chance against the 'Ice Queen of Mean'," I worried out loud. I felt sick inside.

"We can warn him about her, but I don't know if he'll listen," Andrew shook his head.

"What was he thinking?" I asked. Andrew has the ability to read minds so this was not purely a rhetorical question.

"He thinks she's the hottest girl he's ever met. He's determined to get to know her a lot better. He also thinks James is an arrogant womanizer. He doesn't want him anywhere near you. I agree with him there," he said as we walked out to the parking lot that was now nearly empty.

"I'm glad he can see through James' facade, but I'm extremely worried that he'll fall for Psycho Sonya. We have to discourage that. She'll chew him up before he knows what she's planning!" I truly feared for my brother. Was he gullible enough to be fooled by her exquisite exterior? Yeah, of course he was. He was putty in her hands exactly like most of the other clueless males on this planet.

"There's not much we can do, Love. I'll talk to him. I doubt he'll hear what I have to say. You know how persuasive she can be. Eventually, he'll figure it out." He kissed me to make me feel better. I have a hard time holding onto even major misgivings when he does that, and he knows it. He hugged me close and held me there, nibbling on my ear while I listened to his heart and tried to slow my own. Then he kissed me again with more intensity. He stopped, chuckling at my attempt to catch my breath, opened the door of his car for me, jumped in the driver's side and started the engine.

"I just hope he doesn't hand her his heart, so she can make mincemeat of it and bake it in a pie. She kept using food analogies. I think she wanted to eat Mark and Jeremy for an after dinner snack. She looked ravenously boy-hungry tonight," I said, frowning and using a few food analogies of my own.

"Thanks for having other plans." I was relieved that we didn't have to continue to watch as she came onto Mark. Thinking about that made me want to hurl again. Sonya is way more nauseating than the stomach flu. "By the way, what are our plans?"

CHAPTER 2

STARGAZING

He didn't even attempt to answer my question. Instead, he flashed me his gleaming grin with those impossibly irresistible dimples of his. We were climbing up LaVerkin Hill to our favorite stargazing spot. He turned into the overlook parking and brought the car to a stop. Opening the trunk, he pulled out two blankets. I was getting used to his boy scout ways; he was pretty much always prepared. He draped one over the hood of the Mustang. Then he helped me out of the red sports car and lifted me gently onto the blanket. I could have hopped up there easily on my own, but it was fun watching him play a combined Prince Charming and the Incredible Hulk. (Would that make him Prince Hulk or Incredibly Charming?) He is much stronger than ordinary humans, so I often compare him to various superheroes.

We lay back against the blanket cloaked windshield and looked up into the starlit heavens. He covered us with the other blanket and we snuggled together in harmonious silence. I thoroughly enjoyed just being here with his protective arms around me. I was content drinking him in as we gazed up at the glittering night sky.

I remembered the first time he had brought me here to show me the star, Vega, which is Helam's sun. He had explained that Helam was his home planet. His family and friends had escaped to Earth just prior to the hostile takeover by the Hellites. That was on a hot September night.

Tonight was a much cooler evening in late February. It was springtime in the desert. Winters are short here which almost makes up for the long, extra-hot summers when the temperature stays at or above 100 degrees for what seems like forever. We both wore light jackets and melted into each other under the warm blanket, as we looked up into the clear, starry night. There are more stars up there than there are grains of sand in all the countless beaches on Earth. Gazillions of sparkling diamonds were sprinkled lavishly across the black velvet firmament that stretched out above us.

"See that large star just above the southern horizon?" he asked.

"You mean the one that's brighter than all the others?" My eyes followed where his finger was pointing.

"Yes, its name is Sirius, the dog star. It's part of the 'Winter Triangle.' Procyon is above and to its left and Betelgeuse is above and to the right. It's the brightest star in our night sky. We can't see it from here in the summer. It's part of the 'Southern Cross' and is always visible from Australia."

Andrew had lived in Australia for about ten years, and he speaks with an adorable Aussie accent. I could listen to him talk for hours and never get tired of it.

"Is there a reason you're showing me this star now?" I hoped he wasn't going to tell me some odious planet that orbited around it was sending an alien army to conquer Earth and make us into mindless, zombie slaves. Before I had met him, I would have laughed at the idea of such an invasion. Now, I knew it could definitely happen. Yeah, that's one of the scary side effects of being in love with an extraterrestrial whose sworn duty is to help keep Earth safe from malicious alien forces who wish to do us harm.

"I'm getting to the reason. Be patient." He kissed me lightly on my forehead and continued spouting information.

"It is eight and a half light years from Earth. Bob and other agents from the Zariba recently encountered aliens from the planet, Nommo. Sirius is the sun of their solar system. They said they came here to explore the emotions of Earthlings. They have a civilization that is even older than Helam. They've evolved in a more cerebral way than we have. They have tremendous knowledge, but they have suppressed their emotions to the extent that they seem to have difficulty feeling anything anymore.

"Their original plan was to abduct several people from Earth, take them back to Nommo, and study their emotional memories. The Zariba would never allow this. They convinced them to observe for two weeks and then return home. Of course, they were kept under constant surveillance for their entire visit. They left as they were commanded to do, but the Zariba is worried that they didn't actually return to their home planet. They believe the Nommoans are hiding out somewhere in our solar system, and they are planning to come back to perform their original plan.

"Evidently, their race is dying off because they have stopped reproducing and although they are virtually indestructible, they are losing their will to live. It's almost like they're dying of boredom, as ridiculous as that sounds. They are seeking a way to unlock their emotions and they think that if they study ours, they will find the solution. Earth people are known throughout this galaxy for having extra strong emotions.

"The Nommoans have visited the Earth before. A few thousand years ago, they visited the Dogan tribesmen who live on The Bandeara Plateau about three hundred miles from Timbuktu, Mali. According to their religion, these aliens were amphibious extraterrestrials who came in "arks" from the sky. They told the Dogan people that Nommo orbits Sirius and educated them about that solar system. Central to the Dogan beliefs is the fact that Sirius has a companion star that is not visible to the naked eye. They believe this second star holds all creation in place as it orbits around Sirius every fifty years.

"Earth scientists discovered this companion star and its fifty year orbital pattern in the late 1800's, after a more powerful version of the telescope was invented. The Dogan people have known and written about it for over two thousand years. Many anthropologists believe this proves Earth has been visited by aliens. Thank goodness most of the modern world thinks it's just a coincidental legend."

"What does all this mean?" I asked nervously, cutting to the chase. A pang of panic dropped into the pit of my stomach. I remembered that gut-wrenching feeling I had had during the game Foreboding squeezed my heart again,

The Zariba is composed of powerful aliens who came to Earth during Renaissance times. Their home planet, Zarib, was destroyed by a comet. They are ultimately responsible for protecting Earth from extraterrestrial terrorists. The Helamites work with the Zariba to keep us safe and oblivious to threats from outer space.

I knew it probably meant he'd be on patrol duty somewhere in the vast desert of the southwestern United States, watching for amphibious aliens who wanted to abduct Earthlings and perform emotional experiments on them. This stuff would make Sci-Fi aficionados jump up and cheer, if only they knew. Heck, they might even volunteer. Maybe we should go public.

"You're right. It means that after the state basketball finals, I'll be on call again. I'll be gone more than I want to be. We need to enjoy the next two weeks together. If we hadn't won tonight, I'd have had to leave tomorrow. Everyone is on Red Alert." He pulled me closer to his chest pushing my heart into hyper-drive. Yeah, I know it sucks that he can read my mind. I'm not really happy about that superpower, but sometimes it comes in handy when he picks other people's brains and shares the information with me.

"I'm so thrilled you won!" I managed to say before his lips found mine and he thrilled me even more.

"I should get you home," he stopped kissing me just before I could combust spontaneously and turn into a pile of ashes. I had persuaded him to continue a little past the "I'm-going-to-melt-into-a-puddle-of-drool" warning stage that had seriously weakened my willpower, but he has more willpower in his little finger than I have in my whole body.

I should also explain that in his culture there is no premarital sex, extramarital sex, or divorce. He believes that the power to procreate is sacred. His Helamite culture dictates that when he chooses a mate, it's forever. Helamite men generally fall in love only once in a lifetime. They love more deeply than Earth humans do or so they say. He has superhuman self-control. I guess that's a good thing.

"What do these amphibious aliens look like?" I asked, forcing myself to breathe normally. He had insisted that the intelligent life forms that populated the universe were human, even though some of them, like the Hellites, had evolved in ways that were different from how we, Earth humans, are.

"They look similar to us. However, they have webbed feet and gills under their shoulder blades, so they can breathe underwater. Fully dressed, they appear as normal people with crazy, multicolored hair. I guess that isn't really so different from the current fads here on Earth except that their hair is natural, rather than dyed. Their planet is almost entirely covered with water. It is a planet of islands, rather than continents. They spend a lot of time swimming. Many actually live on or in the water most of the time." He explained all this to me as nonchalantly as if we were discussing the latest stock market trends and not incredible spacemen who could walk on the bottom of the ocean.

I was getting used to finding out bizarre factoids about our mysterious universe. It is kind of cool to know stuff that most of Earth's population can't even imagine could be so, with the exception of a few hundred diehard Science Fiction writers with unbelievably creative imaginations. Sometimes truth can be stranger and more disturbing than fiction.

On the way home, I began worrying about Mark and Jeremy again. How was I going to convince them that Sonya Parker was the "Hag from Hades" and not the sweet, gorgeous girl she appeared to be? They couldn't know that she was from another planet. I had kept the whole extraterrestrials-live-among-us and my-boyfriend-is-an-alien secret to myself. I couldn't tell them the truth. It was pointless. They would never believe me. What could I do to convince them that they were in immediate danger from the wickedest, alien witch on this side of the Milky Way without blowing the good, guardian spacemen's cover?

"We'll think of something." He answered my thoughts again. He doesn't often do this. He knows it drives me crazy. I prefer to have him wait until I actually voice my concerns, but sometimes, he just can't help himself. After all, he is only an alien with fantastic superpowers. I wished he had the power to give some of his super-immunity to Mark and

Jeremy. They had no idea they were playing with a fire breathing, draconian temptress. Sonya could pluck out their hearts and burn them beyond recognition before they ever knew what was happening. I had absolutely no idea how to save them and that scared me speechless.

Something bad was coming. I could feel it in my bones. Was it Sonya or evil amphibious aliens? I didn't want to know, so I did what I do so well. I ignored the premonition.

CHAPTER 3

JILLIAN'S BIRTHDAY

We made it back to my house. The two of us were seated at the dining room table, eating Blue Bunny "Cherry Chocolate Bordeaux" ice cream, when Mark and Jeremy arrived. It's my favorite kind that you can get at the grocery store. It has these rivers of frozen chocolate streaming through cherry flavored ice cream. It probably wasn't nearly as tasty as the ice cream Mark and Jeremy had enjoyed, but I prefer mine without a side of the Parkers in way-too-close-proximity. I tend to lose my appetite around them, even when it's something I love as much as ice cream.

"What were your important other plans?" Mark raised an eyebrow and asked as he noted the bowls of ice cream we were contentedly consuming.

"None of your business," I said, sticking my tongue out and crossing my eyes at him. My older brother is often too nosey and overprotective. He thinks I should tell him everything I do.

"I needed some alone time with Tiana." Andrew smiled at my brother, wiggling his eyebrows.

Jeremy rolled his eyes and said, "Some guys have all the luck. Mark has a date with Sonya tomorrow."

"What?" Andrew and I spoke at the same time. I don't think we masked the horror in our voices, but the two of them didn't seem to hear it.

"It's no big deal! She just asked me to go to Jillian's birthday party. She asked Jeremy to come, too," Mark said. He obviously was totally oblivious to our fear for him.

"Yeah, as an afterthought she included me," Jeremy protested, rolling his eyes again more dramatically.

"You don't want to get mixed up with her. She's not what she seems." Andrew's voice was undeniably solemn.

"She's evil!" I exclaimed. "Remember the psycho x-girlfriend I told you about?"

"Sonya was the crazy girl doing the spitting-in-your-face, leave-Andrew-alone-he's-mine bit?" Jeremy asked. His eyes widened with sudden apprehension.

"Exactly," I replied, grateful that I didn't have to retell my first horrendous confrontation with the lovely, but deadly, Sonya Parker.

"Shut up! You've got to be kidding! That was her?" Mark's eyes got extremely big and round. His jaw nearly fell off his face and onto the floor.

"She's the wickedest witch I know. I don't mean wicked in a good way. Of course, she and Alexis could be sisters. We could call them the demonic duo." Andrew said. Alexis was the psychotic cheerleader who had also tried aggressively and unsuccessfully, to win Andrew's affection. We were definitely not friends, but Sonya was far worse. She was my number one arch nemesis. Why do I always have to get on the wrong side of diabolical divas?

"But she's so beautiful, and she seemed so sweet. That is a horrible shame!" Jeremy frowned, looking dazed.

"I know!" Mark said. "That is so unfair! Maybe, I can help her change her evil ways."

"Don't count on it, Bro." I said shaking my head emphatically.

"I think I need to take her out, at least once, to some event on campus where everyone would see us. She'd make a great trophy date, don't you think? My dating cred would skyrocket." Mark insisted. "I think you guys are totally exaggerating or overreacting. She can't be that bad. I'm going to the party."

"Be careful. She *is* worse than that bad. I wouldn't wish her on my worst enemy and certainly not on my girlfriend's brother. Trying to use her like that will backfire and you'll be the one who gets burned. She's smarter than she looks, and if anyone is going to get used, you can bet it won't be her." Andrew tried to dissuade Mark. "If you don't believe me, ask James."

"What's up with him, anyway?" Mark turned his attention to me. "Is he really that crazy about you? You were all he wanted to talk about."

"I think he just wants to irritate Andrew. It's some sort of revenge thing," I said. I didn't want to believe that he was that interested in me. I was certain he just wanted to win out, to triumph over Andrew in any way possible. He had envy issues that went back to their childhood years. I was more comfortable with that idea than believing he had serious designs on me.

"No, he really does like you. He hates me because I've got something he wants desperately and he, like his sister, is used to getting his way." Andrew declared, frowning.

"What does he want?" I asked.

"You, of course."

No, that was not the answer I wanted. I couldn't accept that. It made absolutely no sense to me. I was no prize! There had to be an ulterior motive lurking beneath the surface of his suave exterior.

I had hoped he wanted Andrew's psychic ability, his healing powers, or his ability to read the minds of Earth humans consistently. I knew James could only get a glimpse of my mind. He couldn't heal, know things about the future, or sense when something was happening somewhere else. However, he was a master at manipulating the minds of others and he could put thoughts into your head to make you see things his way. You had to let him into your head first, and I tried hard not to let him or his savage sister, who shared his invasive abilities, into mine.

This aggravating talent worked better on people whose thoughts and emotions they could read well, like their fellow aliens from the planet, Helam. According to Andrew, I have a difficult mind to read because my thought process is somewhat unique. That's a polite way to say my mind is a mixed-up mess. I'm okay with that.

Sonya had only been able to influence me when my defenses had been weakened from lack of sleep or emotional torture at the hands of the Hellites. Her unusual aptitude for controlling the minds of pretty much all of the unsuspecting males of this world was infamous and well documented among the alien population of Earth. I wondered for a moment what it would be like to have that ability. I could see how having such power over others could go to your head. I almost felt sorry for her. Then I remembered she was a vengeful monster who didn't deserve or want my sympathy.

I went to bed that night terribly worried for my brother's emotional well-being. He was in grave danger. I knew that better than anyone. Sonya's most deadly alien superpower was to entice men to fall in love with her. After they were under her influence, she wouldn't hesitate to rip out their hearts and squeeze until she had crushed them into oblivion.

Yeah, she's also much stronger than the average human from our planet. Andrew was somehow immune to her power, but he was the only one he knew of, who had escaped without a badly broken heart. She hated me because Andrew loved me and she hated Andrew because he hadn't succumbed to her shameful, seductive talents. Maybe, she thought she could get back at me by hurting my only brother and while hurting me, she would also get to hurt Andrew by making him feel guilty for exposing me to her in the first place.

At four o'clock, the next day, I was at Jillian's birthday party. We were playing volleyball in the Martin's large backyard which included a spectacular waterfall, a swimming pool, a huge hot tub, and a humongous barbecue grill sturdy enough to feed a small, very hungry army. The volleyball net had been set up on the edge of the grass where special white sand had been trucked in especially for this party. The Martin's spared no expense on Jillian's birthday.

We had been playing a fun game that wasn't too competitive when my brother, Mark, showed up with Sonya. Her brother came in with a beautiful brunette who had enormous, brown, cow eyes. She wore a little too much eye makeup. It wasn't like she needed it. He introduced her as "Kylie, the current Miss St. George." She was totally the beauty queen type: cute, perky, over-the-top smiley and almost too sweet. She seemed a little less than genuine. You know the kind. Can anyone honestly be that enthusiastic about absolutely everything, all the time?

Maybe I was judging her harshly. Feeling a little guilty, I promised myself that I would be extra friendly to the girl. If she could capture James' heart, he would leave me alone. I smiled broadly at her and encouraged her and James to join our team. Mark and Sonya joined the other side.

Sonya made a point of telling all of us that she wasn't skilled at volleyball. She made several attempts to hit the ball over the net without success. Mark took her aside and gave her some pointers.

I looked at Andrew and rolled my eyes. He nodded in response to my thought question, "Is she faking this incompetence for my brother's benefit?" After his pointers, she managed, just barely, to get it across. Then the deceptive-drama-queen jumped up and down like she'd just won the prize for MVP. I wasn't the only one rolling my eyes.

Possession of the serve changed. We rotated positions. To my chagrin, I found myself staring into her hostile, narrowed glare as I shifted my position to stand directly across the net from her. Mark softly hit the ball high in her direction and she spiked it with incredible force right into my face.

I tried to deflect the ball before it connected with my nose, but I wasn't fast or strong enough. I stifled a scream and felt the blood run down from my nostrils. My nose hurt so much, it had to be broken. Andrew had removed his T-shirt and pushed it onto my bloody nose before I could protest. He looks exceptionally good without his shirt, but I promise I wouldn't intentionally get my nose broken just so I could see him that way.

"We're going to sit this one out," he said, as he pulled me away from the game and into the house so quickly, I just barely heard Sonya say she was sorry. It sounded indecently insincere to me. I suspected she was out for my blood. She got what she wanted. The spiteful-volleyball-bully had purposely fractured my face. Score one for the gorgeous gorgon.

When we were inside, my personal healer made me tilt my head back as he used his "magic hands" to fix my broken nose. I tried to blink back the tears that had pooled in my eyes.

"She is way out of control," he said as he wiped away the few drops of moisture that splashed out and ran down my cheeks. "I don't know why Jillian invited her."

Jillian came in at that precise moment and said, "I didn't invite her. Evelyn did. I'm sorry, Tiana. She's just being her rotten, ruthless self. I swear that girl is nine kinds of nasty! She was totally faking being athletically challenged. She plays on a volleyball team in Roswell. We all know that."

"I'm fine. I'm sure it was an accident. I don't think she meant to hurt me," I was lying to be polite. Probably, I sounded more sarcastic than polite. I was sure she knew exactly what she was doing and she definitely wanted to hurt me. Andrew nodded his head, letting me know I was right about her despicable desire to cause me pain. I didn't want to let her win by allowing her to hurt my feelings, but I couldn't help it.

I wished there was something I could do to make her stop hating me. I≈truly didn't want to have to hate her. Hating takes a lot of energy. It's bad for your health. I had been refusing to acknowledge her existence in my world, but now she was invading my personal territory again. I could no longer ignore her evil presence.

Suddenly, Mark, Jeremy, and James were there looking on with worried expressions. This surprised me almost as much as the intentional face spike from Sonya. I struggled to regain my composure. I didn't want them all to see me having an emotional come apart.

"Is she okay?" Mark asked, barely concealing something like panic. Did I mention he's overprotective?

"Is her nose broken?" Jeremy added with his forehead all scrunched up. He's kind of overprotective and brotherly too.

"I am so sorry, Tiana," James said with what sounded suspiciously like actual anxiety in his voice. I was surprised that he left his "famous" date to check on me. What was that about?

"She'll be fine." Andrew assured them. "Go, finish your game. We're done playing."

"Are you sure she doesn't need to see a doctor?" Mark said. "Maybe I should call my dad."

"I'm positive. She doesn't need medical attention. Go back to your dates, guys. Thanks for your concern." Andrew insisted. I waved them off. I didn't fully understand their overly concerned demeanor. Sonya's "accidental" face-fracturing-hit must have looked quite distressing for all three of them to take it so seriously and come to check me out. It was kind of sweet of them. My bruised feelings were warmed.

I had lined Jeremy up with Tiffany. She broke up with Tim a few weeks ago. They seemed to like each other. I was happy about that. They were two of my favorite people. I thought they made a cute couple.

My nose finally stopped bleeding. I managed to suppress the tears. I pushed the lump in my throat back down to my chest. I took deep, cleansing breaths to eliminate the tightness inside and tried to take control of my emotions.

Andrew's shirt was ruined. He didn't care. Material things aren't all that important to him. We had worn our swim suits under our clothes, so we could sit in the Jacuzzi. Did I mention the mammoth hot tub that could accommodate twelve adults or hundreds of small children at once? I'd bought a new one piece swimsuit in turquoise that matched the color of his eyes. It was modest. I thought I looked okay in it. I don't like to reveal too much of my extremely pale skin that simply can't tan, no matter how much I wish it could.

I was just beginning to feel better. We were relaxing in the soothing warm water when most of the group came over to join us. There were six couples: Jillian and Luke, Matthew and Hannah, Mark and Sonya, Tiffany and Jeremy, James and the perky Kylie and Andrew and me. Skylar and Emily were a couple now and they kept playing volleyball against Raven and Coty. Jenna and Ryan were watching from the sidelines, shouting promises to play the winners of that game.

"Oh, it's so bright over here. I'm blinded by the reflection off Tiana's florescent, white skin!" Sonya said and then she giggled like she'd made a super-funny joke. Nobody laughed. The voluptuous viper wore a bikini that showed way too much of her beautifully tanned exterior and no, I don't hate her because she's beautiful. I hate her because she's mean. Oops! Did I say hate? I meant "dislike greatly." No hating here.

"Hey, quit making fun of my little sis. She can't help it that she's half albino." Mark said.

"Tiana has the most beautiful, creamy, porcelain skin I've ever seen," Andrew defended me, giving Sonya a dirty look that said *shut up now.*

"He's right. Tan can be so boring, especially here where everyone has a tan on," James said.

Huh? Where was this kindness coming from?

"I agree. Tiana has her own unique beauty. Her skin is perfect," Jeremy added. Tiffany nodded in agreement. Okay, they were just trying to be nice to the ghostly-white-albino-girl that happens embarrassingly to be me. It was sweet, but unnecessary. I've long accepted the fact that

I'm doomed to be chalky white or red as a beet. There's no brown-in-between for me.

"Quit looking at her skin!" Mark said.

"Guys, hello? I'm right here. You're all very kind except for Mark and Sonya. Quit talking about me. I admit I am part albino. I will never be tan unless I spray paint myself and that doesn't really work on me. Orange streaks are all I get out of a tan in a can. End of discussion!" I was mortified by the conversation. I'm sure my face had turned much redder than any sunburn could have colored it and the heat of it was spreading down my neck. They must be trying to make me feel better, but it wasn't working.

"You're beautiful just the way you are. No spray painting is necessary," Andrew whispered in my ear, so no one else could hear. He kissed me right there in front of everyone.

"Stop that right now!" Mark growled.

"You don't like kissing?" Sonya asked, looking directly at Mark.

"Well, I don't like watching..."

"I don't like watching either," Sonya interrupted. "It's not a spectator sport." She stood up, sat down on Mark's lap, put her arms around his neck, and planted a big, juicy, open-mouthed kiss on his dumbfounded face. An arm shot out of nowhere to snatch her smoothly from the Jacuzzi. The arm belonged to Mr. Parker, her father. Whoa! I didn't see that coming.

"Dad, stop! You're embarrassing me in front of my friends," Sonya said in a pouty voice.

"No, you are embarrassing yourself." Mr. Parker said as he hauled her off toward the house. She was so busted! He handed her a towel and the shirt she had been wearing over her skimpy bikini that she must have gotten at "Skanks-R-Us." My best guess is that she was about to receive a stern lecture on first date etiquette or how not to act in a hot tub when your parents are watching. I couldn't help smiling as I felt somewhat vindicated. There is some poetic justice in the universe. I wanted to get up and give Mr. Parker a standing ovation, but I managed to control myself.

"What just happened?" Mark asked with a stunned look on his suddenly pale face.

"You should run away fast while you still can," James said, laughing at his nervous expression.

"Does your dad blame me for that?" Mark asked with a wide eyed, acutely uncomfortable expression showing on his face.

"No, he knows it wasn't you," James said. "He told her to get rid of that bikini. I think she bought it two sizes too small. She likes to show off all her assets."

"So, why am I running away?"

"To avoid the inevitable pain that will come if you don't bail now," Matthew explained. "She'll claw your heart out, pulverize it, and throw the pieces into cold storage. Later, she'll put it in a blender set on liquefy. Then she'll drink it. She's merciless when it comes to men."

"How do you know that? It sounds suspiciously like you've learned from experience." Hannah looked unhappy. "When did you date her?"

"It was just after you left on your last trip to Australia," Matthew admitted, sheepishly.

"How come I didn't know this? All that time she pretended to be my best friend and no one bothered to tell me? That's so wrong," Hannah looked at Matthew through narrowed eyes.

"I'm really sorry, Hannah. It didn't last long enough to count. I was stupid and weak. You know she's totally evil and doesn't play fair," Matthew apologized profusely.

"Don't be mad at him, Hannah," Jillian said. "You know how she is. She broke Luke's heart too. Didn't she, Luke?"

"Yeah, it wasn't my proudest moment either. She's like those Sirens in Greek mythology. She casts some kind of black-magic-voodoo-spell on you and takes away your ability to resist. Once she gets her hooks into you, you're a goner. There is absolutely no way out without serious suffering. At least, we're no longer susceptible to her charm. We've been inoculated." Luke said. "When we look at her, we just feel sick. It's a lot like holding your hand in an open flame. Once you've felt the burning agony, you never want to do it again. We know to keep our distance. It's just not worth the extreme emotional pain. Looks can only take you so far. Underneath all that physical perfection, she's not a nice person."

"Yeah, she's like a present that's been wrapped up in gold foil with red ribbons by Martha Stewart, but when you open it, you find a rusty can of stinky, disgusting, wormy eyeballs," Matthew added, grinning at his offensive analogy.

"Ew!" All of us girls exclaimed together. Now there's a picture I'd really rather not have burned into my brain. There it was in vivid color.

I understood the "feeling sick" and "being burned" consequences of interacting with the supreme queen of extreme emotional pain.

"Wow, Bro. You nailed it! I totally agree," Luke knuckle punched his brother. "She is so 'stinky-wormy-eyeball-disgusting' inside!"

"I have a list as long as my arm of guys she's cut down, Mark. The only one whose heart she couldn't break is Andrew. He's got some superhuman immunity or something." James shook his head. He didn't seem to disagree with the Allen brothers' distasteful analogy.

Evelyn announced that dinner was just about ready. She and her husband who is Andrew's older brother, Adam, had barbecued almost everything that can be cooked that way. There was chicken, ribs, steak, pork chops, corn on the cob (in February—no less), baked potatoes, vegetable and fruit shish-kabobs, and baked beans. After we stuffed ourselves, we sang Happy Birthday to Jillian and were served red velvet cake and chocolate chip ice cream. Somehow, Sonya's plate ended up in her lap. Hannah grinned at me. Hannah's superpower involves telekinesis. Sonya flashed a dirty look at her. She had apparently guessed it was no accident. I tried not to laugh, but it took some serious self control to stifle the giggles. If I could pick a superpower, I think I'd take that one. Visions of various flying objects pelting her frowning face spun happily in my head.

Jillian had requested no presents be given. I know she meant it. She also knew we would ignore that wish. Her family gave her a brand new Toyota Prius, in powder blue. Tiffany and I got her some genuine turquoise and silver earrings that we had seen her admire while shopping together. Luke gave her an amethyst ring. His family gave her a matching necklace. The Parkers gave her the bracelet and earrings in her birthstone to complete the set. It was handcrafted by Native Americans and was intricate and expensive jewelry. She got an assortment of other carefully chosen gifts from the rest of our friends. Jillian loved everything. She chewed us out for going against her wishes and then graciously thanked us for our gifts.

After the gift giving, we retired to the theatre room in Andrew's basement to watch Jillian's favorite movie, "Eclipse," on DVD. I'd seen it twice already, but it's always fun to watch vampires. I could relate to Bella because I had to keep some secrets about my boyfriend being from another world, but at least he was human and not a mythical character and he didn't want to drink my blood. That would literally suck.

Mark and Kylie invited everyone to go to a dance on Dixie College Campus. Some local band was playing there. They were supposed to be good. Mark and Sonya and Tiff and Jeremy went. Andrew and I declined the offer. I didn't think I could stomach Sonya any longer than I had to. My acting abilities only go so far. I most certainly didn't want to watch her put the moves on Mark. I still had a bad feeling about her sudden attraction to my defenseless brother.

Andrew had his fill of James, as well. They were not on the best of terms. It wouldn't take much for their tempers to flare up and cause damage. Things could get ugly fast. I'd seen it happen before. It could go all "exploding-super-nova" in a matter of minutes. It was best to keep all that testosterone in check.

That night when I went to bed, I said a prayer for Mark. He hadn't come home yet. I didn't know how his date would end. I could visualize her putting a curse on him and turning him into some kind of love-crazed-zombie-slave who would brainlessly perform her selfish wishes and try to fulfill her every painfully demeaning command. It seemed like a perfectly plausible outcome to me, but I didn't like it at all. Maybe I was obsessing over her mysterious attraction to my brother. However, I was well aware of how hazardous this particular infatuation could be if I couldn't find a way to stop her cruel intentions.

CHAPTER 4

MARK'S GOOD INTENTIONS

Mark and Jeremy got home from the dance very late. I was unconscious and completely dead to the world when they came in. My curfew is midnight and I'd tried to stay up until they got home, but somehow I failed, in spite of my frustrating fears for my brother. I finally fell asleep sometime after one thirty. They slept until noon on Sunday. My parents couldn't rouse them in time to go to church, so I had to wait until lunch to hear about their dates.

Tiffany had called and filled me in on her side of things. She said Sonya stuck to Mark like superglue and apparently tripped a girl who asked him to dance while she was in the ladies room. The poor girl was lucky she escaped without serious injury. Tiff liked Jeremy and hoped he'd ask her out again. She commented on noticing that a lot of girls were throwing themselves at James, and his date, the cute and perky Kylie, got miffed and left. She said he hardly realized she was gone.

Evidently, James had grilled Tiffany about me when they went for breakfast. I didn't want to know that, so I quickly swept it out of my thoughts and into the subconscious, basement closet inside my brain where I keep all those things I don't want to think about and would prefer not to know in the first place. I'm really into denial. It has served me well as a way of coping with stress in the past. I wasn't sure what would happen when that closet got full. Oops, there's another thing I didn't want to think about.

After lunch, I finally got my chance to interrogate my brother and his best friend. I was usually the one sitting in the hot seat getting questioned by them, so this was a little different. I wasn't sure what to ask. I couldn't inquire if the vexatious, alien sorceress had enticed Mark to join the dark side. It probably wouldn't be good to ask them, "Can you tell she's from another planet?" If they both had been influenced to think she was the perfect princess, would they even believe me if I told them she was an evil, psychotic, space monster? No, she'd probably been messing with their minds already. It was best not to go there.

"What happened at the dance? Did you enjoy yourselves? Did Sonya do anything crazy?" I wasn't sure I wanted all the horrid, juicy details, but my curiosity was insistent and would not be stifled. I had to ask.

"Yeah, it was fun. You and Andrew should have come. The band was great. Sonya behaved herself, aside from tripping a pretty, little, Asian girl named Kim, who asked me to dance. She apologized profusely and swore it was an accident," Mark explained grinning at me. "She seems to have a lot of accidents. How's your nose, Sis?"

"It doesn't hurt much," I said. I didn't tell them that it had been broken before Andrew fixed it. I would have looked like a prizefighter who lost badly, if Andrew hadn't worked his magic on me. Thank heavens for his healing superpower.

"I had a terrific time with your friend, Tiffany. I'll have to ask her out again when I'm up here next time," Jeremy stated.

"Tiff called and said she'd like to see you again too," I told Jeremy. He looked happy about that. "What time did you get home?"

"It was after two thirty. We went to Village Inn and had pancakes and eggs after the dance," Mark said.

"It's a good thing Tiffany's parents were out of town and her big sister is a sound sleeper. Her curfew is midnight and her parents are strict." I warned Jeremy.

"Good to know. I'll be more careful next time," Jeremy declared.

"James' date didn't go to breakfast with us. She just sort of disappeared. I think she got tired of him quizzing me about you." Mark frowned.

"What did he want to know?" I frowned and really wished James would stop his ridiculous adoration act. I still couldn't believe he was crushing on me.

"He seemed to want your whole life history. It was weird. He acted like he was going to write a book or something. Oh, and he's apparently some kind of celebrity on Dixie campus. Hordes of Girls were constantly asking him to dance."

"That is weird. I don't get it! I mean that he wanted to know stuff about me. I was hoping he was serious about Kylie. She seemed to be his type. He scares me," I admitted.

I didn't care if every girl in the world wanted him. Of course, then I might feel obligated to warn them that he was an evil predator and not to be trusted. That would be a full time job that I didn't want or need.

"You're the one he can't have, so you're the one he wants," Jeremy summed it up with that statement. I didn't want to hear that. Why couldn't he forget me? I hoped one of the girls in the horde would snag and bag his heart and hold onto it indefinitely and that all this would transpire quickly and put an end to his creepy, fake obsession with me.

"Do you like Sonya?" I changed the subject, not wanting to think about James.

"I don't want to like her, but I can't get her out of my head. She has a crazy magnetism that is hard to resist. I've never felt so attracted to a girl before. It's like she's in control of my thoughts. I know it sounds insane, but I think I may be in love with her."

"NO! No, no, no, no, no, no with a side of double-no-way!" I wanted to slap the back of his head to knock some intelligence into it. I wanted to pull my hair out and scream at the top of my lungs. This was beyond bad. This was exactly what I had feared would happen. I had wanted to be wrong about my repellant premonition of doom.

"Chill, Sis. Love scares me to death! I'm not planning on seeing her again. I have better sense than that. Contrary to your obvious opinion, I'm not a total moron. I've been warned by everyone who knows her and I know she's the kind of girl who brings severe emotional heartache. I know when to back away from the beautiful, mesmerizing, scary-hot female. I'm not ready to become romantic road kill."

I breathed a sigh of relief. "Thank heavens! For a minute there, I thought you had lost your mind. I am so relieved that you can see through her attempts to enslave you. Once she has you under her control, she won't hesitate to throw you under a bus and feed your mangled remains to the sharks."

"I hear that! If Andrew can escape from her power, so can I." Mark said with stoic determination.

I hoped he could carry it out, but I still worried. She could be insanely persistent and she was used to getting her way with guys. I was sure this wasn't over. She was probably plotting her next move in her quest to possess my big brother at this very moment. Could Mark resist temptation when it came on full force? Only time would tell. Unfortunately, there was much less time than I had imagined.

The phone rang about an hour after lunch. From the caller I.D., I knew it was Sonya. I stared at it. I froze, afraid to touch it. Mark answered it on the fourth ring, completely ignoring my violent head shaking and my attempts to swat his hand away, stupid, stupid boy!

"What did she want?" I asked after he had a brief conversation with the devil-woman.

"She's coming over to say good-bye. She and her parents are flying back to Roswell late tonight," he answered, giving me a sheepish expression of remorse at ignoring my warning.

"She couldn't just say good-bye over the phone?" Of course not, that would be too easy. She probably couldn't completely overpower him through the phone lines. Oh yes, she could. I was forced to recall how she had called me in the middle of the night, hypnotized me, and sent me into the waiting clutches of barbarian cannibals. However, I thought her magic needed to be in close proximity to the helpless victim, in order to do the most damage. That over-confident, female cobra was going to strike him right here in our own house.

"She says she has something for me and now I'm curious," Mark admitted. "What does a girl give you after one date?"

"A great, big, wet kiss?" Jeremy wondered. "Oh yeah, she already gave you that while sitting on your lap in a hot tub in full view of her father!"

"How about a dog collar and a leash?" I couldn't help it. It slipped out. At least I hadn't said a bite-full of poisonous, space-monster venom that would render you paralyzed and incapable of fleeing from her super-strong alien grasp, but I was thinking it.

"When's she coming?" Jeremy asked. "We've got to head back to Vegas soon."

"She said she'd be here in half an hour," Mark frowned. "Don't leave me alone with her," he begged his best friend. I hadn't seen him look this scared since he wrecked our parents' Saab when he was sixteen and fresh out of Driver's Ed.

The doorbell rang. I knew it wasn't Sonya or I would have run up the stairs and hid under my bed like my cat, Slim, always does when confronted by scary people. It's a conditioned response that I was considering adopting. Bad things happen to me when she's around.

I opened the door and basked in the warmth of Andrew's bright smile. I took his hand, curling my fingers through his and pulling him in the door as he bent over to kiss me, making me forget Mark's difficult situation for an instant. I melted into him and lingered in his arms, feeling the tingling thrill of euphoria that always surges through my insides at moments like this, sending my heartbeat into warp-speed. It was really hard to remember the impending doom that I needed to focus on for my brother's sake. I shivered and forced my attention back to reality and the immediate crisis that was waiting impatiently to be addressed.

"We need to have a sit down," I stated as I remembered the magnitude of the evil that loomed at the edge of my consciousness. Pulling him into the living room, I motioned for Mark and Jeremy to join us. Then I explained the "Sonya dilemma" to him. He could read it in my head, but that would leave Mark and Jeremy wondering what was going on.

"What do you think she's up to?" Mark asked. He looked as nervous as a caged animal with no escape in sight.

"Whatever it is, it can't be good," Andrew frowned. "Watch out. She's indiscriminately devious. Maybe, she wants to brand and shackle you or turn you into a toad. How should I know? She usually brings disaster. She's a catastrophic event building momentum to wreak havoc on the innocent. It's best to stay out of her path of destruction. I think you should avoid even making eye contact with her. Mate, if you want to stay safe, don't even look at her. I've learned to avoid her at all costs. It would be best to leave before she gets here."

"Thanks, Andrew! Okay, now I'm really creeped out. I can't just leave. She made me promise I'd wait for her. How do I not look at her? She's drop dead gorgeous and my eyes have a mind of their own. Dude, is it too much to hope for an autographed picture or a plate of cookies?" Mark's eyes had grown as big as computer discs.

"If she brings anything edible, don't eat it. She's probably put love potion in it or some kind of chemical that would allow her to take over your mind," I warned facetiously, as if she needed to do that when she could just use her superpower of male-mind-domination.

"You guys are ridiculous! She can't be that bad. She's just an extremely good looking, spoiled girl who happens to be interested in Mark. I'd be flattered if she liked me," Jeremy said. He didn't realize that she had worked her magic on him too. He was a delusional fool, if he thought her attention was a good thing.

The doorbell rang again. Andrew and I ducked into the kitchen. Neither one of us wanted to deal with Sonya today. I heard Mark open the door. I heard Sonya and James enter. Slim raced into the kitchen from his usual place under the coffee table to hide behind the fichus tree in the corner of the adjoining dining room. My smart cat can smell danger and he's an amazing judge of human character.

"Where's Tiana?" James asked Mark. We overheard his question from our hiding place on the other side of the wall.

"She's in the kitchen with Andrew," Mark answered. I wanted to kick him. I didn't particularly want to see James either.

"What are you guys doing? You couldn't be hiding from my lovely sister, now could you?" James asked as he entered the kitchen with a huge smirk on his face. We didn't answer.

"Your brother is toast. She's made up her mind. I'm sorry about that. I tried to talk her out of it, but she's got her game face on and you know how impossibly obstinate she can be. I came to offer my condolences. A tornado couldn't stop her now."

"Why Mark?" I had to ask. My stomach was churning with stress. I thought I might really lose my lunch this time. Nausea had become instantaneous every time I got within a mile of that hateful harpy.

"I'm not completely sure. I'm willing to bet she believes it's a good way to exact revenge on the two of you. She's nothing if she isn't petty. She'll talk him into taking her to the airport in Vegas tonight. Another two hours with her and he'll be completely under her power," James spoke apologetically. "I was hoping she'd steal you away from Tiana to leave the door open for me," he said, smiling at Andrew, who didn't smile back.

"Sorry to disappoint you, but that door is closed and locked and you're never getting in." Andrew said, as he pulled me into his arms and held me close as if to shield me from the predatory alien that is James Parker.

"My work is done here. I really am sorry, Tiana. I'll see you both later." James left the kitchen. I heard him say good bye to Mark, Jeremy, and Sonya. I heard the front door open and close. Andrew and I snuck out the back door and left in his car. I just couldn't watch her turn my brother into a spineless, shell of his former self with no will of his own. I had no power to protect him. All I could do was cross my fingers and pray for divine intervention.

I stayed at Andrew's until around ten. I had felt a distinct disturbance in the force when we had left Mark and Jeremy alone with the spacey seductress. Yeah, I was being a wimp, but I hadn't figured out how to stop the "root of all evil" from claiming Mark. I just wasn't strong enough to face off with Psycho Sonya. I wasn't prepared to see the beautiful beast smirk at me triumphantly. I called my brother when I got home to assess the extent of the inevitable damage.

"Mark, are you okay? Did you defect to the dark side? What did she do to you?" I knew he could hear my alarm.

"Tiana, I don't know what happened. I ate her cookies. I tried not to, but they were peanut butter with chocolate chips, all warm and gooey and I couldn't just say no. Do you think there was some kind of mind control drug in them? She's coming to UNLV this weekend. I think I sort of invited her to my basketball game. I don't understand how it went down. It was like she put the words into my mouth and made me say them. What is wrong with me? What have I gotten myself into? Who is she? Is she a real honest-to-goodness witch? Is she a hypnotist?

"You and Andrew have to come down on Saturday to support me. I'm not strong enough to resist by myself. Jeremy was no help at all. He was eating her cookies and I think she was controlling him as well. You have to promise me you'll come!" He sounded desperate.

"Okay, Mark, we'll come. Be strong! You can beat this!" I sounded more confident than I was. I hoped it wasn't too late to stop the horrendous catastrophe that hovered on the horizon from overtaking him, but unfortunately, like an avalanche gathering speed down a steep mountain slope, it was impossible to stop it.

CHAPTER 5

BEST MADE PLANS

I woke up Monday morning shivering in a cold sweat. I had dreamed about my brother and the black-hearted Sonya Parker. In my nightmare, she was a humongous, ugly vulture that swooped down from a black and blue sky, snatching Mark in her long, cruel claws and flying off with an inhuman cry of triumph. She carried him, kicking and squirming in her treacherous talons to the top of a craggy cliff where she proceeded to tear him limb from limb and to swallow him, a piece at a time, while he shrieked in bitter agony. There had to be a way to prevent her from ruining his life, but I didn't know what it was.

Andrew picked me up like always. His angelic face beaming down on me made me almost forget the nagging worries that tugged at my heart. I had to smile back at him. He never stopped making my heart race. He sent a kind of low voltage electrical charge that hummed and vibrated through my circulatory system whenever he was near. We had been dating for almost seven months now. I still felt the full force of his magnetism. I had to struggle to breathe normally for a few minutes while I got acclimatized to his presence.

"Are you still worried about Mark?" His smile faded and was replaced by concern.

"Last night, I dreamed Sonya was a vulture. She tore him apart and ate him while he screamed. It was awful," I shuttered and frowned, remembering how helpless I felt during the horrific nightmare.

"That seems like an appropriate metaphor," he said. "I can visualize her as a vulture. She is a vile, noxious creature who preys on the weakened state of others. We won't let her destroy Mark. We'll think of some way to stop her, Love. No worries." He tried to placate me. It almost worked. He hugged me tightly, resting his chin on the top of my head and then ushered me to his car. It was hard to worry about anything when I was with him.

After school, I sat on the bleachers in the gymnasium while Andrew had basketball practice. I tried to do homework, but most of the time I just had to watch him play. His athletic abilities surpassed all the other members of the team. He didn't hog the ball or try to make all the points. He was a team player who always did his job nearly to perfection. He tried to help the other team members do their assignments to the best of their abilities and offered them constant encouragement. I was so caught up in watching that I hadn't noticed James until he sat down beside me. I was startled by his unexpected appearance. What was wrong with him? This was my safe zone. He shouldn't be here.

"What are you doing here?" I was not altogether polite in my tone. I'm afraid it was more than obvious that I didn't want to see him at my school. He didn't belong.

"Aren't you glad to see me?" He laughed at my rudeness. "I was in the area and thought I might find you here. Can we start over, Tiana? I really don't want you to hate me. Can't we at least be friends? I'm not such a bad guy. I can't help being attracted to you. Do you know how beautiful you are?"

"Stop it! Flattery will get you nothing. Can we be friends? Let me think. You tried to convince Andrew to leave me. You pretended to be his friend and then you stabbed him in the back. You tried to use your superpower to manipulate us both and make us follow your own selfish agenda. You seem to enjoy tormenting him. That certainly doesn't endear you to me. I don't think you would be a very good friend." Why should I try to soft pedal my feelings? I decided to give it to him straight. Honesty is good, right?

"I am sorry about that. My behavior has been inexcusable. Are you going to hold it against me forever?"

"I think you should be apologizing to Andrew. I'm not ready to forgive you for the way you've treated him." I wasn't sure I could ever forgive him his past acts of malice toward my soul-mate.

"Maybe I can help your brother escape from my sister's power before she turns his brain to mush and makes hash out of his heart. Would that help you want to forgive me?" He flashed me his brilliant white grin. I'd think he was addicted to tooth whiteners if I didn't know better. He was stunningly attractive as were all the Helamites I had met. They had tampered with their DNA sometime during the last century. I tried not to think about how unfair that was to those of us who had no such options.

At that moment, the cheerleading squad had begun practicing their cheer routines loudly on the sidelines of the court. I looked down to see Jenna wave at me. I waved back, smiling and to my amazement Alexis smiled and waved also. James wasn't looking at her when she waved. I looked behind me to see if there was someone else that she might be waving to, but there was no one. I gave a timid finger wave back in her direction. What was that about? I was struck dumb for a moment, scrambling to recover my wits. Had she actually been waving at me? What was wrong with her?

"Are they friends of yours?" James asked as he finally noticed they were there.

"Jenna is a friend, but Alexis hates my guts." I was still astonished that she had acknowledged my being here. She usually ignores me or throws dirty looks in my general direction. I prefer the ignoring. It works well with my denial coping strategy.

"Oh, she's the girl that pursued Andrew so aggressively last year, right? She's not hard on the eyes, but she can't compete with you, Tiana. She looks too much like my sister. Let me guess. She's superficial, shallow and selfish. She's a virtual self-serving, materialistic queen who rules the social order here because she looks like a beauty pageant participant and most guys are impressed by the fact that she's attractive on the outside. Teenage boys are such fools for a pretty face," he actually sounded like he meant that. Had he been body-snatched and replaced by a smarter clone?

"Wow, you nailed it! Who are you and what have you done with the James Parker I know? I thought maybe you'd want to meet her. I think she was probably waving and smiling at you." I'd realized that must be her motivation. James was extremely gifted in the looks department. She would love to be seen with someone like him.

"I could line you up. We could double date," I joked, knowing that was never going to happen. Neither Andrew nor I could tolerate Alexis for more than about a minute. We disliked her as much as we disliked James.

"Give me a little credit, Tiana. I'm way past being impressed by girls like her. What? You don't believe me?" He acted as if I had insulted him by doubting his sincerity. "Do you think I'd keep chasing you and enduring this endless rejection if just any gorgeous girl would do?"

"You're wasting your time. I'm taken. I'll bet you could learn to like Alexis if you tried. Okay, maybe not her, but I have many nice friends who would certainly find you very attractive." I smiled at the thought of playing matchmaker. I'd do almost anything to get him to forget me, but I probably wouldn't be able to do that to a friend without feeling guilty for the rest of my life.

"No, thanks, I don't need you to find me a date. However, I do have a plan that may distract Sonya from her obsession with your brother. Hear me out. You and Andrew could pretend to break up. You could act like you liked me and Andrew could appear to be inconsolable at losing you. He could turn to her for comfort. She'd drop Mark like a hot potato. Problem solved!"

"Let me think about that, Aaaah, no! It just doesn't work for me." I shook my head.

I was positively never going to pretend I liked James in a romantic way. Not even if it meant saving my brother and I didn't want Andrew seeking any kind of comfort from Sonya. That idea brought back my gut-wrenching, automatic response to the evil diva. It would be like throwing my boyfriend to a pack of starving coyotes.

"There is no way on this green earth or anywhere else in the universe that I will pretend to turn to your crazy sister for consolation. I'd rather pet a hungry tiger. As for letting Tiana pretend she likes *you*; well, you can forget that right now!" Andrew was finished practicing and was towering over James in a menacing way.

I stood up quickly and sent him a mental message stating my immediate desire to go home. His contempt for James was apparent. His mouth formed a thin, hard line. His eyes were narrowed into slits. His arms were crossed over his chest, and his hands were fisted. He was undoubtedly fighting the urge to punch James squarely in his sparkling white teeth. I sensed the gravity of the situation. I'd seen this look on him before. I thought this might be his conditioned response to James, much like nausea was my immediate reaction to Sonya. I reached out to Andrew, taking his hand, hoping to prevent a physical confrontation before it exploded.

"Look Andrew, I'm really sorry I tried to get you to leave her. I wish you'd let it go. Can we be friends again?" James did his best to look contrite. I wasn't sure I was buying it. Andrew most certainly wasn't. He snorted at James' question.

"You ask if we can be friends after revealing and asking us to participate in your disgusting, impossible, love fantasy. I don't think so! Besides, it would never work. Sonya can read emotions. I wouldn't be able to convince her that I needed anything from her. I'm not that good of a liar. She's smarter than that. She'd know I only feel negative emotions around her."

"Oh, come on! Get real! She wants to believe you like her so badly that she'd ignore your emotional climate and believe anything you said," James retorted and then added, "However, I do have an alternate plan."

"If it's anything like your first plan, I don't want to hear it," Andrew insisted.

"I met a guy in my abnormal psychology class who looks a lot like you. I could talk him into going to Mark's game on Saturday. He might be able to persuade her to lose interest in Mark. She does have a short attention span when it comes to romance. It's worth a try. I still like my first plan best," James said and shrugged his shoulders.

"Bring the guy and make sure he knows all the right things to say. Don't tell him how toxic Sonya is. I know that's unfair to him, but maybe he'll be a willing sacrifice. We'll have to think of a way to repay him if this works," I said, grabbing at the hope that we might find a way to stop the madness. I didn't like the idea of some stranger being caught in her web, but it was better than losing my brother. Desperate times call for desperate measures or anything that has the remotest possibility of success.

"Oh, I'll probably have to bribe him to ease my conscience. He'll think I'm doing him an immense favor until he suffers the consequences. It might work out. She could actually like him and refrain from doing her signature heart-breaking move that she's so good at. Miracles do happen from time to time." James laughed again. Did he actually have a conscience? Perhaps I had misjudged him. Nah, I didn't think so.

The next day, Jenna stopped me in the hall and asked, "Who was that super-hot guy sitting by you on the bleachers yesterday, the one who looks like Antonio Banderas' younger, cuter brother?"

"That was James Parker. I told you about him," I answered.

"He's the guy, who tried to get rid of Andrew, so he could date you?" I could almost see the light bulb go on in her head as her eyes brightened.

"He's one and the same. Don't tell me you're interested in him," I knew Ryan would freak if she was. I'd have to discourage that for her own good.

"No, Alexis thinks he's even hotter than Andrew. She begged me to ask you about him. Do you think he could be persuaded to go out with her?"

"Oddly enough, I actually suggested that. He didn't seem interested, but I'll ask him again when I see him. If he shows up at practice, tell her to come on up. I'll introduce her. I'll even pretend she's a friend, if it will help. I don't know if he'll go out with her, though. He knows about how she stalked Andrew last year."

"Oh, that is bad, but there's no stopping Alexis when she sees something she wants. Maybe, he won't come back. If he does, things could get dicey; more drama for the drama queen. It's about time for her to pitch a fit. I haven't seen her have a tantrum in over a week. Well, I've done what I promised to do. Thanks for the information. I'll filter it and pass it on to Her Majesty," Jenna laughed and hurried off to her next class.

James came back to Andrew's practice the next day, bringing the Andrew doppelganger. The guy did look like my boyfriend. However, I felt no magnetism from him. He wasn't as tall as Andrew. He lacked the dimples and the cleft in his chin. His eyes were more of a wintry, gray-blue color and his thick, artistically disheveled hair was a shade or two darker blond. His smile lacked that distinctive, dazzling quality that drew me to Andrew. It didn't seem to reach his eyes. There were other subtle differences that were obvious to me, but I didn't think others would notice them.

He was certainly attractive. Would he appeal to Psycho Sonya? Everyone in the gym seemed to be staring at him. I could almost hear them thinking that he had to be Andrew's twin or older brother or some long lost relative with an incredible resemblance.

"Tiana, I want you to meet Daniel Thomas. Daniel, this is the girl I told you about, the beautiful and unattainable, Miss Tiana Dawson," James said as they sat down beside me.

"I'm happy to meet you, Daniel," I smiled at him and waited to hear his voice.

"It's my pleasure. You are just as lovely as James said you were," he said in a voice that was nowhere near as alluring as Andrew's and of course, he had no Aussie accent. He had a slight southern drawl instead. It was kind of fun to listen to.

Alexis bravely ascended the stairs to where we were seated on the bleachers. The two boys didn't see her until she spoke to me.

"Tiana, will you introduce me to your friends?" She asked shyly. I knew it was an act. The girl doesn't know shy.

"Of course, Alexis, this is James Parker and his friend Daniel Thomas. James and Daniel, this is Alexis Empey." I kept my voice as warm and friendly as I could manage. I'm a pretty decent actress, myself. I didn't want them to know she was my second-worst enemy on this planet. Well, James already knew.

"Alexis Empty?" James teased, flashing his irresistible grin at her.

"No silly. It's Empey—E-m-p-e-y," she said while batting her ridiculously long false eyelashes shamelessly at the two boys.

"Oh, aren't you charming!" James laughed and rolled his eyes at me. "Isn't she cute, Daniel? She looks a lot like my sister, Sonya."

"Really?" Daniel looked pleased at that and Alexis beamed at him.

"Would you do something for me, Alexis?" James showed her his radiant smile and used his most persuasive voice.

"I'd *love* to," she replied, emphasizing the love.

"First, I'd like you to apologize to Tiana for treating her so rudely in the past. Then, I want you to go down and do your very best cheer for us. Can you do that, Allison?" James beamed all his glamour on her. The poor girl was clay in his hands. He truly had skills as a master manipulator.

"What makes you think I was rude to her? Have you been telling him stories, Tiana?" She asked, acting positively horrified that I might have told him about her past mean-girl actions towards me.

"No, of course not," I lied.

"Was I wrong? I didn't think so," James watched her guilty expression.

"Sorry, Tiana, I'll make it up to you, okay?" She then turned to face James. "My name is Alexis—A-l-e-x-i-s, not Allison. Don't you dare forget it! Now, I'll go do that cheer for you. Be sure you give me your undivided attention, James and Daniel." She turned and pranced back down to join the other cheerleaders who were whispering, giggling and stealing glances up at us.

"Well, at least the girl can spell. I guess she's not a total air head," James said.

"If it doesn't work out with James' sister, do you think you could line me up with her?" Daniel asked me as he watched Alexis' cheering routine with admiration in his adoring eyes. He was a fool. James rolled his eyes so hard at me; I thought they might pop out the back of his head. He didn't even glance at the cheerleaders.

"Sure, I'd love to, if things don't go well with Sonya. Are you positive you don't want to take Alexis out, James? She wants you badly," I grinned at him, trying to direct his attention to her antics on the floor below us.

"I'd rather be boiled in oil or have all my fingernails removed," James exclaimed.

"Wow, what is wrong with you? Look at her cheering. She's so cute and perky. Why don't you like her?" I was amused by his disdain for the Barbie doll who was trying so hard to impress him with cartwheels, back flips and splits.

"You really should give her a chance. She's willing to literally bend over backwards to please you. What's not to like?"

"Tiana, give it a rest. The girl probably hasn't had a meaningful thought in her pretty, little, empty head during her whole superficial life. She's completely forgettable. I've had more than my share of girls like her," James' frown hardened.

"Well, I haven't, and I want some," Daniel was enjoying the show with deep appreciation.

"Oh, you're so going to love Sonya. I hope she's going to love you too!" I exclaimed enthusiastically, clapping my hands. I had found great hope for my brother's future. This scheme might actually work. It was certainly worth the effort. Hey, I was almost willing to forgive James, if this plan of his came to fruition!

CHAPTER 6

MARK'S MAGIC MOMENT

I told Andrew about the particulars of meeting his inferior "twin." He found it all highly amusing and was delighted to hear about Daniel Thomas' affinity for shallow blondes who look like Barbie dolls. He was as optimistic as I was about the "get-Sonya-out-of-Mark's-life" plan. He found it especially funny that Alexis was hot for James. He strongly suggested that I give her James' cell phone number and the address of his apartment in St. George.

We both enjoyed the thought of Alexis persistently stalking James so much, we laughed until we had tears leaking from our eyes. They seemed so perfect for each other, but I knew James didn't think so. I had to give him some points for seeing through her appearance. This was more than most boys were capable of doing. I felt a little sorry for him, but not enough to stop smiling when I thought about her determined desire to steal his heart.

When Saturday came, I was excited to go to Vegas to see Mark and Jeremy play basketball for UNLV. Andrew and I decided to make a day of it. We took a picnic lunch and stopped in the Valley of Fire to eat it. The park lived up to its name. The brilliant red-orange, rock formations resembled burning flames that had solidified into unique shapes with rugged, stone walls and delicate arches that glowed like fire in the bright sunshine. I wondered if the surface of Mars, the red planet, looked something like this. Late February was the perfect time to visit, with comfortable temperatures hovering around sixty five degrees. A few fluffy, cotton-ball clouds floated across the mostly clear, brilliant, aquamarine sky. We hiked, climbed rocks and took pictures until we'd feasted on the startling beauty and unusual landscape that grew out of the desolate, desert wilderness.

It wasn't until we parked in the lot at the Thomas and Mack Center that I heard the warning bells go off with an irritating buzzing in my head. *She's going to win,* that inner voice said the words I didn't want to believe. Surely, it had to be wrong this time, didn't it? This particular voice had never been wrong before. *Mark is going to fall for her. You can't stop it from happening,* it continued to taunt me. I wanted it to shut up, but it kept right on talking to my brain. *"He can't fight this. She's too powerful. Remember the way Andrew drew you to him? It's every bit as compelling as that magnetic magic. Mark won't be strong enough to push her away. No one can stop this. You have to accept it.* Wow, that obnoxious voice was getting so darn wordy. Could it be more annoying? I didn't think so. *Just let it happen. It will all work out eventually.*

Okay, this was getting weird. I actually felt a small drop of peace slip into my terrified consciousness. I didn't understand it. My brother falling in love with Psycho Sonya was a truly horrible thing. How could I feel happy about that? She was undeniably evil. Could something good come from her breaking his heart? I came to a sudden and dramatic realization that it was inevitable like the sun coming up in the morning or the ocean tides rushing further and further onto their respective, sandy beaches and then back out again. I knew I couldn't stop it any more than I could stop night from following day.

"It's going to happen, isn't it?" Andrew said when he opened the door for me. "We can't prevent him from falling for her. You just realized that, right?"

All I could do was nod and then a few tears trickled down my cheeks.

"I'm so sorry, Tiana. It's my fault. I wish I could stop this, but I can't." He looked so forlorn, I felt incredibly guilty that I had once again caused him to blame himself. He held me and kissed my forehead as I tried to recover. Then I felt a second tiny drop of peace. It was just barely enough to give me hope. I dried my eyes and kissed his cheek.

"It's not your fault. You've got to stop blaming yourself for everything that goes wrong. It will be okay. I'm fine," I whispered in his ear. He led me into the massive arena that was filled with rowdy, excited people who had no idea that my brother was doomed.

We found our seats in the middle of the third row. Mark had gotten us primo tickets. Sonya was seated on the first row right behind the players' bench. James and Daniel were there on each side of her. I could tell Daniel was trying hard to gain her favor. She seemed to be enjoying his attention, but she kept her eyes focused on the entrance where Mark and Jeremy would come in just prior to the commencement of the game. This was a big game for UNLV. They were playing UCLA. It would be a monumental victory if they could beat the Bruins.

"What is she thinking?" I had to know.

"You really don't want to know," Andrew squeezed my hand and bit his lip.

"Is it that bad?" I asked, looking into his bright, Indian-turquoise eyes.

"It's worse. She is despicable and very thorough in her pernicious plans. I can't look in her mind again. It's ugly, and it disgusts me. Please don't make me do it anymore tonight. You don't have any idea how malicious and vengeful she is," he pleaded with me.

"Okay, you don't have to go back in there. I understand," I smiled and squeezed his hand. I cringed at the thought that I was causing him such pain.

"Do you know how much I love you, Tiana? I'd do anything for you, but thanks for not making me do that again," he sighed and said the words directly into my ear.

Here was my incredibly brave boyfriend who never even balked at single-handedly taking down malevolent, barbaric, cannibalistic, alien monsters, begging me not to make him read the mind of the gorgeous girl who had decided to make Mark her next romantic victim. What wicked plans were being hatched in that demonic head of hers? I guess I didn't genuinely want to know. The dread began spiking inside my heart. I bit my lower lip.

James turned and looked at us. He shook his head and frowned. I knew he had read his sister's mind too. He was adding his take on it to Andrew's. It was hopeless. Mark was a goner. No, I would not accept this! The dark side was waiting to gobble him up, but not without a fight. I didn't care what the voice said. This wasn't over yet!

The game was exciting and fast paced. Mark and Jeremy made us proud. Sonya squealed like a banshee. I wasn't much better. It felt good to cheer and yell. It was strangely cathartic, kind of like screaming therapy. It was a way to vent my frustration at not being able to save Mark. The effect was almost a cure for my fears. In the end, we won the game, but I still had an intuitive knowledge that we were probably going to lose the battle to keep Mark's heart healthy. The sad part was that he didn't know, and I couldn't find the courage to tell him. I pulled up all my deepest determination. If we were going down, we were going down fighting!

After the game, we were to meet up at Mark's and Jeremy's dorm. We had made our plans to thwart her evil designs on him, through many phone calls, text messaging and e-mail. Our plot consisted of using all our knowledge, and then some, to unimpress Sonya. I had gathered useful information from Andrew, Hannah, Jillian and even James. I now knew most of her pet peeves in regards to dating the opposite sex. We were going to use as many as we could to make her *not* like Mark.

First, since she hated boys who wore sloppy clothes, Mark was going to wear an old, ragged sweatshirt that boasted a few ketchup stains and some grease-stained jeans that he only wore to work on his jeep. The shirt had the words "I'm with Stupid!" emblazoned across the front. She was sure to be offended by that. Who wouldn't be? Since she hated it when she wasn't offered choices, we had the whole evening planned. We were going to surprise the crap out of her. She passionately hated fast food and child-friendly franchises, so "Chucky Cheese" fit the bill. Because she thought video games were a complete waste of time, Mark would make her play the silliest games they had. She always complained about how immature boys were. That meant we'd play at a park on all the playground equipment, and act like we were all spoiled five year olds before going back to his dorm.

Next we would watch all her most hated movies that I had so carefully selected in a marathon of madness that would last most of the night. Because she planned to spend a romantic night here alone with Mark, we all decided to camp out on his floor. If this didn't discourage her, nothing would. Oh, and we were going to stage a popcorn and pillow fight. It sounded like fantastic fun to me! She had to hate it. It had to be the best and most comprehensive plan ever conceived to discourage a girl from liking a boy.

We carried out our devious schemes with excellent, near perfect execution. Something went terribly wrong. Either she was an actress of Academy Award caliber, or we didn't make these adverse activities painful enough. I laughed so hard at Mark's antics to disillusion her. His performance was flawless. Unfortunately, she failed to be horrified. We all had the time of our lives. She seemed to enjoy herself as much as we did. We had sincerely thought she would detest the whole contrived experience. Halfway through "Army of Darkness," she began giggling uncontrollably.

"I used to hate this movie," she said when she finally stopped laughing. "I never realized how funny it is. Bruce Campbell is absolutely hilarious."

This wasn't going according to our master plan. What had we done wrong? Why wasn't she bowled over with disgust? Even James was astonished by this strange turn of events. She didn't even make rude remarks to me. What was wrong with her? I had never seen her play nice with others. I didn't know what to think. Had the Helamites secretly perfected cloning? Maybe, the girl had a robot made to take her place. This version of Sonya loved everything Mark dished out. It was incomprehensible. It disturbed the crap out of me.

The next day, sometime after noon, I woke up thinking it had all been a terrible dream. It couldn't possible have gone down the way I remembered it. Mark and Jeremy had gone to McDonald's and had bought us all Happy Meals for breakfast or lunch. I guess that would be brunch. This was also part of our grand plot. We didn't expect Sonya to love the silly toy panda bear inside.

"I'll treasure this forever," she cooed at Mark.

Our mission was foiled. We all looked at each other with wonder in our wide-opened eyes. Who was this changeling girl? Did we even know her? Where was the back-stabbing, cold-hearted, nasty nemesis that we all knew and disliked immensely? Was she being possessed by a "good" spirit? It didn't make sense.

CHAPTER 7

STATE TOURNAMENT

This was an exceptionally big week for not only the basketball team, but for all the residents of Hurricane. The State High School Basketball Tournament was being held at the University of Utah in Salt Lake City on Thursday, Friday, and Saturday. On Wednesday night, Andrew got special permission to drive there in his own car, so he could bring me. He told the coach that long bus rides made him nauseous. The coach couldn't risk his star player being sick. The Martin's were paying for the hotel for the entire team, so Andrew could do almost anything he wanted. Money talks, even in high school athletics in tiny towns.

Doesn't everyone get nauseous on a bus full of stinky, testosterone driven, teenage Jocks for five hours? The cheerleaders seemed to enjoy it, but most of them aren't what I would consider exactly normal. I guess it could be me who isn't normal. I like testosterone toned down a little.

Maybe, it's just me, but when you get too many boys together they tend to feed off of each other. They posture and act like wild, crazy gorillas. They spend their time beating their chests in competition for the title of Alpha Male. As far as I was concerned, the Alpha Male was mine, and I didn't feel like sharing.

We were going to have a test on Monday, in English, on "The Taming of the Shrew," so I read it aloud on our trip up to the capital city. Andrew half-heartedly suggested that perhaps Mark could tame the shrewish Sonya and help her change into a kinder, gentler girl like Petruchio tamed Katharina, but I don't think he honestly believed that was possible. I argued that Sonya was more like Katharina's sister, Bianca, because she pretended to be nice, but she was shrewish, cold, and conniving under her façade. Katharina was actually pleasant natured and loving under her shrew-like pretenses.

It was that whole appearance versus reality conflict all over again. Who was genuine and who was faking it? Almost everyone seemed to be pretending to be something other than what they truly were. I guess that kind of thing hasn't changed. In our modern world, it's often hard to tell who people actually are, especially on the internet. People can thoroughly reinvent themselves in cyberspace and live out their own fantasies.

The thing that has changed is that women are no longer seen as possessions in most enlightened societies today. Thankfully, we have made some progress since 1592. The "Elizabethan World Order" which placed women beneath men in the "Great Chain of Being" would never fly today, at least not in this country; God bless America!

We know there aren't forty virgins waiting for crazy, religious, fanatical, suicide bombers. Sometimes, I think it would be a kick to see their faces when they find out how deluded they were on Earth. I'd love to greet them and say, "Whoops, you died for nothing! Take the second door on the left. It leads to eternal damnation where you should feel right at home."

"On your planet, did men ever treat women like they were beneath them?" I asked.

"Absolutely not, we've always known you are superior to us in every way," he said grinning at me.

"No, seriously, I want to know. How did your male ancestors treat your female ancestors on Helam?"

"We've always known we are equal. Men may be stronger physically, but women are more in touch with their emotions. We think differently.

Men are much easier to read than women because women tend to be more complex. James tried to manipulate Sonya into not pursuing your brother. It didn't work because Sonya, like most women, knows her own mind and pushed those thoughts right out like she was deleting unwanted, spam e-mail.

"You are also better communicators. In our culture, women have always been treated with respect, with some exceptions. There are bad men on every planet where humans reside. For that matter, there are bad women also. We all make our own choices," Andrew said all the right things. He almost always does. I love that about him.

We were staying at the Marriot Hotel on the university campus. It is a beautiful, expensive place with this fancy purple, glass chandelier, created by some famous artist, that falls from the ceiling of the highest level down to the lowest level in the middle of the building surrounded by the staircases and glass elevators and all the floors which are open to it. The bed linens are divine. My room was a few doors away from the basketball team and across the hall. Andrew said it would be quieter there than right next door. It didn't matter, because by the time I made it there at night, I was so exhausted I fell asleep in about half a second.

Yes, I did get to sit and watch the games, but they were so close and nerve racking that I spent my time jumping up and down and screaming. In between games, while the other players were resting or watching other teams play, Andrew was dragging me around campus. He had decided he would most likely go to medical school here (for the second time) and of course, if he were here, I would be attending also. He insisted on showing me every building until it was all just a blurry place buried somewhere in my memory.

On Saturday, we won the semifinal game against an exceptionally talented Juan Diego High School team. The Soaring Eagles put up a strong fight. Their star player was about seven feet tall. He towered over every other player on either team. His abilities matched Andrew's so closely, it was eerie.

"Did you notice anything different about him?" he whispered in my ear, after the hard-fought victory.

"He was almost as talented as you are, but not quite," I answered. "Is he from another planet? I figured he must be."

"He's a Helamite. He was reading my thoughts all the way through the game. His name is Morgan Smith. We went to elementary school together. He used to be kind of a bully. He was always bigger than everyone else our age. It felt good to hand him a loss," he said.

"The team we have to play for the championship has two Helamites on it. We played together on a team in Roswell before we all moved to Utah. It's going to be tough to beat them. They're really strong players, and they're much bigger than I am."

We had three hours to rest up before the championship game, so we went back to the hotel. Andrew's whole family was coming up for this critical final contest. They had arrived when we got there, so we had lunch with them at the Spaghetti Factory in Trolley Square.

Unfortunately, Matthew and Luke were off investigating some UFO sighting in Nevada, near Area 51 (yes, the government undoubtedly is hiding all kinds of super-secret-alien-stuff there). Jillian said they weren't happy about it, but there had been so much tension after the Nommoans' failed mission to abduct earth people that all possible unexplained events had to be checked out.

Coach Gordon wanted the team dressed, ready to play, and back at the Huntsman Center an hour before the appointed time, so we didn't get to browse through the unique, historical shopping mall. We hurried back, so Andrew wouldn't miss an inspirational pep talk and the warm up drills, not that he needed it.

"Number 7 and number 11 are old friends of ours," Jillian pointed them out to me as we sat in the chair seats, a few rows behind our team.

"We call them the 'twin towers'. They're the Carson brothers. Hannah used to have a crush on Brad. He's number 7. Number 11 is Bryce. He used to date Sonya," she explained.

"Who didn't date Sonya?" Hannah asked, rolling her eyes. "I know Brad dated her too. I'm surprised she isn't here. She seems to have given up on winning Andrew back, not that she ever really had him. Oh no, I forgot! She's focusing all her energy on your brother. My bad! I'm so sorry she wants to add him to her collection of conquests. How's that going, anyway?"

"Not good. He's losing the willpower to resist. She's turned him into putty, and she's molding him into her love-sick puppet. It hurts to watch her power work on him. He knows she's trouble. He just can't seem to escape from her evil plot to hack up his heart. She's got him so confused. The poor boy doesn't know which way to run. I don't know how to help him," I confessed.

"I'm afraid he'll have to suffer the consequences. Sonya is almost a supernatural phenomenon. She's unstoppable. It sucks! There's not much anyone can do to prevent her plans from doing some major damage. He'll need your support when she dumps him in the dirt minus his self respect. It's a terrible thing to have to witness," Jillian declared, shaking her head and frowning at the painful thought of Sonya destroying yet another helpless male member of the human race.

"There is a slight possibility that she might fall in love with Mark. Someone has to bring her down eventually. God is still in his heaven. There is some justice alive and well in the universe. Karma can't let her get away with all this devastation forever. It's got to come back and bite her. Now would be a great time for that to happen," Hannah insisted.

Then the game started, forcing us all to forget about the fate of my poor, pitiful, soon-to-suffer-indescribable-pain, love-struck brother. Instead, we had to watch Andrew bravely battle the six foot seven inch twins for our rightful place as 3A State Basketball Champions.

This game was much harder fought than any other we'd been in so far. The towering twosome was all over Andrew from the start. They were ridiculously accurate shooters. They seemed to anticipate his every move before he made it. They stuck to him like peanut butter sticks to the roof of your mouth. No matter which way he turned, they were in his way. He could hardly get a good look at the basket. Luckily for us, he took a lot of hard fouls from them, and made most of his points from the line. If they kept up this level of aggressive defense, they would both foul out before the fourth quarter.

At half time, we were down by eleven points. It wasn't looking bright for our severely downtrodden Tigers. They despondently dragged themselves off the court to the locker room for some intense criticism from Coach Gordon. He was not a happy man, and the Hurricane team was looking dismal.

Could they pull it together and make up the deficit? Could Andrew find a way around the Grizzly twins? Would we go home without the coveted trophy that we so deserved? This was not going according to our game plan. We were supposed to dismantle and destroy the Grizzlies. Someone forgot to give the memo to this annoyingly persistent and obnoxiously talented team. Having two incredibly tall spacemen with super-human strength and the ability to read our star player's mind gave them a slightly unfair advantage.

The Logan Grizzlies seemed to think they had already won. They proudly bounded off to hear their praises sung by their overweight, balding coach who was smiling almost larger than life. The gleam off his huge display of ivory teeth was shining painfully. We, the Tiger fans, wanted to slap that ugly grin off his face.

Yes, we were a sorry, depressed bunch of worried people. Our team hadn't lost a game all season. We had never trailed by more than five points. We had never even considered that we might lose this contest. It seemed to be the one thing we all could count on this year. It hadn't occurred to any of us that our star player could be stopped. I could see the question burning in every Tiger fan's eye. Who were these relentless Grizzlies and what would it take to defeat them?

I knew the answer to this question. They were aliens from Andrew's own home planet. They were genetically superior to most teenage, basketball stars, and there were two of them to our one. They could read Andrew's mind. Yeah, he could read their minds too, but again, that was two brains he had to listen to and that had to be more difficult than hearing the thoughts in one person's head.

I tried to prepare myself for a possible loss. I began thinking of all the things I could say to console Andrew. He couldn't win this game alone. The whole team would be responsible for the defeat, but I knew from experience that he would blame himself. There was always next year. It was just a game. It wasn't the end of the world. None of this would make him feel any better. He expected perfection from himself. In fact, we all expected it from him, and he nearly always delivered exactly that.

After halftime, the two teams came together to do battle again. Andrew found my face in the audience, and flashed me a determined grin. He had a plan to get around those pesky, freakishly tall twins. Gradually, our team began to catch up. Ryan and Andrew were working together to outscore their opponents. The other Tigers were guarding the Carson brothers like their lives depended on it. Everyone was stepping up to do his job. At the end of the third quarter, we were only down three points.

The fourth quarter began with a ripple of intense excitement that surged through the crowd. The Carson twins were in foul trouble. One more foul on either one would send that player to the bench for the remainder of the game. The Grizzlies knew they couldn't afford to lose one or both of their stars. Andrew stole the ball from Bryce and made his way into the paint for a perfect lay up. The two jolly giants clothes-lined him, sending him to the floor with a thud that echoed through the cavernous building.

The referees blew their whistles and a hush fell over the crowd. Both coaches and an attending physician ran onto the court to see what injuries had been sustained by our favorite Tiger. Andrew made it to his feet, smiling. The foul was called on Brad. Both brothers were benched. They were not happy warming that bench. Bryce yelled something profane at the referee. He was called with a technical foul. He was out of the game, along with his super-sized, twin brother. Andrew made all his foul shots tying the score at sixty two.

The Grizzlies were quickly left in the dust. Without their star players, they were easily deflated and found that they were unprepared and unable to catch up with our talented Tigers who blew them away with precision teamwork. When the final buzzer sounded, the score was seventy eight to sixty five. The impossible goal had been achieved. We were the state champions! Don't you just love a happy ending? In this case, however, the happy ending was not going to last long enough to actually enjoy. There was trouble looming just around the corner. It was coming at us fast!

CHAPTER 8

DOUBLE TROUBLE

We got the bad news as we were packing up the car to head home to happy Hurricane, home of the 3A State Basketball Champions. The spaceship from Nommo had been located in the Nevada desert. Matthew and Luke had called in to say they were about to make contact. That was just before the Championship game. Then it seems they just went and fell off the planet.

Poof! All traces of them were gone just like that. The GPS systems in their phones had disappeared or ceased functioning. Their car had been found abandoned. There was no alien ship anywhere in the general vicinity and the Zariba agents who were looking for it, had all the super high tech searching tools to find it. There was no way to hide from their advanced technological magic. They could penetrate any cloaking devise and see through the dry, desert dirt to depths that reached almost all the way to China. The atmosphere was also empty of anything foreign to our homey corner of the universe for miles and miles. Nothing out of place could be found anywhere in our entire solar system. Where had the Allen brothers gone?

When we left them, Jillian and Hannah had been struggling to remain calm, but I could see the panic they were both working hard to disguise and keep under control. Keeping the Earth save from dangerous aliens is not for wimps.

There were three possibilities. The Nommoans had abducted them and were hiding somewhere in space. They had dropped them off after traveling to a far away, uncivilized spot on this planet. Could they be on their way to the distant planet of Nommo? This third scenario was worse than the other two. The planet, Nommo, was very, very far away.

If they went there, Einstein's Special Theory of Relativity would come into play. Andrew explained this to me on our way home. It took me a while to think through it. It's a little hard to comprehend, so he tried to simplify it. When a spaceship moves at near light speed, time dilation is experienced by the crew. This means that the ship's length shortens in the direction of movement, its mass becomes greater, and time measured on board moves more slowly than the time measured on Earth. Time seems to pass in a completely normal way to the passengers of the ship. This results in a bizarre discrepancy between time on board and time on Earth.

Traveling to Nommo, which is eight and a half light years from Earth, would take the ship about six weeks while eight and a half years would have elapsed on Earth. The return trip would work the same way, so another eight and a half years would pass on Earth, but the occupants of the ship would have only aged a total of twelve weeks. When Matthew and Luke returned, they would be about the same age as they were when they left, but those of us still here would be seventeen years older. We would have been waiting seventeen whole years for them to return.

The Zariba and the Helamites, along with any other interplanetary travelers, know that this theory is a true law as they have all experienced it first hand. This inconvenient and totally scary fact makes moving at light speed through the universe an extraordinarily life altering circumstance, because when you come home all your loved ones will be significantly older and you will have missed out on so much, that it will totally suck to be you. In addition to all of this, if you weren't allowed to tell where you had been, it would be impossible to explain why you hadn't aged. Your life would be essentially destroyed. At least, that's my take on the whole relative-time-and-travel-through-the-universe-at-the-speed-of-light thing.

"Hasn't the government flown any of those alien ships you said it possesses?" I asked.

They had them and were studying them at Area 51. If I had access to those spaceships, I would want to fly at light speed. Who wouldn't? The military must have taken them for a spin around our solar system. They could do that in less time than it would take to travel from coast to coast on a jet.

"Yes, they have, but they haven't taken them too far from Earth because of the ramifications that could occur," he explained lacing his free hand through mine. "There is also the dilemma that if the nations of the Earth can't play nice together, what makes us think that traveling to other inhabited planets would be a good idea?"

"Do other governments besides ours have any light-speed-capable vehicles?"

"The United Kingdom and Australia do. There are some other countries with access to such ships. However, the Zariba has destroyed other alien aircraft they've discovered in many places in the world. They don't trust most other nations to be capable of considering the greater good of our planet, before their own reckless desires.

"Those countries have no knowledge that such things even exist. One rogue government could send out a ship to invade another world that might have greater technology, and that world could retaliate by destroying our whole planet. It's not something to mess around with. The consequences of a few foolish people could mean the annihilation of our entire population."

"How are you going to find Matthew and Luke?" I had never realized how easy it could be to lose someone. People don't fall off the planet every day, at least they didn't in my life before I moved to Hurricane. Okay, I kind of felt like I had dropped off the planet when my family moved to this small resort town on the Utah-Arizona border. That was back when I thought the Earth was safe from space monsters, before I knew that extra-terrestrials walk among us and before I fell in love with one, myself.

This current situation was causing an unease to crawl inside me, grab onto my heart and hang on like taffy stuck to my teeth. For the last seven months, I had managed to block fear's icy fingers from reaching into my consciousness and making me crazy. I had all but refused to see the danger that Andrew had to dabble in as he and the other Helamites worked to keep the Earth safe from suspicious spacemen or alien monsters who meant to do us harm. I hated that this situation had ruined my ability to ignore the frighteningly real, ever-present threats that lurked beneath the comfortable, safety zone of my happy life with Andrew.

He squeezed my hand trying to comfort me and said, "The Zariba is searching in every dark corner of the planet as we speak. They are also combing the skies and searching throughout our solar system. If they've been taken to Nommo, there will be big trouble. The Nommoans were informed on their previous visit that it is a violation of a strict law that prohibits abducting Earth people without their consent. Once they leave our solar system with a kidnapped resident of our planet, they risk retaliation from Zariban forces. When the Zariba is after you, there is no place in the universe where you can hide. They have ways to find you, and they'll make you pay for such serious crimes against the people of Earth."

"Whoa! If I were one of those Nommoans, I'd be very afraid. How can they punish them if they've already gone back to Nommo? Isn't that too far away to just cruise over and arrest them? Wouldn't it take seventeen years off the lives of the arresting officers? Who would volunteer for that kind of duty?"

My brain was squirming around in my head, trying to come up with a punishment that would fit such a crime and to figure out the superpowers the Zariba must have, to be able to hunt down criminals anywhere in the universe and make them pay for their transgressions. I was getting a major headache thinking about the gravity of all this tricky outer space stuff.

"Like I told you before, I can't divulge their abilities. I would have to get explicit permission to tell you how they work. Let's just say they are very effective at tracking violators of the law. They know ways to get around the issue of relativity. Time and space are separate dimensions that the Zariba understand and know how to use the physical laws that govern them to their advantage. They are not subject to the limitations that most of us have to contend with. Don't worry, Love. We'll find Matthew and Luke one way or another and bring them safely home."

It was terribly late when we finally turned off the freeway at the Hurricane exit. The traffic was sparse on the lonesome road that wound past Quail Creek Dam. We had left the main highway and were almost to the turnoff for my house when we saw it! At first, I shook myself, wondering if I had fallen asleep and was dreaming up this thing that had appeared in the heavens.

I opened and closed my eyes several times before I believed that I was actually seeing what I thought I saw! It was enormous and ethereal. The unbelievable, unidentified, flying object grew out of the sky and hovered directly above us. It looked like a large, fat, surreal Frisbee that glowed with a purple florescence. Many orange, oval lights were blinking from its center.

Then as suddenly as it had appeared it vanished again like a fine mist that dissolved into nothing but darkness. It was the kind of strange experience that makes you question your senses and wonder if you are seeing things that aren't really there at all.

"What was that?" I asked.

I was pretty positive it was not of this world. I had only seen one honest-to-goodness spaceship from another planet, and that was in the Martins' pharmaceutical warehouse. I'd never seen an actual UFO in flight. It made my stomach lurch a little with the sudden shock of what I had just beheld. I knew that such things existed, but seeing one with my own eyes still had an eerie, dreamlike effect on me. It didn't seem real.

"You know what it is. The question we should be asking is where did it come from and where is it going?" He said this as he pulled to the side of the road and began punching buttons on his cell phone.

He barked a few sentences explaining what we'd just encountered. When he was finished, he pulled back on the street and drove in silence to my house. He parked in front and looked at me with eyes that were so stone-cold-serious it scared me.

"I have to find the answers to those questions. For now, don't worry and don't say anything to anyone. You didn't see anything. We don't want panic, and we definitely don't want the wrong people searching for a UFO in our own backyard."

He carried my suitcase into the house. He took me into his arms, held me tightly and kissed me with some serious intensity. My body responded to his. He kissed me again. This time I felt an extra urgency in his kiss. The thought that invaded my mind left me speechless. Was he was afraid he would never see me again? No, I must be feeling insecure, but he did seem reluctant to let me go. Of course, I was always reluctant to let him go.

He took a deep breath, pressed his lips to the top of my head and whispered in my ear, "I'll call you tomorrow. I love you, Tiana." Then he was gone. I was alone.

That's when I felt the panic flowing out of the queasy tightness in my stomach. It spread rapidly through my body like an arctic stream running inside me, chilling my blood and freezing my bone marrow. I began trying to talk myself out of this dread. I was being silly, probably over-reacting as usual. He dealt with this kind of stuff all the time. It was no big thing. I was too tired to think rationally. I needed to sleep now. Tomorrow things would look better.

I pulled my suitcase up the stairs to my room. It was two in the morning, and it had been an endless day. We were state champs. That was a good thing. My boyfriend was chasing down a UFO. That was a bad thing. Matthew and Luke had dropped off the planet. That was a very, very, bad thing. I fell on my bed, and despite my ominous feeling of foreboding, I fell asleep.

Even in sleep, I worried. I dreamed that Andrew and I found the UFO we had seen that night on the Arizona Strip (that's the part of Arizona that is separated from the rest of the state by the Grand Canyon). He made me hide in a shallow ravine while he went to investigate. I peered cautiously over the top of the ditch as the door opened slowly and a ramp descended to the desert floor.

In the doorway, Matthew and Luke appeared looking more like mindless robots than real people. They gestured with blank, empty eyes and expressionless faces beckoning Andrew to come aboard. He nonchalantly joined them. The ramp retracted, the door closed. In less than a New York minute, the vehicle fled from my view, winked out of sight, and was swallowed up by the night.

CHAPTER 9

GONE

I woke with an intense sense of foreboding. It permeating my mind and tightening my stomach into knots. I glanced over at my bedside clock radio. It was after ten in the morning. I pushed the sleep away with my covers and rubbed my eyes. I remembered the crisis of last night and felt that icy, ominous feeling spreading out from my chest again. It was joined by alarm bells ringing in my head. Something was wrong. The voice in my head was screaming, *It's bad!* I found my cell and punched number one which connected me to Andrew. It went straight to voicemail. This was not helping my mushrooming anxiety.

"Call me!" was all I could say. I quickly disconnected and punched number two which was the Martin's residence. It rang several times before their machine picked up.

"Hi, it's Tiana. What's going on? I'm worried sick. Call me when you get this message!" I choked on the words and hung up with the anguished apprehension that had pervaded my mind.

"Stop it," I scolded myself, "Everything has to be okay." I didn't believe what I was telling myself. That voice in my mind was shouting at me that something was terribly wrong. It never lied to me. Andrew always answered my calls. I frantically tried his number again, nothing! I pulled myself out of bed and into the shower. I sat my phone on the bathroom counter, so I'd be sure to hear it if it rang. It simply must ring any minute.

I dressed hurriedly and ran downstairs to wolf down an Instant Breakfast, my breakfast of choice when I have no appetite. I was hoping it would chase the nausea away that had crept from my sour stomach up into my throat and was threatening to make me throw up. My parents had left me a note saying they had gone to an art festival in nearby Mesquite, Nevada.

I tried the Martin's home phone again and again the machine answered. I tried texting Andrew. If someone didn't call me soon, I was going to have to drive over and make them tell me what was going on. I was halfway to the front door when the doorbell rang.

I opened the door, hoping to see Andrew smiling back at me. Only his smile could dry up the frigid river of nervous anguish that was rushing around inside me. Instead, James Parker was standing there, frowning at me. The look on his face was one worn only by someone who has bad news to report.

"What is it? What's happened?" I had left worried and hurried into hysterical.

"May I come in?" He asked while looking away from the alarm on my face.

"Of course," I said, allowing him to pass through the doorway and into the living room. Terror had taken a chokehold in my heart, strangling it until I winced from the pain.

"Have they found Matthew and Luke? Where is Andrew?" I wanted to grab him and violently shake him to extract some answers.

"No, and now Andrew is missing as well," he said looking almost as fearful and upset as I was.

Suddenly, my knees turned to the consistency of wet noodles and dissolved beneath me. He reached out and stopped my fall. Then he graciously helped me to the couch.

"I'm sorry I don't have any good news to share. The Martins aren't taking any outside calls. They'll contact you when there is real news. The story is they have had a death in the family and are on their way to Australia. The truth is they are helping in the search for the Nommoan's ship. I volunteered to relay this to you in person. I'm truly sorry, Tiana."

I couldn't reply. I couldn't find any words for the unbearable grief I was feeling. The world was crashing down around me like shattered ice crystals. I felt the blood drain away from my face, leaving me trembling from the chilling trepidation that splashed over me. My skin was covered with goose bumps. I tried to rub them off and felt the clammy dampness of cold sweat. I think I was going into shock.

I forced myself to believe Andrew was okay. The alternative was too painful for me to visit. I braced myself and tried to put on my best, bravest face. I reached deep to search out some courage or faith. At the very least, I needed to act like I had some. I didn't want to have a mental meltdown right here in front of James. I thought I could hold myself together until after he left.

"Are you going to be okay, Tiana?"

James seemed genuinely concerned. I couldn't help myself. I just lost it. He let me sob uncontrollably on his shoulder. I was mortified, but my grief won out over my embarrassment. Why did he have to be the one to bring this horrendous news? His arms encircled me. Their warmth was comforting. However, they were the wrong arms. Finally, I managed to curb the downpour of unwanted tears. I sniffed. He handed me a tissue. I pulled myself from his embrace. I looked up at his solemn, handsome face, begging him to say something that would comfort me.

"We'll find him. Everything will be okay," he promised. "Oh, by the way, you didn't give Alexis my phone number and address, did you?"

"No," I stared blankly up at him. "Why?"

"She's been leaving weird messages on my voicemail. I think I saw her parked outside my apartment yesterday. Do you know anything about that?"

"I don't. We're not friends. I think I'm at the top of her list of people to hate. She doesn't confide in me. Maybe she tracked you down. I'm sure she can't be your first stalker," I said, and I smiled just a little.

I would have laughed, if I hadn't been so miserable. The idea of Alexis following James was pleasantly amusing. It almost cheered me up to think about the drama diva throwing her self at James. I made a mental note to follow up on that when I felt better and could fully appreciate the scenario of James having Alexis as a stalker.

"No, but she's remarkably persistent for a bobble-head. Don't worry about Andrew. This isn't his first rodeo. He's been through worse things. He always comes out on top. I'm sure he'll turn up soon. If there's anything I can do, call me." He said.

I nodded as if I would ever call him. Well, I'd done stranger things. I shut the door behind him. Alone once again, I couldn't suppress my severe depression. I managed to make it into my room before I completely came apart. I soaked my pillow and tried to muffle all those awful crying sounds I make when I lose control in the throes of intense emotional distress. I used up all the moisture I could muster. Then, after suffering all that sorrow, as I so often do, I made the leap to anger.

"Where in the world are you, Andrew Martin? Don't you dare fall off this planet! I will never forgive you!" I screamed at the walls. They didn't scream back so I guess I hadn't lost all my sanity. I punched my pillow a few hundred times and kicked the wall until my foot hurt.

There was no good news over the weekend. I wanted to call in sick to school on Monday, but I had three tests I couldn't miss. I'd probably fail them all. Studying had been nearly impossible. I kept erupting into tears at irregular intervals. I managed to hide my red and bloodshot eyes. When anyone noticed, I complained of allergies. Mostly, I stayed in my room at home, so my parents wouldn't be alarmed by my erratic fits of crying that alternated with many moments of staring off into space. I imagined my life coming to an end, if Andrew was gone forever.

I couldn't tell them anything, so I tried to act normal around them. It was best to hide all my agonizing fears. No good could come from trying to explain. I did tell them about the "death in the Martin family" and their "trip to Australia." They thought I was depressed by Andrew's absence. That was completely true. Although, I think "devastated" was a better description of my emotional status.

I trudged through my classes like the queen of the zombies. I did try to call back my lost mind, attempting to focus on my tests. I think I passed, but, most certainly, not with flying colors. My world no longer registered colors at all.

I sat alone in the black and white lunchroom and listened to my iPod, pushing my unappetizing food around and taking an occasional tasteless bite so as not to look as heartsick as I felt. I wanted to drown in the music and forget my pain. It wasn't working. Tiffany came and sat across the table. I reluctantly pulled out my ear phones. It was time to pretend I was fine and act normal. I wasn't sure I could do it. I had to try.

"Where are the Martins and the Allens today?" She asked.

I sucked it up and rehearsed the cover story again. "They are on their way to Australia to a funeral." I tried hard not to appear as miserable as I felt.

"Who died?"

"I think it was Andrew's father's sister." I didn't even know if Andrew's father had a sister.

I hated to lie, but "filtering the truth" was part of my life now. I couldn't even tell my best friend that Andrew, Matthew and Luke had been abducted by amphibious aliens from the planet, Nommo, because these stupid spacemen were emotional morons who wanted to study Earthlings' memories in hopes that they could reconnect to their inner feelings.

Why couldn't they go see an amphibious, alien psychiatrist? If they were so darn smart why couldn't they fix themselves? Why did they have to screw up my life? Is there no sense of decency in the universe? On what planet was any of this remotely fair? I was so upset at those mental Nommoans. Why couldn't they stay on their own waterlogged world instead of coming to mine? Who invited them? The more I thought about their audacity, the angrier I got. Why couldn't they get in touch with their emotions in some other solar system?

I struggled to shove my anger back down before it could boil over. I didn't want to scare Tiffany by the crazy emotions that were fighting each other inside me. Pain, fear, anger, depression all had to hide in my brain closet and get out of my face for now. I had to pretend to be calm. I couldn't let any of my insanity loose or there would be double trouble.

"What's wrong, Tiana? Are you suffering from separation anxiety? You're even more pale than normal. You don't look well," Tiffany used her concerned friend voice.

I wanted to tell her that I was falling apart. I desperately wanted to scream, sob, vent, and act out. I really, really wanted to confide in her, but I knew I couldn't do that. My life was in the toilet again.

"Yeah, I really miss Andrew. I don't know when he's coming back. I couldn't sleep last night. I think I may have messed up on my History test, and I still have one in English. My life sucks today. I'm sorry I'm grouchy. I'm not very good company. Feel free to ignore me. I won't be offended."

"Girlfriend, I feel your pain. I'm sorry your life is so miserable right now. My life, on the other hand, is looking up. Jeremy called yesterday and said he and your brother are coming this weekend. The good news is he's taking me out on Saturday. The bad news is Psycho Sonya will be here too. We'll be doubling with her and Mark. I guess your big brother is still infatuated with Miss Insanity. What's up with that?"

"That's just one more reason my life totally sucks. My brother is dating my evil- arch-enemy. I'm pleased for you and Jeremy, though. You guys are great together," I said. "I just can't seem to remember what being happy feels like."

"Well hello, Beautiful," a male voice interrupted our conversation. "I hear Andrew had a death in the family. If you're feeling sad and lonely, I'm here for you Tiana." Jordan sat down at our table. "I'd be happy to fill in for him while he's gone," he said showing me his wide, toothy grin.

"I'm fine Jordan. I think Alexis is looking for you," I replied through my own gritted teeth.

"Yeah, you don't want her to see you sitting here. She'll freak out again. She still feels threatened by Tiana. She'll take it out on you with a vengeance," Skylar said as he sat down and punched Jordan in the shoulder. "Hey, on second thought, stay here. We haven't seen her throw a tantrum for a while. We could use some of her special brand of entertainment. Let's give the drama queen a chance to perform!"

"She has a dental appointment," Jordan explained. "She's gone for the rest of the day. Besides, she thinks she's in love with some college jerk that drives a black Corvette, but I'm not supposed to know that. Making her jealous right now might be a good thing."

"You know someone will tell her. She has spies and eyes everywhere," Tiffany added, "and surely you're aware of how fast good gossip flies through these halls."

"Speaking of gossip," Emily joined our table, sitting down with her tray and grinning at Tiffany. "Tim heard about your date to Jillian's party. He is virtually burning up with jealousy; we almost had to use the fire extinguisher on him. You could see the smoke coming out of his ears when Ryan told him."

"That is delicious! I hope he's positively on fire and puke-green with envy. He deserves it after lying to me about sneaking into that dance at Pine View High and hanging all over that Panthera Dance Squad girl." Tiffany clapped her hands with glee.

"Tiana, we're friends, right?" Jordan asked me, changing the subject.

"I guess," I replied wondering what he wanted from me. It didn't bode well.

"Do you know this college guy Alexis is crushing on?"

"Yeah, I think so," I admitted. "His name is James Parker, but I don't think you need to worry about him. He told me that he's not interested in Alexis." I decided to ease his mind. James had made it quite clear that he wasn't attracted to the crazy, mean-girl cheerleader.

"Please, Tiana, won't you help me make her jealous as a favor to a friend?" He asked in his pleading, whiney voice.

"Not even if my life depended on it!" I gave him my worst ask-again-and-I'll-hurt-you stare of death and pushed away from the table.

I mumbled some excuse about having to retrieve something from my car and left the lunchroom. I'd lost my appetite altogether. There was no way I wanted to hear about, let alone get involved in, their on-again-off-again repulsive relationship. Jordan gives me a headache. I think it's psychosomatic. Subconsciously, he reminds me of the car crash that gave me a concussion and the snakebite I suffered running away from him.

The remainder of the week passed at a sluggish speed slower than dial up internet. Does such a thing even exist anymore? I walked around in a gray, mental fog. I kept calling the Martin's house and I kept getting that annoying answering machine. Adam finally called me back on Thursday.

"We found Matthew and Luke wandering around in the desert, east of Lake Mead. They can't remember anything after they called in the sighting. Their short term memories have been wiped clean. I couldn't retrieve even a random thought from their subconscious minds. Whoever did this was meticulous and removed even the smallest details. The Nommoans are more dangerous than we suspected. There is still no sign of Andrew. Try not to worry. If anything were wrong with him, I would know. We don't believe they've taken him off the planet. We'll find him, Tiana. I promise."

I thanked him as graciously as I could, under the circumstances. I asked to be updated ASAP if they found him. He said he would let me know *"when"* they found him, emphasizing the *"when."* He reassured me that he knew he would be found soon. That made me feel a bit better. Adam was psychic, like Andrew, so if he knew something, it had a high probability of being so.

I wished Adam's astonishing ability could be turned on at will so he could know exactly where Andrew was this very moment. Unfortunately, it didn't work that way. Andrew had explained that to me on numerous occasions. What good is being psychic if you can't make it work for you when you need it most? He said it was controlled by our Creator, and only He decides when and how it works.

On Friday night, Mark and Jeremy came home for the weekend. I welcomed the distraction. I wished I could tell them about Andrew's abduction, but again I was forced to reiterate the "death-in-the-family-gone-to-Australia" fiction. They were mildly sympathetic. When Psycho Sonya appeared at my door, she gave me a knowing look. She knew why I was crazy with worry. Then again, she was probably secretly enjoying my pain. I hid in my room for the duration of her visit. Yeah, I'm a total wuss.

CHAPTER 10

THE NOMMOAN ALIEN PRINCE

Another weekend passed by without any news of the illusive Nommoans. It felt like a month. On Tuesday, Adam called to report a new, dire development, like I needed any more bad news. James Parker had investigated another sighting Monday night and promptly disappeared, leaving no trace and no clues. All Helamites were on edge. No one was allowed to go searching for the surreptitious spacemen alone.

My life was set on autopilot. I was going through the motions and demands of school without totally being there. I know a lot of kids do this all the time, but I usually pay attention. I was nearly numb from operating at such a high stress level for half past way too long. I had a constant, dull ache in my head, a strangely hollow, empty feeling in my heart, and I think I was getting ulcers. Little pains like pointy knives seemed to be constantly stabbing at my stomach lining.

I found it difficult to think clearly about anything. Focusing on one thing for any amount of time was next to impossible. It took all of my concentration to do even the simplest math problem. I positively could be the poster girl for Attention Deficit Disorder. In my chaotic consciousness, it was surprising that I even noticed the sinister stranger who was lurking in the shadows of Hurricane High's crowded hallways.

On my way to math, I saw this crazy-looking guy out in my peripheral vision. I turned my face toward him out of pure, morbid curiosity. He was standing so still, he reminded me of a realistic, life-size statue. He looked strangely out of place at Hurricane High.

It was immediately obvious that he didn't belong here. He was dressed in a long, shiny, white tunic-type shirt with some unusual green and maroon insignia which included strange, unrecognizable lettering and a creature that resembled a dragon or maybe a sea serpent on the front. His legs were poured into tight, leather-looking, black pants tucked into heavy, steel toed, black boots that stopped just below his knees. That detail alone screamed that he was a pirate wannabe or posing as one of the three musketeers.

His sand colored hair was streaked with a few strands of blue and purple in front. It was parted straight down the middle and tucked behind slightly pointed ears. It fell in thick waves to his shoulders. His eyes were dark brown. They seemed almost too large for his face, kind of like those Manga-eyed, Japanese cartoons. He resembled a 1970's hippie guru or a medieval, futuristic warrior straight off the cover of a graphic fantasy novel. He wore a faint shadow of facial hair on features that were hard, angular and without expression. They seemed to have been cast in bronze or carved out of granite. He might have been attractive if he smiled, but he looked like his face would fracture should he attempt to produce such a frivolous expression. I concluded that he seldom allowed any such looks to cross his draconian features.

As I passed him by, he fell into step behind me. I thought he could be a foreign exchange student from Bosnia (Is there still a Bosnia?), Estonia, Finland, or somewhere equally distant. I hurried into class, sat behind Jillian's empty seat, and tried hard to pay attention to Mr. Porter's instruction. The mysterious, super-solemn stranger didn't enter the classroom, so I was able to immediately forget this unusual, unhappy, foreign guy, who had to be from some far-away, eastern European country. In so doing, I remained true to form as an A.D.D. poster child incarnate.

When Pre-calculus was finally over, I entered the hall and nearly collided with the same warrior-guy. He looked down at me and almost smiled. I was sure if he had really grinned, it would have cracked his stone-like face. He wasn't much taller than I was, but he was extremely muscular in build. He looked as though he worked out a lot.

I glanced at his face, murmured, "Excuse me," and tried to circumvent his body, so I could hurry away to my next class. He caught my arm in a strong, unyielding grip and held it so tightly; I winced at the pain that shot through me. I was going to have bruises. This halted my progress. My first reflex reaction was to scream, but I opened my mouth and nothing came out. Instead, I just stared at him, willing him to speak and explain himself.

"I've waited so long for you, Tiana," he said in a sing-song way that made me think he might be mentally challenged. Had he arrived on the short bus? How did he know my name?

"Do you know how beautiful you are?" He continued to speak with an unrecognizable accent I had never heard before. He was starting to freak me out.

"I loved you before I met you. How crazy does that sound?" He was beginning to sound certifiably insane to me.

My mind was opened to an electrifying understanding. I had heard these words before, from another source, in another place and time. When I had heard them before, they filled me with joy. Now, they frightened me nearly to death.

I jerked my arm away from his uncomfortable, too tight grasp and sprinted down the hall. He didn't follow as he was very conveniently engulfed by a small army of students who had just filed out of Mrs. Perkins' chemistry class. Their timing was impeccable. I silently thanked God for this divine intervention.

This guy was sending me a message that screamed, "I've just escaped from a prison hospital for the criminally insane" or "I just arrived on a UFO from a planet located light years from Earth." Maybe he came from a distant planet populated by criminally insane, alien prisoners. I ran all the way to the girl's restroom. I ducked inside, pulled out my cell phone and called Adam. The darn machine picked up.

"Adam, there's some guy here at school who acts like he's from another planet. He said things to me that were in Andrew's words. I'm really scared. Please call me back."

After I hung up, I went directly to the office and checked out. I said I was sick. The secretary believed it because I was visibly shaking. The blood had all drained out of my face. I'm sure I looked like I'd just seen a ghost, an axe murderer, or just a super-scary-warrior-guy from outer space.

I was afraid I was going to pass out on the way to my car. I took deep breaths and managed somehow to keep from fainting. I really hate fainting. I do try to avoid it whenever I can. I made it home without hyperventilating, and rushed inside, locking all the doors. My cell phone rang. It was Adam. I answered and again explained what had happened.

"You were smart to call. He matches the description of Raydon, the Prince of the Illdees Islands. That's the one nation that contains most of the population on Nommo. He's the leader of their expedition to Earth. We'll check things out at the school. Stay inside and keep your doors locked. If he comes to your door, don't answer it. Call me immediately. I'll let Bob Zimmerman know. He'll watch your house as soon as he can get there. Don't go anywhere without telling Bob. If we can track the prince, he should lead us to Andrew and James."

I did what he said. What else could I do? Bob came over about an hour later. He explained that they had lost the Nommoan prince's trail. He had vanished into the desert wilderness leaving no tracks to follow. He said the Zariba would be watching Hurricane High. He would personally watch me. Then he reassured me that they would find Andrew and James. He urged me to stay inside as much as possible. I promised to comply.

I had transferred into Speech from Spanish after Christmas, and I joined the debate team. Jillian was my partner. We were the top team to beat. Since she was supposed to be in Australia, I missed out on the meet with Snow Canyon High on Friday. That was probably just as well because my logical thought processes weren't working. Unfortunately, without us, the team had lost. I still had lots of research on the pros and cons of International Migration to keep me busy until my brain completely froze up and crashed. Maybe we should be debating about Interstellar Migration instead.

After dinner, I just couldn't stand being inside any longer. I decided I had to run on the golf course to save my sanity. I knocked on Bob's door and asked his permission. I didn't want to run into that creepy, warrior-prince-guy again. I also wanted him to know where I was going, just in case my body got snatched by that crazy alien-life-form. He said I should go ahead and run.

It was the only dependable thing I could think of to help alleviate the stress I was under so I took off running and I tried to stop thinking about how my boyfriend had been captured by crazy, illegal aliens from outer space. I needed all the help I could get to feel better. Endorphins were my best way to fight off this ever present depression and keep up the ruse that I was still a fully functioning member of society.

I ran the full length of the golf course's cement trail and had just looped all the way around. I was coming back to my backyard when the freaky spaceman came straight out of nowhere and stood directly in front of me, blocking my path. I nearly ran into him before my attention deficit brain could register that he was standing in my way.

He put his hands firmly on my shoulders to stop me and hold me immobile. His touch caused my insides to tingle and not in a good way. He said, "You are even more beautiful than the last time I saw you. How is that possible? Why don't we all go out for ice cream, my treat?" Now he was speaking in James' words. Creepy, much?

That's when I decided that I'd suffered enough of his unwanted, parroting impersonations. I let out a loud scream that should wake the dead if there were any buried nearby and brought my knee up forcefully into his groin. I've practiced this defensive move. I did it with near perfect execution. Huh? It worked just as well on spacemen as it did on annoying boys from Earth. Who knew?

He gasped, let out a string of words that sounded like nonsensical, fighting oaths that I was willing to bet no one on this planet could decipher and then he let go of my shoulders as he doubled over in apparent pain. I ran like I was being chased by the devil himself or a mental, medieval, warrior prince who mimics the words of others. That would teach him to mess with me!

As I neared my backyard, Bob came running up the trail. I told him what had happened. He ran back the way I had come. I turned to watch him go. He vanished. I mean, one minute he was there and then the next minute he was gone, like in a puff of smoke, only there wasn't any smoke. All that remained was shimmering, empty air. He was indeed a mysterious and magic man. Someday, I'd have to ask him how he did that.

On Friday afternoon, on my way home from school, I decided enough was enough. I was sick to death of worrying and wondering about Andrew. I wanted him back. I had to do something, anything to keep from losing my mind. If that meant tracking down that lunatic-warrior-prince-guy, so be it!

Of course, no one else could catch this spacey, amphibious phantom. How was I going to do something that all the super intelligent aliens from advanced civilizations, who now lived on Earth, couldn't manage to do? They had all that superior technological tracking equipment, not to mention all those wondrous and sundry superpowers. I didn't understand why they weren't getting results. They kept reassuring me that everything would turn out okay. Well, I wasn't buying it anymore. I was fed up with all their dubious doubletalk!

When I turned onto my street, I was seething. I honestly hoped that stupid, Nommoan prince would be at my house waiting for me. I wanted to confront him and pull some answers out of his annoying, crazy-talking mouth. I wondered where amphibious aliens hang out when they visit our planet. If they were homesick, I'd guess they would be drawn to a large body of water. I surprised myself by thinking in such a perfectly logical and rational manner.

There were two man-made lakes nearby. Quail Creek Reservoir housed the water treatment plant. Sand Hollow State Park attracted recreating people. It was usually flooded with boaters, skiers, and swimmers. It was kind of like a mini Lake Powell with red, sandy beaches and unusual orange sandstone formations around it. Quail Creek was a state park as well, but it wasn't as popular as Sand Hollow and you didn't have to pay to get in. It would probably be easier to infiltrate by sneaky spacemen who didn't want to attract attention. It was closer, deeper, and free, so I figured it was the best bet.

I stopped at my house, checked the answering machine messages, and went out into the backyard to look in all the places where someone could hide outside. There weren't many. The garage was empty, no one was prowling about on the patio, and nobody was crouched behind the hedge.

I scanned the vegetation on the golf course. No one seemed to be skulking among the tamarisk, ponderosa pines, or palm trees. Nothing else was big enough or sufficiently thick for anyone to hide behind.

The pond wasn't deep enough to conceal even a small amphibious, alien person. I was relatively sure no self-respecting, Nommoan royalty would be caught dead cowering in there. I walked over and looked in it anyway. He wasn't slinking around under the green, slimy, pond scum. The algae covered water was only a habitat for a few tadpoles, some tiny guppies and a handful of assorted ducks that were quacking-mad because I hadn't brought them bread crumbs.

I went in through the back door and started searching the house. I didn't think the Nommoans could walk through walls or teleport themselves into locked houses, but I could be wrong about that. I hadn't been properly briefed on all their abilities. I wasn't taking any chances. I peered cautiously into all the closets, and peeked behind all closed doors and cupboards. For all I knew, they might be able to change their size and shape. I even checked behind the shower curtains in all three bathrooms. I seemed to be utterly alone. Where was that obnoxious warrior-guy when I actually wanted him to be here?

Having settled on joining the search for the stupid extraterrestrials that had screwed up my life, I noticed my stomach was growling. I made myself a ham and cheese sandwich with mayo and mustard and grabbed a coke from the refrigerator. I was going to need all my strength and wits about me to go chasing after the illusive, spacey, kidnapper. Who knew when I'd get to eat again? There is absolutely no legitimate reason to go after crazy aliens on an empty stomach.

I vaguely remembered promising Andrew that I wouldn't go chasing after bad spacemen, but this was the exact scenario that I had told him was the exception to my vow. He had been abducted by aliens who could be torturing him. I was wholly justified in taking this course of action. I proceeded to my car with my nourishing protein snack and liquid energy. Nothing could stop me now.

I decided to drive out past Quail Creek Reservoir. I had to do something. I just couldn't stand playing this waiting game anymore. What could the crazy prince do to me? If he kidnapped me, I'd at least be held hostage with Andrew. Maybe I could talk him into letting us go. I can be highly persuasive. I've proven that I can be an excellent, logical debater.

Yeah, I was fully aware that hunting for a rogue, cerebral spaceman was extremely dangerous. I'd already been captured and tortured by an evil group of cannibalistic, barbarian, Hellites. I didn't think the prince was out to kill and eat me. His declared mission was to study the emotions of Earthlings. The fact that he wanted to take us home with him was disturbing, but if he were taking Andrew off the planet, then he had better be prepared to take me along as well.

I finally reached the turnoff for the reservoir. I drove past the picnic tables and stopped just off the road near the deserted marina. There were only a few boats out on the water today. They were far away from me. The people on them looked like normal, everyday humans from the planet, Earth, as far as I could tell.

The surface of this manmade lake was a smooth, silver mirror as it reflected the sun and sparkled with tiny ripples. There was a cool breeze coming off the water that carried a faint, fishy and musty smell as it blew against my face. I looked down into the murky water as I stood on the deserted dock. A rainbow trout swished by and disappeared. It was followed by a larger, ugly, gray catfish that looked like it had been caught and released a few too many times.

As I watched it slip down into the dingy, dirty depths, I caught a glimpse of something much larger than the fish that were at home here. Suddenly, the water cleared. There, below the gentle waves, the open, staring eyes of a human face were staring up at me.

CHAPTER 11

THE PERFECT PLACE TO HIDE

The human face, just below the surface of the still water, had glassy, wide-open, bulging, gray eyes that were staring straight up at my own horrified expression. I shrieked as a bony, iron hand came out of the dark, murky water and fastened itself onto my ankle before I could shrink instinctively back away from the lake's edge. Desperately, I attempted to shake it off. I kicked at it with my other foot until another strong hand shot out of the lake and grabbed the foot doing the kicking. I crouched down and tried zealously to pry those cold, firm, slimy fingers off my shuttering body. They encircled my ankles like locked shackles made of unbreakable chains.

It was no use. Fighting against the creature in the dark water wasn't working. The heavy hands were determined and unyielding. In a little more than half a second, the hands jerked and I was instantly swept off the dock. I plunged into the frigid reservoir. I managed to fill my lungs with air just before I hit my head on the wooden planks and was dragged under.

The pain of my collision with the dock shot through me like a piercing, angry arrow of hurt that gave me the mother of all migraines. Unfortunately, it wasn't hard enough to knock me out, so I had to remain conscious in my misery and deal with my impending death by drowning.

Why was this happening to me? Why do these unbelievably awful things keep tormenting me? A crippling paralysis crept through me as panic poked at my brain with a sharp, stinging agony accompanied by the sinking pain of despondency. I was being pulled deeper and deeper into the dismal, watery pit. My lungs began to ache for air.

My body went numb. I quit struggling against the terrifying, malignant creature that had attached itself to my appendages. It seemed determined to tow me to my destruction. There are probably a lot of worse ways to die than drowning, but, at that moment, I couldn't think of any. I wasn't ready to die. At least it would be a quick and relatively easy death. Somehow, I wasn't consoled by that fact. I had lost the all strength to fight against the monster that was pulling me down faster and faster. I became nothing but a dead weight, a heavy stone rapidly descending into a black, bottomless abyss.

After a few, long, agonizing minutes that felt like hours, I saw what must be the bottom of the lake. Resting there, a row of dim, orange, oval lights was blinking out of a blurry, purple haze. The ominous glow was the last thing I saw. I gasped, unable to hold my breath any longer, and let the dirty water into my lungs. I choked, trying to expel the dark liquid. Then I succumbed to the black void, losing consciousness at last.

While I was unconscious, I saw all my most memorable life moments march through my mind like an endless movie. They say you see your life flash before your eyes just before you die. I guess they were right. I always thought that was supposed to make you realize all you had done that was wrong, so you could beg forgiveness from the God. Then He would either let you in the pearly gates or direct you to the elevator that only went down.

It wasn't like that. I saw both good and bad memories without feeling guilty, proud, or saddened by my actions. The scenes kept changing so rapidly I couldn't form any reaction at all to what I observed. It was like I was just an innocent bystander viewing someone else's life on fast forward. I wanted to slow it down, but I couldn't find the right button. Then the movie ended. *I'm dead,* I thought, as everything went black.

When I came to, I was reclining in what looked amazingly like a typical, dentist chair. It was a stark, matte white, well padded, with both a head rest and foot extension. The comfortable chair was tilted back to give me an excellent view of the unremarkable, silver, metal ceiling. I strained to look around at the small room I inhabited and realized that this chair was equipped with restraints that were connecting my wrists, ankles, and waist tightly to it.

If I were dead, this couldn't be Heaven. Going to the dentist has never been a particularly pleasant experience for me, and no dentist I've visited has ever tied me up. If I were waiting for a dentist, it had to be a dentist from Hell. He must be coming directly from that down elevator to torture me in ways I didn't even want to think about.

I scanned the room for more clues as to my current whereabouts. The shiny medical machinery around the chair did not resemble any dental equipment I had ever noticed. Even the walls were made of polished metal chrome. On the opposite side of the room, I saw six tube-like, see-through, glass chambers. Three of them were filled with a cloudy steam or gas. I could just make out the forms inside these odd compartments. I gulped when I realized those forms were human bodies. If they were alive, they must be asleep or unconscious because no one can hold that motionless and be awake especially when crammed upright in a standing position inside a glass tube. Maybe, I was the one who was sleeping and dreaming up this frightening place. Nothing I saw here made any sense in my world.

My mind squirmed and was suddenly opened and flooded with the memory of my recent traumatic inevitable death by drowning. Was I dead? I didn't feel dead. My lungs seemed unobstructed. I was breathing without pain. There should be pain. I should be soaking wet, if I'd just gotten here. I wasn't dripping. There was no water on the floor. My hair was bone dry as was the rest of me. I wasn't in one of those ugly, green gowns that fail to cover your butt, so I knew this wasn't some kind of regular, hospital room. I was dressed in the same clothes I was wearing when I drove to the reservoir. How did they get dry?

Where was I? How long had I been here? Why was I stuck in this stupid chair? Who tried to drown me and why? Had I been rescued or was I being held hostage and who were those people in the crazy, foggy tubes that looked like something straight out of a lousy, B-list horror flick? I could think of a hundred questions, but the answers evaded me.

I stared into the round, misty, shower-like, glass stalls, hoping to get a glimpse of a face or something I could recognize. The gas inside kept whirling around them obscuring their features from my view. My neck was beginning to ache from having to crane it up as I tried to see who the bodies buried in the vapor of the circular boxes were. Then I made out a face that I knew as well as my own.

I caught my breath and swallowed hard. It was Andrew. This had to be the ship belonging to the villainous Nommoan prince who wanted to experiment on Earth people. Was I to be their next unwilling guinea pig? What had they done to Andrew?

I prayed desperately that he was alive. As I continued to stare into those chambers, I recognized James Parker as one of the remaining humans. The other one appeared to be female. I couldn't make out her face as her head was turned away from me. She had long, glossy, nearly black hair and her skin was a warm brown, almost the same color as James' was. There was something extremely familiar about her.

I heard the door open and the alien-prince-guy burst into the room, flanked by three, seven foot tall underlings dressed entirely in black. They could have been ninjas without the head and face rags that generally hide their identities. One of the three was the ugly creature who had tried to drown me. He reminded me of a frog with bulging eyes and some kind of skin condition that looked like warts. His coloring was a grayish tan. His hair was dirty, dishwater blond and his eyes were nearly the same exact washed out color. The tips of his hair were bright orange.

The other two men were dark skinned. If they were from Earth, I would think they were of African descent. Their hair didn't fit with that ethnicity, however. One had short, white, spiky hair with streaks of fire engine red running through it. The other's hair was long, with loose curls of florescent lime green. I wondered if it were an exceptionally awful fashion trend on their planet to dye your hair weird, tacky colors or if, through some bizarre mutation, they were born that way. These aliens would never be able to blend into the ultra-conservative, general population in Hurricane, Utah.

The huge men all had a tattoo emblazoned across their foreheads. It was the same insignia on a much smaller scale, as the prince wore on his shiny, white shirt. I thought it might identify them as his henchmen, sort of like having his royal symbol engraved there for the entire world to see.

The prince looked like the boy next door when compared to his strange, scary-looking, samurai soldiers. They were all taller and bulkier than their much better looking leader. I expected they must work out and lift exceptionally heavy weights on a regular basis. Their biceps bulged so big, they almost made their massive arms look deformed like those oiled up "Mr. Universe" types or those bodies with exaggerated muscles and veins that stand out in the pictures of anatomy books.

I'd only seen humongous, muscled men like that on TV. Nobody I knew looked anything like that in real life. These oversized-alien-goons wore utility belts around their waists that were outfitted with several lethal-looking weapons of various kinds. I didn't want to know how they worked. I hoped I wouldn't find out. What did they need those weapons for anyway? They could just pick me up and break me in two or threaten me and scare me to death.

"I'm so happy you are awake, Tiana," the prince talked like we were old friends. "I am Raydon, Prince of the Illdees Islands on the planet Nommo in the Sirius Star system. These are the members of my guard. Brazzo brought you here. The others are Sadvik," he gestured to the man with white and red hair, "and Nafe," he indicated the man with the impossible to miss, glimmering, green locks. They each bowed slightly as their names were spoken, but none of them uttered a word.

"Do you think you could unfasten me from this chair? Am I a prisoner?" I decided not to beat around the bush about this apparent hostage situation.

"My apologies, I thought it best to keep you from injuring yourself while we examined the memory banks of your mind. You kept thrashing around in your sleep," he said as he pushed a button on the back side of the chair that immediately eliminated the restraints. Well, that was highly civilized of him, but I didn't like the idea that he'd been snooping around inside my brain, messing with my personal memories. That explained the weird parade of my life experiences I had dreamed about while unconscious.

"Why were you inside my head? Do you realize that on this planet kidnapping is a federal offense and delving into people's intimate memories is an extremely rude invasion of privacy and just plain wrong? Why are Andrew and James in those glass, tubular compartments? Why are you holding them against their will?" I tried not to sound as perturbed and violated as I felt. I thought it would be best not to antagonize this alien aristocrat, but I couldn't stop the words from pouring out of my unruly mouth.

"We are on an important mission. We are here to save our race from extinction. We feel this gives us the right to take such necessary liberties as we search for a cure for the entire dwindling population of Nommo. We are working for the greater good. They will be released with no serious damage done to them. We have done no harm. Our procedures have been tested and are proven to be safe," he spoke with an arrogant authority. He seemed to think he was perfectly justified. We all existed to be experimented upon by his infinitely superior, alien race.

"Well then, I think it's time to let us all go. You've had your fun. You've got your data. We need to get back to our insignificant lives, so you can go home and save your race from disappearing from the universe. I assume you got what you came for." I got out of the dentist chair and walked purposely over to the tubes. No one moved to stop me. I looked into the one containing the female occupant. I gasped as I recognized my best friend, Tiffany Martinez.

"Why do you have my best friend in here? I demand that you release these people at once! You have no right to detain any of us!" I was through playing nice.

"I wanted to examine her memories of you. They will all be safely and promptly released on one condition," he said with an evil smirk on his stony face. "You must agree to accompany me back to Nommo."

"What are you talking about? Are you insane? I'm not going anywhere with you, and I'm most certainly not leaving this planet. What's wrong with you? You've already been inside my brain without being invited. Who do you think you are?" I was fuming. I couldn't believe the nerve of this bigoted intruder. He shouldn't even be here, and he thought he had a right to get into our heads and trample our psyches.

"You are destined to be my queen. I have examined the emotional memories of these humans. I have felt love for you. I have never felt this emotion before. It is better than I could have hoped for. We will return to my people. We will teach them of this love that they may repopulate the planet, Nommo," he said this calmly and as matter-of-factly as reciting multiplication tables or reading names out of the phone book.

"Excuse me? I will never be your queen! You're crazy! You should be locked up in a padded cell. You can't fall in love with someone through other people's memories. Those memories don't belong to you! I'm in love with Andrew. He is my one and only soul mate. You need to go home and make your own memories with someone from your own planet. I'm sure there are countless Nommoan women who would just love to be your queen. Go home and marry one of them." I rolled my eyes dramatically. I hoped I had communicated the futility and ridiculousness of his appallingly demented proposal.

"You will bend to my will. It is necessary. Once we have left your life here on Earth behind, you will choose to be with me. It is the only logical option. I am offering you a wondrous gift, a chance of a lifetime. If you refuse to accompany me back to my people, you and your friends will be killed, liquefied and left on the bottom of this lake. Is this what you want to happen?"

"You are barking mad, aren't you? How can you calmly tell me that I have to go fly the unfriendly skies with you to some dying, distant planet or you're going to murder innocent people? What is your problem? Have you no concept of morals or ethical behavior? What happened to 'we have done no harm'?"

"I'm sure you will make the right decision. Then I will release your friends, so you can say your good byes. I am not without compassion. Well, perhaps I am, but I have seen this emotion in your memory cells. I am trying to emulate it.

"These humans all love you in different ways. It has been very enlightening to study their feelings. I am sure they will miss you, but they will survive. I am sorry if this causes you pain, but you will recover. You will have an excellent, carefree life on Nommo. I will see to your every desire. You cannot logically choose death over the huge honor of being my queen."

"Are you kidding? I'm too young to get married! I would rather die than marry you, even if I get to be queen of the whole universe!" I declared this with absolute conviction. This would unquestionably be defined as a fate much worse than dying. Falling off the planet is never a smart thing. I sincerely didn't want to do it now or ever.

"You may feel this way now, but I am confident your feelings will change in time. I am sure you would not want your friends to have to die with you. Do you see these?" He pointed to five, different colored, square buttons on the glass door of each chamber. "If I were to push the purple one, the sedating gas would be replaced by a lethal chemical mist that would kill them instantly. Pushing yellow causes a blast of coherent phonons that will destroy all biological allergens, germs and impurities and it will reduce humans to a puddle of water on the floor. It's a sort of sonic cleaning and sterilization process that eliminates anything of an organic nature. The green will stop their suspended animation, and they will regain consciousness. The red button is the one that caused them to be suspended in this dreamlike state in the first place. The blue opens the door.

"Which ones would you like me to push? I will give you five minutes to decide. Will it be green and blue or would you prefer the purple and yellow?"

CHAPTER 12

LETHAL GAS OR LIGHT SPEED

The minutes were quickly ticking by while I tried to think of a way out of this sticky situation. Neither of the gut wrenching choices he had offered me was in any way acceptable. If only I had a third option of letting Andrew, James and Tiffany go and dying alone or better yet, a fourth where we all went home, forgot this ever happened, and pretended we were safe and alone in the universe. Yeah, I'm the true queen of denial.

I thought I might be able to willingly die to save Andrew and Tiffany, but I didn't think I wanted to die for James. Heck, I didn't relish the whole dramatic dying thing at all. Dying can be so over rated. However, I guess it would be the Christian thing to do. I couldn't justify letting anyone die because of me. I just didn't understand why I had to be the one making the hard decisions between the death of my loved ones and a destiny that was worse than death.

If I had a few superpowers of my own, I might be able to think of a way to get us all out alive. I racked my brain anyway, trying to come up with a viable plan. I'm usually adept at thinking on my feet, but under the duress of all this radical death talk, I came up almost empty.

If I could just get this spacey prince to linger here on the bottom of this man-made lake a little longer, the other Helamites or the Zariba might find and rescue us. My car would give them a clue. Weren't they supposed to be brilliant, after all? I hadn't noticed anyone following me to the reservoir, but they could still have me under protective surveillance. I frantically hoped they did.

I still didn't know exactly how I was supposed to detain these delusional extraterrestrials. I couldn't suggest that they needed to abduct more Earthlings to examine because that would put more innocent people in jeopardy. I had nothing to barter with and no idea of how to persuade them to leave this planet without me. How could I make the Spock-like Mr. Logical, who had no emotional experience or maturity, understand that I would never love him and that he didn't really love me? I might as well attack the muscle-bound, royal, body guards, as try to convince Prince "I-am-the-Center-of-the-Universe" to listen to reason. Both were equally impossible tasks.

The hopelessness of all this came crashing down, causing me to shake as it began freezing my insides. My heart was thundering loudly in my ears as it struggled to pump the river of frozen blood through my shivering body, chilling me all the way to my now gelatinous bones. I was surprised that I was still standing. I should be collapsing as my legs turned to jelly. I felt like I would soon be reduced to a pile of organic material on the floor even without the aid of his sonic cleaning machine.

How does my life keep getting more and more complicated? I don't actually enjoy confronting impossible people. I have a hard enough time dealing with difficult folks from this planet, why do I continue to get mixed up with these stubborn lunatics from places that are light years away from Earth and why do they have to be so intent on totally messing up my life?

I guess I shouldn't have followed my instincts to Quail Creek. This was my fault. Why didn't I consult Bob and Adam about my suspicions concerning the Nommoans' whereabouts? I'd acted foolishly, thinking I could convince a bunch of brainiacs from the outer limits to release Andrew. I made a colossal mistake. Now I was going to have to pay the penalty for my idiocy by my untimely death, or by accepting an insane, marriage proposal to a royal, nut-job from another solar system. This was not only harsh; it was utterly unfair!

The bossy king of space bullies cleared his throat and said, "Your time is up. What is your decision?"

"I can't decide in five minutes! I don't want to take either option. Both are cruel and ridiculous choices. Killing us makes no sense. You are supposed to be highly intelligent, aren't you? How can you expect me to turn my back on my loved ones and my life and leave my world and go with you to yours? Try looking at this from my point of view. I'm sure with your superior intellect you should be able to understand that Andrew's memories belong to him. You can't fall in love vicariously! It's not possible.

"What you feel for me is not love. It's something else that won't last. It's like a hologram. It appears to be real, but it lacks substance. It's an imitation. It doesn't really exist."

I was probably talking to the walls, but I had to try to change his inflexible mind. Did I mention that I'm quite skilled at impromptu arguments? Too bad this insane alien wasn't listening to me. My deductive reasoning was flawless. If this debate were being judged, I would surely win, hands down.

"I appreciate your insolent opinion, but I have chosen you to be my queen. I have spoken it. It is now the law. I will soon be crowned King of the Illdees Islands of Nommo. You will rule my people with me. It is a great honor. You should be immensely grateful for this momentous opportunity. You must choose to go with me, or to die along with these unimportant, inconsequential humans. Which buttons will you have me push?" The power-monger prince had a one track mind. His skull was too thick for my brilliant logic to penetrate. I couldn't stop myself. I continued to pummel him with perfect rationality.

"Even if I agree to go with you, I can't promise to marry you. Marriage is a sacred commitment. Let's say, for the sake of argument, that I didn't already love Andrew, I still couldn't make a decision like that in five minutes. No one in their right mind would be able to make such a far-reaching commitment in that short of a time. I don't know you. I don't love you! I never will. I love someone else. Do you really want to have a wife who doesn't love you?" How could anyone want that?

I kept trying to talk some sense into this impossible, pain-in-the-butt, emotionally-stunted madman who reminded me a lot of Petruchio in Taming of the Shrew. He seemed to think he was doing me some kind of tremendous favor by forcing me to go to his world and become his spouse. I was not about to be treated like an object to be possessed or manipulated into marriage by some chauvinistic guy just because he's the royal prince of Nommo! Well, if he was going to act like Petruchio, then I guess I was going to be a shrew. There was no way he was going to tame me!

I started stalling. I just kept on talking, trying, without success, to make him understand that we don't do that kind of thing on this planet. The apathetic alien kept looking at me blankly like he couldn't care less. It was like hitting a brick wall with my head over and over again. I drew myself up to my full height, straightened my spine and started unleashing all my inner fury. I tried to hold back the fire of my anger and attack him first with logic, but if he didn't start listening, I was going to hit him full force with my unbridled wrath. I'm generally good at that kind of attack.

"You can't just abduct me and make me marry you! Besides being erroneous thinking on your part, it's really wrong. It won't work. We're not even from the same solar system. We have no connection to each other. What if you meet someone on your own planet that has so much more in common with you, and you fall in love? Where does that leave me? Would you then discard me like an old toy that you grew tired of? The culture shock alone is going to cause me some pretty major depression. Seriously, I may never be happy again. Do you want to be tied to a sad, resentful, suicidal, wife, who will grow to hate you for dragging her away from home? Heck, I'm starting to hate you already!

"What about my family? They won't know what happened to me. Will you deny them the closure that they need to move on with their lives? They will be searching for me for decades. Is that fair in any galaxy? You are completely demented if you think I'm going to stand by and let you take me off this planet!" My voice had steadily increased in volume. I sincerely wanted to wring his royal neck.

"Silence, I don't wish to hear any more of your disrespectful and impudent words. All these emotions that you speak of mean nothing to me. They are completely irrelevant and ultimately unimportant. It is time to make your final decision," he said as though he hadn't heard anything I said. An alarming noise that had been beeping in the background began to increase in volume.

"I'm disrespectful and impudent? Listen to yourself! Have you looked in a mirror lately? You are a self-centered, insensitive, sexist, control freak who thinks you have the right to ruin other people's lives! You must think the universe revolves around you! You're a monster!" All my logic went out the window as I let the insults fly. The cocky commander didn't even blink.

"They are coming, my lord," the henchman, called Nafe, interrupted my tirade and informed us. "They have discovered our location. In approximately thirteen minutes, they will be upon us. We must prepare for departure at once."

"Choose now," Raydon demanded.

"Okay, okay, let them go," I whispered. I could hardly get the words out as a lump had begun to grow, constricting the muscles in my vocal chords. My anger had been replaced by extreme sadness as I realized the futility of my situation. The presence of unwelcome tears was accumulating behind my eyes, getting ready to spill over and gush down my cheeks. I bit my lower lip until I could taste blood, as I tried not to give in to the intense sorrow that was squeezing and strangling my heart as it crawled up into my throat. I didn't want to give him the satisfaction of seeing me cry. I watched as the three bodies came back to life and the doors opened to release them from their cloudy prisons.

Andrew immediately encircled me in his arms and pulled me close to his chest. "What are you doing here?" He whispered in my ear, looking and sounding puzzled at my obvious distress. My throat was already thick with my negative emotions. I couldn't answer. He kissed me soundly and urgently. Then he lifted my chin and looked into my eyes as the tears started to flow. The others looked confused like they had just awoken from an unbelievably ugly dream.

"Tiana will be accompanying me to Nommo. She has agreed to do this in exchange for your lives. You must leave now. Sadvik and Brazzo will show you out. We will equip you with flotation devices. I think you call them lifejackets. You must leave at once," the prince commanded with no emotion whatsoever.

"I'm not leaving without Tiana!" Andrew insisted, defiantly holding onto me.

"Neither am I," James added, frowning and looking dangerous. He's devilishly good at looking dangerous. I think it's one of his superpowers.

"Where are we? What's going on here? Where did you say you were taking Tiana? I'm calling the police. Where's my cell?" Tiffany said searching her pockets.

"We destroyed your communication devices," Raydon announced.

"That was an i-Phone. Are you insane? Do you have any idea how much that phone cost? Who do you think you are? I'm sending you a hefty bill, Mister High and Mighty!" Tiffany said angrily. "Who died and made you king, anyway? What gives you the right to destroy my property? You're so not getting away with this!"

"I don't think the US Postal Service delivers to the planet Nommo," James said.

"Well, I don't care where you're from. My father is the prosecuting attorney for Washington County. He'll have your head, and he'll put your butt in Purgatory. Are you mentally impaired? What were you thinking? Who destroys an iPhone?" Tiffany was glaring at the aliens with barely contained contempt.

"What is this Purgatory?" The prince asked the guardsmen.

"I think they are referring to the underworld where the spirits of evil men go when they die, sir," said Sadvik.

"Is this a death threat?" The Nommoan eyed Tiffany with scornful distain. He looked as if he might order her to be beheaded on the spot.

"Purgatory is the county jail! Of course, I might have to kill you if you don't pay for my phone and let us all go immediately! Did you all escape from an asylum for the criminally insane? What's up with the hideous hair? Why are you dressed like three giant troll ninjas and their extremely rude, fearless leader? What are these things on your tool belts?" Tiffany reached out to touch one of the weapons attached to Brazzo. That's when the royal guard pulled out their big, scary guns. I began to sob like a baby.

"You must leave now," Raydon ordered and then commanded his warrior guards. "Escort them out! Shoot them if they resist."

"Do you want us to wipe their memories, my lord?" Nafe asked.

"No, there isn't time. Just get rid of them." The arrogant aristocrat waved them away.

Andrew pulled me closer to him and whispered in my ear, "Don't be afraid. I'll come for you. Be strong, patient, and don't lose faith. We'll be together soon, I promise." He kissed me with a fierceness that I felt all the way to my toes. Sadvik and Nafe pulled us apart and the three armed Nommoan giants marched my friends away, leaving me alone with His Majesty, the unfeeling prince of pain. I fell to my knees. My legs had turned to the consistency of soggy pasta. This caused me to slip to the floor as panic and grief overcame me. I was suddenly rendered spineless as well as legless.

Any normal, caring person from our planet would have felt guilt or sympathy as they watched me drop and dissolve into an emotional stupor. Prince Raydon merely lifted me to my feet and deposited me in one of those tubular chambers, closing the door. I couldn't see which button he pushed. I wondered for a moment if I were going to die or fall off the planet. It didn't matter. Both seemed equally tragic to me.

CHAPTER 13

NIGHTMARE OR REALITY

When I became conscious, I found that I felt dazed, dizzy and disoriented. I was seated in my car with my forehead resting against the steering wheel. Had I fallen asleep in my car? That was too weird. I'd never done that before. Was there really a spaceship resting at the bottom of Quail Creek Reservoir? Did that crazy Nommoan prince want me to marry him? Was it all just a neurotic nightmare? Were Andrew, James, and Tiffany being held hostage in giant, glass tubes? It had all seemed so real. Had I dreamed up all those delusional details? If I had, I could probably become a best selling author of Sci-Fi fantasy. Was I honestly that big of a dork? Don't answer that!

I decided not to go looking into the murky, mysterious waters of the manmade lake. Why tempt fate? I looked at it through my car window and shivered. Everything looked different somehow. I swear there were more docks and more picnic tables than I remembered. The beaches that had been rocky and gray were now smooth, white, and sandy. The water treatment facility seemed larger. Was I imagining all these discrepancies or had I just not been paying attention? Maybe I genuinely do suffer from A.D.D.

I started my car and drove toward State Route 9. When I got to the intersection, I turned left onto a road I didn't recognize. I remembered it as having only four lanes. Now there were eight. The traffic had greatly increased. It was more like I was driving in Las Vegas than Hurricane, Utah. Even the vehicles were strange. Where were all the sports utility vehicles and mini vans? Most of these cars seemed sleeker and smaller than usual. A few that whizzed by looked like they hovered above the road without any wheels at all. I must be imagining that. Perhaps all my recent stress had caused my mind to play cruel tricks on me or maybe I needed some professional psychiatric help in a hurry.

As I drove further toward the turn off leading to my family's residence, I noticed many more new houses and businesses. Hurricane had apparently grown into a thriving, heavily populated metropolis while I was napping in my car. How was that possible? Something was terribly wrong with this scene. I felt an unwanted seed of anxiety take root and sprout in the pit of my sinking stomach. I found my street as I was wondering about all of these bizarre alterations to my perceived reality.

The homes in my neighborhood looked older. Some were run down and shabby. My house had been painted a horrible shade of puke-yellow-green. My artistic mother would never allow such an ugly color to dry on the outer walls of our tastefully decorated home. Something was very, very wrong. My tummy anxiety had grown and branched out through my entire body, sending a familiar feeling of foreboding winding itself around my consciousness, making my breath hitch as it tightened its vine-like tendrils of terror around my confused brain.

I stopped in front of the ugly, disguised house and exited my car. The yard was all different. It no longer had grass and flowers. It was now covered with multicolored rocks and pea gravel. A few cacti and yucca plants dotted the desert xeriscape. Xeriscape is what people do in the desert to avoid watering the grass. It made sense to me, but my father considered it a cop out for lazy, cheap homeowners. He swore he'd never replace our small patch of grass. It represented his ability to conquer the wilderness.

I was beginning to think I had stepped through time and space and entered a parallel universe or else this was an overly outlandish dream. I pinched myself hard on my arm that was covered with raised goose flesh, but I didn't wake up. I gathered my wits, as many as I could find under the present circumstances, walked up to the front door and tried it. It was locked, so I took out my key and attempted to insert it in the lock like I had done about a thousand times before. This time it didn't fit!

This couldn't be happening! My hand started to shake. I dropped the key. Cold perspiration broke out and covered my forehead. I brushed it away with the back of my hand as I stared at the key on the cement. Retrieving it from the doorstep, I braced myself, and tried to stop trembling. I knocked on the door with the apprehension that had grown almost as big as a house, afraid of what might be waiting on the other side. A slightly familiar, older, Asian woman with graying hair and granny glasses opened the door and peered out at me questioningly.

"Do the Dawson's still live here?" I asked, trying to act like nothing was wrong. This was incredibly hard because my heart was hammering so loudly in my ears, I could hardly hear myself speak. I managed to keep my voice from squeaking like it sometimes does when I'm stressed out of my mind.

"You must be related to them. You look almost identical to their daughter, Tiana, who disappeared seventeen years ago. It was a terrible tragedy that they never found the poor girl. She was a friend of my Jenna," the woman sadly explained, shaking her head. "Oh no, you most certainly know this already, being a relative and all. I'm so sorry to have brought it up, dear. I'll get you their new address. When Dr. Dawson retired, they moved to a condo in Sun River. That's in South St. George by Bloomington, dear. Do you want me to call and tell them you're coming?"

"No thank you, Mrs. Chun," I said. "I want to surprise them," I added, feeling flustered by all this impossible information. If what I suspected was true, I wondered who I could pretend to be. If I'd gone missing seventeen years ago, no one would believe I *was* me. This was getting confusing and complicated. I was having difficulty processing this bewildering situation.

"Have we met? How did you know my name?" She questioned me.

"No, I met Jenna at the Dawsons' when I was a child. For some reason, I still remember her name. I'm Tiana's cousin, Trish. I've been out of the country for several years. Do you know what happened to the Martins who used to live up on the hill?" I had to ask, fearing the answer.

"Oh, yes. Let me think. I believe Andrew married that blond girl who used to date Mark Dawson. Her name was Sasha or Sarah or something like that," she said this while she copied an address on a piece of scratch paper. I was glad she missed the pained look of shock and grief that now had to have registered on my terrified face.

"Sonya?" I spat out the name. I didn't want to believe what I heard. The horror of it made my jaw almost drop off my head and hit the floor. I was immediately filled with a sick comprehension that pushed outward from my heart so hard I thought I might faint from the force. I could feel an attack of the dry-heaves coming on. My left eye began to twitch. My legs turned to rubber and started to wobble. I had to get away before I collapsed on her floor. I gulped and then took silent, deep breaths, trying to calm myself, so I wouldn't betray the emotional havoc that now warred in my mind.

"Yes, that was her name. Hannah married Matthew Allen and the other girl married his little brother. The whole family moved back to Australia about ten years ago. The last I heard they still live there." She handed me the paper with my parents' new address on it.

"Thanks again," I managed to mutter as I hurriedly escaped to my car before my knees gave out altogether. I heard her shut the door behind me. I climbed in and burst into tears. I banged my head against the steering wheel several times, scarcely feeling the pain. I closed my eyes. I didn't want to live in this world. Something had gone horribly awry. Had I actually gone to Nommo and returned to find that half my life had passed me by? Had they wiped my memories of the trip?

I remembered, all too clearly, Einstein's Special Theory of Relativity. Had I just experienced the fact that time is relative? I had not aged and yet seventeen years seemed to have flown by here on Earth. My whole future had been erased. I no longer could be me. What was I supposed to do? How could Andrew marry Psycho-Sonya? In what universe would he do that? This was a nightmare! I wanted to wake up, and I wanted to do it now! I hit my head a few more times, pounded my fists on the dashboard and prayed that I could leave this disturbingly dream and never visit it again.

I opened my eyes and found that I was no longer in my Honda. My prayer had been answered, but not exactly the way I wanted it to be. I was staring into the huge, indifferent, brown eyes of Prince Raydon through the glass of one of those tubular prisons in the Nommoan spaceship.

For just a moment, extreme relief flowed through my system. Then I realized that the nightmare I had just experienced could undoubtedly have happened. If we were about to land on Nommo, I had probably been asleep for just over a month's time. That meant eight and one half years had passed on Earth.

My poor parents had probably accepted the fact that I wasn't coming back. My classmates at Hurricane High had graduated, married, and started their own families or careers or both. My car was either recycled or rusting at the county landfill or in a local junkyard where they sell parts off antique clunkers. My cat, Slim, might be dead and buried in the backyard. His sweet and timid, little cat spirit could be padding off into the light to find the giant cat box in the sky. Mark could have married and had children. I could be an aunt to kids I'd never meet. He could be playing basketball in the NBA, and I'd never see him do it! Had Andrew given up on finding me and married someone else? That last question made me shudder.

His majesty opened the door to the chamber, took my hand, pulling me out as I contemplated my ruined and shattered life. I went with him without a fight. I felt alone and empty inside. All my relief had been replaced by deep despair.

He led me to a small room with an attached bathroom. A large television screen covered one wall. It made me feel like I was sitting on the front row at the movies. I had to stand back to see the whole picture. It showed a blue-green planet that was spotted with light brown and gray dots. Wispy, white Clouds swirled around it. It resembled Earth without the recognizable, large landmasses that are visible from space. Instead, there were many small puzzle pieces scattered on the surface of the globe like multicolored confetti. We seemed to be slowly orbiting this strange world that I, and probably no one from Earth, had ever seen before. Despite my extreme emotional pain, I couldn't help being curious. I decided to latch onto that curiosity as a way to ignore the despair that wanted to eat me alive.

"I thought you might want to freshen up before we land. My people are waiting anxiously to meet their new queen." He smiled like life had never been better.

I stifled my sudden desire to choke him. This was his fault. My life had been torn into pieces. He was the pig-headed person who had done the tearing. This audacious alien thought the universe revolved around his royal personage. He was the bossy bigot who ripped it up, sending it through the paper shredder. Oh, how I loathed him for it!

He pushed a button on the screen and the picture changed to a partitioned area, roped off and guarded by more ninjas with those super-scary guns. Beyond the ropes, a massive crowd of people formed an ocean of human faces. The camera zoomed in on many of the owners of those faces. They were yelling something. He adjusted the volume. I could hear the people calling his name over and over. I guess they missed him. They apparently loved him or something. I couldn't understand why. Were they a bunch of ignorant fools? Who would have guessed that all this intense adoration was meant for their egotistical emperor, the very same galling, egocentric guy who dragged me kicking and screaming off my own planet and brought me here against my will? Okay, maybe I didn't kick and scream out loud, but I was certainly yelling and kicking on the inside.

As I watched in utter disbelief, I was filled with a brand new fear, a sort of stage fright. I don't actually enjoy the spotlight even in front of people I know and love. I certainly didn't want to be paraded out to be ogled and judged by this crowd of chanting aliens. Oops, I guess they weren't the aliens here, I was. This thought made me freak out even more. What would they think of me? Crazy me! Why did I care?

He left me there to shower and try to make myself presentable so I could be introduced to his loving, loyal subjects. I automatically stripped down and got into the shower. The water spurted from numerous holes in the sides and ceiling of the stall and was controlled by buttons on a panel. I couldn't find the soap or shampoo. I squinted at the buttons that were labeled with pictures. I pushed the one that looked like bubbles. I was instantly doused all over with rich foam that smelled like citrus and jasmine. I rinsed off and stepped out onto the heated bathmat that was situated in the thick archway.

When my feet were both planted on the mat, warm air came from openings in the archway and blasted me dry from my hair to my feet in less that a minute. I wouldn't mind having a shower like this at home I thought and then I felt that much-too-familiar sinking feeling wash over me again. I might never see my home again. I put that unwelcome thought out of my mind for now. I had more pressing things to worry about like meeting the entire population of an alien planet.

I went in the small bedroom to redress and found that my clothes had magically turned into a pale-green, ankle-length dress with the royal insignia embroidered in maroon and black across the bodice. My underwear seemed to have been laundered and laid beside it. That was weird. I wondered if stealthy laundry elves snuck in on tiptoes to steal and wash my undies while I showered. Who does that? My sneakers had disappeared and in their place were delicate sandals that matched the soft, sea-foam green of the silky gown. Everything fit perfectly. Had he measured me in my sleep? Were these clothes delivered via air mail? Did he just have them lying around? Did those sneaky, space-elves make the clothing too?

I had lost weight. I guess not eating for six weeks will do that to you. I was too distraught to care. My face looked gaunt. I studied my reflection in the mirror and realized I was intensely irritated by the stupid insignia emblazoned across my chest. It made me look like I'd been branded or labeled as his property just like his mutant ninja soldiers, who had the same sign stamped on their foreheads.

A knock on the door interrupted my deepening disgust. I opened it to find a short, plump woman standing there with a makeup case and hair brushes in her hands. She was dressed in flamboyant, flowing, silver, gauzy material that seemed to be wrapped haphazardly around her ample body. Her hair was a bright, bubblegum pink streaked with soft, violet highlights. It was artistically arranged in a strange up-do like you see in those hair magazines at beauty salons. It was secured with rhinestone-studded clips. You've seen those wild hair-dos. No one in their right mind would dare walk outside and let people see them looking like that.

"I am Lanu. I am here to get you ready for your official presentation to the people of Nommo. They have been waiting many years to greet you. You are as beautiful as Prince Raydon reported. Is this your natural hair color?" She sweetly asked as she examined a strand of errant hair.

"Yes," I answered. She acted like she had never encountered a natural redhead before. I found that idea to be odd. Then I remembered she was from a different planet and gave myself a mental slap to my forehead. Odd was probably normal here. That made me the strange one.

"On Nommo, no one is born with hair this color. It's lovely! Your skin is such a creamy white. I have never seen this unique, translucent, glowing skin tone," she continued.

Her comments made me cringe and want to run away and hide under the bed. I was going to stand out even worse than I did on Earth. I'd be a redheaded, albino freak again. Why worry about that? The gravity of my predicament jolted me to face facts as I came to the unpleasant realization that I would be the freak from another planet no matter what I looked like.

She made me sit in front of the mirror while she applied touches of miscellaneous makeup. She twisted my hair up on top of my head in a style that reminded me of old movie stars like Audrey Hepburn and Lana Turner. I think they both had died before I was born, but my mother used to make me watch their ancient, black and white flicks with her when my dad and Mark went on fathers and sons campouts.

Thinking about my mother made me tear up. I told myself to behave and not cry because it would ruin my face. I had to be marched out in front of the entire population of a planet that had never seen an albino freak from Earth with red hair before. They were all going to hate me when I refused to marry their royal leader, but today I was inclined to go along with the flow of things and try not to make too many waves. I was sure I would bring on a tsunami when I went public with my disrespectful rebellion against the most powerful and beloved tyrant in their world. I didn't think they were going to take it well. I wasn't ready to rock that boat right now and "dis" their fearless leader in public. I'd need to work myself up to committing what would probably constitute high treason.

I hoped that today I would only have to smile demurely and wave and then be rushed off to His Majesty's castle where I could barricade myself in my quarters and refuse to come out. I wanted to escape into a catatonic stupor, so I wouldn't have to think about how I was going to get myself out of this monstrous mess without being executed, or thrown into some stinky, dark, damp dungeon to rot for the rest of my pathetic existence.

"Relax, dear," Lanu seemed to pick up on my fearful thoughts. "They will all accept you! The entire planet has learned your language, so they can make you feel welcome. They believe you will save them from extinction."

Okay, now I felt worse than I did before. Was this whole world completely wacky? I wasn't capable of saving anyone. I was the one who needed to be saved and soon!

CHAPTER 14

A WHOLE DIFFERENT PLANET

I reluctantly stepped outside of the spaceship. I walked slowly down the steps to make my momentous first official appearance on the planet, Nommo. The air was filled with a sweet, fruity fragrance that had a hint of honeysuckle and gardenia. Prince Raydon guided me to a raised and covered platform where he would address his people, who were still loudly chanting his name like we were at a concert waiting for the famous rock star to begin his long awaited performance.

I was actually standing on another planet. This was a huge step for me. I couldn't help being intrigued. I looked up at the azure sky. It was just as blue as the sky on Earth, but it was so bright, it hurt my eyes. Lanu was standing behind me. She handed me a pair of sunglasses like she had just read my mind, or noticed me squinting. I hastily put them on and then I located their sun, Sirius, and halfway across the sky was another brilliant orb. Sirius was about twice the size of our sun and the other one was significantly smaller. There were a few puffy, floating clouds that looked more pink than white, like cotton candy at the circus.

I kind of felt like I was at a circus. The people assembled here reminded me of circus or carnival people. You know those really strange people who seem to come out only to visit carnivals and circuses. They are the same ones who do their grocery shopping in the middle of the night. Yeah, I've been to the mega-marts after midnight. It's a zoo! I'm sure that's where and when those pictures of the "Mega-mart Martians" are taken and displayed on the internet to make all us more conservative people wonder how anyone would choose to appear in public that way. Maybe they're all from other planets. That makes perfect sense.

Their hair styles ranged from moderately crazy to flat out Looney Tunes or punk rock on mind altering medication. Most of these Nommoans seemed to like the multi-wild-colors look. I think a streak of color here and there can be flattering, but most of these hairdos were way over the top, making them far past all semblance of fashion sense. Some of these people could pull it off, but others looked just plain silly.

The clothes they wore were weird, flamboyant, skimpy, and as brightly colored as their hair. The combination of random patterns was enough to give me a migraine, if I made the mistake of looking at them too long. Many wore strange swimwear with flimsy cover ups that shimmered, changing colors in the sunlight which was everywhere, seeing as they had two suns shining down from different positions in the sky.

The climate was humid and tropical. The atmosphere was warm, moist and very different from the dry air I had grown used to in Hurricane. Oh, how I missed Hurricane. I now realized, without a shadow of a doubt, that it was not only the happiest place on Earth, but the best place in the whole known universe. Would I ever see it again? There was an aching feeling in my heart. It reminded me that I wasn't here of my own volition. I had lost all control over my own recently destroyed life.

In the distance, I could barely make out some colorful squares hovering above the crowd of Nommoans on the ground. As I looked closer, I could see blue balloons attached to the corners of these squares. Lanu, bless her little helpful heart, read my thoughts again and handed me a pair of high powered binoculars. I peered through them at the buckets or baskets that seemed to hang in midair. Each one contained a person, who was peering through a spyglass right back at me.

Yeah, that was awkward and a little creepy like being caught staring at someone's disability or seeing something you shouldn't be viewing at all. Embarrassing, much? Well, I would be mortified, if I actually knew any of those brightly colored, floating Nommoans. The balloons must contain a gas more buoyant than helium to hold them there. I didn't have a chance to ask any questions as a hush had fallen over the crowd. I handed the binoculars back to Lanu. The real show was about to begin.

His Majesty, the narrow-minded narcissist, began to speak to them in a language I didn't understand. His voice was being broadcast through the crowd. I heard it echo back from somewhere far away. He would pause every so often and they would cheer and applaud. They even laughed once or twice. I hadn't thought these ultra-serious, super-intelligent, space people had senses of humor. I'd never seen their egotistical, leader crack a real grin before.

At the end of his speech, he smiled. It transformed his face. He actually looked almost happy and human. I took his cue and smiled. I gave the "parade" wave. You know, the side-to-side, graceful wave beauty queens always use. A few of the people waved back. As I was being whisked away into some flying machine that resembled a helicopter without the turning blades, I heard the crowd yelling another name. It was my name. Now that was freaky.

Flying above the masses, I could see that the island we were on was shaped like a colossal amphitheater. We had been positioned near the "stage" which was a raised area with a massive snow crested mountain as a backdrop. The people had arranged themselves on grass and stone terraces that rippled out from the center like stairs. Beyond those steps was a humongous parking facility that was filled with all sorts of strange machines that must have been their miscellaneous means of transportation. At the base of the scenic mountain, behind where the prince had delivered his speech, stood a military complex, complete with barracks, an army of ninja soldiers like those I had met, and a vast arsenal of armored vehicles and machinery.

Lush green hills ringed the rest of the island. Streams and rivers sliced through the thick vegetation. Some of those hills were covered with unusual fruit trees and flowers. On the outer side of the ring of hills, there were many small hamlets along the coastline. Lots of multi-sized boats were docked all the way around the edges. At one bay that cut into the circle shaped island, there were three Titanic-sized-ocean-liner ships parked.

We flew over several other islands before landing on a small one that was guarded like a fortress. A massive stone wall stretched all the way around our target island. It reminded me of the Great Wall of China. I could see the heavily armed henchmen walking on a path on top. They waved their guns as we passed over them.

"Do you have a lot of dangerous criminals running around loose on your planet?" I summoned the courage to speak to Lanu, who sat beside me. Raydon was up with the pilots in the cockpit or whatever they called that place in this unusual plane.

"There are some, why do you ask?" She looked surprised by my question.

"Why are there so many guards with big guns and what's that wall supposed to keep out?" I asked.

"That's to keep us safe from the rebels and to keep the convicted servants from running away," she explained.

"Who are these rebels? What are convicted servants and why do they want to run away? Where would they run to? This place is surrounded by water."

"On Nommo, when someone is accused of committing a crime they are exonerated, executed, exiled or sentenced to a life of servitude. We have no prisons. Most of those who are exiled join the forces which oppose our government. We refer to them as rebels. They sneak into our cities to cause mayhem. They steal from us. They try to incite the general public to rise against the established bureaucracy.

"Those sentenced to serve, make up the manual labor force of our planet. They are not mistreated, but they have forfeited their freedom to live where and how they choose, so they sometimes try to escape and join the rebels. The government considers them to be infinitely inferior to rest of us. They are deemed unworthy to live among us. Being surrounded by water does not keep Nommoans from getting out or in. We can all swim for many hours without tiring. We can breath underwater. There is also a force field on top of that wall that extends thousands of feet up, so no flying machines can land here without permission."

"Okay, I get it. You hate the rebels and are afraid of them."

"Hate and fear are strong words. We do not resort to hating or fearing anyone. We merely distrust their behavior. Those who rule us prefer to keep us separate from those who indulge in illogical, erratic and emotional actions. The rebels are motivated by extreme passions and sentimentality that are considered uncouth and unacceptable by our current government standards."

"That doesn't make any sense. I thought you were trying to get back in touch with your emotions. I mean, I was under the impression that you lacked passion and were seeking a way to feel it again. Wasn't that the whole purpose of the prince's visit to Earth?"

"Well, yes, but we only want to have the good emotions. We want to feel love and happiness; not fear, hate, anger or sorrow," she insisted.

"I don't think you can pick and choose. They sort of go together in a package deal. You can't really know love or joy if you never suffer sorrow or pain. It's true that we all have to learn to control our negative passions like hate and fear, but we can't completely turn them off without losing the positive ones," I tried to make her understand, but she didn't seem to be getting it. Her face had gone completely blank like she could only hear "blah, blah, blah." I could tell she'd totally zoned out. I had always thought that smart people paid attention when spoken to. Did any of these people actually listen and try to understand?

Our conversation was interrupted when the flying machine touched down next to the "castle." The ginormous structure didn't, in any way, except maybe in the magnitude of the square footage, resemble the castles of fairytales in storybooks. It was more like a gargantuan display of geometric shapes stacked and shoved together in no obvious order or design. I was reminded of those modern art sculptures that are so utterly random, it's hard to know what the artist was thinking about.

There was a hexagon in the center that consisted of five stories of mirrored glass. Attached to that were several three story rectangles. At the ends of three of those were circular stone towers of varying heights and sizes. The tallest tower was at least ten stories high. It was topped off with a large triangular shape that looked a little like the crow's nest on a pirate ship. It had a balcony all the way around it. I was sure the view would be incredible. I wanted that to be my room.

Ha! I realized I would probably end up a prisoner in the basement dungeon when I refused to marry His Mighty Majesty. Maybe, I could pretend to like him for a few weeks and demand that space. Nah, that wasn't going to work. I've never been very good at pretending to like arrogant, unfeeling, tyrannical kidnappers from other planets. However, I figured I'd better not show any animosity yet, or I'd probably be cast out into the sea with the rebels. Unlike them, I can't breathe underwater.

I was ushered from the vehicle and rushed into the castle. Lanu introduced me to Mara and Shan, who were to be my personal servants. They wore the prince's insignia on their right hands instead of their forehead. Lucky for them, they didn't have their faces disfigured like the male servants I'd met.

I couldn't help wondering what horrible crimes they had committed, to be sentenced to serve me. Mara was a petite girl with shoulder length light brown and maroon curls. She had fairy-like features and bright blue eyes. Shan was tall with straight white-blond hair that was streaked with an orange-copper color. Her eyes were that exact coppery, orange-brown and matched her hairstreaks perfectly. Her striking appearance and the dignity with which she carried herself reminded me of the Helamite women I had met on Earth. They were both about my age or a little older. Shouldn't they be in school? Had they done something so terrible that they had lost their right to learn?

I was overcome with awe as I beheld the area just inside the enormous doors of the royal palace. There were two magnificent spiral staircases that wound up to a floor past the tall ceiling that had to be over thirty feet high. Everything in this entrance hall was in varying shades of white except for the lacey greenery that filled about a hundred silver, statuesque, opalescent urns on marble pillars.

The two girls led me to an enormous closed door between the two grand staircases. Mara pushed a button. The door slid into the wall. A glass elevator was revealed. It hugged the outside of the tallest tower. She pushed another button, and we climbed to the crow's nest that I had observed from the plane. We stepped out onto the balcony that surrounded the triangular area. The view was just as spectacular as I had imagined it would be. We walked around the space. It was divided into three suites.

Shan opened the door to what was to be my living quarters. The room was as big as my whole house on Earth. It was the most opulent and ostentatious room I had ever seen. Everything in it was blue, green, white or silver. There were three, silver and blue, crystal chandeliers that glittered and looked like waterfalls reflecting the sun. The bed was massive and covered with bedding made out of some kind of sumptuous, white silky fur. I hoped it wasn't real fur. There was so much of it; I feared a whole herd of something had been slaughtered for their hides. Where were the animal rights activists? The furniture was extremely artsy, futuristic and upholstered in the same fur or a soft and supple, luxurious, blue, leathery material.

The two girls pulled me into a walk-in closet that was as big as my bedroom at home. It was well stocked with clothes and shoes in my exact sizes. Cool! I was in Shoe Heaven! I'd never seen so many shoes in one place before, except for shoe stores, and I seriously love shoes. I couldn't help slipping out of my sandals and trying on a few pairs of truly topnotch works of artistic footwear. They could compete with Prada or Jimmy Choos. They were amazingly comfortable! Even the stiletto-heeled ones had some kind of stabilizer in them that kept my feet from wobbling. How cool is that? Yeah, I can't help myself. I'm easily distracted by a pretty shoe.

The two girls giggled as they showed me some of the outrageously glamorous outfits. They displayed the gown I was supposed to wear to a function the next evening in the capital city. It was white and completely covered with rhinestones. The neckline was outlined in fluffy, white feathers. I wondered what poor bird had sacrificed its life, so I could wear this precious plumage. The skirt was long and shaped like a mermaid's tail.

On Earth, I wouldn't be caught dead in such a gown, but here I didn't care. I was just going through the motions, doing what was expected of me, until I found the courage to defy Raydon and refuse to marry him. I had to make him understand that I could never love him. Then I could die. I dismissed the girls, fell on the bed, and in spite of the many lovely shoes, I proceeded to bawl my eyes out.

Okay, don't judge me harshly. I'm not normally such a cry-baby, but I seemed to have lost all control over my tear ducts when I left Planet Earth. Oh yeah, I guess it was even before that earth shaking event. It was when Raydon had kidnapped Andrew. I could trace it all back to Nommo's favorite fearless leader. He'd invaded Earth, and I'd lost all control over my own life.

I felt the silver ring on my little finger and wondered if my bond with Andrew had been broken by the light years that now separated us. I could see no escape from this unfixable, monumental mess and I couldn't think of a reason to cling to a life that was already over.

When did I become such a fatalist? Well, traveling astronomical distances though time and space can do that to a girl. I hoped the abrasive aristocrat would just kill me fast, so I wouldn't have to suffer. I hate suffering.

CHAPTER 15

WHO'S YOUR DADDY?

I must have fallen asleep during my fit of despair. How could I be tired after sleeping for over a month on board the Star Ship Nightmare? I woke up to an extremely noisy someone knocking furiously on my door.

"Go away!" I shouted above the persistent pounding, "Nobody's home!"

"The prince says you have to come down to dinner," Shan insisted as she and Mara burst into my room when I didn't get up and answer the door. Evidently, there's no respect for privacy on this planet, especially for those who have been abducted by an annoying monarch.

"I'm not hungry," I growled at them. The last thing I wanted to do was sit at a table and try to make polite conversation with the pompously irritating guy who had dragged me off my home planet, forced me to come to his and totally ruined my life.

"Tell the stupid prince to suck rocks and die! I hate him! I'm never coming out of this room! I want to go home!" I pulled the blankets over my head.

"We cannot tell him such things!" Mara said with a note of terror in her voice. "He'll have us executed!"

"You will have to come and tell him yourself, my lady," Shan laughed. "I'd really like to see you talk to *him* like that." She must have thought I was joking.

I decided I liked Shan. At least, she had a sense of humor and didn't seem to think I was awful for hating on the conceited, crown prince. Of course, she probably didn't know the meaning of "hate," since that was one of those "unpleasant" emotions that Nommoans don't want to experience.

"The king is waiting to meet you," Mara continued to look worried by my angry words. Anger, there's another negative emotion. I was just full of them today.

"You mustn't keep him waiting. He could have you killed!"

"That's just fine with me. His son already destroyed my life. Do you have any idea how angry that makes me? Tell him to step right up and kill me now. I'm ready to die!"

I gave them my most defiant, narrow eyed, frowny face, which made Shan collapse in uncontrollable giggles. She was really starting to grow on me. We could be best friends if I were still on Earth, hadn't been abducted by aliens and wasn't about to be executed by their Head Honcho.

"Please, my lady. You must obey the king!" Mara tried to pull me off my bed. "Shan, stop laughing! This isn't a joke!"

"Why must I? He's not my king! I'm a U.S. citizen and a legal resident of the planet, Earth. Prince Raydon committed a grievous crime and broke a universal law when he kidnapped me and brought me here against my will. He's the one who should be executed!" I retorted. "I'm the victim here! Doesn't anyone get that?"

"My lady, Mara's right. You must come with us. We will be beheaded if we fail to bring you to meet the king," Shan implored, still smiling at my theatrics.

"How can you not love the prince? Any girl on Nommo would be thrilled to receive any kind of attention from him. Don't you find him irresistible?" Mara asked with total amazement.

"You're kidding, right? Do you think that self-important, egotistical, aggravating, irritating, overbearing, royal pain-in-the-butt is irresistible? Are you as insane as he is? Is this whole stinking planet insane?"

"Please, my lady, do not speak ill of His Majesty!" Mara begged. She looked even more shocked at my intense outburst. I think she wanted to wash my mouth out with soap for saying all those naughty things about their beloved ruler. I had a lot of much worse adjectives I could use to describe him. Most of them, they probably wouldn't understand.

"You must come with us at once. He will send his guards to escort you to the dining hall, and they aren't very nice," Shan coaxed.

"Alright already, I'll come, but only if you stop calling me 'my lady.' It makes me feel like some loser, old woman in a tragic, historical novel. My name is Tiana. I don't want to be anyone's lady. I'm not changing into one of those awful, mermaid formals so don't even ask!"

I glared at them, got off the bed and went to look in the mirror. I didn't really care what I looked like, but I thought maybe I'd better not disrespect the king. I didn't want all the servants to lose their heads over me. I looked okay, even though I'd cried all my eye makeup off. I took a minute to wipe at the smudges and splash some water on my face. Then I turned and followed the servant girls out of my room wearing the green dress with the stupid, royal insignia emblazoned across my chest. When I got back, I'd take it off and toss it over the balcony in a symbolic act of rebellion. That defiant thought made me smile. I've always been good at passive aggression.

As we entered the immense dining hall, I noticed an empty seat at the head of the table. Raydon sat on one side. I was led to the seat across from him on the other side. Raydon gave me a curt nod of acknowledgement. I pulled a cross-eyed face and stuck out my tongue at him. I figured I was done playing nice as the docile victim of his unforgivable crime.

Why should I make this easy for him? Tonight, I decided I would make him suffer for his sins. I was already planning on being killed so I might as well exact as much revenge as I could manage before my imminent and certain death arrived. He actually grinned at me. He looked entirely different when he smiled. This made me worry. I didn't know if he read minds like the Helamites did. I wasn't about to ask.

I looked away and pretended to be admiring the ceiling which was covered with a mural of the night sky. All the stars glowed brightly, providing light for the room along with several large, triangular, crystal sconces that lined the two long, parallel walls on either side of the massive stone dining table. It was an awe inspiring room. It was generous enough to throw a banquet for over fifty people. The polished granite table had almost that many posh, elaborately upholstered, red, velvet chairs around it.

After we sat there is silence for about five minutes, a tall, lanky man with silvery white hair and bushy eyebrows came strutting in like a peacock in all his finery. He was wearing red and black striped pajamas with slippers that resembled my monkey house-shoes only his were goldfish. Honest! On his head, he wore a silver crown that had been cut out of cardboard, glued together and covered with tinfoil. I made one exactly like it in first grade to wear every time I pretended to be a princess which was pretty much all the time. I thought how ironic it was that I now could marry a prince, and I wanted no part of it. A purple, velvet cape lined with white fur adorned his shoulders.

His odd apparel reminded me of a little kid playing dress up in Halloween costumes. I'm sure my jaw dropped when I saw him. I quickly closed my mouth and forced a polite smile on my misbehaving lips. I know it's rude to gawk at strange kings. It's an especially bad idea, if they can order you to be beheaded on a whim.

"We can start now. Your king has arrived," he commanded, waving a golden scepter at the servants. They were standing at attention, biting their lips so they wouldn't smile. I wasn't the only one amused by his childish behavior.

"I am Roylin, king of Nommo. How do you like my kingly attire? I have been studying your Earth's fascinating history. This is how kings dress on your planet. Am I correct? You have permission to speak, young lady!" He pointed at me with his magic king wand, tapping my head. I had to bite my tongue to keep from laughing. "Is this indeed how Earthly kings are supposed to look and act?"

"During medieval times, absolutely," I managed to say without cracking up.

"They no longer dress and act this way?" He gave me a gigantic grin. He was apparently extremely proud of his outlandish attire. "That is a shame. I think I look magnificent. What do you think, son?"

"You look ludicrous and insane, Father," His offensive offspring answered without smiling. He was obviously embarrassed by his father's antics. The man has no sense of humor.

"That's good, then! I am certifiably insane, so I should look this way." He winked at me. I smiled back. "There is no use hiding who you are. Many kings on Earth were insane. The French Emperor, Napoleon, was obviously off his rocker. He even had a psychological complex named after him. The British King Henry VIII had two of his wives beheaded because they didn't bear him any sons. Now that's real insanity. King Charles I, also of England, loved to put his eighteen-inch, court dwarf between two bread slices and then he pretended to eat him. He was nutty as a fruitcake. King George I of Greece turned his palace's ballroom into a roller skating rink. They thought he was ludicrous and insane also. You don't mind that I'm crazy, do you my dear?"

"No sir, I rather like crazy people as long as they aren't mean. Many of my favorite folks are. I'm a little insane, myself," I said, smiling brightly at him and then I gave Raydon a "you-disgust-me" look.

"Well then, we are going to be excellent friends. I'm sorry my head-strong son forced you to come home with him. I told him it was wrong to take you away from your planet, but he never listens to me."

"I'm not the only king to have trouble with my son. I have learned about many Earth kings who have had difficult children. King George V once said this to his son the future King Edward VIII: 'You dress like a cad. You act like a cad. You are a cad. Get out!'

"Do you even know what a cad is, Father?" Raydon asked in a conde-scending tone.

"Of course, my son, you are a cad for dragging Tiana away from her Helamite soul mate!" The king answered without missing a beat. "King George III said his son, Prince Frederick, was a 'false, lying, cowardly, nau-seous puppy and the greatest liar and beast in the world.' Raydon isn't quite that bad. Do children on Earth today always obey their parents?"

"Not always, Your Excellency," I replied. "I think we're all prepro-grammed to rebel against parental authority at some point in our lives. I really do wish your son was more obedient to you. Then I wouldn't have to die." Oops, the last sentence just slipped out. I wanted to catch the words and force them back inside my head.

"You don't have to die! Who told you that you had to die? I'll have them killed for speaking such nonsense! Now that would be ironic, wouldn't it? Tell me, my child and I'll put this right." He pounded his fist on the table and seemed genuinely angered by my statement of fact. I thought Nommoans were supposed to be unemotional.

He seemed to read my thoughts and said, "They all think I'm crazy because I keep showing my emotions. Can you believe that? They want to get back in touch with some of theirs, but they're absolutely afraid of mine. Maybe, I'm completely sane, and they're all bonkers. What do you think?"

"That would explain everything," I agreed. It was easy for me to believe everyone on this freaky planet was out to lunch.

"You're very intelligent for an Earth girl, aren't you? Now tell me why you think you have to die," he demanded, folding his arms across his chest and giving me his full, royal attention. This surprised me because his son never listened to anything I said. I thought it would be a family trait.

I took a deep breath and then I bravely told the truth. "I'm not going to marry your son, so I imagine he'll have me executed. He thinks he loves me because he studied my boyfriend's memories and identified with him somehow. I told him his love isn't real. He doesn't believe me. He made me choose between having my friends and myself killed or saving them and coming with him. He's the one who won't accept that reality, so I guess I have to die," I calmly explained this to the king in a matter-of-fact manner. What the heck, what did I have to lose? I'd already lost everything I cared about.

"Rubbish! My supercilious son is often confused because he's never tried to understand things like love. I apologize for his inexcusable behavior. I tried to teach him, but he never paid much attention to me. There is not going to be any dying here, young lady. I won't allow it!

"We'll find a way to fix this. It won't be easy with the whole 'time is relative' thing, but I'll put my best thinkers to work on it and I do have some excellent minds at my disposal. We once knew a way around it, but then everyone stopped caring about time. I'm not sure we still have that information stored among our vast accumulation of knowledge, but I'll have my most competent colleagues search the archives for answers.

"Now let's eat and forget about dying! Bring on the feast, my loyal servants!" He waved his wand at the servants. They sprang into action like frantic toy robots that had been wound too tightly.

The "feast" consisted of platters full of exotic fruits and vegetables, three different kinds of seafood, a fish flavored soup, and a delicious dessert that tasted like cheesecake dipped in milk chocolate and topped with purple berries that had a distinctive flavor like grapes crossed with cherries.

We drank a sparkling concoction in a flavor similar to lime with just a hint of coconut.

I was surprised that I found my appetite. The king's vow to make things right must have given me false hope that my life could be restored to what it had been before it was so rudely interrupted by Mr. "Marry-me-or-everybody-dies".

Following dinner, Prince Raydon insisted upon giving me a tour of the castle gardens. They were breathtaking and full of exotic, colorful and fragrant flowers planted in the shape of the royal insignia. There were so many smells and colors; I found my senses became overloaded. Everything blended together, making it impossible for me to describe all the beauty that surrounded me.

"I should have warned you about my father. He lost his grip on reality when my mother died," he explained.

"I'm so sorry. Did this happen recently?" I asked.

It's always sad when you lose someone close to you. I didn't want to feel sorry for him, but I couldn't help it. I had just lost everyone close to me. I hadn't come to grips with that painful scenario yet.

"My father met my mother on her home planet, Helam, when he led an expedition to that world to obtain their accumulated knowledge. They fell in love, and she came back with him to be his wife. She was an overly emotional woman. She felt sorrow for the people who had been exiled from our country. She took medical supplies and provisions to them twice a year.

"The year that I turned twelve, she journeyed to the less desirable islands where these convicted criminals live. The hovercraft she was aboard had an engine problem and was forced down into the ocean. Everyone survived but her. She was not Nommoan, so she was unable to breathe underwater and consequently drowned before anyone realized what was happening. He hasn't been in his right mind since. His advisors governed the country until I turned seventeen and took over."

"You must have been devastated. It had to be a hard time for both you and your father," I sympathized.

All my plans to make him sorry for what he had done went down the drain as I was filled with unwanted empathy for his loss. I didn't want to feel sorry for him, but I couldn't help it. I'm a pushover for sad stories. I could imagine him as a young boy with those huge, sad eyes who had lost his mother in a tragic accident. I had this "precious moment" picture visualized in my imagination. He did have eyes that a girl could get lost in, if she didn't know he was a control freak. Maybe he had a valid reason for acting like a jerk.

"I was sent away to military school. I was taught to forsake emotion and embrace logic. My father did the opposite. He lost his mind. We do our best to humor him and pretend he still rules Nommo," he replied without showing any emotion.

It was a lovely, warm, moonlit evening. Five full moons were clustered together forming a circle that was just slightly larger than Earth's moon when it's at its largest. I looked up at the flickering stars. They made strange patterns in the unfamiliar sky. I wondered if Andrew were thinking of me. I felt that all encompassing sorrow crush me again. I shuttered. The prince put his arm around me, thinking I was cold. I tried to pull away, but he held me tightly against his side.

"Don't think that my father can help you. He's powerless. I rule this planet. You *will* marry me," he whispered softly, yet sternly, in my ear.

He turned me toward him and kissed me hard. I struggled to pull away. As I did, I impulsively caught him on his cheek with a stinging slap. It echoed through the clear, night air. Nobody kisses me like that without my permission and gets away unpunished, not even the prince of a whole planet!

I turned and ran back to the castle. I fumbled with the front door, made my way through the elevator, went up to my room, ran in and bolted my door. I fell on the bed. I bawled like there was no hope left in the universe. I was surprised I still had tears available after all the crying I'd already done. Then I got angry and dried my eyes. I was done shedding tears.

I no longer felt sorry for the unfeeling prince of darkness. I wanted to make him pay dearly for his unspeakable and ruthless actions! I took off the green dress, slipped into a furry, white robe that hung on the wall by my luxurious bed, walked out onto the balcony and tossed the gown that displayed his royal brand over the edge. I watched as it caught the breeze and drifted slowly downward. Just before it floated to the ground, the prince strolled directly into its path. It dropped onto his haughty head. I ducked out of sight as he ripped it off his proud face, and stared up at the deck.

That night I found myself in my tunnel dream again, only this time I was peering into the darkness from outside. I watched Andrew's glowing eyes moving steadily toward me, as he ran through the tunnel. Just when he came to the end and reached up to take my hand, I was sucked up into the black expanse of sky. Our fingers touched for a brief moment. He called after me as I was carried away by some unseen force to melt into the stars. "Don't lose your faith. I'll find you!"

CHAPTER 16

TELEVISION STAR

Instead of waking up to loud knocking on my bedroom door, I awoke to the enticing smell of something delicious: hotcakes, eggs and some kind of fried meat that smelled like bacon. I sat up in bed and opened my eyes to see Shan and Mara accompanied by a male waiter-guy who was pushing a cart covered with yummy looking breakfast food. If I ate all of it, I'd have to be rolled out of this room, but what did I care. I probably wouldn't be alive long enough to get fat, and after all, I had lost a substantial amount of weight on my trip here. I was almost a walking skeleton. Maybe this was my last meal. I might as well enjoy it. There's a cheery thought!

They all smiled at me and said, "Good morning, Tiana," in unison. They must have practiced the greeting before coming in.

"Good morning Shan and Mara and who are you?" I asked the boy. He was also not much older than me. He was of average height, but that was the only thing average about him. He was rail thin with a sharp featured face. His arched eyebrows made him look forever surprised. He had a wicked scar over his left eye shaped like an arrow that pointed to the royal insignia tattooed on his forehead. It was the same symbol that the royal goons had engraved on their faces. His short, curly, black hair had a wide, gold streak running through it in front and two silver ones on the sides. His ears were almost elf-like. He looked like someone who belonged in some fantastic fairytale.

"I am Thad, my lady," he replied with a bow.

"I'm Tiana not 'my lady.' Didn't Shan and Mara brief you on that?"

"Yes, miss, but it sounds so disrespectful and you are our future queen," he bowed his head in contrite subservience.

"I am not going to marry your pathetic excuse for a prince, so I will never be your queen. Just treat me like anyone else. I'm happy to meet you, Thad. What did I do to rate breakfast in bed? Is this my final feast before I'm executed? Am I grounded for the rest of my mortal life?" I asked my female servants.

I thought they would be more in the loop on my current status with Prince Raydon than I was. Last night, I had slapped his very superior face and I figured I'd have to pay for my insolent, offensive, and downright unacceptable behavior. Perhaps I was to be held prisoner in this room. It was better than being locked in the dungeon, chained to a wall, with rats nibbling on my toes. Wow, I was just full of cheerful brain activity today.

"We told the prince you were tired and wanted to sleep in," Shan explained. "He had royal business to attend to and left early this morning. He won't be back until evening to escort you to the fancy dinner dance in the capital city with all the high-ranking, government officials. The sparkly, white gown with feathers around the neckline is for you to wear to this important function. We must have you ready by sundown." The threesome turned to leave me with the overloaded cart of food.

"Wait, you guys have to help me eat. There is no way I can put away all this food. It's a shame to waste it," I called them back. My dad's words sounded in my head, "There are people in Ethiopia who are starving to death, Tiana." I never understood how eating my yucky broccoli and cauliflower would help them. Thinking of my father brought me fresh pain. I had to stifle this mounting pessimism. I was going to be a basket case again. I'd decided last night that I wouldn't cry anymore.

"We aren't allowed to eat in the same room with royalty. We never get to eat this well," Thad said as he looked longingly at the scrumptious array of edibles.

"I'm not royalty. I'm asking you to eat with me. I don't want to eat alone. Please join me," I coaxed them. I needed a distraction from my despair.

"Well, if you insist, I think we'd better obey you. We've been instructed to follow all your directions implicitly. We'll be found negligent in our duties as your assigned servants if we do not please you. Then we'll be punished and replaced," Shan said and began filling a plate with food.

The others followed her lead. We went through the patio doors and sat at a table on the deck with the spectacular view that overlooked the whole tropical island. The day was sunny with a constant, cool and gentle breeze, so the temperature was positively perfect.

"Do you get paid well to work here in the castle?" I asked, politely. They were probably forced into their current jobs because of some past illegal activity, but I felt funny asking them about their criminal records. I didn't want to offend them.

"We are being punished for offensive past behavior. I forgot to pay for some candy at the grocery store, I disrespected a teacher in my last year at public school, and I missed two days without giving a good excuse," Mara spoke softly with embarrassment like these were horrendous crimes too evil to be repeated.

"That's nothing! I refused a marriage proposal from an eminent official in the king's military service and I ran away from home when my parents tried to force me to accept. I would do it again. He was a disgustingly foul and evil minded man and old enough to be my grandfather." Shan declared.

"I can top that," Thad said, raising his hand to stop these confessions. "I checked out of the orphanage for the children of the executed when I turned sixteen and stowed away on a cargo ship that was traveling to the Coral Islands in the southern hemisphere. I snuck food from the captain's pantry and drank all his favorite virganut juice. He caught me the night before we were to reach our distant destination.

"I almost made it. I was going to hitch a ride to the Exile Islands on a departing freighter and join the rebel forces. I'm lucky they didn't know my intentions or they probably would have executed me. I lied and said I just wanted a change of scenery. They couldn't tell I was lying because I had to practice the art of deception a lot at the orphanage in order to survive and I was very adept at fooling the established authorities."

"These are ridiculously, minor transgressions. On Earth, in my country, Mara might have to spend a day or two in detention, Shan wouldn't be punished at all because you don't have to marry anyone you don't want to, and Thad might have to do a month of community service and possibly pay a small fine. Who sentenced you to a life of slavery?" I was indignant about these unfair judgments.

What kind of planet subjects teenagers, who made a few small mistakes, to a life without freedom? Who goes through their teen years without doing something stupid? Had they never heard of second chances? Didn't they know that growing up is a process and you're supposed to learn from making mistakes? This was the kind of thing that made the founding fathers of the United States declare their independence from Great Britain. No, scratch that. These infractions were much too minuscule to consider at all. The whole thing was lamentably lame.

I wondered how many others had been brutally punished for next to nothing. Did the Nommoan government need to fill some kind of quota to provide manual labor or were they just mean spirited and controlling? If they were anything like their prince, the answer was a definite yes. This was a terrible injustice. The more I thought about it, the more infuriated I became.

"We went before the Juvenile Court of Judgment in Illdeemo, the capitol city. If we'd been over twenty we'd have probably been exiled," Thad answered my question.

"They like to get servants who are young, strong, easy to mold and manipulate," Shan's tone showed her contempt for the arbitrary system under which they had all been enslaved.

"This is so bogus! Who makes laws that punish you for these tiny errors in judgment? Who are the losers in charge? Why are they so cruel? Don't you have any way to fight this?"

"No, we have no legal recourse. We don't have trials here. The court judges can usually detect lies in almost all people's stories. Sometimes they say you're lying when you're telling the truth, so they can get their desired results. No one is allowed to defend us after we turn sixteen," Thad replied, looking somewhat surprised by my strong reaction or maybe it was just his eyebrows that made him look that way.

I was probably scaring them all half to death with my emotional response to their deplorable situation. I knew I should dial it down, but it made me see red. How do you fix stupid on a planet that won't get genuinely upset at such incredible oppression? Maybe the rebels had the right idea. I was ready to incite a revolution.

"Tell me about the rebels. Are they trying to stop this poor excuse for law and order? How do I join them? Where do they live?"

This national injustice was giving me a major case of indignation. I wanted to protest, to take action, to stand up for these defenseless, innocent people who weren't even allowed a defense attorney and a trial. Someone was taking unfair advantage of young people who made a few silly choices. They deserved better.

"Tiana, you mustn't speak this way. They'll call your words treason. You must never repeat what you've said. It is not safe even to think about the rebels. Thad shouldn't have mentioned them to you. Please forget what we've told you," Mara begged.

"How do you forget such blatant abuse of power? I can't stand by and not say something. It's so wrong!"

I was insistent and determined to take a stand against this terrible tyranny. Since I was going to be killed anyway, I might as well do some good before I died. However, I was at a loss as to what I could do that would make a difference. This wasn't even my planet. I was just a teenager. Who would listen to me? The all-powerful prince most certainly wouldn't. So far he had ignored everything I had said to him. Communicating with him was like trying to have a meaningful, two-way conversation with a piece of solid granite.

"There is something we must show you," Shan said when we were finished eating. I think she was trying to distract me from my intense irritation at their government's misuse of power. "It's on the picture maker in your room."

We followed her into my lush living quarters. One wall was partially covered with an immense flat television screen. I didn't know where the remote was stored, so I hadn't even tried to see what Nommoan TV was like. I had a sneaking suspicion that they only watched boring, educational broadcasting. Still, I was intrigued by the idea of watching the Nommoans' idea of entertainment. It could prove interesting. It was a way to pass the time until my untimely demise came to claim me.

Shan showed me how to control it. One clap turned it on. Evidently, there were dozens of channels. You could change them by nodding to go forward. Shaking your head would make them to go back. Two claps would turn it off. I laughed at this familiar use of "clapper" technology. I wanted to sing the song; "Clap on, clap off, the clapper!" My Grandpa Dawson had the "clapper" installed in his house. I loved using it to turn on the lights when I was a kid.

Pointing up would increase the volume and pointing down would decrease it. Of course, its electronic eye had to be able to see you when you did this or your efforts were in vain.

"I don't think you're going to like this." Shan said.

She clapped it on and there on the big screen, larger than life, was my face staring back at me. I gasped. After showing my face, they showed streaming video of me sitting in the dentist-type chair in the spaceship at the bottom of Quail Creek Reservoir.

Prince Raydon was explaining the machine that he'd hooked up to my head. It had a small screen that showed memories that were attached to different emotions. The pictures on the small screen were transferred to the big screen. I was forced to watch as my most intimate, private memories marched across it for everyone on this planet to see.

"Oh no, he didn't do this!" I screamed at the screen. "This is too crap-tastic for even Mister-high-and-mighty-maniac! Who does he think he is? I don't care if he's king of the whole universe, he's going down! Does he have snot for brains? Stupid, insensitive, snobby, loser jerk! Wait 'til I get my hands on that controlling, Nommoan, demon spawn! I'll tear him apart with my bare hands! I'll kick his arrogant, alien butt! He's going to be sorry he did this! I'm going to kill him, and it *will* be painful!

While I was yelling, pacing and cursing at the wall-sized television, the servants snuck quietly out of the room to let me suffer my rapid rise to ignominious fame. I couldn't blame them for ducking out and letting me endure this excruciating humiliation alone. I had probably scared them all senseless by my severe and unstable emotional outbursts. Their ears were undoubtedly burning. I finally ran out of names to call him. I sat down in defeat and proceeded to watch this insidious intrusion into my most private memories.

I watched my first day of Kindergarten, how I got off the bus at the wrong stop, and wandered around sobbing uncontrollably. I was lost for what felt like hours, before my mother finally found me. Why did he include that? I was a baby for Heaven's sake!

I saw the six year old me playing princess, wearing my tin foil crown and waving my homemade, royal scepter at Mark and Jeremy. They pretended to grant my every wish until Mark got fed up, destroyed my crown, broke my scepter over his knee, and ordered me to go to my room. I screamed like a banshee, kicked him in the shins, and ran to tattle to my dad. Again, who would care about my childhood memories? I didn't get it.

I saw a string of my favorite childhood birthdays and Christmases that brought me considerable, though childish, happiness. There was the year I got three Barbie dolls, a great collection of monkey games and "My Little Pony." I felt like the queen of the world that year. Another year, I got my own karaoke machine and spent the day singing, "Girl's Just Wanna Have Fun" over and over and over again. Embarrassing much?

I watched Michael White chase me home from school and kiss me before I could get my front door open. Then I got to see Mark sock him in the nose. There was also footage of Ricky Alder ambushing me in the girl's restroom. He kissed me. I hit him over the head with my math book. He spent the afternoon in the principal's office. That turned into a good day. I so wanted to hit the prince over the head with this stupid flat screen television. I wanted to tell him what I thought of his unforgivable invasion of my private thoughts.

I saw my first date. I was forced to watch as I fell down the stairs and broke my arm because I wore those accursed, although impossibly pretty, emerald-green stiletto-heeled shoes. Then I, once again, suffered rejection from my first crush, Jace Pratt. I never wanted to revisit those excruciating moments.

One of the most mortifying times I had to endure was the replaying of an incident two years ago when Mark hid under my bed wearing a nylon stocking over his head. I had just turned out the light when he reached out and grabbed my ankle. He scared the crap out of me! I shrieked in panic and pulled away. He rolled out from his hiding place. I nearly wet my pants. I was so traumatized; I couldn't sleep for a week. I slept with the light on for several months before I fully recovered. I looked under my bed every night for over a year. Mark thought it was hilarious and laughed at me for over a year. I probably needed therapy.

Did these people really want to study the effect of intense trepidation on my human psyche, or did the prince just want everyone on Nommo to see me suffering in the thralls of extreme fear? That is just wrong!

After those hurtful juvenile experiences, I got to relive meeting Andrew. I observed his valiant rescue as he pulled me from Jordan's car just before it blew up. I had to see Jordan assault me in the cave that contained the pictograph of an alien with eyes that glowed in the dark. I watched the snake bite me when I ran away from him. I went to see Andrew's spaceship the night he first shared his secret life. Then there were some wonderful, private, romantic times with Andrew that I didn't wish to share with the whole population of this or any other planet. Was nothing sacred to the supercilious, stone-faced, unfeeling fiend?

I had to see Sonya that day in Zion National Park when she went all "Cuckoo for Co-Co Puffs" and spit in my face after telling me to leave Andrew to her. The most horribly heinous part was reliving the abject terror I experienced when I was captured by those cannibalistic alien terrorists. Watching the emotional torture I had endured at the hands of the Hellites made me feel sick to my stomach. Of course, the next day when Sonya had convinced me that I should break it off with Andrew, because I was infinitely inferior to him, was much, much worse. I'd locked these painful memories in a vault and buried them so deep in the backyard of my psyche that I hadn't thought about them for months.

Tears were streaming down my cheeks. My breathing had become erratic as I was forced to suffer through all that unbearable agony again. My head pulsed with pain. I wanted to turn it off, but I couldn't stop watching. I was hypnotically fascinated with the abomination of this ordeal. I found myself paralyzed, unable to break away from all those riveting and repulsive memories.

The program abruptly stopped tracing my life and a panel of "experts" began probing, discussing and criticizing all my various emotional reactions to the televised events, what was going on in my mind, and how I should or should not have dealt with those intense feelings. These psychological gurus were kind of like Dr. Phil and Oprah, only completely devoid of compassion. I was the victim here. They enjoyed pointing fingers at all my many faults and sneering at all my emotional instability.

I'd become a walking psychological disease, a self-help book in human form. How could he do this to me? How dare he unbury and display all my worst nightmares? I had been betrayed and stripped bare. My innermost and most guarded privacy had been invaded and violated. Everyone on this whole planet had been invited to stomp around inside my head and leer at my life's triumphs and tragedies as they trespassed on all my most closely guarded secrets. The entire thing was intimately disturbing.

I was overwhelmed with the unbearable affront to my personal space. What personal space? I might as well face it. I had no personal space anymore. My whole existence was left naked, bruised and broken, laid out on the floor for everyone to see, while these so-called "emotional experts" analyzed and dissected my feelings and trampled them in front of millions of people. I had no secrets, no private thoughts, nothing!

I clapped off the TV after they told about some memories that would be analyzed on tomorrow's program. They were then going to explore Andrew's, James', and Tiffany's memories of me. That might be entertaining for me to see, but I cringed at the thought that everyone else in this world would see them also.

I had no tears left. I was so mad; I had an almost uncontrollable urge to destroy something. I wanted to rip off the prince's high and mighty head, drop kick it and watch it bounce off the balcony to be dashed to pieces on the distant ground below. I itched to punch holes in the walls and throw a priceless vase through the TV screen. I wanted to scream until I lost my voice. I didn't do any of these things because I feared they might hook me up to that machine again and show this negative, emotional reaction to everyone on Nommo. Then they would pity me for my inappropriate display of anger.

No wonder they all hid their feelings. Their government had no respect for their private lives. I made a promise to myself that I would make that self-important sovereign pay for this intolerable mountain of abuse. My inner shrew was itching to come out and attack him with blind fury. Prince Raydon was going to be sorry he had brought me to his stupid planet! He was going to regret ever messing with this girl's mind!

CHAPTER 17

HEADS OF STATE

That invasive and painful romp through my previously secret, personal, emotional memories took up most of the day. It's surprising how slow time passes when you're *not* having fun. That could be another way to prove that time is relative. Lunch arrived and was left on the room service cart, as my appetite had evaporated along with what remained of my wounded pride. My self respect had been crushed until it had all but collapsed, curled up and died. I didn't think I'd ever be hungry again. They probably wouldn't even have to execute me because I'd just die of starvation.

The lovely Lanu came tapping on my door a few hours after the indentured servants had taken away the uneaten food. She popped through the entrance when I failed to open it and flowed into the room, followed by a frightening team of make-up mavens, artistic-hairdressing-miracle-workers, and Nommoan fashionistas.

This couldn't be good. They were armed with implements of torture and miscellaneous abhorrent accessories designed to make me beautiful by Nommoan standards. It was going to hurt badly. If I had known they were coming, I would have found a secure place to hide until they all gave up and went home.

I suddenly understood how an unfortunate insect feels when it finds itself stuck in a sticky web with no hope of escape. The spiders were creeping toward me now with dogged determination in their multiple eyes. I realized it was pointless to struggle. I didn't have a way out. There was no way to avoid the unstoppable torment I was going to be forced to endure under their ruse of authoritative beautification expertise.

When they finally finished buffing, polishing, and painting the surprisingly stoic me, they poured my body into that horribly-hideous, rhinestone-bedazzled, white-feathered, mermaid gown. Even the matching silver shoes were covered in sequins. I couldn't hate the shoes.

They then curled and stacked my hair on top of my head and for that extra sparkly touch; they stuck a diamond studded silver tiara in it. I'd zoned out in order to submit to the will of the fashion fiends and tolerate what now seemed like the longest day of my life.

I wouldn't let them change my hair color. I didn't care how hard Lanu tried to convince me to go blonde. I had refused vehemently to wear the short golden wig they had tried unsuccessfully to plant on my head. Have you ever worn one of those things? It feels like your head has been encased in tightly fitted plastic baggies and secured with hundreds of rubber bands. It's a distinctively unpleasant sensation. I had to establish some limits or they would have annihilated my identity with their intense make-over madness. I don't know how I found the strength to fight them. It was the principle of the thing.

They explained that the party's theme was Earth's History. I was supposed to look like the late, Princess Diana of Great Britain. Of course, since I wasn't blonde and I wasn't wearing the hot, uncomfortable wig, I'd have to go as the Earth girl who was going to be the next queen of Nommo, even though that fantasy was total fiction. Evidently, here on Nommo everyone had to get the language, customs and basic history of my planet downloaded into their emotionally starved brains.

One of the Nommoans' superpowers is mastering the intake of vast stores of knowledge. Their emotions are probably deeply buried in all that unnecessary, useless and trivial information. These people are walking encyclopedias of all the inhabited planets that have been visited by their venerable astronauts or, as they called them, "Space Travelers."

This data is available to be checked out at their local libraries or "Knowledge Centers" as well as over their version of the internet, "the Connection." However, to gain access to all this super-pointless stuff, they must be approved by the government officials. These officials don't want it falling into the hands of the rebels or the inferior, exiled, former citizens.

All the highest ranking big-wigs of Nommoan nobility had integrated Earth's "pop culture" into their personal, downloaded information. I don't understand how their heads haven't exploded from the immense volume of trivia they've crammed into their superior brains. Just thinking about it was giving me a headache.

The king had accessed all available Earth knowledge, so he's probably hemorrhaging all kinds of crazy, random tidbits like the ones he shared at the dinner table last night. All of these people probably knew the history of my planet better than I did.

I was starting to feel a major inferiority complex coming on. That fact, along with my brain being an open book, made me really want to bail on tonight's formal festivities. Finally, all of my tormenters left except Lanu, who remained and continued to fuss with my hair and makeup. The exasperatingly overzealous woman didn't know when to stop.

Oddly enough, when I saw my reflection at last, I didn't look half bad. The dress looked much more attractive on than it had on the hanger. It was over-the-top glam. In direct sunlight, it was so bright it could cause temporary blindness, if you looked at it for any longer than thirty seconds. Maybe all that, too-bright-to-look-at-without-sunglasses, glaring luminescence was a good thing. It might discourage everyone from staring at the freaky, redheaded Earthling. I started wishing I hadn't passed on the blond wig after all. I hoped no one would recognize me.

Who was I kidding? Who else would they expect the prince to be escorting to the party? From what I understand, he never goes to any of these functions in costume. He's a far too important and supreme being to go as anyone other than himself, the "Royal Prince of Nommo." I was doomed to be gawked at and psychoanalyzed by everyone I met. I was not looking forward to being seen in public and questioned about all my past faux pas. I wondered if I could avoid all this frightening socializing by having a faux migraine.

"You should not lie about health matters, Tiana," Lanu read my thoughts. "Some of us can spot attempts at deception from across the room and yes, a few of us can read your mind. Most of us with this ability don't often use it because it is considered rude. I have been ordered to check your brain as I deem necessary to insure that your needs are met and to help you navigate the turbulent seas of Nommoan society, so I apologize in advance for any embarrassment this causes you."

"Oh go ahead, feel free to invade my privacy. Think nothing of it. Everyone else already has. That outrageously intrusive television program opened my mind to the masses. Why should I ever expect to keep anything secret again?" I told her as dispassionately as I could manage. I couldn't disguise my underlying bitterness and sarcasm.

"That's all on the prince. I advised him against disclosing so many of your personal memories, but he thinks that you are here to save the populace from extinction. He sincerely believes that every bit of information should be extracted from your brain and served to his loyal subjects on a silver platter. The man has more nerve than anyone else on the planet! He does not understand the female psyche. I think on Earth you would call him totally clueless," she explained.

"What other superpowers do Nommoans have?" I thought it was high time for me to find out the truth about these emotionally challenged people.

"Well, we are stronger, faster, healthier, and smarter than the folks on your young planet. We have long been smart enough to keep our emotions hidden from a government that sends a fourth of our population into exile, executes another fourth, and sentences half of those that are left to a life of enslavement. This is the true reason why our population is dwindling. Who wants to have children if they're just going to end up being slaves to the corrupt powers-that-be?

"You mustn't breathe a word of this to Prince Raydon. As I said before, he's clueless. Everyone else already knows. It's been like this since the king's wife died, and he relinquished his control to certain Heads of State and advisors that he should have never trusted. This regime likes being in control of absolutely everything, so they want things to continue as they are in the status quo. They let the prince think he's the one pulling the strings, but he's merely a figurehead. The king understands this. He deals with it by pretending to be insane."

"Wow! Why doesn't anyone want to tell the prince? He really should know about this," I stated the obvious. I was amazed at a nation that could keep the biggest secret ever from their control freak of a ruler. If they could keep their domineering top dog from figuring out that he wasn't in charge, then they had accomplished a coup that made their deception almost an art form. I couldn't help being kind of impressed by such unscrupulous ingenuity.

"On your planet, I think you have a saying about 'killing the messenger.' Whoever ends up spilling this unpleasant and ugly duplicity will definitely suffer His Majesty's wrath. Believe me. He's stored up enough anger to annihilate this planet. It's hiding just beneath the surface waiting to explode, and you don't want to be there when it does. Besides, the rebels may take over before too long and change everything. It's about time for a revolution, don't you think? Again, mum's the word, Tiana. You must keep this secret for your own safety." She tapped her index finger against her mouth that was tightly closed in a straight line. Her eyes glared at me as she attempted to relay the seriousness of her warning.

"Wouldn't it be bad for you if the rebels took over?" This conversation was expanding my desire to help stop this monstrous political madness.

"Not really. The rebels know who to blame. The Heads of State will all be at this dinner you'll be attending. You'll get to meet Nommo's noble collection of all the master puppeteers. It will be loads of fun, my dear. They're a bunch of control addicted, aristocratic snobs who think they will always rule our world. Oh, and don't worry. You can lie to them as long as they aren't Judges of the Court. The judges have nearly perfected their ability to find the truth in the minds of others. The rest of these imperial idiots lost whatever mind reading talents they had when they became self-indulgent, power-hungry tyrants. Mind reading is a talent that is lost when used with evil intent.

"I want to be there when they're ousted from power. I am eager to see their huge heads roll. My husband, Quill, was exiled ten years ago. My only daughter was sentenced to slavery because she protested this judgment. Layla worked here in the castle until she fell in love with Prince Raydon. When he began showing an interest in her, the king's High Chancellor banished her from the kingdom before Raydon could be smitten by her "ensnaring charms."

"My only son verbally objected to her unfair treatment. He currently serves in the royal household. Perhaps you'll meet him tonight. He's going to be part of your accompanying entourage of servants. His name is Quint. His only crimes were his objection to Layla's exile and his alleged felony of falling in love with the daughter of a hoity-toity, pretentious judge who deemed him unworthy of his high-class offspring."

"Why do you people let them get away with such an abuse of power? Can't you join together and fight for your rights?"

I didn't understand why they didn't unite in protest against all this unfair discrimination. Where were the picketers and the protesters? Had they never heard of civil disobedience? It was time for a tea party like the one in Boston. Maybe we could throw all those corrupt officials into the sea. Oh yeah, that probably wouldn't stop them because they all can breathe underwater. They'd think it was all just an enormous pool party.

"All those who tried to fight have been executed or exiled. Those of us who remain are just trying to survive until the rebels overthrow this administration of domination. Tiana, if you're smart, you'll pretend to like the prince and act like you might marry him. This will buy you some time.

"Your Helamite boyfriend may find a way to rescue you yet or the rebels may sympathize with your plight and help get you back to your own world after they take power. I suspect that the knowledge of time travel is safely buried in a vault somewhere. For now, try not to agitate our Royal Highness. No good will come of that," she warned and left me to think over all this new and troubling knowledge of the inner workings and Machiavellian politics of the Nommoan nation.

About five minutes later, Shan and Mara came back with a machine that was used to insert facts into brains. They explained that this information was compiled to help me know the Nommoan dances, customs and manners that I would need to be aware of at the party. I allowed them to hook me up. Why not? It beat having to read and memorize stuff. I closed my eyes and watched the information flash through my head. It was like a crazy, thick dream set on fast forward that only took about three minutes.

After they had finished, they quizzed me and to my astonishment, I knew all the right answers. I could even show them the dance steps. This would be an excellent way to study for tests! I had to get me one of these miraculous, learning-by-osmosis computers! Soaking up data is so much quicker and easier than having to study things the hard way. Why hadn't the geniuses on my own planet invented a machine like this?

I went out on the balcony when they had gone. I watched the suns go down. The big one set several minutes after the small one. I could see the vivid, billowing pink and orange clouds reflected on the ocean's blue-green, glassy surface. This was a very small island, but I was enthralled by its exquisite beauty as the fading light illuminated the exotic landscape filled with bubbling springs, cascading waterfalls, and lush gardens of unfamiliar flowering plants and lacy-leaved bushes and ferns.

I could hear the strange, musical cries of various rainbow-colored birds. The air smelled fresh with a hint of salt mixed with the unusual perfume of the many strangely fragrant fruits and flowers. The great wall that surrounded the land seemed incongruous, oddly out of place in this island paradise.

The white, sandy beaches beyond the walls sparkled like diamonds as the last sun rays lit the sand. I wondered if I'd have to get special permission to visit a section of that inviting place where the ocean met the shore on the wrong side of the fortified barricade. Were the rebels hiding just beneath the ocean's surface? Were there sea monsters lurking under the gentle waves? There was much I still didn't know about this mysterious and beautiful planet that the government had messed up with ridiculous laws and self-serving politics that made no sense to me.

The prince arrived at my door, looking impressively handsome and distinguished in his black, white and maroon, military uniform. This was the best I'd ever seen him look, but I had no time to marvel at his attractive transformation. The time was rapidly approaching when I would have to meet and mingle with the movers and shakers of his planet. I bit my lip and steeled myself.

First I had to have a confrontation with the infuriating man, no matter how good he looked. He smelled good too, like musky pine needles. I ignored all that. I made him come in and sit down, so I could proceed to express my disapproval of his insensitive broadcasting of my many, too-personal memories.

"We need to talk," I began trying to think of a way to approach the subject delicately so as not to upset him too much. I was afraid Lanu might be right about the rage that must be seething in his soul. You can't ignore negative emotions, shoving them down deep inside, and refusing to deal with them forever. Eventually, something will spill out and open the floodgates. Whoever is unfortunate enough to be in close proximity will drown. Yeah, I knew only too well that, with the way things were going, it would most likely be me doing the drowning.

"Can't it wait until we get to the party?" He seemed extremely eager to leave. Huh? Maybe he wasn't as clueless as I thought. I wondered if he might actually be aware that I was unhappy with his affront to my sensibilities. He had to know he had violated my thoughts and exposed my secret memories. He refused to look me in the eye. I threw caution to the wind and restraint out the window and came straight to the point.

"No, it can't. I'm very embarrassed and upset that you transmitted so many of my private and traumatic experiences to your entire planet. I'm mortified that you chose to parade my personal life in front of your whole world! I'm hurt that you didn't even take the time to ask my permission before you threw me to the lions, so they could pick me apart, discuss all my prior bad acts, and analyze my reactions nearly to death. How am I supposed to look these people in the face without cringing? They know all my most intimate memories. How would you feel if I shared all of your secrets with my whole world? Have you no empathy?" I kept my voice neutral as I tried not to set him off.

"No, I don't *do* empathy. I was raised to be a leader. I serve my people. If your memories will help them, then you should be more than willing to make the sacrifice for the greater good. I'm sorry if I have offended your sensibilities, but I'm completely justified. You'll have to deal with it. Pretend it never happened. Problem solved. We need to go now." He took my arm and pulled me out of my room, through the glass elevator and down to the front lawn without another word or a glance in my direction.

Well, that didn't go the way I had planned. He didn't get angry. In fact, he seemed utterly indifferent to my displeasure. That was infinitely worse. He was more galling than I had originally thought. Not only was he hardhearted, he was a callous, unfeeling, genuine jerk, who was in desperate need of a time out after his recent string of poor choices. He made me so mad I could spit! However, I realized this was not an opportune time to try to invoke a negative reaction from him, so once again I bit my tongue and took deep breathes while I tried to focus on being diplomatic and resisting the urge to gouge out his eyes.

I was beginning to think nothing I said would have any effect on him at all. I tried to think happy thoughts like never seeing his proud and condescending face again in this lifetime or getting the opportunity to embarrass him to death in front of all his high class Heads of State.

I considered throwing something squishy and smelly at him during his speech. No, I'd never be able to pull that off before his bodyguards would have me bound, gagged, and removed in handcuffs. I wished I had Hannah's telekinetic talent, so I could hit him over the head with inanimate objects without suspicion. I visualized him standing in front of everyone, wearing food and being smacked on the back of his head with his dinner plate, or being impaled by an eating utensil. The picture in my mind's eye made me smile. I was trying to be positive. I was positive this scene, if it were only real, would please me no end.

A hovercraft was waiting for us. The king was already onboard, dressed like the French emperor, Napoleon. No surprise there. He had a definite affinity for the crazy general who had a mental illness named after him. There were four brawny bodyguards, the pilot and a steward to see to our needs on the short flight to the capital city, Illdeemo, on the island they called "Central Illdee."

The steward, I discovered, was Lanu's son, Quint. He introduced himself to me as he took drink orders from the passengers. He was tall and easy to look at, with a pleasant face, greenish hazel eyes and ash blond hair with a few navy and powder blue stripes running through his sideburns. He had a quick, winning smile and was probably in his late twenties.

As I watched him see to the king's comfort, I detected an underlying sadness that he was working exceedingly hard to disguise. I could relate to his pain, as I thought about how I had been dragged away from everything and everyone I loved by the aggravating man sitting beside me. That intense sorrow blew through me in an icy breeze of frigid despondency. The unbearable hurt welled up inside me. Our eyes met in joint understanding. This silent empathy was communicated through that connection, as we both read the agony behind each other's eyes. I bit my lip and vowed not to give into my emotions. I'd shed way too many tears. I wasn't going to let Prince Raydon see me weep, not here, not now, not ever.

The flight took less than an hour. Our hovercraft touched down on the front lawn of the capital building where a crowd of people dressed as famous Earth celebrities and historically prominent figures from my home

143

planet were waiting to greet us. I watched it fly off and disappear on top of the roof of the building.

An uncomfortable stirring of nervousness took over my stomach, as we entered the banquet hall. The Prince led me to the head table. I hoped I wouldn't make any unpardonable mistakes. My face reddened as I remembered that these people had already seen me act like a fool when they had viewed my broadcasted memories. They had probably already formed opinions of me and my emotional baggage. I definitely didn't have the luxury of making a good first impression. That realization made me relax. I didn't have to worry about trying to impress anyone.

They all took their seats. The prince rose to address them. He said a few words in the Nommoan tongue and gestured toward me. I watched his lips flapping without understanding a word he said. Everyone clapped. He glowed with satisfaction as he basked in their adulation. I expected that he used his native form of communication to introduce me as his future queen. The man was afraid I would contradict him here in front of his high and mighty Heads of State.

He wasn't going to give me the opportunity to embarrass him. What a smart, cagey, and despicable despot he was! I wished I had a cream pie to throw at his irritating face, but since I didn't, I kicked him under the table, glared and frowned at him, giving him the eye of death to let him know I knew exactly what he was doing.

"Tiana, I know you don't intend to marry me. Please, don't discuss this tonight," he said looking tired. He appeared to have had a bad day at the office. His unbelievably huge, brown eyes pleaded for mercy. I was tempted to twist the knife of his discomfort, but I kept hearing Lanu's words of warning against antagonizing him, so I just listened.

"There is trouble brewing within the government and the rebels have gained some top secret information through traitors who are masquerading as loyal government officials. It is essential to the morale and peace of my country and planet, that we look the part of a happy couple.

"There is a prophecy about a beautiful, red haired, Earth girl who will save our planet from self destruction. The majority of Nommoans believe you are indeed this heroic female who has come to rescue us from ourselves. Please go along with it, just for tonight. I beg you!"

CHAPTER 18

PROPHECY

"Gah! W-w-what are you talking about? What prophecy?" I stuttered as I struggled to understand what he had just divulged.

This unexpected, unbelievable revelation threw my mind into an instantaneous whirlwind of confusion. Thoughts and questions spun around inside my head. Who would make such an utterly preposterous and ridiculous prediction? I had been told that I was the first Earth person to set foot on this planet. I was supposed to think this was a great honor, but I never asked to be here. I had been stolen away from everything that mattered to me. In some sense, I had sort of saved Andrew, James and Tiffany from certain death by allowing the prince to coerce me to come. However, that was the only lifesaving I had ever done.

Did this so-called prophet know something that I didn't or was this just the insane mutterings of a deluded, spiritual leader? Did Nommoans believe in God? Was it the same God I knew existed? Surely, God had not sent me here on a mission to save this world. I was just an ordinary, every-day, Earth girl. I had no superpowers.

No, no, no, their mess was not going to be put on me. He was not going to lay this minefield at my feet. They got themselves into this pre-carious predicament. They could positively get themselves out without any help from me. Not. My. Problem. I wasn't an all-wise-and-powerful leader. The very idea of a teenage girl saving them from themselves was stupid and completely crazy. This was not even my planet. Was this planet overrun by idiots and psychos? I was under the impression that these were supposed to be super-intelligent aliens.

Oh yeah, I keep forgetting that I am the alien here. I'm the one who doesn't belong in this whacked out world. If only I could close my eyes, click my heels together and travel back through space and time, I could get my life back and forget all this Nommoan nonsense.

"My great grandfather had a vision about a hundred and fifty years ago that we would find ourselves separated into two groups that threatened to destroy each other. This would bring us to the brink of extinction. Right now the population has decreased from two billion to only around fifteen million. As you know, your Earth is inhabited by more than seven billion people. You have cities that have more people in them than we have living on our entire planet.

"He saw a girl from Earth, with naturally red hair, come to Nommo with his great grandson. She was to bring the people on this planet together, uniting them in a common cause. She would save our world from utter destruction. You are that girl. With your help, the apocalyptic disaster will be averted."

"Are you sure this deceased ancestor of yours was truly a prophet? What makes you think I'm that girl? There are thousands, if not millions, of girls with red hair on Earth! I'm positive you picked the wrong one. You should take me back and start a new, more thorough search. I'm not here to save your world; I'm here because you pulled me off my planet against my will. You blackmailed me into this massive mess. You blew it, Mr. Majesty. You got it all wrong!"

Burning anger percolated inside me, threatening to escape like hot lava seeping out from the fiery insides of an active volcano. This had to be a case of mistaken identity, a huge blunder on his part and the aggravating

Nommoan Neanderboy had gone and screwed up my whole life in the process. Stupid, delusional prince!

"Tiana, do you remember the memory machine that transmitted your thoughts onto the television screens of everyone in Nommo? Did any of the images in your head seem wrong to you? This machine was invented before my great grandfather died. The prophecy was recorded along with all his other predictions. Every one of his other prophecies has come to pass. It was you! I can show it to you, if you don't believe me."

"It was probably someone who looked like me. I'm not that girl!" I insisted.

I had never gotten the memo that I was supposed to save another planet. This had never crossed my "To Do" list. It wasn't my responsibility. I was not going to buy into his insanity. All that molten lava scorched my insides as it ran from my stomach up to my brain cells and was now threatening to explode out the top of my head. I was so furious; I wanted to break his nose. I clutched my fists together in my lap, afraid one of them would rebel and throw itself into his infuriating face.

"Please calm down. People are staring at us. We'll discuss this later in private. Now, for the good of my planet, we must present ourselves as an adoring couple." He smiled at me as if I had said something he found profoundly amusing.

Huh? Adoring? Not likely! I willed myself to keep my internal, burning magma-like wrath from erupting through my mouth, but all my internal organs were vibrating and churning dangerously. I could feel the stabbing, acidic pain of ulcers forming in my stomach lining as my throat tightened in response to all my inner chaos. I closed my eyes for a moment, fighting to breathe slowly and deeply. I begged my hands to remain clutched in my lap, so they wouldn't go for his throat. I admit it. I wanted to hurt him. I am not normally a violent person, but right now I seriously wanted to punch or strangle him! Does that make me a bad person?

Instead, I shut my eyes tightly. I counted slowly to ten. Then I focused my attention on recalling Andrew's angelic face. I tried to remember his smooth, velvety voice when he had attempted to curb my anxiety in the past. I needed his calming influence to help me cope. In my mind, he was telling me to hang in there, and not do anything rash until it was absolutely necessary. He would come for me. Then I didn't care what happened to the population of this obnoxious planet. They could blow each other up, or whatever. I managed to push the scorching, lava rage down into the bottom of my brain cellar to cool, or burn itself out.

I'd call up my inner actress again. I'd pretend I was just a typical tourist on vacation, enjoying a visit to another planet, much the way I'd enjoy visiting another country on the other side of my own world. I wasn't going to let the fact that I was on the other side of the galaxy and couldn't get home to the right place and time freak me out anymore tonight. There would be plenty of time to go crazy later. I put it on my mental list of things not to think about until I could no longer ignore them. I tried not to dwell on the fact that this particular list was getting really, really long. Right now, I'd have to put on my happy face and act like I was enjoying the festivities.

It's good that I'm such a fantastic actress. I donned an air of cordial dignity and resisted my desire to rip off the royal butt-pain's head, put it on a plate, and serve it to all his government cohorts. I smiled as I visualized removing the cover from such a dish with a flourish. I didn't think it would go over very well with this crowd. Violence was not the answer tonight. I know, I know, it seldom is. Sometimes it just feels like it might be rather satisfying.

Servants began bringing trays of delicacies for us to enjoy. We were served first. The prince had to okay each dish before the rest of the dignitaries were allowed to eat. Everything smelled and tasted fabulous, in spite of my state of mind. There were many kinds of seafood cooked in rich, buttery sauces and three or four different types of succulent white meat that all tasted like chicken to me. It was darned tasty chicken. Oh yeah, there were a couple of meats that tasted more like lobster. I love lobster, but I couldn't eat much of the mild, tender meat tonight.

There was also an abundance of dishes made from pretty vegetables and fruits. The breads were warm, fluffy, and delicious. They came in unusual colors: pastel pinks, purples, and yellows. I had learned that I was required by Nommoan etiquette to take a bite of each item on the menu. This wasn't easy because I didn't have a big appetite for obvious reasons.

After these foods had been consumed, the desserts came out in droves. I tasted them, but I was still too upset to enjoy the sweet concoctions. I had enough to know the pastries tasted heavenly. Whatever else these dwindling aliens might be, they were uncommonly talented chefs and bakers. They may well be dying off, but I didn't think it was from starvation; at least not if they ate as well as these important, government officials and their maddening monarch.

I looked out over the Nommoan dignitaries who were enjoying this magnificent feast and it suddenly registered with me that they were all dressed up like dead Earth people. I saw at least ten Elvises, seven or eight Abraham Lincolns, a half dozen Attila the Huns or other assorted barbarian villains, more than a few Lucille Balls, a couple of Lady Godivas, and hundreds of miscellaneous monarchs, kings, queens, presidents and other world leaders. It was uncanny how they had transformed themselves.

Every nationality was represented. Since I'm not all that skilled at recognizing dead celebrities or historical figures from other countries, I couldn't name them all. I saw a bunch of men who were probably supposed to be William Shakespeare, famous explorers or Renaissance artists. There were an abundance of dead spiritual leaders along with old time movie stars and entertainers. I counted three Ganhis, five Buddas, eleven Michael Jacksons, four Janice Joplins, six John Lennons and thirteen Marilyn Monroes.

None of these famous folks were alive today. This reminded me that the attendees could only come to the party as dead people. It made me feel a little weird, like I'd just died and gone to the other side. Was this Heaven or Hell or somewhere in the middle? As I had this strange thought, a pang of cold, biting sorrow surfaced and clawed at me, making me feel empty and hollow. It couldn't be anything like Heaven for me because Andrew wasn't here. I sent the frosty emotions down to the remnants of molten lava in my brain's basement, where it froze all that remained of my recent fiery fury. I would *not* cry tonight.

Unfortunately, I also felt a sudden case of nausea creep up my throat. As much as I was hating on the presumptuous prince at my side, I didn't really want to barf in his lap. I sat there and tried again to think pleasant thoughts like waking up from a bad dream and finding myself in Andrew's arms or being rescued when Andrew popped out of a huge, multi-layered, chocolate cake and punched Mr. Majesty right in his noble face. I even considered how fun it would be to take the whipped cream covered fruit dessert on my plate and rub it in the hair that covered his over-inflated head.

Having a food fight with all these dignitaries dressed up like dead Earth celebrities would be an enjoyable, although juvenile, way to end this formal event. I suppressed the giggles that wanted to pop out of my mouth as I imagined all these uppity people wearing the vast quantities of food they were now consuming. Yeah, you might say I had a weird obsession with creative food usage tonight. Hey, it kept me from stabbing Raydon with my fork.

When everyone had finished stuffing themselves with the delicious and plentiful culinary masterpieces, the prince arose from his seat, took my hand, and we led the procession into the adjoining ballroom. I put on my most dignified demeanor as we exited the banquet hall. He took me to the center of the immense room where we waited for the music to begin. Harmonious vibrations were coming from a band or orchestra or whatever they call such musical groups on this planet, which played unusual shaped instruments made from wood, metal, and a shiny, glassy material.

The sounds blended together in a lilting melody that made my feet move. I was happy to see that these feet of mine seemed to be programmed to the right steps. We danced effortlessly around the room in a Viennese waltz type dance. Wow, that download into my head had actually worked! There was no way I could have picked this dancing ability up so quickly on my own. I began to feel as if I were on the set of some old movie from the Jane Austin era. I was almost having fun. Raydon was smiling at me and I found myself smiling back.

I closed my eyes and pretended I was in Andrew's arms. As we whirled around the floor, I imagined his brilliant, dimpled smile and his bottomless blue eyes that always looked directly into my soul. If only I could turn Raydon into Andrew. Where was my fairy godmother when I needed her? I was dancing with the wrong prince. My heart was again seized with the awful pain of knowing I might never see Andrew again. I gave myself a mental shake and grabbed onto the small ember of hope still burning within me.

"You look incredibly beautiful tonight, Tiana," the prince whispered in my ear as we flowed gracefully over the dance floor. "I wish you loved me as I love you."

"You don't really love me," I declared with intense conviction, "you just think you do!"

"What can I do to convince you that my feelings for you are real?" He looked at me with those sad, puppy-dog, Manga eyes of his. I decided against telling him that he was a poor, emotionally-stunted fool who didn't even know what love was. I didn't think that would sit well with him, so I just shook my head and said nothing. What could I say?

We did another dance that resembled a tango. Then the men in the room began cutting in. Evidently, I was the most sought after dance partner at the party. I guessed I was a novelty, being from another planet and all. I knew I should be enjoying the attention, but it just made me uncomfortable. I kept remembering that these people knew all my life's significant memories, and I knew absolutely nothing about them. They weren't even wearing their own identities. They were all channeling deceased characters from Earth, pretending to be various, resurrected, dead celebrities. How was that fair?

Benjamin Franklin cut in first, saying, "Dost thou love life? Then do not squander time; for that is the stuff life is made of."

"Okay, I know some Franklin quotations. 'Make hay while the sun shines.' 'Haste makes waste.' You are a very convincing Benjamin Franklin. Flown any kites lately?" I'm not all that good at making small talk with dead people. This was the best I could do.

"Not for a while, but did you know lightning strikes about six thousand times a minute on Earth?" He asked while staring at me through the round lenses of his fake glasses.

"No, I had no idea lightening struck that often. That's very illuminating," I admitted. "Do you have lightning on this planet?"

"Of course, but it only strikes Nommo about a thousand times a minute. You probably didn't know that I designed and printed an eight dollar bill for the American Colonies," he added.

"Well no, but 'a stitch in time saves nine' and 'a penny saved is a penny earned'," I said. "Oh, there's that early to bed thing. That about does it for me. I'm fresh out of Franklinisms. Have you any more?"

"Oh, I could go on all night," he grinned at me, "but, he's a fool who cannot conceal his wisdom."

The next man to cut in wore a white toga and a laurel leave wreath around his head. I wasn't sure who he was supposed to be. I waited for him to introduce himself.

"No man is so thoroughly right as to be entitled to say that others are totally wrong. It is well to affirm your own truth, but it is not well to condemn those who think differently," he orated proudly. I had this crazy feeling that I was a contestant on "Jeopardy" and I didn't know the question. I tried to gather my wits.

"Ah, you must be a Greek philosopher," I said.

"Yes, I lived on Earth from 469 to 399 BC." He gave me a clue. Somehow, I couldn't remember exactly what happened between those years, silly me.

"Plato?" That was the only name that I could think of at the moment. My mind wasn't cooperating.

"Socrates," he said shaking his head at my obvious stupidity. "I was Plato's mentor."

"Of course, how could I make such a mistake?" I pretended to be appalled by my wrong assumption. I hoped I wasn't going to have to guess everyone's identity because I hadn't paid quite enough attention in my history classes for that. I should have taken better notes and memorized the pictures, but how was I to know I'd ever be in a situation like this? It isn't every day that you have to converse with the dearly departed.

The next deceased celebrity on my dance card was none other than John Lennon. My mother would be so jealous if she could only see me now, or maybe it was Grandma who loved the Beatles. My parents had all their music. I felt another little piercing pang of sadness jab at my heart when I thought of my family. I closed my eyes for a moment to keep the pesky tears from spilling out. "I will not cry," I told myself again.

"Living is easy with eyes closed, misunderstanding all you see," the former Beatle began spouting his words of wisdom. "Our society is run by insane people for insane objectives. I think we are run by maniacs for maniacal ends, and I think I'm liable to be put away as insane for expressing that. That's what's insane about it."

"You've got that right. How do you stand it?" I said before I realized my saying such things might seem traitorous to the Nommoan government.

"I get by with a little help from my friends," he laughed.

Then he got all cryptic on me and warned, "You talk about a revolution. You know we all want to change the world. Instant karma is going to get you!" Some of those lyrics could have been written by his friends: George Harrison, Paul McCartney, or Ringo Star. I wondered if those guys were here too. Oops, I meant Nommoans pretending to be those singers. I'd almost started believing I was meeting dead people.

"You think?" I looked into his serious brown eyes and wondered what he could be talking about. Was he a rebel who had infiltrated this elite social event? How could he pass through all the checkpoints? Everyone here, except for our royal party, was required to go through complex x-ray machines. The security had been worse than airport security back on Earth.

The sidelines were full of bodyguards dressed in black military dress uniforms complete with those humongous utility belts full of wicked-looking weaponry.

I danced with Elvis and Michael Jackson. They also spoke in lyrics from their songs. It was amusing. I was surprised at how many of those words were stored in my memory banks, even though I wasn't that familiar with all their music. I'd just picked up random lyrics from my parents' old records, some of which they had inherited from my grandparents, when I was a kid.

Elvis said he had a twin brother who died at birth. He explained that he loved meatloaf. He weighed 230 pounds when he died. He failed his high school music class.

Michael Jackson told me that he had owned the rights to the state anthem of South Carolina. Where did they get this obscure trivia? How did they remember it all?

Winston Churchill, Abraham Lincoln, and Johannes Chrysostomus Wolfgangus Theophilus Mozart took their turns. Who knew his real name was so long? Two infamous Vikings, whose names I forgot, fought over me with swords. Four intensely dramatic Shakespeares held me hostage at the punchbowl and tried to out-quote each other until Queen Elizabeth commanded them to cease and desist. Did you know she was afraid of roses?

Finally, Prince Raydon reclaimed me and put an end to my steady stream of dead dance partners. We did some crazy, jumping dance that reminded me of the bunny hop. Some of the participants were obviously tipsy. I was glad I hadn't drunk any of the stinky, green, fermented fruit juice that many of them seemed to be guzzling like soda pop. A few of those people fell on their butts when we started going backwards. Some of the inebriated, living, dead dudes crashed into each other and yelled what must have been obscenities in their native language as the security staff forcefully helped them back to their seats. I watched a crazy collection of Edgar Allen Poes do a somber line dance with grapevine steps and Russian kicks. Tiffany would have loved this show. I missed her too. I wished for my cell phone, so I could take pictures and send them to her. Yeah, I know how ridiculous that thought was. I couldn't help wondering if they had cell phones here.

Many of the drunken and disorderly were inventing their own bizarre dances. They didn't seem to care that they were attracting attention with their foolish antics. Why should they? They were all wearing disguises that kept their identities hidden. They reminded me of a menagerie of wild animals. Things were just getting interesting, and rather entertaining, when a trumpet-like instrument sounded a blaring halt to the music. This signaled the official end of the dancing part of the program. Just before the final notes were played, the loud, shrieking explosions began. I startled at the noise and fearfully looked toward the doors that led outside.

CHAPTER 19

FIREWORKS

Raydon smiled at my worried reaction, took my hand and pulled me though the double doors that led out to the extensive, lush, manicured lawns in back of the capital building. The exploding sky was ablaze with humongous fireworks that stretched out in every direction. These were not ordinary, normal fireworks like I watched every Fourth of July and sometimes on New Year's Eve. These were gigantic, screaming, exploding, brilliant, rainbow colors that spread across the heavens, leaving glorious, glittering tracks spinning out to light up every corner of the cosmos.

They took several minutes to fade. While they were fading, more ginormous flower patterns had layered on top of the previous ones. This caused the sparkling, intense hues to bleed into each other in an immense work of moving art. The shimmering shades and tints of the radiant sky paints swirled and illuminated the entire visible part of the universe from just yards above our heads to the farthest, twinkling stars. Silver and gold flames shot through the waterfalls of colors making them glow and pulse with an electric, metallic sheen. The fireworks I'd seen and loved on Earth were as dim as mere candlelight when compared to these gargantuan, fiery wonders. These were more like massive, gazillion watt, halogen spotlights than the tiny flames I had witnessed before. The smoke that was left by these dancing fireballs smelled strangely sweet like roasting cinnamon and brown sugar on toast.

"Do you like them? I arranged this display as a tribute to you because you are the most beautiful, intelligent, and compassionate girl on this planet," he proudly proclaimed.

"I love fireworks!" I was astounded not only by the incredible, illuminating sparks shooting through the night sky, but also by his unusual kindness. I'd never known him to do "kind" before. Mostly, he barked orders at me, gave me impossible ultimatums, or dismissed my feelings and thoughts as irrelevant and unimportant in relationship to the grand scheme of things for the "greater good" of his planet.

"I know," he said, almost tenderly. This was a side of him that I hadn't met before. I definitely liked this Raydon better. Where had he been hiding?

"I've never seen anything quite like it. It's beautiful!" I couldn't help being majorly impressed by the remarkable light show above us. Maybe there was hope for the prince. This was genuinely magnanimous of him. I was also surprised by his words. He had paid attention to some of my fondest memories. He knew I loved fireworks. I was hit hard with the sudden understanding that he probably knew more about me than anyone else living in this galaxy with the possible exception of Andrew and my family.

Raydon had access to all my memories, but Andrew had sifted through the thoughts in my head for over seven months. I tried not to think about Andrew. I wanted to lose myself in the vivid colors that drizzled down, leaving trails of glorious, shimmering light. I wanted to be swallowed up in the incredible, dazzling expanse of spectacular brilliance that was streaking through the night and sparkling like scattered diamonds and other vividly colored gems across the black velvet sky. I wished it would burn away the darkness that was left in my mind, heart and soul, when I thought about the absence of the one person in this universe that I didn't want to live without.

So what if the prince was being kind? He'd already reduced my life to ruins. How could I forgive him for that? No mere firework display, however grand, could take away the devastating pain that had taken up permanent residence in my heart. I had to shove all that agony back into the depths of my soul and lock the door before it could overwhelm and destroy me again. I didn't want to go to pieces here in the company of all these high and mighty Heads of State and other prominent Nommoan leaders.

For the second time, I wondered if His Majesty could read my thoughts. I knew some Nommoans had the ability. He was also half Helamite. Most Helamite men could read minds to some extent. If he had the talent, I didn't think he used it very much because he never seemed to care what anyone else thought. To him, the only truly important thoughts were his own. I hadn't seen evidence that he ever cared what I was thinking, but I could be wrong about that.

"I saved the best for last," he whispered in my ear, "and yes, I can read your mind when I want to do so." I cringed at that disturbing bit of enlightenment.

Not only did he know my memories, he knew my thoughts. I was tempted to run away, not caring where, just so I could have my own private pity party without an audience. His gaze never left me as we waited for the finale to burst into the atmosphere above us.

The final fireworks to touch the sky came together projecting the picture of a face, large enough to cover the whole, wide and smoke-filled expanse. I thought it would probably be a portrait of the prince. I squinted up at the glistening image that was staring back at me.

My eyes opened wide with instant and embarrassing recognition. The fiery face that covered the smoky clouds was none other than yours truly. I shook my head, blushed, and looked down at my silver shoes wishing I could dissolve away like my face in the sky. Raydon had gone way overboard with this display. This was much worse than being in the spotlight. I sort of *was* the spotlight. After my firework face finally faded away, everyone applauded, signaling the end of the extremely embarrassing extravaganza.

The crowd began flowing back into the capitol building. Just as Raydon and I approached the double doors, a thunderous boom shook the ground. A shockwave pushed us forward with terrific force, causing me to stumble. Raydon caught me before I could fall to the ground. We turned to see an enormous crater form and explode into flames, shooting debris into the air around us like a geyser. It took out almost the entire park-like grounds. The destruction included the air strip and the hovercrafts that were waiting there to return the dignitaries to their respective homes. The many waiting servants had been blown apart, as well. I tried to shut out that lurid detail.

We covered our heads trying to shield ourselves from the dirt, rocks and organic matter that came raining down upon us. Dense smoke filled the air, making it hard to breathe and to see the extent of the cataclysmic ruins. This smoke smelled bitter and acidic like gunpowder mixed with human carnage. I struggled to remain on my feet as my knees gave out and buckled beneath me.

Raydon grabbed my right arm. One of his burly bodyguards grabbed my left arm. They pulled me into the building and up the staircase to the roof. I was grateful for their support. Our hovercraft was waiting there with engines roaring. The rest of our group was already onboard.

I hoped they had missed seeing my face in the sky. I gave myself a hard, mental kick. How could I be so selfish and superficial? How could I be concerned about my own mortification when bombs were dropping like hailstones and people were being blown to bits?

As we flew away from the disturbing scene of disaster, I heard sirens wailing and the sound of more bombs exploding around us. People were running in all directions on the ground beneath our flying machine, scattering like cockroaches when you turn on the light in a cheap hotel. They zigzagged, leaving serpentine tracks in the dirt, seeking safety that eluded them as more falling fire power claimed them.

In my last view of the capital building, I saw it burst into fifty foot flames. It was hit dead center and reduced to rubble. I shivered uncontrollably, closed my eyes and prayed that most of those dead Earth celebrities hadn't suffered real death from the destructive force of the enormous explosions. There had to be a large amount of fatalities, judging from the deaths I had witnessed and the devastation that destroyed the capital building and its magnificent grounds. This was not the "Grand Finale" that had been planned. It was a war zone. This conflict could be the beginning of the end of Nommo.

"It's my fault! I had the shield that protects the capital taken down so we could enjoy the firework display. The rebels timed their attack perfectly, striking just before the force field could be reactivated." Raydon looked horrified by the attack. I read the devastating pain and guilt on his face. I'd never seen such emotion cloud his expression before.

"How could you have known? I t was completely unexpected. You mustn't blame yourself for the random, evil actions of the rebels!" I insisted. Being exceptionally proficient at the "blame game" myself, I understood how he must feel. "You could just as well blame me. You wouldn't have had fireworks if I weren't here, would you?"

"It's my fault because I brought you here. Blaming you would be ridiculous. You had nothing to do with the rebels attack," he insisted.

"Well, you had nothing to do with their attack either," I replied.

I wanted to make him feel better even though I didn't think I could take away his perceived responsibility for the inflicted damages. Surprised by the empathy that flooded me, I wished I knew the best way to comfort him. The realization that he truly cared about his planet and his people filled my mind with an epiphany of understanding. He wasn't quite as horribly unemotional as I had originally thought.

There was a communication screen on the ceiling of the hovercraft. He switched it on just in time to view a recap of all the demolition and drama that we had already experienced first hand. After our escape, the force field had been successfully reactivated, preventing any further bombs from hitting their targets on the ground. When they struck the shield, they exploded midair and took out the planes that had dropped them. The rebel pilots had been on a suicide mission. I didn't know if that were their intention, but they must have known the consequences would be deadly. The death toll was expected to be upwards of three hundred and fifty, but there were many more victims who were seriously wounded.

The fatalities were mostly those who had been in the capital building when it exploded and collapsed, along with the crews and servants who were waiting in the hovercrafts parked beyond the fine lawns. There had been around five hundred in attendance, so the rebels had taken out more than half of the attendees. It was the equivalent of either the Senate or the House of Representatives or maybe both being assassinated in the United States Government. However, these were appointed leaders, not elected officials. At any rate, it meant the planet Nommo was in a state of emergency and political pandemonium.

On viewing this newsflash, the prince looked even more despondent and crushed. I impulsively took his hand in an effort to comfort him.

He looked up at me with agony clearly written across his facial features. It made me tear up to see his pain.

"How can I fix this? How can I begin to repair this damage? This is a declaration of war. More people will die. We are already on the brink of extinction. We can't afford any future casualties. Is there anyway I can stop this?" He stared into my eyes pleading for an answer. The voice in my head spoke for me.

"Yes, I think there is."

CHAPTER 20

NOMMOAN ARMAGEDDON

"How can I let this horrendously brazen act of war go unpunished? I will appear weak as a ruler if I back down in any way. How can I negotiate with traitors and murderers? Most of my trusted advisors are dead. Many of my top military personnel were also killed by the rebel attack. How can I stand by without retaliating? I need to mobilize our troops immediately!" He raked his fingers through his hair and stared at me waiting for my answer.

I had his full attention now. We were back at the castle, safely sitting at the dining room table in the great hall. He held onto my hand like it was his only lifeline to a successful solution and he hung onto every word I said.

"Do you want more people to die? This war could destroy everyone on your planet. It could be the beginning of a Nommoan Armageddon, a final battle that may put an end to all of your civilization. Do you seriously want to die preserving a government that has killed or banished half of your population and turned countless young people, who made stupid, insignificant mistakes, into slaves?

"Even if the rebels don't immediately confront you again, they will soon outnumber you. Think of all the servants imbedded throughout your kingdom that could be spying for them or giving them aid. Your people don't want to have children who will inevitably make some silly mistakes and then be forced to work for the government for the rest of their lives. Can you blame them? They will eventually get angry and rise against you. Maybe they already have.

"I know you love your country, but I think your closest advisors are not only untrustworthy but also corrupt and shameless. They want to control everyone's lives. They let you think you are the boss because they believe the people will remain loyal to the beloved royal family, and so far it's worked. The population of your planet doesn't need to get in touch with their emotions; they've merely been hiding them from your government, so they wouldn't be exiled or worse." The words tumbled out of my mouth with so much force and conviction, I impressed myself.

"How do you know this? Have the rebels abducted you and put these ideas into your head?" The prince was shaking his head. He was still unwilling to see the truth.

"You said you brought me here to save your planet. I think you'd better listen to me, Mr. I-Know-Everything! Your laws need to be reviewed and revamped. You've got to fix this now before it's too late. You need a new system of government that protects the inalienable rights of the people. That would be the usual stuff like 'life, liberty and the pursuit of happiness,' etc and so forth.

"When someone breaks the law, the punishment should fit the crime. Acting up and disrespecting a school teacher should not result in losing your freedom for the rest of your life. People make mistakes all the time. It's how we learn. Everyone deserves a second chance, a chance to make restitution and a chance to change. Have you people never heard of forgiveness?

Community service is an excellent way to serve a sentence for misdemeanors, but it should be dealt out in a matter of hours or days, not years or lifetimes. Only the most heinous of crimes, if any, should result in execution. Have you never heard of probation or rehabilitation? Also, the government should serve the people. They should have a say in how things go down." I was so convincing, I could see the wheels beginning to turn inside Raydon's head. I thought I might be finally getting through His Highness' extremely thick skull.

"If you need a governmental model, look at my country's system. It's not perfect, but it has provisions to change things when necessary. It was inspired by God, and you don't get any better than that in this life. You need to allow your people to have a voice through representation. You can have a king instead of a president, but you have to have checks and balances. You have to answer to the people. Unchecked power and authority breeds greed and political depravity," I said.

I continued to be amazed at the wisdom of the words that were flowing out of my mouth from that voice in my head. It was telling me all the right things to say. I sounded like an authoritative expert on democracy. I might have actually paid attention in my American History class enough to learn something. Who knew that would come in handy some day?

"She's right, Raydon. I have studied this democratic form of government. It seems to have been divinely inspired. It's absolutely brilliant! I believe we could make a similar system work here on Nommo." The King had slipped into the royal dining hall while I was trying to talk some sense into his hard-headed son. He had changed out of his Napoleon costume and looked sufficiently sane as he spoke confirming what I already knew. The man wasn't crazy.

"She is also right about our government. It has been taken over by power hungry tyrants who have been preying on the common man. It's my fault. I was fooled by their flattery and their willingness to take over my responsibilities while I was blinded by grief over your mother's death. They wormed their way into my confidences and took control because I was so distracted.

"I've been masquerading as a lunatic, so they wouldn't suspect that I was plotting to get my authority back. I have a detailed list of all the current officials and what they have done to denigrate their positions, using their offices for unrighteous dominion and ill-gotten gain. I know who we can trust. I have contacted them. They will arrive at dawn tomorrow. These are the leaders who really care about the Nommoan people."

"Father, you knew all of this and failed to confide in me?" Raydon demanded with incredulity. "How could you let me think you were insane? Why didn't you trust me?"

"I didn't really come to my fully-functioning senses until after you left on your mission to Earth. I had to wait for your return. I've been waiting for the appropriate time when you would be inclined to believe my words," the king confessed.

"You have a bad habit of tuning people out when you should be listening. I know you learned this from me. I am truly sorry I failed you as a father. I don't expect you to forgive me, but I hope that you can work with me for the good of our people."

"Of course, I can forgive you, Father, but how do we fix this disaster? How can we convince the rebels to trust and unite with us in establishing a new improved system of government? What will stop them from just overthrowing us and taking complete control of Nommo? Who knows what kind of government they would establish? The result could be even greater tyranny." Raydon looked to his father for the answers.

I smiled to myself, happy to see them bridging and healing the communication gap and hard feelings that had been festering between them for years. I loved the fact that the prince had regained his faith in his father and that he now trusted his instincts.

"First, we need to call a media conference and explain our desire to sit down with the leaders of the rebels to discuss amnesty and a radical change that will bring us together as one nation. Then we wait for them to contact us. I am sure they are planning to hit us with a long list of demands. We need to show that we are open to negotiating a compromise," the king explained.

I listened to them debate the issues and logistics until I couldn't keep my eyes open any longer. This political stuff was boring me to sleep. I laid my head on the table and shut my eyes for a moment. When I woke up, I was in my bed with no recollection of how I got there or how I got into my pajamas. I didn't have time to figure that out before I instinctively felt that something wasn't quite right.

It was still dark. I could hear the crunch of heavy footsteps outside my door. I hoped it wasn't someone coming to summon me because I was too tired to open my eyes. Ignorance can be bliss. I chose to ignore that feeling of wrongness. I didn't want to know what it was. Let the Nommoans take care of negotiating their future. I had done my part and pushed them in the right direction. Surely, they could take it from there. If I ignored the knocking, it might go away, right?

The knocking I was expecting never came. Instead, I heard someone insert a key in the lock, quietly open the door, and slip inside. For several minutes, I could hear nothing but the sound of my heart pounding in my ears. I lifted my head a hair off my pillow and carefully scanned the room through half-closed eyes without any sudden movements. A dark figure was standing motionless just inside the room, waiting, no doubt, to see if I were deep in sleep-land. I struggled to keep my breathing even.

Who would possibly want to sneak into my room in these early hours before dawn? Was the shadow a friend or a foe? My gut feeling and my inner voice had begun sounding an alarm. This person had to be an enemy. When did I get to be on somebody's enemy list for another planet?

I racked my brain for a way out of this situation. Was there anything I could use for a weapon near my bed? I eased my hand silently and stealthily out from under the covers, reaching toward the bedside table. My fingers grasped the base of the brass reading lamp.

The figure was probably waiting for his eyes to adjust to the dark. I could see that he was wearing dark clothing. His head and face were covered like someone in a ski-mask who was determined to rob a convenience store or a bank. Slowly, with extreme caution, he began inching silently toward my bed. Adrenaline was pumping through my tensed body as I readied myself for the coming confrontation.

Whoever this masked man was, he was going to get a whopping, painful surprise. He would be sorry he had broken into my room in the dead of night! I wasn't going down without a fight. I still had no idea who it could be. Was he a rebel or a ninja assassin come to kill me?

Where was all that security that the prince paid to guard the castle? If I screamed would anyone even hear my cries? I didn't think the other guest suites were occupied. I'd never seen anyone else come or go. Was I totally alone up on top of this secluded tower? Why hadn't I asked more questions? Time seemed to freeze as a finger of cold terror jabbed itself through my heart.

My hand gripped the lamp harder. I took a deep breath, trying to steady my twitching nerves. The shadow stopped when the sound of my intake of air changed. I held my breath for a brief moment and tried to resume a normal, sleep-type, breathing pattern. The dark, mysterious, ninja villain edged closer to my bedside, nearing the lamp that I clutched so tightly.

He removed some sort of gun-like weapon from his belt. Now was my only chance to get the upper hand before he used that weapon on me.

I popped up from my bed like a jack-in-the-box, lifting the dead weight of the heavy lamp at the same time. It connected with his head, sounding a loud thwack as it found its mark in the darkness. The sinister figure stumbled back a few steps but didn't go down.

"I really wish you hadn't done that," he cursed and came at me again, wrestling the lamp from my grasp. He attempted to restrain me and I began shrieking like a banshee. He tried to cover my mouth, probably to save his hearing, and I bit him hard until I tasted his blood. He cursed again, pushed me back on my bed and straddled my body. That's when I kicked at his legs and then kneed him mercilessly in the groin. He rolled off me, doubled over in pain for a brief moment and struggled to get control of his weapon.

I made a last dramatic effort to escape, but he shoved me back, aiming the gun-thing at my chest. I saw a strange flash of light, felt an extra-painful, electrical shocking sensation that surged through my body, instantly paralyzing all my appendages. My heart felt like it had been micro-waved while wrapped in aluminum foil. I opened my mouth to scream "bloody murder" and nothing came out. It must have paralyzed my vocal chords, as well. I helplessly fell backwards onto my bed. Then all the lights went out.

I regained consciousness as I was being tossed onto another bed. I couldn't see. I had difficulty breathing. I realized a pillowcase had been pulled over my head, which throbbed like someone was hammering nails into it. My arms and legs were tied tightly with strong chords that chafed my skin when I struggled against them. The footsteps were walking away from me.

I sensed that I was being left alone aboard a boat of some kind. The room I was in rocked back and forth slowly. Sea birds were crying in the background. I could hear waves splash against a hard surface in the distance. I smelled a faint fishy odor and tasted salt on my lips as I licked them nervously. I was no longer paralyzed, although I might as well have been, since I was bound securely with scratchy ropes.

I thought about screaming, but I was afraid the crazy-ninja-boogieman would come back and shock me with that taser-like weapon again. Besides that, any screaming would be muffled by the bag over my head. My chest still burned like it had been hit by a flame-thrower that had torched my internal organs.

Who was the maniacal mystery man in black? What did he want with me? Where was he taking me and why? How did he get past all the security that guarded the royal island? How did he bypass everyone at the castle? I had a gazillion and one questions swimming through my aching head. I'd probably think up a few billion more that could all have scary answers.

I began to wallow in my misery, feeling sorry for myself. I'm extremely proficient at wallowing and practice has made me close to perfect at whining too. Why did bad things keep happening to a good person like me? I didn't sign up for tribulation. Why do I always have to be the one to get kidnapped by demented, evil-doers who want to torture me and mess up my once happy life? Why couldn't God, Karma, or the Universe beam me back to Hurricane, Utah? Why was I the only person from Earth to get stuck on the one planet in the whole galaxy that was determined to destroy itself?

This kind of thing was only supposed to happen in sci-fi thrillers or blockbuster movies to superheroes that were all-wise-and-powerful with all the right tools to repair the injustice and take down the cruel culprits they faced. Where the heck was my superhuman hero and soul-mate when I needed him? How did I find myself light-years from home with very little hope of ever getting back to my own life, on my own planet, and having it reset to the right time? Could things get any worse? Was there a fate awaiting me that was more painful than marrying the arrogant Prince Not-so-Charming? Right now I realized I would welcome even his condescending face if he would come rescue me from the unknown perils awaiting me.

Then, I started praying. I was willing to make a promise to God, if he would get me out of this predicament. I would strive to be kind to naughty children and small, noisy animals. I mostly did that already. I would stop mocking people I didn't know. That would be dreadfully hard because some people just beg to be mocked, but I was willing to make the sacrifice. I would become more actively engaged in community service and volunteer more of my time to help those in need. I'd donate to all worthy charities if I ever had any money. I would sign up to do whatsoever random acts of kindness I could fit into my life, if I got that life back. Oh yeah, and I would forgive and forget the many past indignities that others had inflicted upon me. I'd work out the specifics later, if I had a later. As if on cue, I started to think of all the people who had made my life a living Hell.

For some reason, Prince Raydon's face popped up on my brain screen, bigger than life as number one on my list of people who had wronged me. Could I forgive him for bringing me to this forsaken planet populated by super-intelligent, idiots bent on their own annihilation? Could I ever forget how he totally screwed up my life, stealing me away from my friends, family, and my one true love? Was I capable of that kind of selflessness? Did he even qualify for forgiveness? I supposed he did.

The next face I saw was Sonya Parker. I had an exceedingly long list of crimes she had committed against me. Was I strong enough to forgive the pain she had poured upon me? I might be able to stop hating her, but I wasn't sure I could ever forget all the evil she had thrust my way. I feared she wasn't done dishing out the drama. I decided I could suck it up if I had too.

I promised God right then and there, I'd sincerely try to forgive both of them if I could just have my life back. My sincere prayer was rudely interrupted by the grating sounds of approaching, clonking footsteps and deep, growly voices arguing angrily.

"Why do we have to keep her alive? She's trouble. She broke a lamp over my head! She bit me and . . ."

"We need leverage. He will agree to almost anything to get her back," another voice explained as it interrupted the first one.

"I say we kill her now. Then we get rid of the inconvenience of keeping her alive as a prisoner. We won't tell him she's dead until after he meets our demands!"

CHAPTER 21

REBELS ON THE RISE

"We're not going to kill her unless we're explicitly ordered to do so! He specifically said to keep her alive. We can't ignore his commands. You're just mad because she saw you coming, and you got spanked by a girl. She's a feisty little thing and resourceful for an Earthling. I wish I'd seen her swing that lamp. That must have been priceless!" The voice laughed loudly at the ninja-bad-guy who wanted to kill me.

"I think I'll just electrocute her and throw her off the ship. I'll say she was trying to escape. It was an accident, or self defense. I've got bruises and bite marks to prove it! All I need is for you to corroborate my story. I know you'll back me up because your head will be on the chopping block along with mine." The growling, mean-man-monster sounded too confident about the whole killing me idea.

"Maybe later," the other nicer voice said, "after we have some fun with her."

Okay, so he wasn't nicer. This was getting seriously disturbing. I thought they were probably just yanking my chain, but I wasn't amused. No one was going to have any fun with me, and I wasn't going to hold still while they killed me either. I was so done with all this torture and death stuff. If I were going to die, it was going to be on my own terms. I had come to the sudden realization that I couldn't die on this planet, or I'd be stuck here forever! I needed some time to think, to gather my wits and to find some other options. There had to be better choices, didn't there? I'd survived this long. I wasn't ready to give up yet. It would help if I could see. I was sick of blindly listening to these two creeps talk about me like I wasn't sitting right here in front of them. Let them tell me their disgusting evil plans while I looked them in their evil eyes. I deserved at least that much dignity.

"Could you take this pillowcase off my head, please?"

I decided to take the direct approach. Perhaps they would listen to reason. It was time for me to use my words. I collected all my persuasive speaking skills and put on my most congenial smile, hoping to sound convincingly cooperative.

"It's really dark inside this bag. I would so like to see your happy faces. I'm sure you feel very good about successfully kidnapping me. Kudos to you both! Let me be of help to you! I am sympathetic to your rebel cause. Let's talk about what you want to get in exchange for my freedom. I'm sure the prince will grant any number of demands to get me back safely. If he won't, then I don't wish to go back at all. After all, this is my second, forced abduction in a relatively short time. I had already been kidnapped from my life on a planet far, far away. This whole snatch, grab and drag me away is getting old fast!"

My words seemed to be working because the pillowcase was removed from my head. I finally saw the faces of my current abductors. My eyes widened with surprise. I knew these guys. They wore the prince's insignia on their foreheads. I was shocked to recognize their familiar faces. I had been kidnapped by Raydon's own bodyguards, Brazzo and Sadvik. How had they slipped their leashes? I wondered if their cohort, Nafe, were around here somewhere.

"You look surprised to see us, my lady," Brazzo laughed at my incredulous expression. "Don't worry; I won't let Sadvik kill you. He's still angry about the nasty bump on the head you gave him. His dignity has been bruised and there are other parts of him that still feel the pain. I wish I had been there and seen that!"

"Shut up, Brazzo!" Sadvik looked sullen, but then he always looked that way to me. "Don't listen to her. She can't be trusted! She's under Raydon's thumb," he insisted in a sulky voice.

"I am not under anybody's thumb! You both know I was brought to this planet by the annoying prince against my will and I'm not the one parading around with His Majesty's mark tattooed on my forehead!" I yelled.

I objected vehemently to Sadvik's accusations. These stupid aliens were such a bunch of super-obnoxious-control-freaks. I was getting fed up with their bad attitudes and their penchant for hijacking my body and taking me places I had no desire to visit.

"I beg to differ, miss. You are now under our own very fortunate thumbs," Brazzo grinned at me, "Well, you're under my thumb; I think you bit Sadvik's thumb nearly clean off his hand. These insignias we wear were necessary to gain the prince's trust. He would never suspect his own royal guards. It was the most daring, perfect and brilliant disguise for espionage. His Highness is a hopeless loser who lives in his own make believe castle on the other side of the realm of reality."

He still reminded me of a frog, but his warts had cleared up. I couldn't help wondering how he cured them. Perhaps that ugly skin condition was an allergic reaction to the planet, Earth. I decided now wasn't the right time to ask such a personal question.

"Perhaps you would be so kind as to take me to your leader?" I stashed my anger away and worked hard to appear cooperative again. It seemed a wiser move at the moment. I wanted to stay alive, so I'd do my best impression of docile.

"Who is your leader anyway? Have I met him? Is it Nafe?" I asked this with my sweetest, sugar-coated voice. This brought more fits of laughter from my two captors.

"Nah, Nafe is back at the castle pretending to head up a search party for you. The prince is beside himself with grief over your unwilling departure from his supposedly secure home. Nafe is covering for us. I'm ill. Brazzo has a family emergency," Sadvik retorted. "We are taking you to the High Commander as we speak. We should reach his headquarters in another hour or so. His name is Quill. I believe you have met his wife and son in the royal household, Lanu and Quint," Sadvik seemed to be accepting my submissive act.

171

"Quill and his daughter, Layla, command the rebel forces. We have sworn our allegiance to bring about the downfall of the current tyrannical empire and to establish a new government. You are but a pawn in the new, improved grand design of things. Your abduction will simply gain the prince's attention and keep him distracted from our real offensive which is scheduled to begin in about forty four more hours." Brazzo said as he looked at a timepiece that hung around his neck.

Nommoan days are twenty two hours rather than the twenty four hours as on Earth. Two days were all I had to escape and warn the prince or to come up with some other plan to get out of this plight. Heck, I didn't even know where I was. I certainly didn't know how to get back to the castle or how to contact the prince.

Did they have cell phones or other communication devices? I should have paid more attention. I had seen the prince talk to something that resembled a pen, but I wasn't sure how it worked. I was completely out of the loop with their technology. It might as well be magic. I felt like my grandparents must feel when they try to surf the web. It seriously sucks to be techno-challenged on any world. I made another promise to God, Karma and the universe that I'd be more patient with technophobes if I survived and ever got back to the place and time where I belonged.

"Could you possibly untie me, please? I promise I won't jump ship. I can't breathe underwater as you well know. I'm not that good of a swimmer. Besides, I would have no idea which way to go. I have no way to contact the prince. I'm completely lost. I have no sense of direction on your planet," I tried more of my "I'm-completely-compliant" ruse to appeal to their sympathy. They had to know that I was at the disadvantage and posed no serious threat to them.

"If you promise to be a good little hostage and mind your manners, we will remove your restraints. You mustn't hit, bite, or kick Sadvik or he might accidentally kill you and that would be most unfortunate." Brazzo smiled and winked at me. "There will be no hitting, biting, kicking, spitting or any other various acts of violence or we will be forced to electrocute you again and that would be dangerous to your health as well as very hurtful. Do you understand? Will you behave?"

"Of course, why would you think I'd resort to such uncivilized actions? As long as you treat me with the respect I so deserve, I'll be a perfect guest. You know, you could have just asked me to accompany you to see your

High Commander. If you had taken the time to explain things to me, I probably would have agreed to come with you. No force would have been necessary." I smiled back innocently and batted my eyelashes at the two humongous, muscled, brawny guys. Were they afraid of me? No, they must be mocking me. I posed no real danger to them.

"Untie her, Sadvik," Brazzo gave the order.

"No, you untie her," Sadvik said.

"No, It's your job," said Brazzo, "and I'm in charge!"

"Who said you were in charge?" Sadvik asked.

"Stop fighting over me," I said. "You sound like you're five years old." Okay, docile was just too hard to maintain for any length of time.

"Just untie her, Sadvik, now!" Brazzo demanded, giving me his death-ray glare.

"I don't trust her. She's vicious. I say we throw her overboard and forget this babysitting job." Sadvik said. He stared at me with the "I'd-rather-kill-than-look-at-you" face he usually wore. I was getting used to it.

He definitely didn't like me much. What had I done to deserve such ardent dislike? Oh yeah, I guess I knew why, but I only hit him with a lamp, bit him and maimed his pride. I was perfectly justified in doing all those things in my own self defense. He was the one who committed the crime. What was his problem? He needed to seek therapy to get rid of his violent tendencies. A little shrink wrapping would do him good.

"I think you threw your head overboard. You need to get a grip! You aren't afraid of a little defenseless Earth girl, are you? You're twice as big as she is and you weigh three times as much!" Brazzo kept taunting Sadvik. "You're such a gutless wimp!"

"That's easy for you to say," Sadvik argued back. "She didn't savagely attack you! She is far from defenseless. She looks all frail, but she's a conniving little demon when provoked."

"I'm sorry I hurt you, but you snuck into my bedroom, tasered me, and dragged me away without my consent. I think you totally deserved the bump, bite, and beat down I gave you! Why are you so determined to kill me?" That anger I had stashed came unstashed and bubbled up to the surface. I wished I could hit him with that lamp again.

"See what I mean," Sadvik declared. "See how volatile she is!"

I was volatile! Seriously? He was the homicidal maniac threatening to murder me.

"Hey man, she's right! You did sneak into her room and abduct her. You're a big baby! Man up, and untie her. She's not going to bite you, are you Miss Dawson?" Brazzo was enjoying this too much.

"I won't bite," I promised, but I truly wanted to kick his sorry butt all the way back to the castle.

Finally, the two dimwitted giants removed the chords that bound me. I had to work hard to keep my composure and resist the terribly compelling temptation I had to knee Sadvik where it would hurt him the most and slap that silly grin off Brazzo's infuriating frog face.

As they finally removed my restraints, there was a sharp, impatient knock on the door of my prison cell and a pretty girl with large violet eyes and bright purple curls danced into the room with a tray of soggy looking food items that smelled like inferior seafood. You know the kind they serve in cheap diners or school lunchrooms. She was almost exactly my height and weight. She looked about my age.

"Dinner for the prisoner," She said, as she placed it on the bedside table.

"Thanks so much, but I'm really not hungry," I replied sweetly. It's never good to antagonize your waitress. She could bring something I actually might want to eat later when I was hungry. I wouldn't want her to spit on it to punish me. I know never to offend the wait staff. They have their ways of getting even.

"It tastes better than it looks, I promise. You should at least try it. Who knows when you'll get to eat again?" She shrugged like she couldn't care less. She stared at me with some kind of morbid curiosity, studying me like I was a life form from another planet, which, of course, I was. Still, I found her intense scrutiny to be rude. She looked at me like I was some kind of alien-devil-spawn. I wasn't all that strange. She was the one with purple hair. I stared right back at her. She narrowed her eyes.

"You must be the infamous Tiana Dawson from the planet, Earth. I expected you to be oozing magnetic charm and boasting beauty beyond words. What magic spell did you use to make Raydon fall for you?" She sneered at me. What had I done to deserve her disgust? Who was she to be judging me so harshly?

"I didn't come to your planet by choice. My only wish is to go back to my own life. I didn't do anything to your fancy-pants prince. I'm in love with someone else. Raydon forced me to come here, not that it's any of *your* business," I retorted.

"Oh, aren't we testy? So you don't love our Royal Majesty? How can you resist him? Every other girl on this planet would die to gain his favor. Are you so much better than the rest of us? Is your boyfriend a prince on your planet?" She spoke, her voice dripping with some severe hostility and obvious sarcasm. Whoa! What had I done to rain on her parade? I'd never even met her, and she hated me with extreme prejudice.

"I just want to go home," I whispered, lowering my eyes from her loathsome gaze. I was seized by an overwhelming fatigue. I was fed up with this abundance of aggravating alien attitude. I wanted them all to go away and leave me alone. Why couldn't this whole bad dream be over and done?

"Well, I'm sorry we can't grant your wish. You may be useful to us yet," she said as she turned and left the room slamming the door behind her.

"Who was that?" I asked, staring after the hateful girl.

"That was Layla. I think she wanted to get a look at you. She doesn't generally bring prisoners their food," Brazzo answered.

"Why would she care what I look like?" I couldn't help wondering out loud.

"She used to have a crush on Raydon before she was exiled. In fact, I think that's *why* she was exiled. She probably wanted to see what his fiancé looks like." Sadvik said with an ugly grin on his even uglier face.

"I'm not his fiancé! I have no intention of marrying him!" I declared with conviction.

"Is that so? I know for a fact he has every intention of marrying you. Perhaps we'll perform you a service and kill him before he has a chance to make you his queen. For him to become King of Nommo, he has to get married. I think the tentative date he has set is in about a month from now."

"What? How could he set a date when I haven't agreed to marry him? Am I the only one who can see that this is wrong on so many levels? That's it! I'm done! Where do I sign up to be a rebel? The nerve of that guy, how can he think he can force me to marry him? What a crock of crap! I've already told him I'd rather die!"

"Relax, princess, he probably won't live that long. We're planning to eliminate all those who don't stand with us. We'll exterminate all the government officials and take out their entire military. We've been stock-piling weapons of mass destruction for years. They won't have a chance to retaliate after we strike," Brazzo remarked with a nasty snicker and a smart-alecky smirk.

As angry as I was at Raydon, I didn't want him dead. Why did everything have to be a matter of life or death on this stupid planet? If they were so smart, how come they kept acting like war mongers and death dealing dummies? Why couldn't they work things out? Don't they have any negotiating skills? Where were the mediators? Why was I the only one who could see this situation clearly for what it was? With their highly developed intellect, how could they not find a reasonable and peaceful way to fix their government? They reminded me of a bunch of immature children who would rather throw tantrums and break their toys than talk to each other. Had they never heard of compromise?

And why did this Layla, the rebel-warrior-princess, hate me so much? I didn't understand her. Was she jealous because the prince planned to marry me? Was she still in love with him? Hey, she was more than welcome to him. I would gladly trade places with her, if that were possible. If I ever got the chance, I'd be sure to suggest it!

CHAPTER 22

REBEL HIGH COMMANDER

I was left alone for the final hour of our voyage. Brazzo and Sadvik had realized I wasn't going anywhere. Yeah, their low-wattage brain power had kicked in. They had given in to my pleas and provided me with some generic clothes to put on. I was relieved that I wouldn't have to appear in front of their leader in my furry white pajamas. I changed into a black shirt and pants that matched the other ninjas on board. I almost felt like I was on their team. Well, not quite!

I stabbed at the soggy seafood on my plate for a while to pass the time. I wondered why they had brought me here to meet their esteemed leader. Was I truly supposed to be a distraction to keep the prince from discovering their plans to destroy him and take over this world, or did they have some other devious plan to make my life more miserable than it already was? Did Layla have an ulterior motive to punish me for Prince Raydon's past sins? How was that my fault?

The food didn't taste quite as bad as it looked and smelled, but the texture was rubbery like it had been cooked too long, so I couldn't force myself to eat more than a few bites.

I didn't think His Royal Highness would care that much that I'd been captured. Of course, his two muscled body guards seemed to think he would care. They could be right. I just had a hard time believing that I was that relevant to the rebels.

I moved to the round porthole that showed me the ocean depths, raised the shade and peered out into the inky sea. We were in some sort of submarine that traveled at high speed. Everything we passed was just a blur in the black, murky water. I was reminded of the space movies when pilots pushed the warp speed button and the stars became streaky lines of light.

We were encased in an air bubble that clung to our watercraft like a clear membrane. After several minutes had elapsed, we began to slow down. The blurry seascape started to take shape before my eyes.

Among florescent, fuchsia, coral reefs were swarms of strange swimming flowers in muted colors of purple and yellow. Reddish seaweed covered with tiny green eyes watched the fishy flowers. Amoeba shaped see-through creatures in neon pink and orange moved among them. Their insides were swirling around like tiny tornados. Glowing, white fish darted in and out of coral canyons, nibbling on the seaweed and taking bites of the swimming flowers.

The amoeba organisms occasionally trapped a fish by surrounding it. They, then, absorbed it into their spinning innards. There were some squid-type things with enormous mouths full of pointy, jagged, shark teeth that came after the amoebas. They ripped the brightly colored amoebas to bits. The water was filled with a rusty brown fluid that oozed from the shredded creatures.

I was stunned by the violence of the working food chain system. I knew it wasn't any worse than the system on Earth. These creatures weren't any stranger than those I'd seen at aquariums and on the pages of National Geographic magazines. Survival of the fittest can be brutal on any world. I closed my eyes for a minute and tried to forget the carnage I hadn't wanted to witness. Then I opened them again, too curious to pass up the wonders I might miss.

Up ahead of us, I began to see enormous structures of glass, bunched together. There were multicolored lights beaming from the odd shaped and domed glass boxes. As we came closer, I could just make out people's faces smashed up against the glass, staring at our vehicle. There was a whole city of shining lights on the floor of this ocean. What better place could there be to hide an entire rebel army than on the bottom of the sea?

As we approached the city, I saw guards with spear guns swimming in front of what must be an entrance. They wore no wet suits or breathing apparatuses. They were shirtless, and there were weird looking gills under their shoulder blades moving up and down like the gills on fish. I noted their webbed feet, churning the water as they swam about. I had known about the unusual evolutionary anomalies these humans had developed over thousands of years on this water world, but it still shocked me to view them with my own eyes.

The entrance opened like a garage door. We entered and settled on the bottom of the enclosure. The door closed and the water began draining away. When the water was gone, another door opened, and more fish-like guards walked toward our craft.

Brazzo and Sadvik burst into the room, declaring that it was time for my audience with their "High Commander." They grabbed onto me and climbed out of the submarine, moving purposely into the attached gleaming glass building. After walking through some airport-like, security gates that x-rayed our persons for concealed weapons, I was led up a glass escalator to the inner chamber of the rebel leader.

The rebel commander rose from his chair as we entered the room. He was tall, slender with shoulder length, unruly, silver hair that was tinged with blue and gold highlights. He had the same pleasant face and greenish hazel eyes as his son, Quint. He nodded at Sadvic and Brazzo and the other guards to move to the chairs that lined the walls. He gestured to me to take a seat in front of his massive, metal desk.

"Welcome to our underwater city, Miss Dawson. I'm Quill, Leader of the Nommoan Rebel Forces. I'm happy to get to meet you at last. What do you think of our fair planet thus far?"

"I think it's pretty messed up. I think you're on the brink of disaster. If you aren't careful, you'll blow up your whole planet and destroy your entire civilization." I decided to call it as I saw it. Why not? What did I have to lose?

He frowned at my insolent words and spoke with a calm, authoritative voice, "Whose side are you on, my lady? Do you favor the pompous, insipid pawn of a prince with his evil political puppeteers who've been pulling the strings and profiting from enslaving the masses while they destroy our freedom? Are you sympathetic to our mission to bring equality back and to restore our God-given rights?" He wasn't dancing around the issues either. I liked that about him.

"I just wish you would talk to each other. The prince is now aware that he has been manipulated by his advisors. He and the King are ready to hear your demands. They want to make concessions that will unite your people with his. They were planning a news conference to invite you to peace talks as I was being abducted and brought here against my will. They're prepared to offer you amnesty and representation in a new form of democratic government."

"How do I know that you are speaking the truth? The prince could have simply told you these things, so you'd be able to deceive us. I can read minds, Miss Dawson, and I know you think you're being honest, but why should I believe that Prince Raydon and the king aren't setting a trap and trying to trick us?"

"Why would he lie? He had no idea that you were going to kidnap and question me. Do you have one of those 'memory machines' around here?" I asked, somewhat astonished by what I was about to propose.

"Hook me up and take a look at my recent meeting with those two. If that doesn't convince you, then go ahead and blow up this crazy planet of yours. If you aren't willing to give them a second chance, your world is doomed anyway. You might as well bring on the weapons of mass destruction and put an end to all of Nommoan civilization."

I'd sworn that I'd never allow anyone to go traipsing around in my brain again, but here I was volunteering to open my mind to him and the other leaders of the rebel army that he controlled. Who would have guessed? I guess desperate times can make me do ridiculously desperate things. I should never say "never' because I often have to eat my words and they don't taste good.

"That's an excellent idea, Miss Dawson. You're surprisingly intelligent for an Earthling," he nodded approvingly at my suggestion.

That was the second time I'd heard that comment on my intellect since I'd landed on this planet. I'd personally found many of these supposedly super-intelligent Nommoans to be super-stupid when it came to practical sense, but I held my tongue. I thought it would be better to keep that opinion to myself. There was no use upsetting the people who held the big guns.

He called his servants with his ballpoint-pen-phone. They wheeled in the dreaded, privacy-invading box. It was attached to a reclining dentist chair just like the one on board the spaceship that brought me to Nommo. I was strapped into the chair and given an anesthesia pill that knocked me out as soon as I swallowed it. Thank heavens; I didn't have to witness them thumbing through my mind again.

When I came to, I found a crowd of people intently watching a massive screen that took up one wall of his office. They'd gone back to see every moment I'd spent with Raydon. I closed my eyes and sadly shook my head. These aliens had positively no respect for a person's privacy. Give them an inch and they take miles. They just didn't understand boundaries.

"I say we can't trust the Prince. We should destroy the royal family and all their entourage of corrupt leaders. We can use the Earth girl as bait and lure them out of their security. We can say we're coming in peace to negotiate a new government. When they turn off their shields, we'll hit them with everything we've got. We can blast the whole Illdee Island and everyone on it, to the bottom of the sea." Sadvik suggested with gusto. He had some serious anger management issues.

"No! Too many innocent people would be killed," Layla responded, giving him a killer look that shut him up in a hurry. "We can't resort to such barbarianism. We're not savages!"

"What do we care if a few thousand innocents die? I'm sure they would gladly sacrifice themselves for the revolution!" Brazzo retorted. "You just don't want your precious prince to die!"

"My wife and son are on that Island. Many of you have family there. Are you willing to let them die? I'm not!" Quill responded with a very stern, "I'm-in-charge-and- don't-you-forget-it" voice. "If we kill that many innocent Nommoans we're no better than the dictatorial government we wish to abolish. The Earth girl is trustworthy. Raydon loves her. He'll do what she tells him."

"Are you sure about that? If she won't marry him, he'll be angry. He may go back on his word to spite her. She's convinced him to negotiate, but what will he do when she refuses his love and publicly humiliates him? His pride could cause him to change his mind and revert to his old ways.

The royals think they are entitled to rule with an iron hand, answering to no one," Sadvik insisted.

"Your argument is valid. Tiana must marry Raydon. It's the only way we can allow him to live. We'll give him a chance to help set up a new government if Miss Dawson will agree to share his power. The people have seen all her memories. They believe in the prophecy. They trust her. If she'll consent to marry Raydon, they'll support a new government with those two as a vital part of the package." Layla shot daggers at me with her eyes as she said this.

She completely baffled me. I'd entertained the thought that she still had feelings for Raydon, but if she did, why would she insist that I marry him? It made no sense. Was she was trying to convince herself and everyone here that she harbored no love for the man?

"Layla's right. We can't force you to marry His Majesty, Miss Dawson. However, if you refuse we'll have no alternative. He'll have to die," Quill stared into my eyes.

"What will you choose? Will you marry Raydon or should we kill him? The fate of our entire population rests squarely in your hands."

CHAPTER 23

WHY ME?

Sure, no problem, I'll decide the fate of your planet. Why not? Who would be more qualified to make that kind of monumental decision than a seventeen year old girl from another world? Hello? Just about anyone would be better at this than I was. That's no pressure. Why does everyone keep expecting me to make all the hard choices?

First it was Raydon, making me choose between leaving the Earth with him so Andrew, Tiffany and James would be saved and released or dying after having to watch them die. Now, the High Commander of the Rebel Forces wanted me to choose to either marry the prince or watch as he and the king were killed along with a big bunch of innocent people.

What was wrong with this picture? Who were these crazy people? I wasn't even from this planet. I didn't want to have to decide these kinds of things. It was so bogus! I shouldn't have to be the decider! Why couldn't

I just abstain on principle? It was their mess. They should clean it up without help from a seventeen year old Earth girl who shouldn't even be here in the first place.

How could I choose either option? I didn't love the prince. I didn't want to marry him, but I couldn't sit by and watch them murder him and other innocent bystanders. As I had grown to know him better, I had started to like him when he wasn't being all bossy and annoyingly arrogant. He had begun treating me with more respect and affection. I couldn't deny that I felt something for him, but was it enough? I knew he loved his people. He only wanted the best for them. Deep down inside, I recognized that he was an honorable leader who had been taken advantage of because of his youth and inexperience. He should get a second chance at ruling his planet with representation from the people.

He didn't deserve to die, but did I deserve to be forced to marry him? It wasn't fair! I know, I know, life is seldom fair on my own planet. Here, it seemed utterly unjust. These people didn't know the meaning of fair. I felt sorry for their complete lack of justice and their difficulty in instigating change without catastrophic annihilation. However, this was not supposed to be *my* problem!

Where was my psychic soul mate? Why hadn't he come to rescue me as he had promised? Was I going to have to spend the rest of my life on this watery world where I didn't belong? Was there no justice in the universe?

I fumbled with the tiny ring on my left hand. Andrew Martin, where are you? I needed you yesterday. My mind was flipping out on overload, bringing up fears I had tried to sweep under my miserable, miscellaneous, cluttered brain cells like dirt pushed under a rug. Would I ever see my own world again? If I did make it back to Earth, would I even have a life, or would I be a complete stranger because I'd lost my place in time. Would my contemporaries have moved on and aged way beyond me. Would anyone remember me? Would they believe I *was* me? Could I fit into a world where technology had progressed past my comprehension? Had Andrew forgotten me? Had he made himself a new life, one that no longer included me?

Perhaps I should give up and resign myself to this unfair and undesirable fate. Marrying a prince wasn't the worst thing that could happen to a girl. Was it? I felt closer to Raydon than any other person on this planet. I had come to depend on him in a way. Wasn't that some kind of psychological disease? I think 'Stockholm Syndrome' was what they called it. Was I identifying with my kidnapper because I was grateful that he hadn't killed or tortured me? Had my mind finally snapped under all this pressure? Was I running down the road to insanity?

Should I forget my dreams and banish my beloved superhero from my thoughts? Could I accept the fact that I was probably never going to see Andrew's face again? Would I never again get to gaze into his intense turquoise eyes, or bask in the warmth of his brilliant smile? The horror of this very probable outcome sent its icy fingers shooting through my veins, snaking their way to my heart where they clutched, squeezed, and rung all the joy out of me and left only intense despair and anguish in its place.

The tears started streaming down my face again. I quickly wiped them away with my fingers. I swallowed the sobs that were clawing at my throat, pushing to escape into the air and become uncontrollably audible for all to hear. No, I wasn't going to lose control. I didn't want to bawl like a baby in front of these unsympathetic rebel leaders.

I wouldn't give them the satisfaction of watching me dissolve into a puddle of human emotion under their unyielding, unfeeling scrutiny. I forced my sorrow back into the bottommost parts of my soul where it could hide out until I was alone. I knew it would come back to haunt me then. I wouldn't give in until the moment when I could break down with some degree of privacy. Right now, I would be strong. I would stand tall. I would lie through my teeth like my life and the lives of others depended on it because they did.

"Don't kill him. I'll marry him," I said softly.

It might not end up being a lie. I might have to do it eventually, but for now I just had to buy some more time. I had to think of it as the truth, so I could fool Quill, if he were trying to read my mind. I kept saying *I will marry Raydon* in my mind over and over, concentrating on making it feel true. He stared into my eyes. Then he looked away from me to the rebels with a satisfied smile. I was sure he'd picked up my thoughts. He thought I was telling the truth. I could read it on his face.

Later, I would need to take time to think about all this madness. I'd give Andrew one last chance to save me. I'd search the recesses of my intellect. I'd try to come up with an escape plan. There had to be a more acceptable solution. Andrew could still make good on his promise. I had to believe he would save me. If he didn't, I'd have to find a way to save myself. I would be strong. I wouldn't let them see my emotions. There had been too much of that already.

I reached inside my soul, picked up some faith, and held onto it tightly in my nearly broken heart with all my might. I closed my eyes. I visualized his face while I twisted the ring of silver and diamonds that was a symbol of his commitment to me. I could hear his voice saying, "Don't give up yet. I will find you and bring you home!" I had to believe. The voice in my head confirmed that this was indeed, the best strategy. At that moment, it was the only thing I could do.

"You have made a wise decision, Miss Dawson," Quill smiled down at me. "I know this feels like a tremendous sacrifice on your part, but the future of Nommo rests in your hands. We will be forever in your debt. His Majesty will be ecstatic that you have agreed to be his wife. Every unmarried girl on this planet will envy you. I'm sure you will grow to love him in time."

"Or not," I mumbled under my breath, but no one seemed to hear me. If they did, they didn't acknowledge the comment.

Layla smirked at me. She enjoyed seeing my obvious emotional pain. I still couldn't quite figure her out. I wondered if she wanted some sort of revenge on Raydon. Was she a woman scorned who radiated Hell's fury as the saying goes? Yeah, I'd seen her fury. It was hellish. Had he spurned her, or had he just been oblivious to her crush on him? Had he wounded her pride and knowingly rejected her romantic attention? Why exactly had she been forced into exile? Had he once cared for her? Then failed to save her from being banished from his kingdom? Was strapping him with a wife who didn't love him, her idea of a fitting punishment for his past offences?

I'd have to try to get the real story out of His Highness. I was pretty confident she wasn't going to tell me. I was sensing some serious hate vibes emanating from her. The crazy rebel princess wouldn't stop sneering at me with obvious distain. She looked at me like I was some foolish twit from another planet. Okay, she was half right. Her dark, dirty looks were starting to unnerve me. I felt like a bug she wanted to squish with her shoe and grind into the floor.

"May I leave now?" I asked their fearless leader. I wanted to get away before the floodgates of my emotional pain broke loose, sending me a river of hysteria that would overpower me and render me inconsolable. I didn't want to entertain Layla by falling apart in front of her. She would undoubtedly enjoy that way too much. I couldn't bear her smug satisfaction at witnessing my misery.

"Before you have enjoyed our hospitality? I don't think so," Layla responded. She wanted to watch me self-destruct. I could feel it in her hairy-eyeball glare.

Her father cleared his throat and replied. "We'll contact the prince and tell him we are ready to meet and negotiate a truce tomorrow. Brazzo and Sadvik will show you to your quarters. You should get some sleep. You will remain our guest until Raydon sets up the meeting. You are dismissed."

My least favorite bodyguards showed me to a small room with a bed in it. One wall was glass and gave me a breathtaking view of the ocean floor. It was like an immense, endless aquarium. It would have been fascinating if I hadn't just been forced to come to grips with my own unfortunate future.

I fell onto the bed. The sobs I had swallowed came exploding out in a raging torrent of negative emotions. I could no longer stifle them. They came out so loud that I had to bury my face in the pillow, so the whole rebel army wouldn't hear me cry. Finally, when I could weep no longer, I fell into a fitful sleep.

I found myself in the dark tunnel that I had dreamed about so often in the past, before I had known that Andrew was from another planet. I was walking in complete darkness, feeling the side of the enclosure with my right hand and using my left to push out in front, praying that I could find the way out. As I edged my feet cautiously forward, I heard faint footsteps behind me. I turned to see who or what followed me, but all I could see was a black void. I increased my speed and stumbled on until I could just make out a dim light which must be the opening at the end of the pitch black cavern. I was filled with hope as I moved faster and faster toward it. When I was nearly there, someone or something grabbed me from behind. I screamed and woke up in a cold sweat.

"Are you all right?" Someone yelled as he knocked incessantly at the door to my room. "Open the door, Tiana!" I had heard that voice before, but I couldn't remember where or when I had heard it. I reluctantly got off the bed and opened the door.

"Thad, how did you get here?" I asked the servant who had delivered my breakfast with Shan and Mara at the castle.

"I followed Brazzo when he kidnapped you and I snuck on board the submarine," he explained. "I wanted to be sure you weren't going to be harmed. I also suspected they were taking you to the rebels. It seemed like a good opportunity for me to join. We get to take a grand tour of Aguatia and Exile Island. We leave in about thirty minutes. We get to see the cyborg factory! You do want to come, don't you?" He now looked surprised and excited.

"Of course," I replied. I realized that I wanted see how the other half of the Nommoan population lived. Who would turn down a chance to see a place where they made cyborgs? I thought that was make-believe stuff from science fiction movies. Had these exiled Nommoans actually found a way to construct androids that were part machines and part organic living matter? This I had to see! If my brother were here, he'd think he was in Sci-Fi heaven.

"Good! I'll be back to get you then." He turned and left and I shut the door.

A short time later, we were in a smaller submarine moving along the ocean's depths. With the glass city of Aquatia behind us, I saw an immense mountainous shape come into view. We began to ascend and finally reached the surface next to another tropical island. We were transferred to a small boat and ferried to the dock. Then our ninja guards ushered us onto a beach where an open aired hover vehicle awaited. They handed us over to a friendly woman.

Our tour guide was a tall, gaunt lady with long curly turquoise hair and eyes that matched, who looked a lot like my Grandma Simmons, minus the blue-green hair, during her hippie days before she became my granny. I'd seen pictures. I think she had an eating disorder back then. Now she was a normal, round, middle-aged woman. It seemed odd to be reminded of someone I knew well by a person on another planet. Her name was Nila.

She explained that our driver was a cyborg. They had created these human robots to do the most mundane manual jobs like sewage treatment, garbage disposal, harvesting crops, driving tour buses, doing laundry, etc. All the dirty, dangerous and boring stuff that most humans didn't want to be stuck doing. These were the same type of menial jobs the indentured servants who lived on the Ildees Islands had to do. This was great! When the prince freed all the slaves, he could get cyborgs to do their work unless they wanted to keep doing the mindless jobs for money. Some people actually seem to like those mundane tasks that bore me stupid.

Most of the island was dedicated to producing crops. This made perfect sense because land was in short supply on this water dominated world. There were acres of fields of giant vegetables and grains along with orchards of trees bearing nuts and fruits. There were many workers in the fields, picking the various natural foods. They worked in a robotic, zombie way that suggested that they were indeed machines. They were quick and efficient.

After traveling across miles of farms, we found ourselves in a large, lush park where many people were playing weird sports. One game involved hitting a hover-Frisbee between players. They eventually batted it through a floating net. The other team tried to steal it away and then proceeded to their flying goal. There were hills, gardens and forests crisscrossed with nature paths that were crowded with hikers and people peddling hover bikes and riding hover boards. Children played on crazy playground equipment that changed colors and moved like multiple, kiddie-carnival rides connected together.

There was a petting zoo that contained unusual breeds of tiny horse-like animals in vibrant colors. They galloped about and made sounds like little, barky puppies. They chased smaller animals that looked like dragons with red spotted, white fur- lined bodies. Just when I thought the horse things were going to catch them, they would spread their hidden wings and fly up into the trees.

The aviary was full of birds that looked more like fairies with cat-like faces that smiled intelligently back at you. They warbled haunting wild songs that made me want to stay and listen forever. There were some tall ostrich-size orange birds that looked more like flamingos with purple peacock tails and skinny yellow legs. They made a piercing, shrieking sound like the cry of a newborn baby.

On the other side of the island, there was a large, sterile looking facility that reminded me of a medical center. Finally, we made it to the cyborg factory. After a brief tour, we were escorted into a laboratory where we could see many gas filled tubes along one wall. Inside each compartment was an incredibly human-looking body. It was so creepy, I shuttered. It reminded me of those tubes onboard Raydon's spaceship where I'd discovered Andrew, James, and Tiffany. I thought of the tube that I was forced into when I was abducted and brought to this planet. I had to close my eyes, and tell myself not to run screaming from the room.

"This is where we make our labor force," Nila explained, gesturing to the tube lined wall. "It's much better than forcing young people to become slaves." She had already shown us the place where the mechanical parts for the robots were made and where the artificial intelligence computer chips were programmed for different capacities. We had just entered the place where the human parts were developed. This lab reminded me of those old, black and white, mad scientist movies like "Frankenstein." It was weird and creepy seeing the bodies in different stages of development from fetuses to full grown adults.

A distinguished man who had salt and pepper hair with a few strands of green highlights approached us, smiling. "Ah, you must be Thad Evers and Miss Tiana Dawson. I am so happy to meet you. I am Tovin. These are my children," he said, giving me a small bow and gesturing toward the many strange bodies. "Are you enjoying your tour of our laboratory?"

"Very much, thank you sir!" Thad exclaimed.

"How about you, Miss Dawson?" His amber colored eyes stared into mine as I answered.

"I find it a little disturbing. Can these creatures think for themselves?"

"Only as far as we program them. They only look human. They are machines. However, it can be hard to recognize them for what they are when they're encountered outside this lab. They appear human to the untrained eye. If you look into their eyes, you can see that they have no spirit there, no soul. They look empty because they are merely machines with an organic camouflage. They are kind of like the zombies you earth people enjoy watching in movies or killing in video games. However, they are harmless. They don't eat brains or try to kill humans."

Wow, even here among the rebels he knew all about Earth. I was a little surprised by that. He must have picked up on my shock, because he looked amused and continued. "Yes, we all downloaded your planet's history into our brains just like those who live in the prince's domain. We actually have surpassed their technology."

"How is that possible?" I asked.

"The best and brightest minds were exiled or ran away from the established tyranny of the empire. The most brilliant minds tried to stop the insanity. They were either killed or banished. We have profited by the government's feeble attempts to punish those who had the superior intellect and the bravery to rise up against them. The most intelligent people prefer to be free to choose how they think and what they do."

"This android looks like my father!" Thad had stopped in front of one of the tubes and was staring intently at the body inside.

"Yes, we have your father's DNA on file. We made this one look like Josen Evers. He was a rebel hero. He died trying to save a busload of condemned teens that were being shipped off to work in the virganut orchards."

"So, you use real people as a pattern for making these robots?" I was forming an idea in my head. There might be a way out of my impossible marriage to Raydon. "Could you make one that looks like me?" I tried not to let on how excited this idea made me.

"Of course, I would be honored to produce a cyborg in your image. All I would need is a sample of your DNA, and I'd need to have you step into my imaging machine over here," he smiled and pointed to a chamber that looked like a small shower stall.

"How much would something like that cost?" I knew I didn't have any Nommoan currency. I didn't have anything to barter with, but I had to ask.

"For you, Miss Dawson, I will do it for free! Please allow me to grant your wish. I can finish it in a week's time and have it delivered to the royal palace. I assume you will be on your way back there in a few hours. May I ask what you want it for or would you prefer to keep that a secret?" His eyes met mine. What I saw in them made me pretty sure he could read my mind. He probably knew why I wanted it, and I was pretty sure he suspected what I was planning. These rebels had all received the memo that I had agreed to marry His Majesty to further their cause. They also knew that I didn't particularly want this marriage.

"I just think it would be fun to have a clone that could do some things that I'd really rather not do," I answered with as much vagueness as I dared. "I'd also prefer that no one else know about it."

"I'll disguise the package. I can label it as a case of some rare fruit juice that you asked for, my dear, if that will help you."

"Thank you so much! I won't forget your kindness." I gave him my brightest smile.

"It is my pleasure to serve you, my lady," he said, giving me a knowing grin and a wink in return. "If you will just step inside, we will get your dimensions. Then I will need to swab your mouth for DNA." He led me to the imaging machine. I entered the circular chamber. A light flashed. I think my entire body had been x-rayed. "Stand perfectly still. It takes only about a minute and a half." The light flashed several times before stopping. He helped me out. He swabbed my mouth with a giant Q-tip that he immediately bagged and tagged as they do in all those CSI shows.

"What?" He had noticed my surprise.

"I'm amazed that you do it the same way as it's done on Earth."

"Actually, my dear, we used to have people spit into the bag. When we downloaded your entire world's knowledge, we decided your method was somewhat less disgusting. It works just as well. We have managed to learn a few things from you. Your world is full of free thinkers, and even though our technology is much more advanced, your scientists are creative geniuses. You have given us a different perspective which is invaluable. We are also impressed by your country's democratic government. We want to adopt a similar system. We are indebted to you for suggesting this to the king and the prince of the Ildees. It makes much better sense to negotiate and unite with them than to exterminate them. I am a pacifist, but many among us are not."

"We need to get you back to Aguatia," Nila motioned to us to follow her out.

"Don't give up, Miss Dawson. He will come for you." Tovin stabbed my heart with those words as I turned to go. I glanced back with astonishment, but he had already disappeared into his office. I wasn't sure I had heard him correctly.

CHAPTER 24

NOMMOAN NUPTUALS

When our supersonic submarine docked on the edge of Castle Island, I was surprised to see the prince waiting there for me looking like he hadn't slept in a week. When I climbed out, he stepped forward and hugged me. He kissed the top of my head and then held me by my shoulders and gazed into my disbelieving eyes with genuine concern. Who was this guy? Had someone kidnapped the real prince and left a loving clone in his place?

"Are you okay, Tiana? Did they hurt you? I've been sick with worry. I'm so relieved to have you back!" He looked strangely close to tears. I didn't think that was possible. He hugged me again for a long minute. This was too weird. I hugged him back.

"I'm fine," I smiled at this stranger. I was kind of glad to see him. I'm not sure why. It must have been that "Stockholm Syndrome" thing again. He was the closest thing to a caring friend or family member that I had on this planet.

He knew me well. That was comforting on some level. I still didn't believe his feelings for me were genuine. Thinking about that made me feel alone.

I wondered about Layla and Raydon. Had he loved her once? I was almost certain she still had feelings for him. She had some serious jealousy issues, if I were reading her correctly. When we were alone, I asked the question that had been nagging so persistently at my mind.

"Were you in love with Layla? Do you still have feelings for her?" I bravely asked. I had nothing to lose, so why not push the envelope? He looked surprised by my query and then he looked uncomfortable.

"Yes, I think I might have been. I didn't understand love then. I was sad when she was exiled. The High Chancellor said it was for the best. I was young. He said she wasn't good enough for me. I was a prince. I had a responsibility to the people of Nommo. Not long after that, he sent me to Earth on the quest to find the red haired girl in the prophecy. That was you. I love *you* now. You are meant to be my queen. I may harbor some feelings for her, but they will fade in time as will your feelings for the Helamite, you call Andrew." He seemed quite sure about that. I was too surprised by his confession to correct him.

That night I contemplated my future. I had been formulating a plan in my mind during the journey back to his kingdom. I was going to have my own personal robot that looked exactly like me aside from the empty eyes. I was sure I could program it to play my part in the upcoming wedding. If Nommoan brides didn't wear veils over their faces, I could claim that it was an earth tradition and insist that I wore one. That would hide the vacant eyes until the end of the ceremony. But as I tried to plan my escape, I realized that I had nowhere to escape to.

The rebels were going to unite with the kingdom. All the people wanted me to marry Mr. Majesty. Who could I trust? Where would I go? How could I survive? I hadn't even graduated from high school yet. I had no job skills. No one would hire me anyway because I would be a fugitive from justice, running away from a fate every other single girl on this planet had probably fantasized about. It seemed unbelievably futile to conceive that I could make any sort of life for myself here if I didn't do exactly what everyone wanted me to do. The only two options I had were to go ahead and marry Raydon and resign myself to living out the rest of my pitiful life away from all the people I loved or sit tight, stall, and hope to be rescued by Andrew or the Zariba.

This whole impossible situation was so messed up! I was beginning to falter in my belief that my superhero would intervene in time to save me from a union I dreaded more than placing my hand in a garbage disposal while someone flipped the switch.

What if he came too late? Could I leave after making those wedding vows? Would Andrew still want me if I'd officially gotten myself hitched to the prince? Could I get an annulment or a quickie divorce? Would Andrew's strict cultural moral code make an allowance for my being forced into a marriage that was not of my choosing? If I went back to Earth, would forced vows, taken on this planet, be valid?

No, I was not going to give up and sink like a stone into this pool of negativity. Another friend popped into my head. Shan would help me. I was sure of it. I would drag my feet as long as I could. Then I'd dress my twin cyborg in my wedding ensemble, and send it out to marry the unsuspecting king to be. He would get the shock of his life when he looked under that veil.

I might even stick around incognito just so I could see his face. It would be priceless. No, it would be sad. I felt a few pangs of guilt wash through me. I didn't want to hurt him. I had some feelings for the man. When the moment came that he realized he'd been tricked, would he play along, not wanting to make a scene in front of his whole planet? Would he immediately call his military to arms and set them on my trail to hunt me down and make me pay for my audacious act?

I'd ask Shan to hide me until my real prince came to take me home. I could do this! No one was going to make me get married at seventeen to anyone, especially someone I didn't want to marry! There was always a choice. Andrew was my soul mate. I had to choose him. I had to believe that he would come. I wasn't going down without a fight, or in this case, an escape plan.

A month rushed by in almost a total blur. The prince was ecstatic when he learned that I had agreed to marry him for the sake of the new alliance with the rebels. He was also heavily invested in helping create a new democratic government that would join the two factions of the population together. That took up all of his days. The evenings I spent with him usually consisted of diplomatic interviews, meetings and parties with Nommoan dignitaries and rebel leaders.

He continued to treat me with loving adoration. I tried to play the part of a dutiful fiancé. Mostly, I just followed along, stayed in the background, and kept my mouth shut with a frozen fake smile plastered across my lying face. I was like those stepford-wives of presidential candidates who had to act their perfect part as the supportive, irreproachable mates. I do so hate politics!

I spent my days with Shan and Thad. The prince had promoted them to be my companions. Their job was to keep me entertained. They were free now, but they stayed in the royal household as paid employees while they decided what futures to pursue. Mara had moved back in with her parents on another island.

They took me to all the most beautiful beaches and other nearby, scenic, tourist places. I saw the incredibly spectacular Eruption Island with over one hundred active volcanoes that spewed red, hot lava into rivers of fire. The molten streams flowed into the ocean causing steam to flare up and fill the air with hot humidity that burned my lungs. Being there was like spending an entire day in a sauna.

We visited another island, called Bridal Veil Isle, which was covered with an amazing, erosion carved canyon. It was thick with lush vegetation and a myriad of fantastic waterfalls that fell to incredible depths from high, intricately ornate cliffs and poured through cracks and crevices in the colorful jade-green, rock walls.

It looked kind of like our Bryce Canyon, another national park in southern Utah, which is filled with similar "hoodoos" (delicate rock columns that are often topped off by odd-shaped balancing boulders). I told them about the park that looked a lot like this canyon and related the Paiute story of the "Legend People."

"The Paiutes believed that before there were any Indians on Earth there were many kinds of wildlife like birds, lizards and animals who looked like people. These creatures lived at Bryce Canyon. They were evil and were at war with each other. Because they were so bad, the all-powerful coyote turned them into stone. These are now the "hoodoos" that look like eroded rock formations. If you look closely, you can see their faces still painted with war paint as they appeared before being changed into giant rocks."

"Do Native Americans still believe this primitive story?" Shan asked.

"I don't think so," I admitted, "but it's one of their more imaginative legends. They have a rich culture that is very fascinating." Talking about

Native Americans made me homesick again. Who knew I'd miss Indian culture?

"I wish I could visit your planet and meet these people. Do you know any of them personally?" Thad asked.

"My friend, Raven, is of the Paiute tribe. She told me the story last October when Andrew and I went to visit Bryce with her and her boyfriend, Coty." I missed Raven. I had to find a way to get back to Earth. I threw myself into admiring the scenery, so I wouldn't have to deal with that impossibility.

Instead of the rusty red, white and gold soil, this Nommoan canyon had stripes of turquoise and black that ran though the light green rock. It had much more water everywhere. The erosion process was faster here than at Bryce Canyon.

It was a tropical paradise full of strange animal life like large, black, furry gerbils that hop like rabbits, green, hairless monkeys with humongous, yellow eyes, and ostrich sized birds with bright, purple feathers and blue, duck bills, rather than a pine-tree forest landscape, inhabited by chipmunks, prong horns, deer and coyotes. Despite all the differences, the "hoodoos" were similar in everyway except color.

They took me in a hover plane to "Forbidden Island." It was a wildlife reserve where all the most dangerous animals on Nommo roamed. This was a sort of floating zoo in the middle of a sea that was separated from the rest of the ocean by some kind of magnetic electrical shield.

The "Serpent Sea" was filled with brontosaurus sized monsters that had heads like hammerhead sharks. They swallowed whale-sized fish in one big gulp. Piranha type flying fish, the size of small dogs, leaped into the air to catch sea birds. It was frightening to watch.

The island was home to the green and brown spotted "Camocat" which was hard to see at first because its fur was excellent camouflage for the giant elephant-sized feline. This enormous animal had razor sharp teeth and claws the size of electric chain saws. We watched as one sliced and diced another vicious creature that resembled a giant red spider with a long snake-like neck and head.

There was also an enormous bird thing that looked like a pterodactyl crossed with a vulture. It was as big as a diesel truck and had a wingspan almost the same size as a jet plane. Luckily it could only fly short distances at an altitude of about thirty feet off the ground. This place was full of things that should only exist in nightmares. Nommo had some unusually scary, indigenous wildlife.

After my tour of the wonders of this watery world, I had to face the wedding planner. Lanu was overjoyed to have her husband and daughter back and to have her son, Quint, free at last. She and her devoted staff were planning the upcoming nuptials. She kept asking me for my opinion as she used her many talents to plan the "Royal Wedding" that was supposed to be the ceremony of the century. It reminded me of the "Royal Wedding" I'd watched on television of Prince William to Kate Middleton. I'd felt kind of sorry for them because everything they did had to have an audience. I'd never in my wildest nightmares, imagined that I'd find myself in a similar situation.

I usually told her to go with her creative urges. I didn't care how crazy she got with the details. I was no "Bridezilla". I didn't even want to think about the marriage that loomed around the corner of too little time. Finally, when I couldn't placate her anymore, I was forced to be fitted with the outrageously glamorous gown.

On Nommo, wedding dresses are traditionally a bright turquoise blue signifying the fresh, clean waters and bubbled up from underground springs that quenched the lush, verdant vegetation, along with the oceans of salt water that covered the planet. The veils are a pastel green lace which symbolizes the land that was in limited supply and provided much of the food that nourished all life.

My veil consisted of long layers of delicate lace and was topped off with a lacey, emerald and sapphire studded tiara made from the finest gold. The bodice of the dress was covered with hundreds of tiny blue seed pearls interspersed with glittering white rhinestones. It was a beautiful dress, but each time I looked at it, my eyes filled with tears and I had to choke on the sobs as I struggled to hold down the thick emotions that clustered in my throat. It represented the fact that I was going to hurt Raydon. Andrew was probably going to be too late in his promised rescue if he made it at all.

The evening before the cursed event was to take place, I spent the night tossing and turning. Prince Raydon had again pledged his undying love to me when he walked me to my door. I had an odd reaction to his words. They sounded almost true. He seemed to mean them. Did he genuinely love me? Our eyes met for an electric moment. He kissed me softly and tenderly. I surprised myself and kissed him back. I felt something stir within me. My heart responded to the kiss by quickening my pulse. Was I falling in love with him? My insides tingled ever so slightly.

Then I felt guilty. I forced myself to think of Andrew as I closed the door on Raydon. I leaned back against it and twisted my pinky ring. All the intense emotions that I felt for my lost boyfriend rushed into every cell in my body. Andrew was my soul-mate, my life, my true love. He was my anchor in a universe that spun around me, out of my control.

Was it possible to love two guys at the same time? The love I felt for Raydon was a lit match, but my love for Andrew was a forest fire. Should I settle for the tiny flicker and try to feed that small flame, hoping that it would grow over time? Lots of people in the past had to settle for marriages of convenience or weddings arranged by their parents. Some of them found happiness and love in such unions. Could I make the best of this unwanted bonding?

I went to bed with chaotic thoughts knocking around in my head, making it hurt. I closed my eyes and watched my past life experiences flash by in an unending loop stuck on continuous playback. I saw Andrew, my parents, my brother, my friends, my home and the town of Hurricane with its rocky red cliffs and purple plateaus. I had never been so homesick in my whole short life.

Was that chapter of my existence closed and gone forever? Should I write a new story, a tale where I marry a prince and become the queen of an entire planet or one where I become a fugitive from the law, running and hiding away, always hoping to be rescued by a superhero that never came?

I woke with red, puffy eyes and the aura of a growing migraine headache. It felt like someone was beating my brain against the inside of my skull. Shan came in bringing me breakfast. She gave me a pill that instantly killed the pain in my head. They did have excellent remedies for pain on this planet. I wished I could take something that would stop the pain in my heart.

She reassured me that our plan would be successful. We pulled the cyborg from its crate in my closet and set to work preparing it for the ceremony. Shan and Thad had programmed it for me already, using the instructions from Tovin, the kindly, mad scientist I'd met at the cyborg laboratory. I nervously hoped that no one else had learned I was in possession of the android. Whoa! Was I being paranoid much? How could anyone, aside from my trusted friends, possibly know?

"I can't believe how it's a perfect copy of you, Tiana! No one will be able to tell the difference! No one will guess that it isn't you." Thad exclaimed when he came to examine our handiwork.

"It creeps me out. It's sort of like an out-of-body experience where you die and look down at your body while your spirit floats on the ceiling. At least I think that would feel like the weird sensation I get every time I look at that thing," I responded, shivering. Hey, don't say you wouldn't be freaked out if you had an identical twin that was a machine.

We waited on the deck outside my room. The cursed ceremony was to take place at noon. I sat there staring out at the small island, the nearby ocean, and up at the pinkish clouds that drifted between the two suns, contemplating my unknown future. Shan and Thad left me alone and went to check on some wedding details.

As I gazed out over the finely manicured lawns and gardens beneath my tower, something fuzzy caught my eye. The air began to shimmer like a mirage on a desert highway and believe me; I've seen plenty of those. I kept watching it in wonder as it solidified before my astonished eyes. It took the form of a circular cylinder a bit bigger than a port-a-potty. The way it simply came out of the air to appear behind a tree with a thick trunk reminded me of Dr. Who's TARDIS spaceship. I closed my eyes and opened them again in disbelief. I thought the stress might be getting to me, making me see things that weren't there, in an effort to conjure an easy way out of my present predicament.

The door to the structure opened and out stepped the one person in the whole universe that I wanted to see more than anyone else. Yes! It was a long way down there, but I knew immediately that I was not mistaken. I could feel him. My insides tingled, jubilant bells sang inside my head and my pulse started racing with heady, ecstatic excitement. Someone else followed him out. I couldn't recognize that person from so far away. It didn't matter who was with him. He was here! My heart did a happy jig and nearly jumped out of my chest and off the balcony in an effort to close the distance.

Andrew looked up at my tower and waved. I waved back. Then as I watched the two men walk away from the port-a-potty, everything disappeared back into nothingness. It had all vaporized into a delicate mist that dispersed into the atmosphere leaving me staring at the empty space. I sat down on a deck chair in frustration. Had I just imagined that my boyfriend was here to rescue me? Was I finally losing my sanity? Was the looming ceremony the last straw that had caused my mind to snap?

Out of nothing, the two men materialized not two feet away from my chair. I gasped and then I was in his arms. This time I cried tears of relief mixed with intense joy. He held me tightly and kissed my forehead and then my lips were burning as his mouth found mine and passionately told me how much he'd missed me too. I buried my face in his chest as he whispered assurances in my ear that everything was going to be alright. My "Sun, Moon, and Stars" had arrived. He was really here in the flesh. I didn't have to be crazy anymore.

CHAPTER 25

SURPRISE CEREMONY

I had just finished reiterating the weird stuff that had transpired here on Nommo since I had arrived. I gave them the short version, promising to fill in the details when we got back to Earth. Andrew and Bob Zimmerman had explained that they had overshot time by two months. Bob being an alien from the planet, Zarib, was a man of many unusual and diverse talents. One of those talents is his ability to travel through time and space, taking objects and other people with him when necessary. It was that whole "time is relative" thing again. He tried to explain how he did it, but all I heard was "blah, blah, blah." My brain just couldn't take it in with any degree of understanding at that precise minute. I really wanted to get out of there before we were found and I was forced to walk down the aisle. I just wanted to be done with this planet, its super smart inhabitants and their somewhat lovable, but impossible, monarch.

"It's tricky to predict and calculate the exact time and place where you wish to land when you're traveling such extraordinary distances through the galaxy. I now know the true coordinates. I'm relatively sure I can get us back to Earth at the right moment in time, when you're ready to leave this place," Bob assured me.

"Please stop talking nerdy! Let's just get out of here." I didn't have any patience left. I'd used it all up while I had waited nearly forever to be rescued.

"You're right. I'll explain things later. Do you have any loose ends you need to tie up before we go? We need to make our move before the wedding ceremony starts. As much as I'd love to see His Majesty's face when he discovers that it isn't you under that veil, I think we should be on our way. We don't want to start an intergalactic incident. I probably should arrest him and take him back to Earth for trial, but as long as he never returns I think it wise to let things be."

"This android is amazing," Andrew said as he appraised my wedding gown on the lifelike, me-twin mannequin. "It really looks like you or rather, an empty shell of you. It's lovely to look at, but your true beauty comes from within." He said, still clutching me like I might disappear if he loosened his hold. I didn't want to let go of him either. I had spent too many sleepless nights worrying that I might never see or touch him again.

Shan and Thad returned. I introduced them to Andrew and Bob. They got ready to escort my robot down to the flamboyantly decorated and specially prepared castle gardens to recite the marriage vows. I felt a bit guilty about the subterfuge I had planned, but it wasn't my fault. It was Prince Raydon and the rebels who had brought this on themselves.

Using force to get what you want from others is unethical. It should backfire and burn those doing the forcing. I know it doesn't always work out that way, but I have to believe that there is an accounting that takes place eventually, if not in this life then in the next. Everyone deserves to make their own choices. Those choices have natural consequences that are often inescapable. When we make mistakes we nearly always have a chance to make things right, but we still have to deal with the things we have set into motion. I hoped that someday Raydon would understand this. Wow, when did I get so wise?

I hugged my two friends and thanked them for their bravery in helping me pull off this necessary deception. I had written a letter to Prince Raydon explaining that I was sorry I hurt him, but I wasn't the girl he thought I was and I didn't belong in his world. I hoped he would forgive me someday and realize I was right about that.

Okay, I know I'm not the one who should be asking for forgiveness, but I was trying to see things from his point of view. After all, I'm the one with natural empathy. I could step up and be the noble one. It was exceptionally big of me, if I do say so myself. I left the apology note with Shan and instructed her to say she found it on my bed after he discovered it wasn't me in the wedding gown.

We were about to dematerialize with Bob's help when Layla burst into my room flanked by her over-sized, steroid-mutant-henchmen complete with huge, scary guns that were all drawn and pointed directly at us. She had escorted Thad, Shan, and my perfectly coifed cyborg, not so gently, back into my room.

She announced, "If you send that machine in your place, you will still be married to Raydon. There is a responsibility that comes with owning a cyborg of yourself. You are held accountable for anything your android does, so Raydon will still have a claim on you. You will be his legal and lawful wife. Did Tovin neglect telling you that? Sometimes he's a bit absentminded, mad scientist that he is. He accidentally told me that he had created a masterpiece for you. I figured out what you wanted it for. I can't let you deceive our prince like this. You'll marry him as promised or you'll all die!"

"I can't marry him, Layla. I only said I would so you wouldn't kill him. You, of all people, should get that! He still loves you. I know you care for him. You can't deny that you are totally jealous. You are the one who should be marrying him today! We're about the same size. This dress will fit you," I said, amazing myself with the perfect solution to this problem. The voice in my head gave me the inspiration. There was no doubt in my mind that this was the thing to do.

"Me? I couldn't marry him. He betrayed me and had me exiled," she protested. "I'd rather chain him up by his ankles and throw knives at him!" Her muscle-bound minions laughed at that picture. I laughed a little inside because I had wanted to do almost the same thing on numerous occasions. I had a pretty funny visualization of the prince hanging upside down, screaming for mercy as I pelted him with water balloons, preserved in my mind. The knives were a tad too violent for my imagination, but I guess that worked for her. I struggled to remain serious and persuasive.

"No, it was the High Chancellor who set that in motion. He had nothing to do with it. Please Layla, this was meant to be. You should be the one to unite the rebels with the people of the Ildees Islands. You know this is the right course of action. I promise he won't be disappointed. I know he loves you! He said he did. It's a win-win proposition."

"No, I can't take that chance. I'm afraid," she admitted, suddenly looking vulnerable and insecure. I'd never seen her that way before. The way her guards looked at her with shock on their faces told me this was definitely out of character for her. I would have bet my life that no one had seen this look on her face before. She had always appeared to be as confident and arrogant as Raydon. Heck yes, they so belonged together! This had to happen! I wanted it! The universe, fate, destiny and God wanted it! The whole population of Nommo wanted it, they just didn't know it yet.

So, how come they didn't get it? Why was I the only one to see the beauty of this obviously perfect outcome? These super-intelligent aliens could be so dense sometimes. I wanted to slap them up the side of their heads and tell them to get a clue, but I needed to be diplomatic in this intensely delicate, political situation. After all, these trigger-happy, military-minded morons had very frightening automatic weapons aimed at our heads. I figured we'd be instantly dead if I didn't hold my sarcastic wit in check.

"Listen to your inner voice," I tried again to convince her. "It will tell you this is supposed to happen. Deep down inside you know I'm right! Listen to your heart."

"She's right, Layla. You should be the queen!" Sadvik declared.

"It makes perfect sense," Brazzo added. I guess they were smarter than I gave them credit for.

"Yes! Long live Queen Layla!" Nafe chimed in. The rest of her guards erupted in energetic affirmations and sheathed their guns. I took in a deep breath that ballooned my cheeks and then exhaled in an audible sigh of relief. I had no strong desire to meet with instantaneous death today. I had my real prince back. I wanted to go home to my real life on my own planet. Hurricane was right up there with Shangri-La, Paradise and Heaven in my book. I wanted to be there yesterday.

She scanned her men with disbelief as if they had all escaped from an insane asylum or had just sprouted horns. Then she closed her eyes and touched her temples like she was trying to receive instructions from somewhere deep inside of her or had to hold a tension headache at bay. When she opened them, they were full of understanding. I was sure she finally saw the truth in my statement. She broke down and began crying.

I tried to comfort her by patting her arm and saying, "It's okay. This is your date with destiny" or something wise and sort of trite like that. I made the men turn around (I didn't want them staring at my droid in my underwear). I undressed the robot in my closet, and handed my discarded clothing to Layla. She went in my bathroom and changed into the wedding dress. With the veil in place, she looked so much like me, it was eerie. I hugged her and sent her down to become the rightful queen of Nommo. Shan and Thad grinned at me. They both gave me a double thumbs up sign. This was going to work out. The big men with the big guns safely back in their big utility belts marched out like an honor guard behind her, saluting us as they left.

Andrew pulled me to him. We each took one of Bob's hands and disappeared, reappearing at the door of the spaceship port-a-potty. I felt like I was being sucked into a black hole for a fraction of a second, my stomach dropped like it does when riding a fast elevator down to the lowest level of a hundred story building, and then I was in front of the silly looking ship. I must have looked mystified because Bob muttered something about breaking down our molecular structure and then pulling it back together. I only understood the part where he said, "Teleporting is a complicated process."

We ducked through the door and just as Dr. Who's TARDIS is superroomy inside, this spaceship was a little larger than it looked. It didn't matter how roomy and comfy it was because Bob set the coordinates, and before I could blink twice, we landed in his backyard in Hurricane, Utah, USA, on Planet Earth.

I was home! I was really and truly home on Earth! I thought back at how I had longed to see home again and how I had worried and wondered if I ever would. I wanted to kiss the ground, but I kissed Andrew instead. That was much better. He kissed me back. I felt every cell in my body heat up until I was on fire. I had missed him so much, it hurt. From the way he kissed me, I was pretty sure he had missed me a lot too.

"You are my here and now, my always and forever, no matter how far apart we are," he whispered in my ear, "I will always find you and bring you home."

I know, I know, it was completely cheesy and super sentimental. I loved every word.

"Okay you two, we need to debrief. Stop with the hot romance already! Come inside the house before my backyard goes up in flames," Bob laughed as he pushed us toward his back door.

We talked again about all that had happened in the time that I was away. I found out we had returned in the evening of the same day I had left, so no one had time to miss me. That made things easier. I didn't have to try to explain my absence to my parents. The Helamites and the Zariba were the only ones who knew about my extended, forced vacation to a planet located light years from here.

"If Raydon shows his face on this planet again, we will arrest him. He will have to stand trial," Bob promised.

"I don't think he'll make any more trips to Earth. He has a lot of work to do, revamping the government and all. That and being a newlywed should keep him occupied for a very long time," I agreed, "I don't think Layla will let him out of her sight. I'm sure she won't allow him to go cruising around the universe any time in the near future. I think Earth will be off limits forever." I remembered how much she hated me when we met. Now, I thought it was probably just the jealousy she couldn't control. I forgave her. I was getting good at forgiving people.

I was happy with how things had turned out. The people of Nommo would have their second chance with a new democratic government where they would have the freedom of choice to live lives of their own choosing. Raydon would get his second chance to lead his people with their input. He and Layla would get a second chance at love and I, Tiana Dawson, an insignificant earth girl had played a part in the grand scheme of things. I had helped save their planet from blowing itself up. I felt extremely happy about that!

CHAPTER 26

DOWN TO EARTH

It's funny, but saving millions of lives on another planet can certainly give you an appetite. It was Friday evening. I was starving. Andrew and I entered my house to the smell of Mom's special teriyaki chicken with fried rice and snow peas.

"Where have you two been?" My dad said, "You look like one of you swallowed a canary and the other can't believe it!"

What did that mean? I guessed Andrew did the swallowing. I was the one still in shock. I reassessed my boyfriend's face. He did look remarkably pleased with himself. I wondered what my dad thought we'd been doing, but I wasn't going to think about that.

"We were next door talking to Mr. Zimmerman. He wanted to show us the new shed he built in his backyard," Andrew explained, grinning sheepishly. That particular look probably resulted from the fact that, as usual, he knew what my dad was thinking.

"So, what did you think about it? Was it as fantastic as most of Bob Zimmerman's building projects? His family room renovation was more than spectacular with the wall-sized movie screen and the futuristic sound system that shakes the entire neighborhood. The man's a techno-genius!" My dad declared as he questioned us further. My dad was in awe of Bob. If only he knew the wide spectrum of Bob's many alien talents, he would be even more amazed.

"Yeah, Bob's awesome, but his shed looks like an oversized port-a-potty to me," I laughed. "Of course, I didn't tell him that. It's small, but surprisingly roomy inside. He's very proud of it." I grinned at Andrew. He winked and nudged me, taking my hand and squeezing it. Yeah, I got the whole wink-wink-nudge-nudge-Bob's-your-uncle warning. Of course, I didn't tell my dad it was a time travel machine. Some things are just better left unsaid. It would have taken too long to explain. I didn't think my parents were ready to learn about the aliens-are-real-and-some-are-dangerous world that I lived in.

"I was sorry to hear about your aunt's death, Andrew," My mother hugged him.

"Was it sudden?" My father added in a sympathetic tone.

"No, she was my great aunt. She was very old," Andrew adlibbed solemnly. "Thank you for your concern. She lived a long life. She was ready to join her husband, who has been dead for many years. My family lived with her for a while after my parents were killed. She was a great lady. We'll miss her."

This was not an out-and-out lie. He did have a great aunt in Australia who died last December. His family had lived with her for a few months. She was one hundred and fifty two years old when she died. She didn't look a day over thirty five. I'd seen pictures. Helamites age well.

After dinner, I hugged my dad and then my mom. They looked stunned by my sudden, unusual show of affection. I mumbled something about not taking them for granted. I volunteered Andrew and myself for clean up duty. I sent them out of the kitchen. Before she left, Mom spoke and dropped a bomb about Mark.

"Mark's on his way home. He should be here about ten o'clock. He has some important news that he wouldn't tell us over the phone. He wants you to be here, Tiana."

"Okay, do you know what it's about?" I couldn't think what could be so majorly significant that he had to tell us in person.

I was happy that he was coming, but there was an inkling of foreboding trying to insinuate itself into my consciousness. I ignored it. I'd lived under constant stress for too long. I couldn't make myself worry. The two months I had spent on Nommo had made me appreciate my family more than I ever had before. I guess when you think you may never see them again; you realize how precious they are to you. Yeah, sometimes you don't know what you've got until it's gone. I was just too happy I had my life back to stress about what my brother wanted to tell us.

"We'll just have to wait and see," Mom answered from the hall. She didn't sound happy. Okay, I guess I could worry just a little.

"What do you think that's about?" I asked Andrew when we were alone. I was actually asking him what my mother thought it was about, since he would surely know that.

"She seems worried that it's a girl."

"Not Sonya? Do you know what's going on with her and Mark?" I didn't think he'd know much because he'd been captured right after the state basketball tournament. I'd been too wrapped up in my misery over his disappearance to stay up to date on the status of my brother's romance with the abominable-queen-of-mean.

"I've been too focused on finding you and bringing you back. I haven't kept up on her progress in her sordid quest to conquer his heart. It's got to be bad news if it involves her latest attempt at controlling your brother's emotional life. Your guess is as good as mine," he said as we finished putting the dishes in the dishwasher. "It's too bad Raydon didn't kidnap her and take her to Nommo instead of you. I'm not sure anyone would miss her. I know I wouldn't."

"You know, that is kind of sad, but I totally agree." I suddenly felt a bit sorry for the malicious-mistress-of-mayhem. She desperately needed an intervention. Maybe she could change if she wanted to, but I didn't think she was going to want to trade in her malevolent ways anytime during this millennium. I had come to the realization that we all make mistakes. We all deserve second chances, but only if we sincerely want to straighten out our lives, forsake wrongdoing, and try to be better people. I was pretty confident that didn't include her.

Repentance was the word I was searching for. I didn't think Sonya knew the meaning of that term. I couldn't see Sonya wanting to change anything about her malicious mischief. She seemed to get off on destroying others. She'd tried hard to torture and terminate me. Her efforts had almost paid disastrous dividends. If she'd had her way, I'd be dead and buried, or in the clutches of her scary big brother. Since I'd survived the Hellites' torture and been rescued by Andrew, she had seemed determined to bring Mark down in her twisted plot for revenge. I still felt partly responsible for her depraved designs on him.

"Tiana, it's not your fault. You've got to stop blaming yourself. If you have to blame someone, blame me. I brought her into your life. If it weren't for me, you would have been spared from all that agony," Andrew answered the thoughts in my head again. He had that pained look of guilt and grief that I hated to see clouding his face.

"Not. Your. Fault. You're the one who needs to stop feeling guilty!" I kissed the grievous expression off his face. "I got the prize. It was worth the pain. I love you. If that means I have to deal with the meanest girl on Earth, so be it! Mark's strong, he'll recover." I sounded more sure about that "recovering" thing than I felt.

"You wouldn't have been kidnapped by Raydon if it weren't for your association with me!" The stubbornly grim look was back. I wanted to order it gone.

"No, I don't think that had anything to do with you. There was this prophecy about me saving their planet. I'm beginning to believe it was all supposed to happen. I'm seriously glad it's over." I shrugged and kissed him again in an attempt to chase his undeserved guilt away at last. This time he held me close and kissed me back with a fierce fervor that left me weak in the knees.

"Do you think that prophecy was really true? Do you think I was supposed to save that planet? Did God send me there?" A swarm of questions flew from my mouth as I pondered the significance of all I'd been through.

"Do you think that God would create worlds, populate them with people, and then abandon them? In the eleventh chapter of Hebrews, Paul says, 'Through faith we understand that the worlds were framed by the word of God...' Notice that he said 'worlds' not 'world.' In the 147th Psalm, King David said, 'He telleth the number of stars; he calleth them by their names.' God knows his creations. He loves all his children. He works through us to bring about his miracles.

FALLING OFF THE PLANET

"I wouldn't be at all surprised if he had a hand in your adventure. We all have important missions to achieve while we're in this mortal life. The trick is to figure out what they are and how to accomplish them. Things happen for a reason. You're not half as happy as I am that it's over and you're back where you belong," he whispered into my hair. Peace flooded my soul.

We left my parents, promising to be back by ten, so we'd be there for Mark's "important news." We drove to Andrew's house. Before we got to the door, Jillian and Hannah came running out to greet us.

"Thank heavens, you're alright!" Jillian said, hugging me. Then Hannah took her turn.

"We were worried sick. That stupid, Nommoan prince had better never show his face on this planet again!" Hannah exclaimed as she and Jillian hugged their brother.

"I don't think he'll be back," I smiled at them. "I think we insured that he'll have to stay put. His new wife has a jealous nature. She probably won't allow him to travel to Earth again. I'm thinking he's going to be grounded for the rest of his noble life."

"I hate that he has a life-size, doll-robot of you, though," Andrew mumbled under his breath, so only I could hear. "We should have destroyed it, or brought it home with us."

"Yeah, that would have been cool. I could have made it do all my chores. I could have sent it to school when I wanted to ditch classes. Why didn't I think of that?" I wondered.

The Allen brothers came over. Adam and Evelyn joined us, while I recounted my misadventures on the amphibious planet that orbited Sirius. I regaled them with tales of the fancy-dress, dead-celebrity ball and the uprising of the rebels. They applauded my logical persuasion that led the prince to recognize the need for a new democratic government. I told them about being abducted by the rebels and taken to the underwater city. They all loved the part where I plotted to send the cyborg to be the prince's bride They cheered when I told them how I convinced Layla to take my place and marry her one true love. The story would make a thrilling science fiction fairytale. I could call it, "How I avoided marrying Prince Not-So-Charming and saved the planet, Nommo, from certain self-destruction" or something like that, only shorter.

"So, his great grandfather prophesied about a red-haired Earth girl who came and saved Nommo? That is so awesome! You're like a

213

super-hero-chick!" Luke smiled at me. At that moment, I kind of felt like one even though I still don't have any real superpowers to speak of.

"Do you know who Raydon's mother was?" Adam asked smugly. "She was Evelyn's and Jillian's aunt. His father talked her into marrying him and moving to Nommo when he visited Helam. That makes Raydon their cousin."

"Wow, I guess it's a small galaxy after all," I declared with surprise at the connection between families. Perhaps we could invite the Nommoan couple to dinner sometime or maybe not.

Before we knew it, it was time to go back to my house to find out Mark's "important" mysterious news. There was an anxiety attached to thinking about what he might want to share that had taken root in my stomach and started to grow. I quizzed everyone to see if they had any inside information about the relationship between Sonya and my brother.

"I know she and her parents have been staying at the Bellagio in Vegas for a while," Adam frowned, trying to remember. "I'm not sure how long they've been there. They conducted a bunch of seminars. Sonya begged to accompany them, so she could spend time with Mark. Oh, and they found a house in St. George that they're supposed to close on soon. I know they're staying until after that. Then they'll go back to Roswell to get ready for the move. They plan on moving the end of April."

"Oh that's just great!" Hannah complained. "We'll have to act all nice and supportive of Sonya. I'd really rather not!"

"I hear that! Now might be a good time to take a trip to Australia, or pretend we did." Matthew chimed in. We all nodded except Evelyn who always insisted on looking for the best in all people, even Sonya.

"Now, now," Evelyn soothed. "She's just a misguided girl with an ugly past. We need to help her want to change. She's not all that bad."

"Oh yes, she is," Jillian said, "Just ask Tiana. She's been horrid to her. You know she sent her straight into the hands of the Hellites, pretending to be you. Oh, and then there's the way she treated Luke and Matthew. She broke their hearts. She used both of them to build her enormous ego. She's beyond bad."

"That's right, and she manipulated me to try to break Andrew and Tiana up because Andrew wouldn't succumb to her charms," Hannah added venomously. "She has a bad habit of using people to feed her own selfish desires. The girl doesn't deserve our support! Why can't she go back to Roswell and stay there?"

"Better yet, can we send her to live with Cousin Raydon on Nommo?" Jillian asked. We all laughed.

"I understand how you feel, but everyone deserves a chance to change. I'm only asking you to give her another chance," Evelyn persuaded.

"Evelyn's right. Everyone deserves a second chance," I surprised myself by saying that. Huh? I was being incredibly tolerant today. "However, if she crushes my brother, I'm afraid I will be fresh out of compassion. Mark's coming home to bring us some 'important news.' My mom thinks it's about a girl. He's been dating only her, as far as I know. I can't help being nervous about it."

"It doesn't sound good," Luke mused, "but maybe it's something else. I wouldn't wish that she-devil on anyone, at least, not anyone I like."

When it was time for us to return to my house, the biting anxiety inside me was churning acid. I could feel it chipping and eating away chunks of my stomach lining. Sonya Parker seemed to be giving me ulcers from a distance. What was she doing to Mark?

CHAPTER 27

LOVE AND HEARTBURN

Right after we parked in front of my house, Mark pulled up alone in his jeep, and took giant strides across the grass to greet us. At least he didn't have the manipulative monster-girl in tow. He had a gigantic grin pasted across his face like he'd just been asked to join the NBA, or had been given several thousand dollars worth of pocket change. He slapped Andrew on the back and hugged me. He was so obviously happy; maybe his special "secret" was going to be really good news and nothing to do with Sonya.

We walked inside to join my parents in the living room. Mark had started talking basketball with Andrew. He was telling anecdotes about his coach and fellow players. He had played some crazy pranks like super-gluing their shoes to the bottom of their lockers and filling the coach's desk drawers with shaving cream. This was after they filled his locker with stinky gym socks and the coach duck-taped Mark's shorts to the ceiling.

I didn't realize college jocks could be so juvenile. I was under the erroneous impression that his coach was a grown up, silly me.

"Well, you're probably wondering what my special news is," Mark smiled radiantly at us looking like he was about to share a magical secret of the universe. His face was all lit up like a Christmas tree. Then he dropped the S-bomb. "I've asked Sonya to marry me. She said yes."

For a moment, the room fell deadly silent. No one moved. No one spoke. It was as if he had cast a spell with those wicked words that instantly froze us into individual ice sculptures. We just sat there in cold shock and awe with dropped jaws and disbelief written across our incredulous, frozen faces. Had the nefarious, female, space alien gone and secretly lobotomized my brother's brain? I watched my parents' eyes move to look at each other. It was as if Mark had spoken unfamiliar words that made no logical sense to them. They looked at him like he'd flown in from another planet and was speaking gibberish. My mother looked scared. My father proceeded to get angry.

"What? Isn't she seventeen? You're too young to get married! What are you thinking?" Dad asked. He wasn't quite to the "I'm-about-to-blow-a-gasket" stage of his controlled, though growing, rage. His glowing eyes had started pulsing like quasars, radiating the look of death in Mark's direction. I was familiar with this warning level from a few of my past blunders. I knew what was coming next. I always tried to avoid any degree past this phase of my Dad's fury. I was glad he hadn't turned his death-ray-glare on me.

The rest of us stared at Mark with our mouths gaping open, waiting for our brains to catch up and process what had just happened. He seemed totally oblivious to the simmering boatload of anger that was evident under the barely composed facade of my father's facial expression. He must be operating his brain activity under Sonya's influence, or he'd know it was time to cut his losses and activate escape velocity to rocket away from Dad's wrath.

"No, she just turned eighteen. She's already finished high school. She's seriously smart. She's even taken some college courses. She's been accepted at UNLV for Fall Semester. Don't worry; we're not going to do the deed right away. We're thinking maybe during Christmas break. That's almost nine months away. You'll have plenty of time to get used to the idea. Her parents have hired me to help with their seminars. I can start right away, now that basketball season is over. We're saving up for the big event.

"I was wondering if I could give her Grandma Dawson's diamond, the one you've been saving for Tiana. I need to give her a tangible symbol of my undying love for her. I'm sure Andrew will give Tiana a newer, bigger one when he gets around to it. What do you think?" He asked this cheerfully like we should all be positively thrilled by his news. I wondered what color the sky was in the alternate universe where he must currently reside.

"I thought she was Tiana's age. Eighteen isn't much older. You're both babies! You're not mature enough to get married! You don't know what 'undying love' is!" My mother had turned white and was shaking. I thought she was going to scream, have a coronary, or something worse.

Andrew and I knew the tenacious temptress was actually older than that, but Mark wasn't even twenty yet. What had she done to him? Why had she said yes? Was this part of her evil plan to enslave him and then pluck out his heart, pulverize it and trash the pieces? This was way over the edge of the vengeance-is-mine scenario. What evil deeds was she plotting? Had he completely lost his mind? Did she have his brain pickled in a jar and hidden away in her "hope" chest? What did she "hope" to accomplish by this marriage charade? Was she planning to embarrass him to death by standing him up at the altar? Would she let it go that far? Would my brother be destined to be miserable and emotionally scarred for the rest of his mortal life?

The way he had said "tangible symbol of his undying love" made me extremely afraid for him. My brother doesn't say things like that. She had to have ensnared his brain cells and was holding them hostage. Maybe she'd sent them on a permanent vacation to somewhere outside our solar system. I was willing to bet those had to be her words. She must have used her superpower to plant them in his young, inexperienced and impressionable mind where they had taken root and grown into full blown insanity.

"Son, this is unacceptable. It's highly irresponsible. You need to finish school first. You haven't even decided what you want to be when you grow up. You haven't declared a major at college yet." Dad said.

My dad's words were uttered in a slow, restrained manner. Their sound was still at a relatively calm decibel level, but the veins in his forehead were enlarged and visibly throbbing. His blood pressure looked to be rapidly on the rise. His right eye had started to twitch. The death rays emanating from his enlarged pupils were gathering energy and growing in intensity. I could feel the heat from across the room. I hoped he wasn't going to have a stroke.

"Your father's right, Mark. You're not even twenty until November. You're not old enough to make such a life changing decision," Mom's voice was increasing in volume as it had reached a higher than normal pitch. I could tell she was trying hard to keep it under control. Her hands were balled in fists. Her knuckles were turning whiter than her face.

"Do Sonya's parents know? Surely they can't be happy about this? Shouldn't you both date more before you jump into matrimony? What's the rush? You just met this girl. How do you know your feelings for her won't fade when the infatuation dies?"

"They know! They're happy about it! They want me to be their son-in-law! I love her! I've never known a girl like her before. I'm not infatuated. This is so real it hurts. I can't think of anything but her. We're meant for each other. We want to be together forever. You were only twenty one when you married Mom. She was only nineteen. You'd known each other for how long when you got engaged? Oh yeah, it was only six short weeks. You're such hypocrites! You always said I would know when I found the right girl. Well, I've found her. Why can't you be supportive? You said you trusted my judgment. Why can't you accept this and be happy for me?"

Mark's face was beet-red with his own rage now. His voice was starting to squeak like it always does when he's passionate about something that the rest of us think is ridiculous. He looked exactly like this when he wanted to hitchhike to Disneyworld when he was thirteen. Then there was the time just after he got his driver's license when he wanted to drive Mom's Saab all the way to Mexico with Jeremy. This was worse than any of his past bouts with stupidity. His mind was plainly not firing on all cylinders or he'd realize his logic was lost somewhere in deep space.

Andrew and I sat there speechless. We stared at each other in stunned silence. What had happened to my brother's common sense? I knew from sad experience that Psycho-Sonya had the power to get inside your head and make you do things you wouldn't normally do. Her prowess at winning the hearts of men was legendary and unprecedented. She was also known for her blatant, disastrous disregard for those whose hearts she had stolen. Breaking hearts was her favorite competitive sport. The thing I couldn't understand was why her parents had joined the poison party. I was relatively certain that they didn't condone the torment she was infamous for inflicting on the male population of Earth. Even her brother,

James, had seemed repelled by her deviant behavior when it came to her ruthless game of demolishing members of the opposite sex.

"Tiana, you haven't said anything. I know Sonya hasn't treated you well. She's planning to grovel and beg for your forgiveness. Will you give me Grandma's ring? I can't afford to buy one right now. Please Sis, I'm begging here."

"Let me get this straight. You want me to give you the ring my grandmother willed to me, so you can give it to Sonya Parker. Isn't this the crazy, rude, vindictive girl who hates me and treats me like I'm her worst enemy in the whole known universe? The very same girl who spat in my face and told me that I wasn't good enough for Andrew? The mean things I've shared with you don't amount to even a fraction of the evil that girl has shoved in my face. How can you ask me to let you give her my ring?"

I liked the visual of Sonya Parker on her knees pleading for me to forget that she had very nearly ended my life and had caused me much more than considerable and agonizing degrees of suffering. I just couldn't see that happening any time this decade or even during this lifetime.

"Tiana, please give her another chance. She's promised she'll never treat you badly again. What if I give it to her temporarily until I can afford to buy one? Then I'll give it back to you, I swear!"

"Are you sure you want to do this, mate? The girl has a terrible track record. She's never cared about anyone but herself before. She hasn't a compassionate or empathetic bone in her body. How can you be sure her love for you is genuine? You deserve better!" Andrew added when I appealed to him by pushing my thoughts in his direction, begging him to help me dissuade Mark.

"This is what I want more than anything else in the world! She swears she loves me. I believe her. I can't live without her." Mark declared with conviction. "Andrew, you should understand that. I know you feel the same way about my sister."

"Mark, your sister is nothing like Sonya. You can't compare the two. It's like comparing two totally different species. Sonya is a conniving, master-manipulative predator with an evil agenda all her own." Andrew vehemently insisted.

"She's not, I swear! I don't know how you could possible believe that about her. You must not know her the way I do!" My poor deluded brother protested.

Mark was in complete denial. It hurt me to see the extent of the damage he had already incurred. He'd lost all ties to reality and had taken up permanent residence in Crazy Town with the Parkers.

"I need to think about this," I said as I took Andrew's hand and pulled him toward the front door. "I'm not saying no. I'm just not saying yes. We'll be back in an hour. We'll discuss my ring then, if you can talk Mom and Dad into going along with your impossible insanity. Good luck with that!"

My parents looked immediately despondent and disappointed in me. I was bailing on them. I had to get out of there before I came unglued, or got careless and dropped the atomic "alien-with-cruel-superpowers" bomb. We got in Andrew's car and drove up to the top of LaVerkin Hill. It's a good place to think about things and contemplate the big picture.

He killed the engine. We sat there in silence while I stewed in my intense anxiety over my brother's unfortunate fate. He got out, came around to my side and opened the door. He helped me out into the star-filled night and folded me into his arms. As we looked out over the twinkling city lights and up at the broad expanse of heavenly stars, he rocked me side to side, kissing the top of my head. He acted as if I were a child who needed comforting. Then he turned me toward him. He cupped his hands around my face, kissing me with such intensity that my heart burst into flames as the warmth of his love filled me.

I'd sincerely missed the way he always makes me feel loved. I was relieved and happy to be home in his arms where I belonged. Together, we could face anything.

I didn't want to think about the dark queen of evil who had abducted my brother's heart. I just wanted to melt here in Andrew's embrace, knowing that I wasn't alone. I had someone who would never knowingly hurt me, someone who did know the meaning of 'undying love,' and someone who was completely committed to me forever. We kissed for several minutes before that nagging itch snuck back into my head, niggling me and demanding that I pay attention and scratch it.

"We have to tell him," I finally whispered. "He has to know that she has that nasty superpower of manipulating others. He needs to understand where she's coming from and where she actually came from. If by some small chance they really love each other, he's going to have to find out anyway."

"You're right, but how are we going to convince him? You can't just say, 'Brother dearest, your girlfriend is an evil alien from another planet who is controlling your mind and making you think you love her.' How about 'Sonya is way older than you, she's capable of turning your brain to jelly, and she breaks hearts for fun and recreation! Oh, and all this is just an attempt to get revenge on me and Andrew because she's the Harpy from Hell who holds vicious grudges when her evil plans fall short of the catastrophic annihilation of those she loathes.'"

"You could read his mind. That should work, shouldn't it? If he has any recent basketball injuries, you could heal them. I wish you could cure his romantic insanity," I said.

I started brainstorming. It wouldn't be easy. I hated to ask him to show Mark the spaceship. It was his family's most guarded secret, but I realized it might take drastic measures to get my stubborn sibling to see the truth. I thought that might be our last ditch effort if nothing else worked. I was desperately afraid nothing else would. I looked into Andrew's eyes, pleading for his cooperation in bringing my brother into his family's confidences.

"I can't say no to you," he sighed and pulled me in for another long, passionate kiss before guiding me back into his car.

He started the engine. We made our descent back into the Hurricane valley to tell my unsuspecting brother the full truth about his fiancé and about not being alone in the universe. When we stopped in front of my house again, he whipped out his cell phone and made a quick call to Adam.

"I've got to ask for permission," he explained, frowning.

While he argued with his brother, I wondered how things had gone after we left. I suspected my parents had used their vast worldly experience in an attempt to squeeze out every ounce of logic they could argue to get him to see their point of view. I also realized Mark wouldn't crack. They would have to leave the decision up to him in the end, after begging him to think about his future, long and hard, before going any further with this ridiculous marriage business.

They might use their financial "trump card." He had a scholarship that paid for college classes and books, but they still paid for his room and board. They gave him a hefty allowance, so he wouldn't have to work. If they brought that up, he would be forced to rebel by insisting that they loved me more than they did him. He often used this ploy in arguments.

Well, I'd been known to use that one too, only it was him that they loved more in my assertions.

Then he'd throw in the fact that Andrew and I were practically engaged already. Why weren't they opposed to our exclusive relationship? I'd get him back somehow if he used that argument! I didn't need my parents scrutinizing *my* love life.

They would then back off, fearing they might estrange their only son. He was stubborn enough to walk away from their financial support. He would unreservedly disregard their futile warning, and proceed to do exactly as he pleased. Mark was worse than I was at being incredibly obstinate. That's saying a lot. I used to be the most stubborn one, but he caught up and passed me when he became a teenager. I blamed testosterone for that.

Later, when Sonya pulled the proverbial rug out from under him, and his whole world came crumbling down in utter chaos, he'd ask us all why we hadn't stopped him when we had the chance. Of course, he would never give us half a chance.

Yes, I knew my family well. I could predict the outcome of this power struggle. Hopefully, I might still be able to play my ace and save the day. It would be up to Andrew and me to stop all this marriage madness. I tried to get hold of some bravado to stop myself from balking at the thought of the mountain we'd have to scale in order to make Mark believe our accusatory defamation of the beautiful, devious spacewoman he thought he knew and loved.

Andrew took my hand, gave me a stoic glance and said, "Let's do this!" We walked back into the house to face my poor, lovesick and brainwashed brother.

CHAPTER 28

ENLIGHTENMENT

We entered the living room together holding hands and our collective breath. My mom was crying softly in the corner. My dad was pacing nervously. Mark was in the kitchen raiding the refrigerator. That's my brother for you. The apocalypse could be commencing, and he'd have to stop and have a snack. He must think he had the situation under control. Maybe he was making himself a victory sandwich. Not many things can take away my brother's appetite.

If he thought he had lost this power struggle, he would have left already. Yes, I know my brother. His stubborn pride would have dictated that he would have to storm out until my parents had time to realize he was right, or until he became aware that he might be wrong, or he needed money, or a home cooked meal, whichever came first. At any rate, he always came back. The fact that he hadn't left spoke volumes as to the state of his current mindset.

"You don't have to give him the ring, Tiana. My mother wanted you to have it. She wouldn't approve of this." My dad spoke in a loud whisper, stopped pacing and sat down by Mom to comfort her.

"Sweetheart, You do what you think is best," Mom said quietly, nodding toward the kitchen and wiping her eyes. "He'll come to his senses and realize he's not ready to get married. If we push him too much, he'll just rebel more. We need to pretend we trust him to make the right decision. We'll make sure you get the ring back."

"It might not be necessary, Mom," I told her. "Andrew and I are going to take him on a field trip. We're going to help him see the error in judgment that he's made. We'll try to steer him back toward sanity. If this doesn't work, nothing will." My parents looked hopeful.

Mark came out of the kitchen, eating a peanut butter and grape jelly sandwich, his favorite comfort food. He finished it in three big bites, washing it down with a full glass of milk.

"What's this about a field trip?" He asked as he wiped his mouth with his sleeve.

"Andrew and I are going to show you something. I guarantee you'll find it fascinating!" I used my most charming smile, hoping he had missed my comment about his faulty decision making skills.

"Sis, about that ring…" he started, but I interrupted him.

"Of course, you can have it, if you still want it when we get back."

"Does this have something to do with my fiancé?" Mark frowned at us.

"You could say that," Andrew answered. "Trust me, mate; it's something you should know about. We're going to have a little show and tell session you won't want to miss." He took one of Mark's arms. I linked my arm through the other. We led him out to the car. We all got in and fastened our seatbelts. This could prove to be a bumpy ride for my elder brother.

"What's this about? Where are you taking me?"

"This is sort of an intervention. If you are truly planning to marry Sonya, these are things you need to learn," Andrew spoke with solemn authority.

"Okay, then. Start talking! Let's get it over with! Say what you want to say, but you won't change my mind about her." Mark folded his arms across his chest taking a defensive posture in the back seat while Andrew proceeded to drive to his family's pharmaceutical warehouse. I turned in my seat, so I could face him.

"Do you remember when we went camping last September on Cedar Mountain? We were sitting around the campfire. You and Jeremy were drilling me about Andrew. I said he was really strong, he seemed to heal me with his hands and he had the uncanny ability to read my thoughts. Do you remember what you said?"

"Let me think. Oh yeah, I remember. Jeremy said he thought Andrew was a superhero. I said he had to be an extraterrestrial from a distant planet in a galaxy far, far away. You called me a dork or something. So what? Australia is far away, but it's hardly another planet. What does that have to do with Sonya? She never lived in Australia. Where are you going with this?"

"You were half right, mate, different planet, same galaxy. Your girl-friend is from the same planet I'm from. She has her own unique skill set. It involves mesmerizing men with her special brand of very potent mind control. She specializes in getting guys to fall in love with her. Then she twists out their hearts, cooks them slowly over an open flame and eats them for breakfast," Andrew said as we pulled to a stop in front of the spaceship garage.

"Oh you guys are hilarious! What's the punch line? Are you punking me because I used to believe in UFOs when I was a kid or what? Are you making fun of my love for sci-fi thrillers? You can't convince me that Sonya is an evil alien who is controlling my private thoughts. If she wants to abduct me and experiment on my body, I'm totally okay with that!" Mark laughed loudly. He thought he was making a super funny joke. He looked disappointed when we didn't laugh. He didn't know the joke was on him.

"You are closer to the truth than you think!" Andrew said.

I turned to stare Mark down without humor. For once, I wanted him to be serious. How was I going to make him recognize the truth when it was so darned unbelievable? It was time for some undeniable proof.

"Maybe, you'd like a demonstration. Think of some things that Andrew couldn't possibly guess. Visualize and hold onto them. He'll read your mind right here, right now."

"What kind of things?" Mark asked, looking like he never had an original thought in his life before.

"Memories, goals, things you have done or want to do. Make it as complicated as you want. Your mind is pretty easy to read," Andrew explained.

"Hey, does that mean you've read my mind before? Okay, I'll bite. Wait a minute while I form some completely unreadable, random thoughts." He closed his eyes, raised one finger in the air to make us stop talking, so he could concentrate for a few minutes.

He took a deep breath and let it out slowly. Then he said, "I'm ready. Do your best. You'll never get this right!"

"Ug! Lose the make out session with Sonya. I don't want to view your intimate, and extremely nauseating, memories. Hanging me upside down from my toes is a bit gruesome. Forcing Tiana to beg your forgiveness and kiss your feet is way over the top. It will never happen. Do you harbor some kind of foot fetish? Winning the MVP in the all-star college basketball game is a stretch too. Talking us into going for a hot fudge sundae after this might be doable, if you still have an appetite when we're done with you. I must say you have a particularly vivid imagination for an Earthling. No offense, but your mind is a little attention deficient. It's sometimes hard to keep up with the rapid fire of constantly changing thoughts."

Andrew was still driving. He didn't even have to look at Mark to delve into his mind. Yeah, he's absolutely that good at mind reading. Mark had to be impressed. I sure was.

"Wow, you're great at reading minds, dude!" Mark admitted. "Remind me not to get on your bad side. I'll have to be extra careful about what I think around you. But hey, that's just a neat parlor trick. There are people from this planet who do that for the entertainment of others. You should get your own talk show. You could interview celebs and tell everyone what they're really thinking. We could call you *The Amazing Andrew*, or something more mysterious like *Andrew Martin, Mind Reader Extraordinaire*. What else have you got?"

"Well, I could use my exceptional strength to throw you a few hundred yards and let you collide with the pavement. Then I could heal your injuries. What's your preference? Do you want me to break your arm or your leg? I'll put it back together when I'm done. I could knock out your front teeth and replace them, or give you two black eyes. All of these things would hurt, but you're not afraid of a bit of suffering are you? After all, you want to marry the queen of pain, don't you mate?"

"No, let's just take him to see the proof," I interrupted Andrew's teasing tirade. I knew he was kidding, but my brother was starting to look nervous. My boyfriend was doing a perfect imitation of "bad cop," so the least I could do was play the good one.

"Oh come on, Love," Andrew begged, "Let me have some fun here. I won't do too much damage. I promise I'll fix him when I'm through. If we let Sonya have at him, he may never recover. She's not much for fixing what she breaks. We need to show him some tough love now to save him from some hefty heartache later."

"Just show me the proof already? I don't believe you could really hurt me, but just in case, I'd rather see whatever it is you want to show me that proves you and Sonya are from another planet, like that's even possible. It should be mildly amusing, if nothing else." Mark folded his arms and rolled his eyes at us.

We got out of the car and escorted him through the many doors and the impressive security system. Mark kept rolling his eyes and snorting at every successive entry.

"What's with the ridiculous barrage of locked doors? What could possibly warrant such security measures? What are you protecting inside? No, let me guess. There are giant-green-android-monsters stored inside that you are programming to take over the U.S. government. How about a secret laboratory with tiny micro-organisms that you can plant in unsuspecting human brains, so you can control Earthlings like robots and make them into a zombie army to fight opposing forces in your plot for complete world domination?"

"You'll see," Andrew answered. "If I tell you, it won't be a surprise. You'll be the second Earth person to see it."

He stopped before the last door and said, "You have to promise not to disclose this to anyone. I really don't want to have to kill my future brother-in-law. Wiping your brain clean might leave some serious holes in your long term memory."

"Okay, you have my word. I won't tell a soul." Mark crossed his heart. He kept chuckling to himself and shaking his head. He apparently thought this was some monumental, elaborate prank we were pulling on him. Was he in for a rude awakening or what?

"Dude, you are one great actor! I almost believe there's something worth seeing stored inside. Are you growing new bodies in there, so evil,

invisible aliens can come and possess them to help you and Sonya exterminate all the current inhabitants of Earth? I've got it! You're cross breeding
grizzly monsters from your planet with polar bears, so you can sick them
on industrial polluters and save the Earth from global warming!" We both
rolled our eyes at my sibling. He has an overactive imagination. Even I
stand in awe at the stuff he can and does think up.

Finally, we made it through the maze and into the huge, cavernous
room. Andrew flipped on the lights. We watched as my brother laid eyes on
his first and only real sighting of an honest-to-goodness, flying saucer from
another planet. Mark's eyes nearly popped out of his head. His jaw dropped
to the floor. He wobbled and went completely silent. I thought he might
be about to pass out. Then he got this enormous, silly smile on his face. His
eyes lit up with sudden delight.

"Holy stinkin' crap! What the heck? It's awesome! Am I hallucinating?
Are you making a movie or what? Where'd you get it? Did you hypnotize
me or something? Is it a genuine, alien spaceship? It's amazingly realistic!
I can't believe it! I need to touch it. Can I touch it? Is it going to disappear
if I do? Can we go inside? Does it actually fly? Let's take it cruising! I can't
imagine how Tiana managed to keep this a secret, especially from me. You
know how much I've always wanted this alien stuff to be real! You knew,
and you didn't tell me! How could you two leave me in the dark until now?
You didn't trust me, did you? That is so wrong! I am extremely offended
by your lack of trust."

"Sorry Mark, but everything is on a need to know basis with our kind.
We do try to avoid mass hysteria at all costs. You understand, don't you?
We can't let information about us leak out. What would people think?
More importantly, what do you think they would do? It's the spaceship that
my family and fellow Helamites used to escape from our home planet and
set up residence on yours," Andrew told him calmly.

He gave Mark the guided tour, complete with all the smallest details.
My brother had more questions than I can even remember. He was so
into science fiction. He grew up believing in aliens the way the rest of
us believed in Santa Claus or the Tooth Fairy. This was his wildest dream
come true. When he knew all the history of the Helamites and had seen
all the wonders of the magnificent machine, we left the facility. We sat
in Andrew's car to discuss the reasons why we had chosen to let him in
on our big secret.

"Tell me everything! I want to know all the juicy, spacey stuff. Don't leave anything out. This is so flipping awesome! It's a shame I can't tell anyone. Jeremy would freak out! Are you sure I can't tell Jeremy? He can keep a secret. Well, maybe not. There was that time we...oh, never mind.

"Seriously, this is just too uber-fantastic for words. I have a hard time believing that all intelligent alien life is human, though. How could you possibly know that? Have you visited every inhabited planet in the known universe? I really wish you were insects, reptiles, or something a bit more exciting. I'll bet there's some semi-intelligent life out there that you don't know about. Well, at least you have superpowers, right? How did you manage to keep this all on the down low, Tiana? I never knew you could keep a secret. You never could before."

"You wouldn't have believed me, if you hadn't seen the evidence with your own two eyes," I answered, barely masking my irritation at his insinuation that I wasn't good at keeping secrets. I kept secrets from him all the time. Just because I couldn't think of any besides aliens walking among us, didn't mean I couldn't be totally discreet. Anyway, this space thing was the biggest secret ever. I hadn't told anyone until tonight. I deserved an award for super secret keeping!

Andrew told my brother about my unpleasant torture experience with the Hellites, and how Sonya had sent me there hoping they'd kill me. He explained how she could enter your mind and manipulate you into doing whatever she wished. He told him the difference between manipulators and motivators. He even shared some of the other talents his fellow aliens possessed. Mark seemed to be pondering everything he said. He kept saying things like, "No way!" and "Shut up!" and "Shut the front door!"

When Andrew finished, he finally grinned ear to ear and said, "Dude! So, have you been to any other planets lately?"

"Actually, I just rescued your sister from the Planet Nommo in the Sirius star system. She was kidnapped by the prince, who planned to make her his wife. She saved their world from destroying itself. Your sister is a superhero in her own rite."

"Nuh-uh! You've got to be kidding! How come nobody noticed she was gone?" He scoffed at my superhero status. I tried not to take offense. I seldom get the respect I deserve from my older brother. I've learned to live with that.

"I had to do some time travel to get her back to the right place at the right time and to avoid scaring your parents. She was gone nearly two months. By using a fellow alien's 'Time and Space Relativity Machine,' I was able to keep her absence under wraps. You do understand that time is relative. Am I right? Your mom and dad don't know about any of this. I strongly suggest that you don't share what you know."

"Oh, don't worry. I'm very good at keeping secrets from my parents. Yeah, I know Einstein's Special Theory of Relativity. Any self respecting connoisseur of science fiction is aware of that. This is just so incredible! I want to know all about your trip. Give it to me straight. I can take it. I've been fantasizing about this kind of stuff for most of my life!"

He turned to me and asked, "Tiana, why didn't you want to marry the Nommoan Prince? No offense, Andrew, but she could have been the queen of a whole planet! Who would willingly give that up?"

"Very funny! Maybe I should throw you at a wall, just to show you what I'm capable of with my superior strength and healing powers," Andrew said with narrowed eyes.

"No thanks, I'm good. You made a wise choice, Sis! Who wants to marry a prince and be the queen of some old watery world that's light years away from here, anyway? You'd miss me too much!"

I told him about my adventures on the planet, Nommo. He was duly impressed by my escapades with His Eminency, Prince Raydon. I described the weird wildlife, the strange landscapes, the super-smart, Spock-like, supposedly unemotional Nommoan people, and how I convinced them to make a new government with equality for all and second chances for the young people who had made unfortunate mistakes that led to their unjustified enslavement.

It sounded like a surreal dream to me, now that it was over, and I was home. I explained about the machine that scanned my memories and the one that I used to download the knowledge of Nommoan culture that I needed to attend the ball with the fake, dead Earth celebrities. Darn it! I should have smuggled one of those machines that programmed knowledge into brains off that planet. It would have made school so much easier. It could have freed up a lot of my time. Anyhow, Mark was eating up everything I said. It felt good to confide in my brother and have him actually believe me.

"This is freaking fantastic! My sister's dating a spaceman; she's literally fallen off this planet and gone to one nobody from Earth has ever seen or heard of. Best of all, my fiancé is a gorgeous extraterrestrial with super powers! I feel like I've died and gone to Science Fiction Heaven!"

"This is serious, Mark. Think about it! We told you all this, so you could avoid getting used. She may be playing with your emotions, plotting to destroy you to get back at us. She hates Tiana and me. She could be driven by her need for revenge. Don't you find that disturbing? Don't you want to know the truth about her intentions? Are you sure she's being honest with you? Every romantic relationship she's had has ended badly, with her dumping the poor guy and ripping his heart to shreds. I'm the only one who ever dumped her. She hates me for it. Do you feel lucky? Do you think you're different from everyone else?" Andrew asked him the hard questions.

"Whoa! I never thought of it like that." Mark seemed to be considering Andrew's solemn words. He suddenly looked sad and deflated, as he contemplated what this all meant to his love life. His abrupt mood change from exuberant mania to depressed despondency was hard to watch. Then his face changed again to somewhere in between the two contrasting emotions.

"I still think you're wrong about her feelings for me, but you could be right. That is seriously scary. And yes, I am definitely different from everyone else on this planet. However, I still need time to think about this."

Did I tell you my brother has an exceptionally high opinion of himself? Yeah, he's never had any self esteem issues to speak of. Whatever happened, I was confident he would recover.

"What we're telling you is that you need to make sure your feelings for her are genuine and that she's not playing you for a fool by using her manipulative abilities. Make sure she really loves you before you get yourself in too deep. We won't tell you what to do. It's your life. We just want you to know what you may be getting into. We don't want you to get hurt." I told him.

"If you still want Grandma Dawson's diamond, it's yours. If you can honestly say that Sonya has changed her evil ways, I'll support you. I'm willing to forgive all the pain she has pushed on me, if she can truly make you happy. Please just make sure that she really loves you and you really love her before you hand over your heart!"

Mark nodded and gulped. All the blood had drained from his face. He didn't say another word on the way home. When we got there, he muttered his "thanks" and ran into the house where he went directly to his room. My parents begged to know what had happened.

"He has a lot to think about," Andrew told them.

"Yeah, give him some space," I added. "I don't know if he's going to want the ring after all. We filled him in on Sonya's history, which is less than stellar, when it comes to men. He's got some hard decisions to make. He'll have to confront her with her past before he can plan his future."

CHAPTER 29

FORGIVENESS

Andrew and I sat on the leather sofa in my living room which sounds like a mundane, ordinary sort of thing to do. I'd done it thousands of times before, so many times, in fact, that I took it for granted until now. Now it was the best place on Earth as long as Andrew was here, sitting beside me. I had thought I might never see Andrew or home again while I was stuck on Nommo. Falling off the planet had been hard on me. I realize not many people can relate to that, but I don't recommend it. Going to another planet involves some serious culture shock, especially when you think you might be staying there forever.

My parents had gone to bed leaving us with some time alone at last. We hadn't had a chance to talk, one on one, about my trip off the planet. I wondered if he were mad at me for going to Quail Creek Reservoir looking for the Nommoans who had kidnapped him, James, and Tiffany. I'd do it again if I had too, but I remembered our discussion after the Hellites had tortured me and how I'd promised not to go looking for bad spacemen. I also recalled that I had voiced the exception that if he were being held captive, I just might have to break that promise without remorse.

I wondered what had happened with Tiffany. Did she retain her memories of being abducted? There was much to discuss. I didn't know where to begin. It felt so right just to snuggle on the couch and feel his arms around me. I let the contented relief encompass me as I took in the perfection of this moment. I hated to ruin it by speaking.

"I'm not mad at you," Andrew read my thoughts. "How could you think I would be? You saved me this time, Love. I'm not sure what would have happened to us if you hadn't figured out where the Nommoan's ship was hiding. It was terribly clever of you. I wish you hadn't come alone, however. If there's a next time, and I seriously hope there isn't, please bring backup. Call Bob or Adam. Okay? I need you to promise me. I'm not sure I'm strong enough to go through losing you again! You could be the death of me yet."

"Okay, I'll try to remember that. I don't want to cause your death," I sighed. "I wasn't confident enough that I knew what I was doing to ask for back up. I was just following a whim, trying to take some action to distract me from the world of worry that had taken up residency in my over-active imagination. I couldn't just sit around and do nothing like everyone told me to do. What happened with Tiffany?"

"James and I took her to Bob. We used your car and drove her home, after Bob gave her a slight case of amnesia that erased all memories of her abduction. We thought it best to make her forget. Our truth is a hard secret to keep. You know she's the 'gossip girl' of Hurricane High."

I glared at him. I was appalled at the suggestion that she would give us away. "You didn't trust my best friend to keep our secret?"

"It's not like she'd want to tell, but she's a teenage girl. She was bound to let something slip out! Are you willing to bet our lives on her ability to keep secrets?"

"I guess not," I admitted reluctantly with a shoulder shrug. It would have been so fabulous to be able to confide in my BFF.

"I'm still a little nervous about telling your brother, but I understand he had to know. I think we can trust him. He has a stake in this. I'm glad you left your keys in your car back at the reservoir because the prince had destroyed all our cell phones. Tiffany thinks she lost hers. She's very angry about that. If we hadn't erased her memory of Raydon, our princely Nommoan kidnapper, she probably would have gone back to the bottom of that lake looking for him with a baseball bat. She was persistently determined to find her personal property. She seemed completely fearless in the face of the injustice of losing it."

"Yeah, I think she inherited that trait from her father, the district attorney. What do you think is going to happen with Mark and Sonya?"

"Let's not talk about that anymore tonight," he said, touching a finger to my lips and then proceeded to help me forget about everything except us. I closed my eyes, inhaled his uniquely musky-spice-mixed-with-sunshine intoxicating scent, and melted into him. I wanted nothing more than to experience his strong, comforting arms embracing me. A few of his white hot kisses trailing from his lips down my neck and back to my mouth caused me to lose all my fearful memories of Nommo. His touch was sending that potent electrical excitement surging through me, keeping pace with the increased pulse rate of my happy heart. His own was drumming in response to mine. He whispered all the words I hungered for with a low growl in my right ear. He's certainly talented at helping me live in the moment and causing me to shut out everything except the two of us. I was home again, in the right time and in the right place where I belonged. I had my life back.

That night, I dreamed about Sonya. I was back on Nommo, sitting bolt upright on a red, velvet-covered throne at court, wearing fancy, flowing robes that shimmered an opalescent blue-green. An intricately cut, gleaming, golden crown set with emeralds and sapphires adorned my head. Around my neck, I wore multiple strands of pearls in assorted colors and my fingers dripped with silver and diamonds. In this very vivid dream, I must have married Raydon because I was most definitely and undeniably a queen. Two guards in their black ninja uniforms brought the hated Helamite to stand before me.

"This woman stands convicted of inflicting emotional and physical pain on Your Majesty, the Royal Queen of Nommo and your brother, Mark Dawson. Her crimes are evil and loathsome and might I add, totally unacceptable. It is your duty to decide the punishment for her many vicious and grievous transgressions," one of the ninja guards said bowing his head respectfully.

"What will it be, Your Highness? Shall she be executed, exiled, or sentenced to a life of servitude? Your will is our command and will be swiftly enforced," the other ninja guy spoke.

The crowded courtroom, which looked more like a packed football stadium, began to chant, "Kill her! Kill her!" over and over. I was leaning toward that particular penalty myself. It seemed a perfectly plausible and fitting end to the evil entity that stood cowering before me. Just as I was about to make the ruling and give a thumbs-down order, the voice in my head stopped me from making the gesture or speaking.

Everyone deserves a second chance. Even Sonya should have the opportunity to clean up her act and change her life. To err is human, to forgive divine! Who said that? What was Alexander Pope doing in my head?

Why do I always have to be the divine one? I didn't want to have this internal dialogue now. I deserved justice. I should at least get some payback in my own dream! I told that voice to shut up. I wanted my revenge. I wanted her to pay the price for all the pain and suffering she had caused me and my brother and all those unfortunate, victimized boys who innocently gave her their poor, unsuspecting hearts, the ones who had to watch as she smashed and obliterated them before their sad, horrified eyes. Her mere existence was a menacing threat to the male population on any planet. I wanted to strike a blow for all mankind! I didn't think Sonya qualified for forgiveness. I thought it was majorly magnanimous of me to carry out this execution, to rid the universe of this brazen, bitter Barbie-look-alike.

I looked into her big, blue-gray eyes. That was an ginormous mistake. She was crying and begging me for mercy. "I love Mark. I really do! I'm sorry for all the agony I've caused. Please forgive me, Tiana! Please, I'm pleading for mercy. You have to believe me! I've lied in the past, but I swear I'm telling you the truth now. Originally, I had wanted to hurt him to get back at you. Then everything changed when I fell in love with him. Your brother has made me want to be a better person." She approached my throne and dropped to her knees, wrapping her arms around my legs. The ninja guys tried to pull her off of me, but she was too strong. The stupid alien was using her superpowers on me. I wanted to be done with her super-badly! I tried to pry away her clutching claws, but it was no use. I started struggling and screaming.

She flashed me a wicked grin. She wasn't sorry. She just wanted me to look mean, cruel and unforgiving in front of absolutely everyone on the planet. Ever the manipulator, she was carrying out her own abhorrent agenda once again! I heard comments around me, "Oh the poor dear! She's sorry for her misdeeds. She deserves another chance. She's too beautiful to be that bad! Show some mercy! Exonerate the lovely, sweet girl! Free her! Free her!"

I woke up with a start. I tried to understand the nightmare. Was it nonsense or was it a warning of things to come? Had she truly been acting remorseful in my dream? Why had the voice in my head taken her side? Was I fighting with my conscience? Should I forgive her for all her horrendous, abominable acts against me and those I loved? I wanted to extinguish this inner turmoil. It was distressing enough that I had to deal with her in real life, now she was invading my dreams. The reality that she might even infiltrate my family by marrying my brother made me want to throw things.

Later that morning, Mark and I sat across from each other at the breakfast table. Dad was making pancakes and Mom had fried up some eggs and bacon. They had on their everything-is-going-to-be-fine faces complete with oversized, fake smiles. Dad was trying to draw Mark into a conversation about "March Madness." It was about halfway through the "Big Dance." That's college basketball talk for the NCAA tournament. UNLV was already out, having won only their first game, much to my brother's disappointment.

Mark didn't even feign an interest in the final four. He was uncharacteristically sullen and unresponsive. His answers to my father's questions were bordering on robotic. I could tell this baffled my dad. He didn't know Mark was despairing over Sonya. I was sure my brother was trying to decide how to approach her to elicit the absolute truth about their relationship. He had to contemplate what the whole aliens-are-real-and-I'm-dating-one reality would mean for him and for his relationship with her.

"I want you and Andrew to come with me to James' apartment. I'm meeting her there. I need to know what she's thinking so I'll know for sure whether she's manipulating me or not." Mark leaned across the table and whispered to me.

"I don't know if that's a good idea. If she sees Andrew she'll get suspicious. Her guard will go up. She can shield her thoughts when she wants to," I whispered back.

"How about if I take her to the Pizza Factory for lunch and you guys are waiting there? You can keep out of sight, staying within earshot. I need back up on this, Sis. I have to know the truth. I tend to turn stupid around her. Keeping my focus is hopelessly hard. Sometimes I do crazy things. I never understood it before, but now it makes perfect sense that she was exerting some freaky mind control over me with her alien, manipulation powers."

"I'll ask Andrew," I said reaching for my phone on the kitchen counter. It started ringing when I picked it up.

"It's him. He's psychic." I thought Mark would laugh at that, but he just nodded his head as though he'd believe anything I shared with him today. He'd never endowed me with so much credibility. It made me feel unusually powerful.

"Hey," I answered the call.

"Are we going to play spies today?" Andrew inquired. I don't know why he bothered to ask.

"Absolutely, your psychic abilities are unsurpassed on this planet, Mr. Smarty Pants. Bring your James Bond persona and get over here fast, so we can plot our undercover course of action."

"I'm already there," he chuckled. "Look out your window. I'm parked out front."

"Come in and have breakfast. The folks have whipped up a cheer-up-because-everything's-normal feast of eggs..."

"Don't tell me! Bacon and pancakes with strawberries and whipped cream are also on the menu!"

"No fair! You're too perfect today. Stop it now. You're totally going to freak Mark out. This is all new to him." I laughed as the doorbell rang and I went to let him in.

My brother stared after me like I'd introduced him to a new parallel dimension. I remembered how unnerved I had been when I found out I was dating a genuine, card-carrying spaceman. I could relate to my brother's fragile state of being. His situation was worse because he couldn't be sure of his feelings or hers since her peculiar brand of powers might be messing with his mind.

My parents finished. They left Mark and me with the responsibility of clean-up duty. Dad was going fishing with Bob. Mom had some serious shopping to do. They needed to take their own therapeutic measures to get past the stress of last night.

We welcomed the privacy to discuss and plot our next move. My brother wanted so badly to know that Sonya honestly did love him. He also needed to be sure that his feelings for her were real and not conjured up by her mind-boggling powers of persuasion.

If she were deceiving him, how would we know? Our best chance was to have Andrew read her thoughts. She couldn't know he was eavesdropping, or she would shield her intentions. He had to get a read on her and stay in her mind long enough to understand fully what her romantic relationship motivation entailed. It wasn't going to be easy. Going into Sonya's mind was never fun.

"If I do this, you are going to owe me big-time," Andrew sighed. Her psyche was one of his least favorite places to boldly go. "Are you sure you want to know what's going on in her head?"

"It's better to find out now," Mark said. He didn't look altogether sure of that. "The pain will just escalate, the longer I hold onto the hope. I need to know if any of this is real. If it's not, it needs to end now, before I lose my ability to walk away. I don't trust myself to be strong enough to say goodbye if it goes on any longer."

Three hours later, we were seated in a secluded booth at the Pizza Factory. We saw Mark and Sonya enter and take a booth where we could see my brother's face and the back of the siren's head. Sonya was speaking animatedly about how they could make their upcoming nuptials work while they attended college. She kept on chattering contentedly, explaining how her parents would help them with finances and how they could live in married student housing while they finished their education. Andrew's eyes were closed as he tried to sift through the things in her head. After a few minutes, he opened his eyes. His brow was furrowed with puzzlement.

"As far as I can tell, she seems to mean everything she's saying. She isn't making any attempts at controlling Mark's mind. If this is an act, it's undetectable. For all intents and purposes, I think she's telling the truth. She appears to believe her own words. Either that or she's better at deception than we ever guessed."

"Are you sure she's for real?" I looked at him with amazement.

"As positive as I can be. If she were anyone else, I would be absolutely sure. Since it's her, I still have my doubts, but there's nothing to substantiate my suspicions. As far as I can tell, she's in love with your brother and she's telling him the truth. What do you want me to say?"

"I guess you'll have to tell him what you've told me. If she really loves him, I think we'll have to back off and let it play out. It's his life and his choice. We shouldn't interfere," I replied without conviction.

I wanted to interfere. I wanted to shield my brother from her seductive charms. Was he even strong enough to make the hard choices? I couldn't believe this would end well. Even if she loved him, I wasn't sure it was enough to keep her from destroying him. She was not now, nor had she ever been, a nice person. This love affair could be doomed to bring him some extreme heartache. I knew in my heart that he had to decide for himself. The choice was his, not mine, to make. It was his life. He had to live it. I wasn't sure I wanted to watch. What else could I do?

CHAPTER 30

ACCEPTANCE

As we watched my brother and his fiancé, we saw their euphoric mood change dramatically as the scene played out for us. Mark related some of his secrets, telling her things he had never told anyone before. I knew most of them. They were mostly silly and inconsequential. Things like how he got arrested once for malicious mischief when he toilet-papered some girl's house whose father was a municipal judge, and the time he forgot where he parked our dad's Acura, so he pretended it had been stolen.

He told her about the incident when he threw an egg at an off-duty police officer. This cop pursued Mark through stop signs, red lights, etc. He was finally surrounded and stopped by six police cruisers. When he got out of the car, he said, "Was this really necessary?" That prompted the police to shove him spread eagle against the car as they roughly patted him down. He had his license suspended, and had to do community service for a year. I think he might have told a few people about that grand adventure.

Of course, my favorite was the episode when he water-ballooned couples at a rival high school's prom. He got caught and suspended from school. Okay, everyone at Northridge High knew about that. He also related some embarrassing moments like losing his swimming trunks at the city pool when he dove off the high board to impress Becky Knudsen. Darn, I missed that one. I wondered why she always looked at him funny. How did he manage to keep that a secret from me? I can't believe no one told me.

When he finished baring his soul, he asked her point blank if she had any secrets or regrets to share with him. She didn't skip a beat, swearing she couldn't think of anything. Then she remembered one time taking James' corvette without asking permission, running out of gas and then calling him to demand that he drop everything to come get her. She laughed at her own ironic, erratic behavior. After relating that, she promptly said she had no "real" secrets from him, at least nothing of any importance. Liar, liar, pants on fire! I swear I saw her nose grow an inch or two with that whopper!

"I'd never keep any significant secret from you," she purred as she lied flirtatiously through her pearly, white teeth. I could feel her flaming panties burning hot from where we sat. How could she blatantly lie so convincingly? I guess she'd had plenty of practice. Heck, I'd have believed her if I didn't know any better.

"Are you absolutely sure about that?" His tone became instantly somber and brutally serious. Even the queen of liars should have noticed the change. The temperature plummeted by at least ten degrees.

"Of course, how could I keep anything from you, Sugar-lips?" She said that with a teasing gleam as she batted the eyelashes attached to her lying eyes.

I had a sudden urge to giggle. I put a hand over my mouth to suppress the laughter that threatened to sneak out and give away our hidden position. She called Mark "Sugar-lips." Seriously? How lame is that? It was just plain wrong, but, at the same time, it was totally hilarious! I was choking on my mirth. I could positively get some mileage out of that ridiculous, although kind of sweet, nickname, if I ever dared repeat it. Mark didn't seem amused by the silly, affectionate pet-name she had bestowed on him. Go figure.

He looked her straight in her big, blue eyes and said, "You're lying to me! I'm going to give you one more chance to tell me the truth. If you don't, I'm walking. If you can't trust me with your secrets, I can't trust you with my future!"

Bravo! I wanted to clap and cheer like crazy. I held my breath instead, waiting to hear the Mother of All Liars' reaction. My brother had just grown a spine. My respect for him had doubled.

"What are you talking about? Did Tiana tell you lies about me? Don't you see? She hates me! She's been insanely jealous of me since we first met. I don't understand why she's always had it in for me! I've never done anything to deserve her loathing. I'm totally blameless. I'm the victim here. You must see that. Your sister has some gigantic trust issues. She wrongly thought I was trying to steal Andrew from her, as if! Is Tiana paranoid much? You can't possibly listen to her.

"That insane, insecure girl resents me for no good reason. She's been trying to sabotage our relationship from the beginning. She'd say anything to keep us apart. She just doesn't want us to be happy. She's willing to go to considerable lengths to insure that we break up! I know she's your sister and all that, but surely you can see what a little liar she is?"

I saw Mark's jaw tense and his eyes narrowed as he answered. Wow! She had said all the wrong things. My brother has a license to harass and criticize me, but he doesn't look kindly on anyone else bad-mouthing his only sister.

My own blood was boiling as I watched her disrespect me, calling me the liar. The irony was palpable. I wanted lightening to strike her false heart. I wanted her lying tongue to die, dry up and fall out of her prevaricating mouth. I found myself fighting the urge to march over there and slap her across her deceptively beautiful face. The desire to deck her was so strong; I started to rise to my feet. Andrew reached across the table, grabbed my hands, holding me back, as he shook his head at me.

"My sister isn't a liar, you are! She was right about you. You don't care about me! You've been manipulating me, using me, playing me for a fool. You planned to get revenge on her because you couldn't have Andrew. You wanted to break my heart and taunt her while you did it. Were you planning to break up soon, or did you want to draw things out to humiliate me by standing me up on our wedding day? Well, you win! I think I do love you, but I'll get over it. We're done here! It's over!"

With those words, he got up, slammed some money on the table and stormed out of the restaurant. Everyone stared after him. A hush fell over the restaurant. Then all eyes went automatically back to Sonya. She hastily arose and took off after him.

"Wait, I'm sorry! Let me explain, Mark! Please!" She called after him, but he was already out the door. She ran to catch him. Her spiked heals clattered noisily on the wooden floor.

I don't know if she caught up with him. Andrew and I sat there dumbfounded in silence for a long while. When I recovered from the harsh trauma and shock of witnessing that unpleasant scene, I whipped out my phone and called his number. He didn't answer. That was a bad sign. I texted him. I got nothing back. Either they were still fighting, or he had driven off too fast and too recklessly as was his habit when he got extremely angry.

"Well Love, do you think he can walk away?" Andrew inquired.

"I don't know. I'm not sure what to think. He won't answer his cell or text me back. That probably means he's more upset than I've ever seen him."

"He definitely meant what he said. Let's wait a few minutes. Then I have an idea as to where he went."

We waited for what felt like hours. According to my watch, it was only ten minutes. I tried calling Mark another five times and texted him twice more. He still didn't pick up. He didn't text me back. Since I didn't want to run into them when we left, we waited another five minutes just to be quite sure they were gone.

We exited the restaurant in time to see James pull into the parking lot to pick up a seemingly miserable Sonya. The lousy liar was sitting on the curb with her head in her hands, shaking and sobbing uncontrollably which was completely out of character. Was she indeed that despondent, or was it an act and just another lie? People were staring as they passed by. James pulled her up, helping her into his black corvette. They sat there having an intense conversation while we found Andrew's car.

She was wallowing so deep in her sorrow that she didn't even notice us at all. Andrew had just started the engine when James came running over. He began knocking on the driver's side window. Andrew frowned at me before opening the glass to talk to him. I shrugged.

"She has it really bad for your brother. I've never seen her like this," James addressed me. "She's having a major anxiety attack. I guess Mark called her a manipulative liar. He said he never wants to see her again. I have to hand it to him. It took some real courage to say those words and walk out on her. The thing is, he's right. She knows it. No one's ever talked to her like that. He gave her a heavy dose of her own bitter brand of medicine. Who knew it would be Mark who did the dumping? The man has guts!" He whistled through his teeth. Then he steeled himself, adopting a more appropriately solemn expression before he walked back to console his devastated sister like a dutiful, caring brother.

"Where do you think Mark went?" I asked Andrew.

"I saw it in his mind. I'll show you," he said as he drove out of the parking lot. We followed a street that went up the Red Hill to Skyline Drive. We drove along the red-rocked, elevated road that towered above the town below. He turned into the parking area just past the three foot white letters that spell "DIXIE" on a massive rust-colored rock formation at the entrance to Pioneer Park. This park is part of Red Cliffs Desert Preserve which is filled with petrified orange sand dunes, red sandstone walls, and miniature, dusty pink, rocky canyons. It is also home to the highly protected, endangered, desert tortoise. There are all these six inch high, orange plastic fences designed to keep the little buggers off the highway and out of harms way. I'm not kidding. They must work because I've never seen any desert tortoise road kill.

Sure enough, there was Mark's empty jeep. We got out and started looking for him. Andrew spotted him across the road on the brink of a craggy, vermillion cliff that overlooks the entire city of St. George and beyond. He seemed to be swaying in the breeze on the edge of the precarious precipice. He had climbed over the cement barriers that were there to save cars from veering off the pavement and falling to imminent and total destruction.

My breath caught in my throat. Was he thinking about jumping? Our father had told us about a high school friend of his who committed suicide at this very spot. No, my brother would never do that. Still, I went cold inside as we rushed across the street to where he was standing.

"Mark!" I yelled frantically. He glanced over his shoulder in our direction and stepped back carefully from his perilous perch on the extreme edge. I ran to him and hugged him tightly. When I looked into his eyes, I winced at his apparent anguish. He was hurting. I didn't know how to comfort him.

"Don't worry, Sis. I'm not going to jump. This is just a good place to think. The view goes on forever. It helps me see the bigger picture. You know, the eternal scheme of things, how this moment relates to the rest of my existence which right now feels very long and empty."

"Whoa Mark, that's some deep thinking," Andrew put his hand on Mark's shoulder. "Are you going to be alright?"

"Yeah, I think so, sometime in the future. In another year, I'll probably feel a whole lot better."

"Do you want to talk about it?" I asked, biting my lower lip as I saw the obvious pain in his eyes that he couldn't conceal.

"Not yet, I need to be alone for a while. Please understand. Don't worry about me. I'll survive. I promise I won't do anything stupid, at least nothing nearly as stupid as falling in love with a lying, manipulative, albeit gorgeous, girl from another planet. It could be worse, I guess. I could have married her. Nah, she probably would have stood me up. I don't think that was part of her plan to control and destroy my life."

"Are you sure you don't want to go somewhere and talk about this," I asked again, already knowing the answer. He only shook his head sadly, staring blankly out into space.

"At least, move away from the ledge, please," I begged.

Andrew and I left him there after my boyfriend checked Mark's intentions in his thoughts. He nodded to me as a sign that it would be okay. He had left his original spot to sit on a gigantic, sandstone boulder that was a short distance back from the cliff. Seeing him there, made me feel better about leaving him alone. He didn't plan on jumping, but he could have lost his balance and plunged off that rocky ledge to a certain, accidental death from where he had been previously standing.

We went back to Pioneer Park where we decided to hike and do some moderate rock climbing. This natural setting contained some extremely enormous rocks for scaling. I needed to work off the adrenaline that had rushed though me as a reaction to my fear. The giant sandstone shapes were pock-marked and riddled with holes. This made the formations look like orange Swiss cheese. The holes made excellent hand and foot holds. On this precise, picturesque spot, three ecosystems converged. The Mohave Desert, the Great Basin, and the Colorado Plateau came together. Yeah, I read the sign. It was highly informative.

Hiking and climbing was excellent therapy for me. Exercising was a way to stop dwelling on my brother's misery. Getting physical helped me focus on something other than Mark's pain. The beauty around us was breathtaking. When we were both physically spent (well, probably just me, Andrew could go on forever), we sat at a picnic table and talked about this turn of events.

"Are you feeling better, Love?"

"Yeah, I guess, but I wish there was something I could do to help Mark through his inevitable grief. I'm so helpless and inept," I admitted feeling like a failure. I didn't know what to do.

"Tiana, you saved an entire planet from self-destruction. You are hardly helpless or inept."

"What good is saving a planet of people I don't even know from themselves, if I can't help my own brother recover from a broken heart?"

"There are some things you can't fix. He'll have to work through the misery. Grief is a process. When he's ready for support, we'll be there for him. For now, you have to let it go. What he's feeling is a common side effect of allowing oneself to love. Pain is the price we often have to pay when we open our hearts to the hope that we'll receive love in return."

Andrew always knew what to say to make me feel better. Between his comforting touch and the warmth of the sun on my face, I felt somewhat lighter. My brother was strong. He would get through this. My inner voice assured me that he would live to love another day.

We went back to Andrew's house and watched the last Sherlock Holmes movie. I love Robert Downey Jr. We ate warm, gooey, chocolate chip cookies that Evelyn had just taken out of the oven with cold milk. Now that's a recipe for feeling good. Robert Downey Jr., chocolate chip cookies and some passionate kissing from Andrew and I was ready to face the world again with a conviction that my brother would indeed be okay.

I made it home just before my curfew of midnight. Mark wasn't there. I decided to read for a while, hoping he'd be home soon, so we could talk if he were ready. There was a timid knock on my front door. Had Andrew returned because he wanted to wait with me? I smiled at that pleasantly delicious thought. There were some definite perks to having a psychic soul-mate.

I opened the door expecting to see my favorite spaceman. Instead, I was met by my least favorite alien. Sonya peered down at me through puffy eyes and a tear-stained, pain-stricken face. I just barely recognized the girl. This was a whole new look for her. It wasn't pretty.

"Please Tiana," she whispered, "You have to help me!" She stumbled into my living room and sat down on the couch without being invited. Huh? I thought you had to invite vamps into your house before they could come inside. Oh yeah, Mark had already made that mistake at least twice that I knew of. I gave up trying to keep her out.

"Your brother won't talk to me. I've tried to explain. He won't answer my calls, my texts, or my e-mails. I can't find him. I'm worried sick. Please Tiana, you have to tell him to talk to me. He'll listen to you!"

I had followed her in. I sat across from her on the loveseat, folding my arms in a defensive motion across my chest as I braced myself for whatever disagreeable thing she was going to throw at me. Who knew what she was up too now?

"What makes you think so?" I responded.

"He trusts you! I know what you think of me. I don't blame you. I'm so sorry! I realize I don't deserve your help, but I don't know who else to turn to. I love Mark! I know you don't believe me, but it's true. I honestly do love him. It started out as a vengeful game. I admit I wanted to hurt you by hurting him, but he stole my heart. I've never known anyone like him.

"I thought I loved Andrew, but I was just mad because I couldn't control him when he didn't fall for me. He hurt my pride. No one has ever refused me before. Boys have always succumbed to my feminine charms. I've never had to work hard to get the guy I wanted. You can understand that, can't you?"

Huh? Was she suggesting that I never had anyone reject me? I was not a fellow member of the Irresistible Club. Was this her way of flattering me into agreeing with her? Okay, I could understand having your pride hurt, but the rest of it was Greek to me.

"I know I have a lot to make up for. I've treated you horribly. We may never be friends, but I really need your help. I want to change. I'm begging for your forgiveness. Please tell him to give me another chance!" She sobbed out the words. She looked at me with pleading eyes that were streaming tears down her cheeks.

She seemed sincere, but I was still wary. She was an unscrupulous and accomplished liar. All my past experiences with her had brought me intense pain. She taught me to question her motives, to expect the very worst. Just being this close to her made me nauseous. I could feel an unwanted case of the dry heaves creeping up into my throat as my stomach went into another freefall. It was difficult for me to consider trusting that she might be telling me the truth this time. It would be a first.

I hesitated for another few moments, weighing my options: a) I could force her out the front door, lock it, and turn my back on the evil wench forever, b) I could call her names, order her back to the underworld from whence she came, and hope my brother would quickly get over his broken heart, or c) I could give her a chance to change her ways, and pray that she would make Mark happy.

That still, small voice prompted me. It confirmed that c was the correct answer, even though the first two choices appealed to me more. Darn it! I didn't want to listen to that dumb voice in my head. It had to be wrong. It went against everything I knew about this girl who had used her super-powers countless times to dominate and inflict misery on others, especially me. I had emotional scars to prove it.

"I'll tell him," I said. "I don't know if it will help, but everyone deserves a second chance." I totally shocked myself. I just opened my mouth and the sentence jumped out.

How had those words escaped through my tightly pursed lips? What was wrong with me? I considered her the meanest girl ever born. She was the same girl who had tried to take away my boyfriend, get me killed and shatter my life. I'd just agreed to deliver a message that might help her get my brother back under her complete control. What was I thinking?

"Thanks Tiana, I knew you'd help me! You're a much better person than I am or ever hope to be. You and Andrew deserve each other. You're good together. I'm so sorry I tried to come between you." She smiled through her despair. She hugged me. Yeah, I'm not kidding. She actually wrapped her arms around me and squeezed. I almost passed out on the spot. I didn't hug her back. I was too startled by her complete change in behavior. Who was she?

"I'm staying at James' place," she said. Then she walked out my front door and disappeared into the darkness like an apparition, a ghost or a figment of my imagination. She could have been any of those fictitious beings for all I knew. She certainly didn't act like the Sonya Parker I knew and disliked greatly.

I closed the door and leaned back against it. Did that actually happen? Was she for real? Was she seriously in love with Mark? Did she sincerely want to change? I didn't want to believe her. I still wanted to beam her back to her home planet, so I'd never have to deal with her again. Did she even deserve another chance? *Yes, she does.* My inner voice had spoken softly, but unmistakably to my mixed up mind again.

About ten minutes later, I heard the sound of Mark's jeep pull up in the driveway and stop. I heard his familiar, though slower than usual, footsteps come haltingly dragging through the front door. He looked miserable.

"You just missed Sonya," I said quietly as I hugged him.

"Good! I never want to see her again," he tried to sound convincing, but I caught the pain that crossed his face before he looked down at his feet.

"Yes, you do. You can't lie to me. I know you too well. You need to give her another chance. I think she genuinely loves you. She's willing to change for you, or so she says. Both Andrew and James think she truly does love you. They can read her mind. As much as I distrust the girl, I think you need to at least talk to her. She's staying at James' apartment. Go see her. She's waiting for you."

His eyes widened. I saw the glimmer of hope in them. He turned abruptly and fled out the door into the dark and gloomy night. Okay, I'd done my part. It had been a terribly long, trying day. I hoped I wasn't sending my brother to his emotional demise. Oddly enough, I didn't think I was. I was so totally confused by this unusual change in the order of the cosmos that I couldn't think about it anymore.

I slowly ascended the stairs to my bedroom. My energy had all ebbed away. I felt like a deflated balloon. I dropped onto my comfy mattress and almost instantly fell asleep without bothering to change, wash my face or brush my teeth.

Sometime in the middle of the night, someone kissed me lightly on the forehead and gently shook me.

"Wake up Sleeping Beauty!" A voice whispered in my ear.

I was stupid with sleep. I groaned at the noise that had so rudely disrupted my slumber. I deserved a decent night's sleep after all I had endured. For crying out loud, was that too much to ask?

I opened my eyes into narrowed slits. I found myself looking at a much too familiar face, a face I thought and hoped I would never see again. My frightened eyes flew all the way open. As my eyes adjusted to the dark, moonlight bled into the room under and around my curtains, illuminating the big, sad, puppy dog eyes that were staring into mine.

Prince Raydon was hovering over me in the flesh. I was filled with immediate, chilling dread that made my blood go stone cold. It began to sour and curdle inside me. I must be having some kind of horrible, terrifying nightmare. I was still groggy from the sleep induced coma I had been enjoying. I rubbed my eyes and looked up at him again. I touched his face, hoping it would vanish into vapor and fade away. It didn't. I felt the stubble on his chin. It appeared I was awake, but I so didn't want this to be reality.

"What are you doing here?" My mouth was cracked and dry. My voice was tight, oozing with panic and denial. I closed my eyes. I begged the universe to swallow him up and make him disappear, but to my chagrin, he was still there when I opened them again.

"Aren't you happy to see me? Did you really think you could run away from the Royal Prince of Nommo? Did you actually believe I'd let you get away with leaving me on our wedding day? I love you too much to let you run away from me. You did me a grave injustice, my queen, and I've come to rectify the situation."

CHAPTER 31

PREMONITION

"How did you get here?"

"You really should lock your windows," he shrugged. "Anyone could climb in."

"That's not what I meant. You can't be here! It would take eight and a half years for you to travel to Earth. It's just not possible!" I blurted, trying to argue his existence away from the here and now and back to his proper place in the cosmos where I had left him.

"It's a funny thing I learned about your friend, Tovin. Did you know he's a genuine genius? He invented a time machine in his basement. He was still testing it, but as you can see, it works! I'm here! We are reunited, together again, and all is forgiven. I've traveled halfway across the galaxy to find you. You don't look so well, Tiana. Aren't you happy to see me?"

"No! This is not happening. I'm going to close my eyes. You are a figment of my imagination, a hallucination, or a bad dream brought on by Post Traumatic Stress. I want you to be gone when I open them." I shut my eyes tightly, scrunching them up, refusing to look into his oversized, chocolate-brown, Manga eyes. My sleep-numbed brain couldn't process all this disturbing information. I had to be dreaming. He was a nightmare.

"Sorry, I'm not going anywhere without you!"

"Ah, yes, you are!" Another voice retorted. I looked toward my open window, seeing another dark figure enter my bedroom. When had my second story bedroom window become such an inviting entrance? Was there a giant neon sign out there flashing the words, "Come on in and join the party" in bright pink and purple letters? That random irritation fluttered away as relief took its place. I recognized and loved this particular dark figure.

"Andrew?" It had to be him. His voice had finally registered as my brain unfroze itself and rebooted.

"Yes Love, the prince is just leaving!" He said, coming nearer.

"No, I'm not!" Raydon turned to confront Andrew. "Tiana and I have unfinished business that doesn't include you."

"Everything that concerns Tiana *is* my business! *You* have no business even being on this planet. *You* committed a serious crime when you took her away from Earth. *You* are going to pay for that felony."

"Shhhhh! Keep your voices down, please," I begged. I didn't want all this loud, conflicting, testosterone-fueled talk waking my parents. They would not understand. I did not want to try to explain it to them.

"She agreed to accompany me to Nommo! That is not a crime." The prince drew himself up to his full stature, but Andrew still towered over him.

"You threatened her with death. She only agreed in order to save Tiffany, James, and myself from being killed by your mutant guards!"

"I would never have had anyone killed. You can check my thoughts. My intentions were pure. She was destined to save my planet. I did what I had to for the greater good of my people!"

"Well, she saved Nommo already, so you need to back off now!" Andrew had both his hands on Raydon's chest, pushing him away from my bedside.

"She's the one who committed a crime. She agreed to marry me and reneged on that promise. She left me standing at the alter. The entire population of my planet watched in horror!" Raydon pushed back. I hoped they weren't going to start throwing punches.

"Again, she was forced to make that promise to save *your* life! The rebels would have killed you if she hadn't agreed to marry you. Her intentions were to save the lives of those who remained loyal to you, as well. You owe her for saving your planet, your friends and yourself from certain death." Andrew got right up in Raydon's face as he delivered that speech. The Royal Nommoan Nuisance had enough sense to back away from the angry, authoritative Helamite.

"You were supposed to marry Layla." I stood and got between them, whispering loudly as I joined in the maelstrom. I tried desperately to get them to lower their voices and play nice with each other.

"What are you talking about? Layla had nothing to do with your treacherous betrayal," the clueless monarch insisted, giving me his look of death.

"I sent her down in my wedding dress. She loves you. I know you have feelings for her. You were made for each other. Don't you see? It was to be the perfect union between the rebels and the established government. I don't belong on your planet. The two of you should rule it together with input from the people!" I answered him, ignoring his evil-eye stare.

"That's not what happened. She brought your clone and explained how you had planned to deceive me. I was made to look a fool in front of my whole planet!"

And there it was! His Majesty's arrogance was showing. He was mad because he had been embarrassed. He was willing to drag me back to Nommo just to prove that he could. He was attempting to save face. He wanted to punish me because I had escaped his manipulation. Was he a crazy control-freak or what?

I suddenly felt incredibly sorry for him. He didn't realize what he was doing. I was surprised that I was finding it easy to forgive him for everything he had done to me. As I let go of my anger, a sense of peace flowed into me. Who knew forgiveness could bring such perfect peace with it? I could only feel pity for the maniacal madman. He had so much to learn about real love, leadership, what mattered and what didn't. Wow, who was I, and when did I start sounding like I was a grown up?

"What's going on in there, Tiana?" My father demanded from outside my door. I was pulled back into the immediate and too real drama that was playing out in my bedroom. I wasn't grown up enough to face my dad with two boys in my room in the middle of the night.

"Hush, you two," I whispered with pleading in my voice. "You do not want to get caught by my father."

"Open this door, Tiana. I need to talk to you." He sounded seriously pissed.

"What do you want, Dad?" I asked in my best sleepy voice. "I couldn't sleep. I was watching TV. I'm sorry the noise woke you. I just turned it off. I'll go back to bed now."

"You do not want to meet her father under these circumstances," Andrew whispered to Raydon as he dragged him toward my closet door. Raydon acted like he wanted to refuse, but then he thought better of it, nodded and followed Andrew into my closet. He's not a complete idiot.

"Tiana! Open! The! Door! Now!"

I got to my feet. The room started spinning. I was dizzy from experiencing so much intense trepidation. I hadn't yet recovered from the shock of being awoken from deep sleep by the unwelcome presence of Raydon. I definitely couldn't think of a rational reason why two boys would be fighting over me in my bedroom at two o'clock in the morning, at least not one my father would buy.

I could feel the blood, which was still running cold from shock, pumping through my body at an accelerated pace. It pounded so loudly in my ears that I could hardly hear myself think. This situation was potentially worse than being abducted by an alien prince, and having my brother's heart kidnapped by my former worst enemy. If my father found two guys hiding in my closet, it would be the end of the world as I knew it. I wasn't altogether sure that two boys would be worse than one, but I didn't want to find out. I took several deep breaths. I tried unsuccessfully to steady my nerves. My hands shook as I opened the door.

"What do you want, Dad? I turned off the television. I'm sorry it was too loud," I yawned and stretched as I tried my best to mask my fear with a sleepy face. "I think I can go back to sleep now."

"I heard a male voice. It didn't sound like the TV." He said, as he stooped and looked under my bed.

"You can't really think someone's hiding under my bed, Dad!" I acted appalled at the very suggestion. This was going to be severely disastrous if he found them. He put his hand on the closet door. I had to do something fast. I considered hurling myself out of my open window, but I realized that wasn't a viable solution. I'd probably break my neck or something else that was equally painful and unpleasant. I tried to harness all my brain cells. I needed to think of some way to keep my secret world from spinning out of my control. I hoped that someday I'd be able to share my knowledge of that hidden world with my father, but I didn't think this was the proper time or place to clue him in. There would need to be much preparation before I dropped that bombshell in his lap. I had nothing but pseudo-indignation to throw at him now. I decided to pull out all the stops.

"You don't trust me!" I exclaimed. "I can't believe you think there's a boy in my bedroom!" I was pouring it on. I wasn't ready to let my dad know of the dangers that I knew were out there waiting to wreak havoc with the Earth and its inhabitants. The alternative was dangerous enough to get me grounded for the rest of my life. In either scenario, my father would probably do everything within his power to keep me away from Andrew for my "own good." I couldn't let that happen. I threw myself into the part of the incensed victim of undeserved injustice with enthusiastic and aggravated passion.

"If you open that door, I will never speak to you again! My word should be enough. I have never given you a reason to doubt me. I have always been responsible and trustworthy. Why would I hide a boy in my closet? Do you think I'm a total idiot?"

I certainly had acting ability. I might consider the theater as a career, if I could pull this off. That was if I didn't die from a coronary or a stroke, or if I didn't become a murder victim of my father's unbridled wrath tonight.

"Not *a* boy," he said, "*the* boy! I don't trust Andrew. I know he's in here. Don't deny it!" Where was all this mistrust coming from? I thought he had accepted and even grown to like my very-nearly-perfect boyfriend. I wondered if Andrew knew how much my father didn't trust him. He had mercifully kept that knowledge to himself. I instantly felt compelled to defend my extraordinarily admirable boyfriend's honor.

"Dad, you don't know what you're saying. Andrew is the most reliable, responsible and trustworthy boy I know. He would never..."

He interrupted my tirade of indignation by jerking the closet door open with a quick motion as if he were going to catch a thief by surprise. I was ready to pass out. I was waiting for the inevitable. I wondered what excuse we could use. Would we have to come clean by telling the frightening and incomprehensible truth that my dad would probably refuse to accept? Would he ever believe this truth? I was pretty sure he was much more likely to believe something else entirely. I waited for my father's perfectly justified fury. I waited for the sword to fall. I waited for what felt like an eternity.

Nothing happened. I peered cautiously into the closet. There was no one there. I caught my gasp in my throat before it became audible. Dad searched behind my clothes. The space contained my wardrobe, more than enough shoes (well, can you ever actually have enough shoes?), a few purses and nothing more. I breathed an inaudible sigh of relief.

"See, Dad! Are you satisfied now? How could you doubt your own daughter? I'm the most responsible, mature and incredibly trustworthy daughter you've got. Why don't you trust me?"

Someday, in the faraway future, I would have to explain everything to my dad, but it wasn't going to happen tonight. Heck, I didn't even understand what had just happened.

"I'm sorry, Tiana. I should have trusted you. I was so sure I heard his voice. I'm sorry I suspected your 'all-too-perfect' boyfriend. I know he's in love with you. That makes me very nervous. Someday, when you have children, you may understand just how scary that can be. Forgive me for doubting you," he said, as he left my room and closed my door.

I locked it, leaned against it and then sank to the floor. I forgave my father. There was honestly nothing to forgive except his mistrust. I fully understood where that was coming from. I couldn't blame him. Well, maybe I could, but I felt like being generous with forgiveness tonight.

I just sat there for a few minutes as the last of my adrenalin seeped away leaving me still stunned and thoroughly drained of energy. Life had been much more than fair with me tonight. Andrew had foiled Raydon's attempt to re-abduct me. Then he and the prince had disappeared from my closet, saving me from an explanation that my father would not believe without more proof than I could muster at the moment.

Where did they go? I finally found enough strength to arise from my place on the floor. Curiosity drove me into my closet. I looked up at the ceiling. I'd seen a movie once where someone had hidden up there and went undetected because people don't usually expect anyone to be hanging out over their heads. They weren't there. I went back out and turned out the lights. I glanced back at my bed. Andrew was casually seated on it with a brilliant on his smug face. Raydon was gone. Yay! My heart started up again doing its happy dance in my chest.

"What? How did…"

"Your questions can wait until tomorrow. Let's just say I had a premonition. I acted upon it. I've learned a few new tricks from Bob. I went into the future just far enough to disappear. I moved Raydon outside and left him in Bob's very capable hands. Right now, order has been restored to the heavens. You are in desperate need of a good night's rest. I'll stay until you fall asleep, if it will make you feel safer."

I nodded and joined him on my bed. He held me in his arms while a whole world of trouble fell away. I let the unanswered questions go. I would revisit them in the light of day. My real prince was here. We were safely wrapped in each other's embrace. I was home. Nothing else mattered tonight. As I peacefully drifted off into dreamland, I was confident that all the planets had been realigned. The cosmos was calm once more.

I know, it probably won't stay that way for long, but just for now, it was all good. Just for now, I was back in the right place, at the right time, and I planned on staying here. There would be no more "falling off the planet" for me. My "sun, moon and stars" was within my grasp. I was holding onto him. I would not let go. All was well in the universe.